'Sapper'

BULLDOG DRUMMOND

PUFFIN BOOKS

PUFFIN BOOKS

Published by the Penguin Group
27 Wrights Lane, London W8 5TZ, England
Viking Penguin Inc., 40 West 23rd Street, New York, New York 10010, USA
Penguin Books Australia Ltd, Ringwood, Victoria, Australia
Penguin Books Canada Ltd, 2801 John Street, Markham, Ontario, Canada L3R 1B4
Penguin Books (NZ) Ltd, 182–190 Wairau Road, Auckland 10, New Zealand

Penguin Books Ltd, Registered Offices: Harmondsworth, Middlesex, England

First published by Hodder & Stoughton Ltd, 1920.
Published in Puffin Books 1988

Made and printed in Great Britian by
Cox & Wyman Ltd, Reading, Berks
Filmset in Linotron Palatino by
Rowland Phototypesetting Ltd, Bury St Edmunds, Suffolk

CONTENTS

Prologue

In the month of December, 1918, and on the very day that a British Cavalry Division marched into Cologne, with flags flying and bands playing as the conquerors of a beaten nation, the manager of the Hôtel Nationale in Berne received a letter. Its contents appeared to puzzle him somewhat, for having read it twice he rang the bell on his desk to summon his secretary. Almost immediately the door opened, and a young French girl came into the room.

'Monsieur rang?' She stood in front of the manager's desk, awaiting instructions.

'Have we ever had staying in the hotel a man called le Comte de Guy?' He leaned back in his chair and looked at her through his pince-nez.

The secretary thought for a moment and then shook her head.

'Not as far as I can remember,' she said.

'Do we know anything about him? Has he ever fed here, or taken a private room?'

Again the secretary shook her head.

'Not that I know of.'

The manager handed her the letter, and waited in silence until she had read it.

'It seems on the face of it a peculiar request from an unknown man,' he remarked as she laid it down. 'A dinner of four covers; no expense to be spared. Wines specified, and if not in the hotel to be obtained. A private room at half-past seven sharp. Guests to ask for Room X.'

The secretary nodded in agreement.

'It can hardly be a hoax,' she remarked after a short silence.

'No.' The manager tapped his teeth with his pen thoughtfully. 'But if by any chance it was, it would prove an expensive one for us. I wish I could think who this Comte de Guy is.'

'He sounds like a Frenchman,' she answered. Then after a pause: 'I suppose you'll have to take it seriously?'

'I must.' He took off his pince-nez and laid them on the desk in front of him. 'Would you send the *maître d'hôtel* to me at once?'

Whatever may have been the manager's misgivings, they were certainly not shared by the head waiter as he left the office after receiving his instructions. War and short rations had not been conducive to any particular lucrative business in his sphere; and the whole sound of the proposed entertainment seemed to him to contain considerable promise. Moreover, he was a man who loved his work, and a free hand over preparing a dinner was a joy in itself. Undoubtedly he personally would meet the three guests and the mysterious Comte de Guy; he personally would see that they had nothing to complain of in the matter of service at dinner . . .

And so at about twenty minutes past seven the *maître d'hôtel* was hovering round the hall-porter, the manager was hovering round the *maître d'hôtel*, and the secretary was hovering round both. At five-and-twenty minutes past the first guest arrived . . .

He was a peculiar-looking man, in a big fur coat, reminding one irresistibly of a codfish.

'I wish to be taken to Room X.' The French secretary stiffened involuntarily as the *maître d'hôtel* stepped obsequiously forward. Cosmopolitan as the hotel was, even now she could never bear German spoken without an inward shudder of disgust.

'A Boche,' she murmured in disgust to the manager as the first arrival disappeared through the swing doors at the end of the lounge. It is to be regretted that that worthy man was more occupied in shaking himself by the hand, at the proof that the letter was bona fide, than in any meditation on the guest's nationality.

Almost immediately afterwards the second and third members of the party arrived. They did not come together, and what seemed peculiar to the manager was that they were evidently strangers to one another.

The leading one – a tall gaunt man with a ragged beard and a pair of piercing eyes – asked in a nasal and by no means an inaudible tone for Room X. As he spoke a little fat man who was standing just behind him started perceptibly, and shot a bird-like glance at the speaker.

Then in execrable French he too asked for Room X.

'He's not French,' said the secretary excitedly to the manager as the ill-assorted pair were led out of the lounge by the head waiter. 'That last one was another Boche.'

The manager thoughtfully twirled his pince-nez between his fingers.

'Two Germans and an American.' He looked a little apprehensive. 'Let us hope the dinner will appease everybody. Otherwise –'

But whatever fears he might have entertained with regard to the furniture in Room X, they were not destined to be uttered. Even as he spoke the door again swung open, and a man with a thick white scarf around his neck, so pulled up as almost completely to cover his face, came in. A soft hat was pulled down well over his ears, and all that the manager could swear to as regards the new-comer's appearance was a pair of deep-set, steel-grey eyes which seemed to bore through him.

'You got my letter this morning?'

'M'sieur le Comte de Guy?' The manager bowed deferentially and rubbed his hands together. 'Everything is ready, and your three guests have arrived.'

'Good. I will go to the room at once.'

The *maître d'hôtel* stepped forward to relieve him of his coat, but the Count waved him away.

'I will remove it later,' he remarked shortly. 'Take me to the room.'

As he followed his guide his eyes swept round the lounge. Save for two or three elderly women of doubtful nationality, and a man in the American Red Cross, the place was deserted; and as he passed through the swing doors he turned to the head waiter.

'Business good?' he asked.

No – business decidedly was not good. The waiter was voluble. Business had never been so poor in the memory of man . . . But it was to be hoped that the dinner would be to Monsieur le Comte's liking . . . He personally had superintended it . . . Also the wines.

'If everything is to my satisfaction you will not regret it,' said the Count tersely. 'But remember one thing. After the coffee has been brought in, I do not wish to be disturbed under any circumstances whatever.' The head waiter paused as he came to a door, and the Count repeated the last few words. 'Under no circumstances whatever.'

'*Mais certainement*, Monsieur le Comte . . . I, personally, will see to it . . .'

As he spoke he flung open the door and the Count entered. It cannot be said that the atmosphere of the room was congenial. The three occupants were regarding one another in hostile silence, and as the Count entered, they, with one accord, transferred their suspicious glance to him.

For a moment he stood motionless, while he looked at each one in turn. Then he stepped forward . . .

'Good evening, gentlemen' – he still spoke in French – 'I am honoured at your presence.' He turned to the head waiter. 'Let dinner be served in five minutes exactly.'

With a bow the man left the room, and the door closed.

'During that five minutes, gentlemen, I propose to introduce myself to you, and you to one another.' As he spoke he divested himself of his coat and hat. 'The business which I wish to discuss we will postpone, with your permission, till after coffee, when we shall be undisturbed.'

In silence the three guests waited while he unwound the thick white muffler; then, with undisguised curiosity, they studied their host. In appearance he was striking. He had a short dark beard, and in profile his face was aquiline and stern. The eyes, which had so impressed the manager, seemed now to be a cold grey-blue; the thick brown hair, flecked slightly with grey, was brushed back from a broad forehead. His hands were large and white; not effeminate, but capable and determined: the hands of a man who knew what he wanted, knew how to get it and got it. To even the most superficial observer the giver of the feast was a man of power: a man capable of forming instant decisions and of carrying them through . . .

And if so much was obvious to the superficial observer, it was more than obvious to the three men who stood by the fire watching him. They were what they were simply owing to the fact that they were not superficial servers of humanity; and each one of them, as he watched his host, realized that he was in the presence of a great man. It was enough: great men do not send fool invitations to dinner to men of international repute. It mattered not what form his greatness took – there was money in greatness, big money. And money was their life . . .

The Count advanced first to the American.

'Mr Hocking, I believe,' he remarked in English, holding out his hand. 'I am glad you managed to come.'

The American shook the proferred hand, while the two Germans looked at him with sudden interest. As the man at the head of the great American cotton trust, worth more in millions than he could count, he was entitled to their respect . . .

'That's me, Count,' returned the millionaire in his nasal twang. 'I am interested to know to what I am indebted for this invitation.'

'All in good time, Mr Hocking,' smiled the host. 'I have hopes that the dinner will fill in that time satisfactorily.'

He turned to the taller of the two Germans, who without his coat seemed more like a codfish than ever.

'Herr Steinemann, is it not?' This time he spoke in German.

The man whose interest in German coal was hardly less well known than Hocking's in cotton, bowed stiffly.

'And Herr von Gratz?' The Count turned to the last member of the party and shook hands. Though less well known than either of the other two in the realms of international finance, von Gratz's name in the steel trade in Central Europe was one to conjure with.

'Well, gentlemen,' said the Count, 'before we sit down to dinner, I may perhaps be permitted to say a few words of introduction. The nations of the world have recently been engaged in a performance of unrivalled stupidity. As far as one can tell that performance is now over. The last thing I wish to do is to discuss the war – except in so far as it concerns our meeting here tonight. Mr Hocking is an American, you two gentlemen are Germans. I' – the Count smiled slightly – 'have no nationality. Or rather, shall I say, I have every nationality. Completely cosmopolitan . . . Gentlemen, the war was waged by idiots, and when idiots get busy on a large scale, it is time for clever men to step in . . . That is the *raison d'être* for this little dinner . . . I claim that we four men are sufficiently international to be able to disregard any stupid and petty feelings about this country and that country, and to regard the world outlook at the present moment from one point of view and one point of view only – our own.'

The gaunt American gave a hoarse chuckle.

'It will be my object after dinner,' continued the Count, 'to try and prove to you that we have a common point of view. Until then – shall we merely concentrate on a pious hope that the Hôtel Nationale will not poison us with their food?'

'I guess,' remarked the American, 'that you've got a pretty healthy command of languages, Count.'

'I speak four fluently – French, German, English, and Spanish,' returned the other. 'In addition I can make myself understood in Russia, Japan, China, the Balkan States, and – America.'

His smile, as he spoke, robbed the words of any suspicion of offence. The next moment the head waiter opened the door, and the four men sat down to dine.

It must be admitted that the average hostess, desirous of making a dinner a success, would have been filled with secret dismay at the general atmosphere in the room. The American, in accumulating his millions, had also accumulated a digestion of such an exotic and tender character that dry rusks and Vichy water were the limit of his capacity.

Herr Steinemann was of the common order of German, to whom food was sacred. He ate and drank enormously, and evidently considered that nothing further was required of him.

Von Gratz did his best to keep his end up, but as he was apparently in a chronic condition of fear that the gaunt American would assault him with violence, he cannot be said to have contributed much to the gaiety of the meal.

And so to the host must be given the credit that the dinner was a success. Without appearing to monopolize the conversation he talked ceaselessly and well. More – he talked brilliantly. There seemed to be no corner of the globe with which he had not a nodding acquaintance at least; while with most places he was as familiar as a Londoner with Piccadilly Circus. But to even the most brilliant of conversationalists the strain of talking to a hypochondriacal American and two Germans – one greedy and the other frightened – is considerable; and the Count heaved an inward sigh of relief when the coffee had been handed round and the door closed behind the waiter. From now on the topic was an easy one – one where no effort on his part would be necessary to hold his audience. It was the topic of money – the common bond of his three guests. And yet, as he carefully cut the end of his cigar, and realized that the eyes of the other three were fixed on him expectantly, he knew that the hardest part of the evening was in front of him. Big financiers, in common with all other people, are fonder of having money put into their pockets than of taking it out. And that was the very thing the Count proposed they should do – in large quantities . . .

'Gentlemen,' he remarked, when his cigar was going to his satisfaction, 'we are all men of business. I do not propose therefore to beat about the bush over the matter which I have to put before you, but to come to the point at once. I said before dinner that I considered we were sufficiently big to exclude any small arbitrary national distinctions from our minds. As men whose interests are international, such things are beneath us. I wish now to slightly qualify that remark.' He turned to the American on his right, who with his eyes half closed was thoughtfully picking his teeth. 'At this stage, sir, I address myself particularly to you.'

'Go right ahead,' drawled Mr Hocking.

'I do not wish to touch on the war – or its result; but though the Central Powers have been beaten by America and France and England, I think I can speak for you two gentlemen' – he bowed to the two Germans – 'when I say that it is neither France nor America with whom they desire another round. England is Germany's main enemy; she always has been, she always will be.'

Both Germans grunted assent, and the American's eyes closed a little more.

'I have reason to believe, Mr Hocking, that you personally do not love the English?'

'I guess I don't see what my private feelings have got to do with it. But if it's of any interest to the company you are correct in your belief.'

'Good.' The Count nodded his head as if satisfied. 'I take it, then, that you would not be averse to seeing England down and out.'

'Wal,' remarked the American, 'you can assume anything you feel like. Let's get to the show-down.'

Once again the Count nodded his head; then he turned to the two Germans.

'Now you two gentlemen must admit that your plans have miscarried somewhat. It was no part of your original programme that a British Army should occupy Cologne . . .'

'The war was the act of a fool,' snarled Herr Steinemann. 'In a few years more of peace we should have beaten those swine . . .'

'And now – they have beaten you.' The Count smiled slightly. 'Let us admit that the war was the act of a fool if you like, but as men of business we can only deal with the result . . . the result, gentlemen, as it concerns *us*. Both you gentlemen are sufficiently patriotic to resent the presence of that army at Cologne I have no doubt. And you, Mr Hocking, have no love on personal grounds for the English . . . But I am not proposing to appeal to financiers of your reputation on such grounds as those to support my scheme . . . It is enough that your personal predilections run with and not against what I am about to put before you – the defeat of England . . . a defeat more utter and complete than if she had lost the war . . .'

His voice sank a little, and instinctively his three listeners drew closer.

'Don't think that I am proposing this through motives of revenge merely. We are business men, and revenge is only worth our while if it pays. This will pay. I can give you no figures, but we are not of the type who deal in thousands, or even hundreds of thousands. There is a force in England which, if it be harnessed and led properly, will result in millions coming to you . . . It is present now in every nation – fettered, inarticulate, uncoordinated . . . It is partly the result of the war – the war that the idiots have waged . . . Harness that force, gentlemen, co-ordinate it, and use it for your own ends . . . That is my proposal. Not only will you humble that cursed country to the dirt, but you will taste of power such as few men have tasted before . . .' The Count stood up, his eyes blazing. 'And I – I will do it for you.'

He resumed his seat, and his left hand, slipping off the table, beat a tattoo on his knee.

'This is our opportunity – the opportunity of clever men. I have not got the money necessary: you have . . .' He leaned forward in his chair, and glanced at the intent faces of his audience. Then he began to speak . . .

Ten minutes later he pushed back his chair.

'There is my proposal, gentlemen, in a nutshell. Unforeseen developments will doubtless occur; I have spent my life overcoming the unexpected. What is your answer?'

He rose and stood with his back to them by the fire, and for several minutes no one spoke. Each man was busy with his own thoughts, and showed it in his own particular way. The American, his eyes shut, rolled his toothpick backwards and forwards in his mouth slowly and methodically; Steinemann stared at the fire, breathing heavily after the exertions of dinner: von Gratz walked up and down – his hands behind his back – whistling under his breath. Only the Comte de Guy stared unconcernedly at the fire, as if indifferent to the result of their thoughts. In his attitude at that moment he gave a true expression to his attitude on life. Accustomed to play with great stakes, he had just dealt the cards for the most gigantic gamble of his life . . . What matter to the three men, who were looking at the hands he had given them, that only a master criminal could have conceived such a game? The only question which occupied their minds was whether he could carry it through. And on that point they had only their judgement of his personality to rely on.

Suddenly the American removed the toothpick from his mouth, and stretched out his legs.

'There is a question which occurs to me, Count, before I make up my mind on the matter. I guess you've got us sized up to the last button; you know who we are, what we're worth, and all about us. Are you disposed to be a little more communicative about yourself? If we agree to come in on this hand, it's going to cost big money. The handling of that money is with you. Wal – who are you?'

Von Gratz paused in his restless pacing, and nodded his head in agreement; even Steinemann, with a great effort, raised his eyes to the Count's face as he turned and faced them . . .

'A very fair question, gentlemen, and yet one which I regret I am unable to answer. I would not insult your intelligence by giving you the fictitious address of – a fictitious Count. Enough that I am a man whose livelihood lies in other people's pockets. As you say, Mr Hocking, it is going to cost big money; but compared to the results the costs will be a flea-bite . . . Do I look – and you are all of you used to judging men – do I look the type who would steal the baby's money-box which lay on the mantelpiece, when the pearls could be had for opening the safe? . . . You will have to trust me, even as I shall have to trust you . . . You will have to trust me not to divert the money which you give me as working expenses into my own pocket . . . I shall have to trust you to pay me when the job is finished . . .'

'And that payment will be – how much?' Steinemann's guttural voice broke the silence.

'One million pounds sterling – to be split up between you in any proportion you may decide, and to be paid within one month of the completion of my work. After that the matter will pass into your hands . . . and may you leave that cursed country grovelling in the dirty . . .' His eyes glowed with a fierce, vindictive fury; and then, as if replacing a mask which had slipped for a moment, the Count was once again the suave, courteous host. He had stated his terms frankly and without haggling: stated them as one big man states them to another of the same kidney, to whom time is money and indecision or beating about the bush anathema.

'Take them or leave them.' So much had he said in effect, if not in actual words, and not one of his audience but was far too used to men and matters to have dreamed of suggesting any compromise. All or nothing: and no doctrine could have appealed more to the three men in whose hands lay the decision . . .

'Perhaps, Count, you would be good enough to leave us for a few minutes.' Von Gratz was speaking. 'The decision is a big one, and . . .'

'Why, certainly, gentlemen.' The Count moved to-wards the door. 'I will return in ten minutes. By that time you will have decided – one way or the other.'

Once in the lounge he sat down and lit a cigarette. The hotel was deserted save for one fat woman asleep in a chair opposite, and the Count gave himself up to thought. Genius that he was in the reading of men's mind, he felt that he knew the result of that ten minutes' deliberation . . . And then . . . What then? . . . In his imagination he saw his plans growing and spreading, his tentacles reaching into every corner of a great people – until, at last, everything was ready. He saw himself supreme in power, glutted with it – a king, an autocrat, who had only to lift his finger to plunge his kingdom into destruction and annihilation . . . And when he had done it, and the country he hated was in ruins, then he would claim his million and enjoy it as a great man should enjoy a great reward . . . Thus for the space of ten minutes did the Count see visions and dream dreams. That the force he proposed to tamper with was a dangerous force disturbed him not at all: he was a dangerous man. That his scheme would bring ruin, perhaps death, to thousands of innocent men and women, caused him no qualm: he was a supreme egoist. All that appealed to him was that he had seen the opportunity that existed, and that he had the nerve and the brain to turn that opportunity to his own advantage. Only the necessary money was lacking . . . and . . . With a quick movement he pulled out his watch. They had had their ten minutes . . . the matter was settled, the die was cast.

He rose and walked across the lounge. At the swing doors was the head waiter, bowing obsequiously . . .

It was to be hoped that the dinner had been to the liking of Monsieur le Comte . . . the wines all that he could wish . . . that he had been comfortable and would return again . . .

'That is improbable.' The Count took out his pocket-book. 'But one never knows; perhaps I shall.' He gave the waiter a note. 'Let my bill be prepared at once, and given to me as I pass through the hall.'

Apparently without a care in the world the Count passed down the passage to his private room, while the head waiter regarded complacently the unusual appearance of an English five-pound note.

For an appreciable moment the Count paused by the door, and a faint smile came to his lips. Then he opened it, and passed into the room . . .

The American was still chewing his toothpick; Steinemann was still breathing hard. Only von Gratz had changed his occupation, and he was sitting at the table smoking a long thin cigar. The Count closed the door, and walked over to the fireplace . . .

'Well, gentlemen,' he said quietly, 'what have you decided?'

It was the American who answered.

'It goes. With one amendment. The money is too big for three of us: there must be a fourth. That will be a quarter of a million each.'

The Count bowed.

'Yep,' said the American shortly. 'These two gentlemen agree with me that it should be another of my countrymen – so that we get equal numbers. The man we have decided on is coming to England in a few weeks – Hiram C. Potts. If you get him in, you can count us in too. If not, the deal's off.'

The Count nodded, and if he felt any annoyance at this unexpected development he showed no sign of it on his face.

'I know of Mr Potts,' he answered quietly. 'Your big shipping man, isn't he? I agree to your reservation.'

'Good!' said the American. 'Let's discuss some details.'

Without a trace of emotion on his face the Count drew up a chair to the table. It was only when he sat down that he started to play a tattoo on his knee with his left hand.

Half an hour later he entered his luxurious suite of rooms at the Hôtel Magnificent.

A girl, who had been lying by the fire reading a French novel, looked up at the sound of the door. She did not speak, for the look on his face told her all she wanted to know.

He crossed to the sofa and smiled down at her.

'Successful . . . on our own terms. Tomorrow, Irma, the Comte de Guy dies, and Carl Peterson and his daughter leave for England. A country gentleman, I think, is Carl Peterson. He might keep hens and possibly pigs.'

The girl on the sofa rose, yawning.

'*Mon Dieu*! What a prospect! Pigs and hens – and in England! How long is it going to take?'

The Count looked thoughtfully into the fire.

'Perhaps a year – perhaps six months . . . It is in the lap of the gods . . .'

CHAPTER 1

In Which He Takes Tea at the Carlton and is Surprised

I

Captain Hugh Drummond, DSO, MC, late of His Majesty's Royal Loamshires, was whistling in his morning bath. Being by nature of a cheerful disposition, the symptom did not surprise his servant, late private of the same famous regiment, who was laying breakfast in an adjoining room.

After a while the whistling ceased, and the musical gurgle of escaping water announced that the concert was over. It was the signal for James Denny – the square-jawed ex-batman – to disappear into the back regions and get from his wife the kidneys and bacon which that most excellent woman had grilled to a turn. But on this particular morning the invariable routine was broken. James Denny seemed preoccupied, *distrait*.

Once or twice he scratched his head, and stared out of the window with a puzzled frown. And each time, after a brief survey of the other side of Half Moon Street, he turned back again to the breakfast table with a grin.

'What's you looking for, James Denny?' The irate voice of his wife at the door made him turn round guiltily. 'Them kidneys is ready and waiting these five minutes.'

Her eyes fell on the table, and she advanced into the room wiping her hands on her apron.

'Did you ever see such a bunch of letters?' she said.

'Forty-five,' returned her husband grimly, 'and more to come.' He picked up the newspaper lying beside the chair and opened it out.

'Them's the result of that,' he continued cryptically, indicating a paragraph with a square finger, and thrusting the paper under his wife's nose.

. . . 'Demobilized officer,' she read slowly, 'finding peace incredibly tedious, would welcome diversion. Legitimate, if possible; but crime, if of a comparatively humorous description, no objection. Excitement essential. Would be prepared to consider permanent job if suitably impressed by applicant for his services. Reply at once Box X10.'

She pushed down the paper on a chair and stared first at her husband, and then at the rows of letters neatly arranged on the table.

'I calls it wicked,' she announced at length. 'Fair flying in the face of Providence. Crime, Denny – crime. Don't you get 'aving nothing to do with such mad pranks, my man, or you and me will be having words.' She shook an admonitory finger at him, and retired slowly to the kitchen. In the days of his youth, James Denny had been a bit wild, and there was a look in his eyes this morning – the suspicion of a glint – which recalled old memories.

A moment or two later Hugh Drummond came in. Slightly under six feet in height, he was broad in proportion. His best friend would not have called him good-looking, but he was the fortunate possessor of that cheerful type of ugliness which inspires immediate confidence in its owner. His nose had never quite recovered from the final one year in the Public Schools Heavy

Weights; his mouth was not small. In fact, to be strictly accurate only his eyes redeemed his face from being what is known in the vernacular as the Frozen Limit.

Deep-set and steady, with eyelashes that many a woman had envied, they showed the man for what he was – a sportsman and a gentleman. And the combination of the two is an unbeatable production.

He paused as he got to the table, and glanced at the rows of letters. His servant, pretending to busy himself at the other end of the room, was watching him surreptitiously, and noted the grin which slowly spread over Drummond's face as he picked up two or three and examined the envelopes.

'Who would have thought it, James?' he remarked at length. 'Great Scott! I shall have to get a partner.'

With disapproval showing in every line of her face, Mrs Denny entered the room, carrying the kidneys, and Drummond glanced at her with a smile.

'Good morning, Mrs Denny,' he said. 'Wherefore this worried look on your face? Has that reprobate James been misbehaving himself?'

The worthy woman snorted. 'He has not, sir – not yet, leastwise. And if so be that he does' – her eyes travelled up and down the back of the hapless Denny, who was quite unnecessarily pulling books off shelves and putting them back again – 'if so be that he does,' she continued grimly, 'him and me will have words – as I've told him already this morning.' She stalked from the room, after staring pointedly at the letters in Drummond's hand, and the two men looked at one another.

'It's that there reference to crime, sir, that's torn it,' said Denny in a hoarse whisper.

'Thinks I'm going to lead you astray, does she, James?'

Hugh helped himself to bacon. 'My dear fellow, she can think what she likes so long as she continues to grill bacon like this. Your wife is a treasure, James – a pearl amongst women: and you can tell her so with my love.' He was opening the first envelope, and suddenly he looked up with a twinkle in his eyes. 'Just to set her mind at rest,' he remarked gravely, 'you might tell her that, as far as I can see at present, I shall only undertake murder in exceptional cases.'

He propped the letter up against the toast-rack and commenced his breakfast. 'Don't go, James.' With a slight frown he was studying the typewritten sheet. 'I'm certain to want your advice before long. Though not over this one . . . It does not appeal to me – not at all. To assist Messrs Jones & Jones, whose business is to advance money on note of hand alone, to obtain fresh clients, is a form of amusement which leaves me cold. The waste-paper basket, please, James. Tear the effusion up, and we will pass on to the next.'

He looked at the mauve envelope doubtfully, and examined the postmark. 'Where is Pudlington, James? And one might almost ask – why is Pudlington? No town has any right to such an offensive name.' He glanced through the letter and shook his head. 'Tush! tush! And the wife of the bank manager, too – the bank manager of Pudlington, James! Can you conceive of anything so dreadful? But I'm afraid Mrs Bank Manager is a puss – a distinct puss. It's when they get on the soul-mate stunt that the furniture begins to fly.'

Drummond tore up the letter and dropped the pieces into the basket beside him. Then he turned to his servant and handed him the remainder of the envelopes.

'Go through them, James, while I assault the kidneys,

and pick two or three out for me. I see that you will have to become my secretary. No man could tackle that little bunch alone.'

'Do you want me to open them, sir?' asked Denny doubtfully.

'You've hit it, James – hit it in one. Classify them for me in groups. Criminal; sporting; amatory – that means of or pertaining to love; stupid and merely boring; and as a last resort, miscellaneous.' He stirred his coffee thoughtfully. 'I feel that as a first venture in our new career – ours, I said, James – love appeals to me irresistibly. Find me a damsel in distress; a beautiful girl, helpless in the clutches of knaves. Let me feel that I can fly to her succour, clad in my new grey suiting.'

He finished the last piece of bacon and pushed away his plate. 'Amongst all that mass of paper there must surely be one from a lovely maiden, James, at whose disposal I can place my rusty sword. Incidentally, what has become of the damned thing?'

'It's in the lumber-room, sir – tied up with the old humbrella and the niblick you don't like.'

'Great heavens! Is it?' Drummond helped himself to marmalade. 'Do you think anybody would be mug enough to buy it, James?'

But that worthy was engrossed in a letter he had just opened, and apparently failed to hear the question. A perplexed look was spreading over his face, and suddenly he sucked his teeth loudly. It was a sure sign that James was excited, and though Drummond had almost cured him of this distressing habit, he occasionally forgot himself in moments of stress.

His master glanced up quickly, and removed the letter from his hands. 'I'm surprised at you, James,' he remarked severely. 'A secretary should control itself. Don't forget that the perfect secretary is an it: an automatic machine – a thing incapable of feeling . . .'

He read the letter through rapidly, and then, turning back to the beginning, he read it slowly through again.

My dear Box X10 – I don't know whether your advertisement was a joke. I suppose it must have been. But I read it this morning, and it's just possible, X10, just possible, that you mean it. And if you do, you're the man I want. I can offer you excitement and probably crime.

I'm up against it, X10. For a girl I've bitten off rather more than I can chew. I want help – badly. Will you come to the Carlton for tea tomorrow afternoon? I want to have a look at you and see if I think you are genuine. Wear a white flower in your buttonhole.

Drummond laid the letter down, and pulled out his cigarette-case. 'Tomorrow, James,' he murmured. 'That is today – this very afternoon. Verily I believe that we have impinged upon the goods.' He rose and stood looking out of the window thoughtfully. 'Go out, my trusty fellow, and buy me a daisy or a cauliflower or something white.'

'You think it's genuine, sir?' said James thoughtfully.

His master blew out a cloud of smoke. 'I *know* it is,' he answered dreamily. 'Look at that writing; the decision in it – the character. She'll be medium height, and dark, with the sweetest little nose and mouth. Her colouring, James, will be –'

But James had discreetly left the room.

II

At four o'clock exactly Hugh Drummond stepped out of his two-seater at the Haymarket entrance to the Carlton. A white gardenia was in his buttonhole; his grey suit looked the last word in exclusive tailoring. For a few moments after entering the hotel he stood at the top of the stairs outside the dining-room, while his eyes travelled round the tables in the lounge below.

A brother-officer, evidently taking two country cousins round London, nodded resignedly; a woman at whose house he had danced several times smiled at him. But save for a courteous bow he took no notice; slowly and thoroughly he continued his search. It was early, of course, yet, and she might not have arrived, but he was taking no chances.

Suddenly his eyes ceased wandering, and remained fixed on a table at the far end of the lounge. Half hidden behind a plant a girl was seated alone, and for a moment she looked straight at him. Then, with the faintest suspicion of a smile, she turned away, and commenced drumming on the table with her fingers.

The table next to her was unoccupied, and Drummond made his way towards it and sat down. It was characteristic of the man that he did not hesitate; having once made up his mind to go through with a thing, he was in the habit of going and looking neither to the right hand nor to the left. Which, incidentally, was how he got his DSO; but that, as Kipling would say, is another story.

He felt not the slightest doubt in his mind that this was the girl who had written to him, and, having given an order to the waiter, he started to study her face as unobtrusively as possible. He could only see the profile but that was quite sufficient to make him bless the

moment when more as a jest than anything else he had
sent his advertisement to the paper.

Her eyes, he could see, were very blue; and great
masses of golden brown hair coiled over her ears, from
under a small black hat. He glanced at her feet – being an
old stager; she was perfectly shod. He glanced at her
hands, and noted, with approval, the absence of any
ring. Then he looked once more at her face, and found
her eyes fixed on him.

This time she did not look away. She seemed to think
that it was her turn to conduct the examination, and
Drummond turned to his tea while the scrutiny continued. He poured himself out a cup, and then fumbled
in his waistcoat pocket. After a moment he found what
he wanted, and taking out a card he propped it against
the teapot so that the girl could see what was on it. In
large block capitals he had written 'Box X10'. Then he
added milk and sugar and waited.

She spoke almost at once. 'You'll do, X10,' she said,
and he turned to her with a smile.

'It's very nice of you to say so,' he murmured. 'If I may,
I will return the compliment. So will you.'

She frowned slightly. 'This isn't foolishness, you
know. What I said in my letter is literally true.'

'Which makes the compliment even more returnable,'
he answered. 'If I am to embark on a life of crime, I would
sooner collaborate with you than – shall we say? – that
earnest eater over there with the tomato in her hat.'

He waved vaguely at the lady in question and then
held out his cigarette-case to the girl. 'Turkish on this side
– Virginian on that,' he remarked. 'And as I appear
satisfactory, will you tell me who I'm to murder?'

With the unlighted cigarette held in her fingers she
stared at him gravely. 'I want you to tell me,' she said at

length, and there was no trace of jesting in her voice, 'tell me, on your word of honour, whether that advertisement was bona fide or a joke.'

He answered her in the same vein. 'It started more or less as a joke. It may now be regarded as absolutely genuine.'

She nodded as if satisfied. 'Are you prepared to risk your life?'

Drummond's eyebrows went up and then he smiled. 'Granted that the inducement is sufficient,' he returned slowly, 'I think that I may say that I am.'

She nodded again. 'You won't be asked to do it in order to obtain a halfpenny bun,' she remarked. 'If you've a match, I would rather like a light.'

Drummond apologized. 'Our talk on trivialties engrossed me for the moment,' he murmured. He held the lighted match for her, and as he did so he saw that she was staring over his shoulder at someone behind his back.

'Don't look round,' she ordered, 'and tell me your name quickly.'

'Drummond – Captain Drummond, late of the Loamshires.' He leaned back in his chair, and lit a cigarette himself.

'And are you going to Henley this year?' Her voice was a shade louder than before.

'I don't know,' he answered casually. 'I may run down for a day possibly, but –'

'My dear Phyllis,' said a voice behind his back, 'this is a pleasant surprise. I had no idea that you were in London.'

A tall, clean-shaven man stopped beside the table, throwing a keen glance at Drummond.

'The world is full of such surprises, isn't it?' answered

the girl lightly. 'I don't suppose you know Captain Drummond, do you? Mr Lakington – art connoisseur and – er – collector.'

The two men bowed slightly, and Mr Lakington smiled. 'I do not remember ever having heard my harmless pastimes more concisely described,' he remarked suavely. 'Are you interested in such matters?'

'Not very, I'm afraid,' answered Drummond. 'Just recently I have been rather too busy to pay much attention to art.'

The other man smiled again, and it struck Hugh that rarely, if ever, had he seen such a cold, merciless face.

'Of course, you've been in France,' Lakington murmured. 'Unfortunately a bad heart kept me on this side of the water. One regrets it in many ways – regrets it immensely. Sometimes I cannot help thinking how wonderful it must have been to be able to kill without fear of consequences. There is art in killing, Captain Drummond – profound art. And as you know, Phyllis,' he turned to the girl, 'I have always been greatly attracted by anything requiring the artistic touch.' He looked at his watch and sighed. 'Alas! I must tear myself away. Are you returning home this evening?'

The girl, who had been glancing round the restaurant, shrugged her shoulders. 'Probably,' she answered. 'I haven't quite decided. I might stop with Aunt Kate.'

'Fortunate Aunt Kate.' With a bow Lakington turned away, and through the glass Drummond watched him get his hat and stick from the cloakroom. Then he looked at the girl, and noticed that she had gone a little white.

'What's the matter, old thing?' he asked quickly. 'Are you feeling faint?'

She shook her head, and gradually the colour came

back to her face. 'I'm quite all right,' she answered. 'It gave me rather a shock, that man finding us here.'

'On the face of it, it seems a harmless occupation,' said Hugh.

'On the face of it, perhaps,' she said. 'But that man doesn't deal with face values.' With a short laugh she turned to Hugh. 'You've stumbled right into the middle of it, my friend, rather sooner than I anticipated. That is one of the men you will probably have to kill . . .'

Her companion lit another cigarette. 'There is nothing like straightforward candour,' he grinned. 'Except that I disliked his face and his manner, I must admit that I saw nothing about him to necessitate my going to so much trouble. What is his particular worry?'

'First and foremost the brute wants to marry me,' replied the girl.

'I loathe being obvious,' said Hugh, 'but I am not surprised.'

'But it isn't that that mattters,' she went on. 'I wouldn't marry him even to save my life.' She looked at Drummond quietly. 'Henry Lakington is the second most dangerous man in England.'

'Only the second,' murmured Hugh. 'Then hadn't I better start my new career with the first?'

She looked at him in silence. 'I suppose you think that I'm hysterical,' she remarked after a while. 'You're probably even wondering whether I'm all there.'

Drummond flicked the ash from his cigarette, then he turned to her dispassionately. 'You must admit,' he remarked, 'that up to now our conversation has hardly proceeded along conventional lines. I am a complete stranger to you; another man who is a complete stranger to me speaks to you while we're at tea. You inform me that I shall probably have to kill him in the near future. The statement is, I think you will agree, a trifle disconcerting.'

The girl threw back her head and laughed merrily. 'You poor young man,' she cried; 'put that way it does sound alarming.' Then she grew serious again. 'There's plenty of time for you to back out now if you like. Just call the waiter, and ask for my bill. We'll say goodbye, and the incident will finish.'

She was looking at him gravely as she spoke, and it seemed to her companion that there was an appeal in the big blues eyes. And they were very big: and the face they were set in was very charming – especially at the angle it was tilted at, in the half-light of the room. Altogether, Drummond reflected, a most adorable girl. And adorable girls had always been a hobby of his. Probably Lakington possessed a letter of hers or something, and she wanted him to get it back. Of course he would, even if he had to thrash the swine within an inch of his life.

'Well!' The girl's voice cut into his train of thought and he hurriedly pulled himself together.

'The last thing I want is for the incident to finish,' he said fervently. 'Why – it's only just begun.'

'Then you'll help me?'

'That's what I'm here for.' With a smile Drummond lit another cigarette. 'Tell me all about it.'

'The trouble,' she began after a moment, 'is that there is not very much to tell. At present it is largely guess-work, and guesswork without much of a clue. However, to start with, I had better tell you what sort of men you are up against. Firstly, Henry Lakington – the man who spoke to me. He was, I believe, one of the most brilliant scientists who have ever been up at Oxford. There was nothing, in his own line, which would not have been open to him, had he run straight. But he didn't. He deliberately chose to turn his brain to crime. Not vulgar, common sorts of crime – but the big things, calling for a master criminal. He has always had enough money to allow him to take his time over any coup – to perfect his details. And that's what he loves. He regards crime as an ordinary man regards a complicated business deal – a thing to be looked at and studied from all angles, a thing to be treated as a mathematical problem. He is quite unscrupulous; he is only concerned in pitting himself against the world and winning.'

'An engaging fellah,' said Hugh. 'What particular form of crime does he favour?'

'Anything that calls for brain, iron nerve, and refinement of detail,' she answered. 'Principally, up to date, burglary on a big scale, and murder.'

'My dear soul!' said Hugh incredulously. 'How can you be sure? And why don't you tell the police?'

She smiled wearily. 'Because I've got no proof, and even if I had . . .' She gave a little shudder, and left her sentence unfinished. 'But one day, my father and I were in his house, and, by accident, I got into a room I'd never been in before. It was a strange room, with two large safes let into the wall and steel bars over the skylight in the ceiling. There wasn't a window, and the floor seemed to be made of concrete. And the door was covered with curtains, and was heavy to move – almost as if it was steel or iron. On the desk in the middle of the room lay some miniatures, and, without thinking, I picked them up and looked at them. I happen to know something about miniatures, and, to my horror, I recognized them.' She paused for a moment as a waiter went by their table.

'Do you remember the theft of the celebrated Vatican miniatures belonging to the Duke of Melbourne?'

Drummond nodded; he was beginning to feel interested.

'They were the ones I was holding in my hand,' she said quietly. 'I knew them at once from the description in the papers. And just as I was wondering what on earth to do, the man himself walked into the room.'

'Awkward – deuced awkward.' Drummond pressed out his cigarette and leaned forward expectantly. 'What did he do?'

'Absolutely nothing,' said the girl. 'That's what made it so awful.'

'"Admiring my treasures?" he remarked. "Pretty things, aren't they?" I couldn't speak a word: I just put them back on the table.

'"Wonderful copies," he went on, "of the Duke of Melbourne's lost miniatures. I think they would deceive most people."

'"They deceived me," I managed to get out.

'"Did they?" he said. "The man who painted them will be flattered."

'All the time he was staring at me, a cold, merciless stare that seemed to freeze my brain. Then he went over to one of the safes and unlocked it. "Come here, Miss Benton," he said. "There are a lot more – copies."

'I looked inside only for a moment, but I have never seen or thought of such a sight. Beautifully arranged on black velvet shelves were ropes of pearls, a gorgeous diamond tiara, and a whole heap of loose, uncut stones, and in one corner I caught a glimpse of the most wonderful gold chaliced cup – just like the one for which Samuel Levy, the Jew moneylender, was still offering a reward. Then he shut the door and locked it, and again stared at me in silence.

'"All copies," he said quietly, "wonderful copies. And

should you ever be tempted to think otherwise – ask your father, Miss Benton. Be warned by me; don't do anything foolish. Ask your father first."'

'And did you?' asked Drummond.

She shuddered. 'That very evening,' she answered. 'And Daddy flew into a frightful passion, and told me never to dare meddle in things that didn't concern me again. Then gradually, as time went on, I realized that Lakington had some hold over Daddy – that he'd got my father in his power. Daddy – of all people – who wouldn't hurt a fly: the best and dearest man who ever breathed.' Her hands were clenched, and her breast rose and fell stormily.

Drummond waited for her to compose herself before he spoke again. 'You mentioned murder, too,' he remarked.

She nodded. 'I've got no proof,' she said, 'less even than over the burglaries. But there was a man called George Dringer, and one evening, when Lakington was dining with us, I heard him discussing this man with Daddy.

'"He's got to go," said Lakington. "He's dangerous!"

'And then my father got up and closed the door; but I heard them arguing for half an hour. Three weeks later a coroner's jury found that George Dringer had committed suicide while temporarily insane. The same evening Daddy, for the first time in his life, went to bed the worse for drink.'

The girl fell silent, and Drummond stared at the orchestra with troubled eyes. Things seemed to be rather deeper than he had anticipated.

'Then there was another case.' She was speaking again. 'Do you remember that man who was found dead in a railway-carriage at Oxhey station? He was an Italian –

Giuseppe by name; and the jury brought in a verdict of death from natural causes. A month before, he had an interview with Lakington which took place at our house: because the Italian, being a stranger, came to the wrong place, and Lakington happened to be with us at the time. The interview finished with a fearful quarrel.' She turned to Drummond with a smile. 'Not much evidence, is there? Only I *know* Lakington murdered him. I *know* it. You may think I'm fanciful – imagining things; you may think I'm exaggerating. I don't mind if you do – because you won't for long.'

Drummond did not answer immediately. Against his saner judgement he was beginning to be profoundly impressed, and, at the moment, he did not quite know what to say. That the girl herself firmly believed in what she was telling him, he was certain; the point was how much of it was – as she herself expressed it – fanciful imagination.

'What about this other man?' he asked at length.

'I can tell you very little about him,' she answered. 'He came to The Elms – that is the name of Lakington's house – three months ago. He is about medium height and rather thick-set; clean-shaven, with thick brown hair flecked slightly with white. His forehead is broad and his eyes are a sort of cold grey-blue. But it's his hands that terrify me. They're large and white and utterly ruthless.' She turned to him appealingly. 'Oh! don't think I'm talking wildly,' she implored. 'He frightens me to death – that man: far, far worse than Lakington. He would stop at nothing to gain his ends, and even Lakington himself knows that Mr Peterson is master.'

'Peterson!' murmured Drummond. 'It seems quite a sound old English name.'

The girl laughed scornfully. 'Oh! the name is sound

enough, if it was his real name. As it is, it's about as real as his daughter.'

'There is a lady in the case, then?'

'By the name of Irma,' said the girl briefly. 'She lies on a sofa in the garden and yawns. She's no more English than that waiter.'

A faint smile flickered over her companion's face; he had formed a fairly vivid mental picture of Irma. Then he grew serious again.

'And what is it that makes you think there's mischief ahead?' he asked abruptly.

The girl shrugged her shoulders. 'What the novelists call feminine intuition, I suppose,' she answered. 'That – and my father.' She said the last words very low. 'He hardly ever sleeps at night now; I hear him pacing up and down his room – hour after hour, hour after hour. Oh! it makes me mad . . . Don't you understand? I've just got to find out what the trouble is. I've got to get him away from those devils, before he breaks down completely.'

Drummond nodded, and looked away. The tears were bright in her eyes, and, like every Englishman, he detested a scene. While she had been speaking he had made up his mind what course to take, and now, having outsat everybody else, he decided that it was time for the interview to cease. Already an early diner was having a cocktail, while Lakington might return at any moment. And if there was anything in what she had told him, it struck him that it would be as well for that gentleman not to find them still together.

'I think,' he said, 'we'd better go. My address is 60A, Half Moon Street; my telephone is 1234 Mayfair. If anything happens, if ever you want me – at any hour of the day or night – ring me up or write. If I'm not in, leave a message with my servant Denny. He is absolutely reliable. The only other thing is your own address.'

'The Larches, near Godalming,' answered the girl, as they moved towards the door. 'Oh! if you only knew the glorious relief of feeling one's got someone to turn to . . .' She looked at him with shining eyes, and Drummond felt his pulse quicken suddenly. Imagination or not, so far as her fears were concerned, the girl was one of the loveliest things he had ever seen.

'May I drop you anywhere?' he asked, as they stood on the pavement, but she shook her head.

'No, thank you. I'll go in that taxi.' She gave the man an address, and stepped in, while Hugh stood bareheaded by the door.

'Don't forget,' he said earnestly. 'Any time of the day or night. And while I think of it – we're old friends. Can that be done? In case I come and stay, you see.'

She thought for a moment and then nodded her head. 'All right,' she answered. 'We've met a lot in London during the war.'

With a grinding of gear wheels the taxi drove off, leaving Hugh with a vivid picture imprinted on his mind of blue eyes, and white teeth, and a skin like the bloom of a sun-kissed peach.

For a moment or two he stood staring after it, and then he walked across to his own car. With his mind still full of the interview he drove slowly along Piccadilly, while every now and then he smiled grimly to himself. Was the whole thing an elaborate hoax? Was the girl even now chuckling to herself at his gullibility? If so, the game had only just begun, and he had no objection to a few more rounds with such an opponent. A mere tea at the Carlton could hardly be the full extent of the jest . . . And somehow deep down in his mind, he wondered whether it was a joke – whether, by some freak of fate, he had stumbled on one of those strange mysteries which up to date he had regarded as existing only in the realms of shilling shockers.

He turned into his rooms, and stood in front of the mantelpiece taking off his gloves. It was as he was about to lay them down on the table that an envelope caught his eye, addressed to him in an unknown handwriting. Mechanically he picked it up and opened it. Inside was a single half-sheet of notepaper, on which a few lines had been written in a small, neat hand.

> There are more things in Heaven and Earth, young man, than a capability for eating steak and onions, and a desire for adventure. I imagine that you possess both: and they are useful assets in the second locality mentioned by the poet. In Heaven, however, one never knows – especially with regard to the onions. Be careful.

Drummond stood motionless for a moment, with narrowed eyes. Then he leaned forward and pressed the bell . . .

'Who brought this note, James?' he said quietly, as his servant came into the room.

'A small boy, sir. Said I was to be sure and see you got it most particular.' He unlocked a cupboard near the window and produced a tantalus. 'Whisky, sir, or cocktail?'

'Whisky, I think, James.' Hugh carefully folded the sheet of paper and placed it in his pocket. And his face as he took the drink from his man would have left no doubt in an onlooker's mind as to why, in the past, he had earned the name of 'Bulldog' Drummond.

CHAPTER 2

In Which He Journeys to Godalming and the Game Begins

I

'I almost think, James, that I could toy with another kidney.' Drummond looked across the table at his servant, who was carefully arranging two or three dozen letters in groups. 'Do you think it will cause a complete breakdown in the culinary arrangements? I've got a journey in front of me today, and I require a large breakfast.'

James Denny supplied the deficiency from a dish that was standing on an electric heater.

'Are you going for long, sir?' he ventured.

'I don't know, James. It all depends on circumstances. Which, when you come to think of it, is undoubtedly one of the most fatuous phrases in the English language. Is there anything in the world that doesn't depend on circumstances?'

'Will you be motoring, sir, or going by train?' asked James prosaically. Dialectical arguments did not appeal to him.

'By car,' answered Drummond. 'Pyjamas and a toothbrush.'

'You won't take evening clothes, sir?'

'No. I want my visit to appear unpremeditated, James, and if one goes about completely encased in boiled shirts, while pretending to be merely out for the afternoon, people have doubts as to one's intellect.'

James digested this great thought in silence.

'Will you be going far, sir?' he asked at length, pouring out a second cup of coffee.

'To Godalming. A charming spot, I believe, though I've never been there. Charming inhabitants, too, James. The lady I met yesterday at the Carlton lives at Godalming.'

'Indeed, sir,' murmured James non-committally.

'You damned old humbug,' laughed Drummond, 'you know you're itching to know all about it. I had a very long and interesting talk with her, and one of two things emerges quite clearly from our conversation. Either, James, I am a congenital idiot, and don't know enough to come in out of the rain; or we've hit the goods. That is what I propose to find out by my little excursion. Either our legs, my friend, are being pulled till they will never resume their normal shape; or that advertisement has succeeded beyond our wildest dreams.'

'There are a lot more answers in this morning, sir.' Denny made a movement towards the letters he had been sorting. 'One from a lovely widow with two children.'

'Lovely,' cried Drummond. 'How forward of her!' He glanced at the letter and smiled. 'Care, James, and accuracy are essential in a secretary. The misguided woman calls herself lonely, not lovely. She will remain so, so far as I am concerned, until the other matter is settled.'

'Will it take long, sir, do you think?'

'To get it settled?' Drummond lit a cigarette and leaned back in his chair. 'Listen, James, and I will outline the case. The maiden lives at a house called The Larches, near Godalming, with her papa. Not far away is another house called The Elms, owned by a gentleman of the name of Henry Lakington – a nasty man, James, with a nasty face – who was also at the Carlton yesterday afternoon for a short time. And now we come to the point. Miss Benton – that is the lady's name – accuses Mr Lakington of being the complete IT in the criminal line. She went even so far as to say that he was the second most dangerous man in England.'

'Indeed, sir. More coffee, sir?'

'Will nothing move you, James?' remarked his master plaintively. 'This man murders people and does things like that, you know.'

'Personally, sir, I prefer a picture-palace. But I suppose there ain't no accounting for 'obbies. May I clear away, sir?'

'No, James, not at present. Keep quite still while I go on, or I shall get it wrong. Three months ago there arrived at The Elms *the* most dangerous man in England – the IT of ITS. This gentleman goes by the name of Peterson, and he owns a daughter. From what Miss Benton said, I have doubts about that daughter, James.' He rose and strolled over to the window. 'Grave doubts. However, to return to the point, it appears that some unpleasing conspiracy is being hatched by IT, the IT of ITS, and the doubtful daughter, into which Papa Benton has been unwillingly drawn. As far as I can make out, the suggestion is that I should unravel the tangled skein of crime and extricate papa.'

In a spasm of uncontrollable excitement James sucked his teeth. 'Lumme, it wouldn't 'alf go on the movies, would it?' he remarked. 'Better than them Red Indians and things.'

'I fear, James, that you are not in the habit of spending your spare time at the British Museum, as I hoped,' said Drummond. 'And your brain doesn't work very quickly. The point is not whether this hideous affair is better than

Red Indians and things – but whether it's genuine. Am I to battle with murderers, or shall I find a house-party roaring with laughter on the lawn?'

'As long as you laughs like 'ell yourself, sir, I don't see as 'ow it makes much odds,' answered James philosophically.

'The first sensible remark you've made this morning,' said his master hopefully. 'I will go prepared to laugh.'

He picked up a pipe from the mantelpiece, and proceeded to fill it, while James Denny still waited in silence.

'A lady may ring up today,' Drummond continued. 'Miss Benton, to be exact. Don't say where I've gone if she does; but take down any message, and wire it to me at Godalming Post Office. If by any chance you don't hear from me for three days, get in touch with Scotland Yard, and tell 'em where I've gone. That covers everything if it's genuine. If, on the other hand, it's a hoax, and the house-party is a good one, I shall probably want you to come down with my evening clothes and some more kit.'

'Very good, sir. I will clean your small Colt revolver at once.'

Hugh Drummond paused in the act of lighting his pipe, and a grin spread slowly over his face. 'Excellent,' he said. 'And see if you can find that water-squirt pistol I used to have – a Son of a Gun they called it. That ought to raise a laugh, when I arrest the murderer with it.'

II

The 30 hp two-seater made short work of the run to Godalming. Under the dickey seat behind lay a small bag, containing the bare necessities for the night; and as Drummond thought of the two guns rolled up carefully in his pyjamas – the harmless toy and the wicked little automatic – he grinned gently to himself. The girl had not rung him up during the morning, and, after a comfortable lunch at his club, he had started about three o'clock. The hedges, fresh with the glory of spring, flashed past; the smell of the country came sweet and fragrant on the air. There was a gentle warmth, a balminess in the day that made it good to be alive, and once or twice he sang under his breath through sheer light-heartedness of spirit. Surrounded by the peaceful beauty of the fields, with an occasional village half hidden by great trees from under which the tiny houses peeped out, it seemed impossible that crime could exist – laughable. Of course the thing was a hoax, an elaborate leg-pull, but, being not guilty of any mental subterfuge, Hugh Drummond admitted to himself quite truly that he didn't care a damn if it was. Phyllis Benton was at liberty to continue the jest, wherever and whenever she liked. Phyllis Benton was a very nice girl, and very nice girls are permitted a lot of latitude.

A persistent honking behind aroused him from his reverie, and he pulled into the side of the road. Under normal circumstances he would have let his own car out, and as she could touch ninety with ease, he very rarely found himself passed. But this afternoon he felt disinclined to race; he wanted to go quietly and think. Blue eyes and that glorious colouring were a dangerous combination – distinctly dangerous. Most engrossing to a healthy bachelor's thoughts.

An open cream-coloured Rolls-Royce drew level, with five people on board, and he looked up as it passed. There were three people in the back – two men and a woman, and for a moment his eyes met those of the man nearest him. Then they drew ahead, and Drummond pulled up to avoid the thick cloud of dust.

With a slight frown he stared at the retreating car; he saw the man lean over and speak to the other man; he saw the other man look round. Then a bend in the road hid them from sight, and, still frowning, Drummond pulled out his case and lit a cigarette. For the man whose eye he had caught as the Rolls went by was Henry Lakington. There was no mistaking that hard-lipped, cruel face. Presumably, thought Hugh, the other two occupants were Mr Peterson and the doubtful daughter, Irma; presumably they were returning to The Elms. And incidentally there seemed no pronounced reason why they shouldn't. But, somehow, the sudden appearance of Lakington had upset him; he felt irritable and annoyed. What little he had seen of the man he had not liked; he did not want to be reminded of him, especially just as he was thinking of Phyllis.

He watched the white dust-cloud rise over the hill in front as the car topped it; he watched it settle and drift away in the faint breeze. Then he let in his clutch and followed quite slowly in the big car's wake.

There had been two men in front – the driver and another, and he wondered idly if the latter was Mr Benton. Probably not, he reflected, since Phyllis had said nothing about her father being in London. He accelerated up the hill and swung over the top; the next moment he braked hard and pulled up just in time. The Rolls, with the chauffeur peering into the bonnet had stopped in such a position that it was impossible for him to get by.

The girl was still seated in the back of the car, also the passenger in front, but the two other men were standing in the road apparently watching the chauffeur, and after a while the one whom Drummond had recognized as Lakington came towards him.

'I'm so sorry,' he began – and then paused in surprise. 'Why, surely it's Captain Drummond?'

Drummond nodded pleasantly. 'The occupant of a car is hardly likely to change in a mile, is he?' he remarked. 'I'm afraid I forgot to wave as you went past, but I got your smile all right.' He leant on his steering-wheel and lit a second cigarette. 'Are you likely to be long?' he asked; 'because if so, I'll stop my engine.'

The other man was now approaching casually, and Drummond regarded him curiously. 'A friend of our little Phyllis, Peterson,' said Lakington, as he came up. 'I found them having tea together yesterday at the Carlton.'

'Any friend of Miss Benton's is, I hope, ours,' said Peterson with a smile. 'You've known her a long time, I expect?'

'Quite a long time,' returned Hugh. 'We have jazzed together on many occasions.'

'Which makes it all the more unfortunate that we should have delayed you,' said Peterson. 'I can't help thinking, Lakington, that that new chauffeur is a bit of a fool.'

'I hope he avoided the crash all right,' murmured Drummond politely.

Both men looked at him. 'The crash!' said Lakington. 'There was no question of a crash. We just stopped.'

'Really,' remarked Drummond, 'I think, sir, that you must be right in your diagnosis of your chauffeur's mentality.' He turned courteously to Peterson. 'When something goes wrong, for a fellah to stop his car by braking so hard that he locks both back wheels is no *bon*, as we used to say in France. I thought, judging by the tracks in the dust, that you must have been in imminent danger of ramming a traction engine. Or perhaps,' he added judicially, 'a sudden order to stop would have produced the same effect.' If he saw the lightning glance that passed between the two men he gave no sign. 'May I offer you a cigarette? Turkish that side – Virginian the other. I wonder if I could help your man,' he continued, when they had helped themselves. 'I'm a bit of an expert with a Rolls.'

'How very kind of you,' said Peterson. 'I'll go and see.' He went over to the man and spoke a few words.

'Isn't it extraordinary,' remarked Hugh, 'how the eye of the boss galvanizes the average man into activity! As long, probably, as Mr Peterson had remained here talking, that chauffeur would have gone on tinkering with the engine. And now – look, in a second – all serene. And yet I dare say Mr Peterson knows nothing about it really. Just the watching eye, Mr Lakington. Wonderful thing – the human optic.'

He rambled on with a genial smile, watching with apparent interest the car in front. 'Who's the quaint bird sitting beside the chauffeur? He appeals to me immensely. Wish to Heaven I'd had a few more like him in France to turn into snipers.'

'May I ask why you think he would have been a success at the job?' Lakington's voice expressed merely perfunctory interest, but his cold, steely eyes were fixed on Drummond.

'He's so motionless,' answered Hugh. 'The bally fellow hasn't moved a muscle since I've been here. I believe he'd sit on a hornets' nest, and leave the inmates guessing. Great gift, Mr Lakington. Shows a strength of will but rarely met with – a mind which rises above mere vulgar curiosity.'

'It is undoubtedly a great gift to have such a mind, Captain Drummond,' said Lakington. 'And if it isn't born in a man, he should most certainly try to cultivate it.' He pitched his cigarette away, and buttoned up his coat. 'Shall we be seeing you this evening?'

Drummond shrugged his shoulders. 'I'm the vaguest man that ever lived,' he said lightly. 'I might be listening to nightingales in the country; or I might be consuming steak and onions preparatory to going to a night club. So long . . . You must let me take you to Hector's one night. Hope you don't break down again so suddenly.'

He watched the Rolls-Royce start, but seemed in no hurry to follow suit. And his many friends, who were wont to regard Hugh Drummond as a mass of brawn not too plentifully supplied with brains, would have been puzzled had they seen the look of keen concentration on his face as he stared along the white, dusty road. He could not say why, but suddenly and very certainly the conviction had come to him that this was no hoax and no leg-pull – but grim and sober reality. In his imagination he heard the sudden sharp order to stop the instant they were over the hill, so that Peterson might have a chance of inspecting him; in a flash of intuition he knew that these two men were no ordinary people, and that he was suspect. And as he slipped smoothly after the big car, now well out of sight, two thoughts were dominant in his mind. The first was that there was some mystery about the motionless, unnatural man who had sat beside the driver; the second was a distinct feeling of relief that his automatic was fully loaded.

III

At half-past five he stopped in front of Godalming Post Office. To his surprise the girl handed him a wire, and Hugh tore the yellow envelope open quickly. It was from Denny, and it was brief and to the point:

Phone message received. AAA. Must see you
Carlton tea day after tomorrow. Going Godalming
now. AAA. Message ends.

With a slight smile he noticed the military phraseology –
Denny at one time in his career had been a signaller – and
then he frowned. 'Must see you.' She should – at once.

He turned to the girl and inquired the way to The
Larches. It was about two miles, he gathered, on the
Guildford road, and impossible to miss – a biggish house
standing well back in its own grounds.

'Is it anywhere near a house called The Elms?' he
asked.

'Next door, sir,' said the girl. 'The gardens adjoin.'

He thanked her, and having torn up the telegram into
small pieces, he got into his car. There was nothing for it,
he had decided, but to drive boldly up to the house, and
say that he had come to call on Miss Benton. He had
never been a man who beat about the bush, and simple
methods appealed to him – a trait in his character which
many a boxer, addicted to tortuous cunning in the ring,
had good cause to remember. What more natural, he
reflected, than to drive over and see such an old friend?

He had no difficulty in finding the house, and a few
minutes later he was ringing the front-door bell. It was
answered by a maidservant, who looked at him in mild
surprise. Young men in motor cars were not common
visitors at The Larches.

'Is Miss Benton in?' Hugh asked with a smile which at
once won the girl's heart.

'She has only just come back from London, sir,' she
answered doubtfully. 'I don't know whether . . .'

'Would you tell her that Captain Drummond has
called?' said Hugh as the maid hesitated. 'That I

happened to find myself near here, and came on chance of seeing her?

Once again the smile was called into play, and the girl hesitated no longer. 'Will you come inside, sir?' she said. 'I will go and tell Miss Phyllis.'

She ushered him into the drawing-room and closed the door. It was a charming room, just such as he would have expected with Phyllis. Big windows, opening down to the ground, led out on to a lawn, which was already a blaze of colour. A few great oak trees threw a pleasant shade at the end of the garden, and, partially showing through them, he could see another house which he rightly assumed was The Elms. In fact, even as he heard the door open and shut behind him, he saw Peterson come out of a small summer-house and commence strolling up and down, smoking a cigar. Then he turned round and faced the girl.

Charming as she had looked in London, she was doubly so now, in a simple linen frock which showed off her figure to perfection. But if he thought he was going to have any leisure to enjoy the picture undisturbed, he was soon disillusioned.

'Why have you come here, Captain Drummond?' she said, a little breathlessly. 'I said the Carlton – the day after tomorrow.'

'Unfortunately,' said Hugh, 'I'd left London before that message came. My servant wired it on to the post office here. Not that it would have made any difference. I should have come, anyway.'

An involuntary smile hovered round her lips for a moment; then she grew serious again. 'It's very dangerous for you to come here,' she remarked quietly. 'If once those men suspect anything, God knows what will happen.'

It was on the tip of his tongue to tell her that it was too

late to worry about that; then he changed his mind. 'And what is there suspicious,' he asked, 'in an old friend who happens to be in the neighbourhood dropping in to call? Do you mind if I smoke?'

The girl beat her hands together. 'My dear man,' she cried, 'you don't understand. You're judging those devils by your own standard. They suspect everything – and everybody.'

'What a distressing habit,' he murmured. 'Is it chronic, or merely due to liver? I must send 'em a bottle of good salts. Wonderful thing – good salts. Never without some in France.'

The girl looked at him resignedly. 'You're hopeless,' she remarked – 'absolutely hopeless.'

'Absolutely,' agreed Hugh, blowing out a cloud of smoke. 'Wherefore your telephone message? What's the worry?'

She bit her lip and drummed with her fingers on the arm of her chair. 'If I tell you,' she said at length, 'will you promise me, on your word of honour, that you won't go blundering into The Elms, or do anything foolish like that?'

'At the present moment I'm very comfortable where I am, thanks,' remarked Hugh.

'I know,' she said; 'but I'm so dreadfully afraid that you're the type of person who . . . who . . .' She paused, at a loss for a word.

'Who bellows like a bull, and charges head down,' interrupted Hugh with a grin. She laughed with him, and just for a moment their eyes met, and she read in his something quite foreign to the point at issue. In fact, it is to be feared that the question of Lakington and his companions was not engrossing Drummond's mind, as it doubtless should have been, to the exclusion of all else.

'They're so utterly unscrupulous,' she continued, hurriedly, 'so fiendishly clever, that even you would be like a child in their hands.'

Hugh endeavoured to dissemble his pleasure at that little word 'even', and only succeeded in frowning horribly.

'I will be discretion itself,' he assured her firmly. 'I promise you.'

'I suppose I shall have to trust you,' she said. 'Have you seen the evening papers today?'

'I looked at the ones that came out in the morning labelled 6 p.m. before I had lunch,' he answered. 'Is there anything of interest?'

She handed him a copy of the *Planet*. 'Read that little paragraph in the second column.' She pointed to it, as he took the paper, and Hugh read it aloud.

'Mr Hiram C. Potts – the celebrated American millionaire – is progressing favourably. He has gone into the country for a few days, but is sufficiently recovered to conduct business as usual.' He laid down the paper and looked at the girl sitting opposite. 'One is pleased,' he remarked in a puzzled tone, 'for the sake of Mr Potts. To be ill and have a name like that is more than most men could stand . . . But I don't quite see . . .'

'That man was stopping at the Carlton, where he met Lakington,' said the girl. 'He is a multi-millionaire, over here in connection with some big steel trust; and when multi-millionaires get friendly with Lakington, their health frequently does suffer.'

'But this paper says he's getting better,' objected Drummond. '"Sufficiently recovered to conduct business as usual." What's wrong with that?'

'If he is sufficiently recovered to conduct business as usual, why did he send his confidential secretary away yesterday morning on an urgent mission to Belfast?'

'Search me,' said Hugh. 'Incidentally, how do you know he did?'

'I asked at the Carlton this morning,' she answered. 'I said I'd come after a job as typist for Mr Potts. They told me at the inquiry office that he was ill in bed and unable to see anybody. So I asked for his secretary, and they told me what I've just told you – that he had left for Belfast that morning and would be away several days. It may be that there's nothing in it; on the other hand, it may be that there's a lot. And it's only by following up every possible clue,' she continued fiercely, 'that I can hope to beat those fiends and get Daddy out of their clutches.'

Drummond nodded gravely, and did not speak. For into his mind had flashed suddenly the remembrance of that sinister, motionless figure seated by the chauffeur. The wildest guesswork certainly – no vestige of proof – and yet, having once come, the thought struck. And as he turned it over in his mind, almost prepared to laugh at himself for his credulity – millionaires are not removed against their will, in broad daylight, from one of the biggest hotels in London, to sit in immovable silence in an open car – the door opened and an elderly man came in.

Hugh rose, and the girl introduced the two men. 'An old friend, Daddy,' she said. 'You must have heard me speak of Captain Drummond.'

'I don't recall the name at the moment, my dear,' he answered courteously – a fact which was hardly surprising – 'but I fear I'm getting a little forgetful. I am pleased to meet you, Captain Drummond. You'll stop and have some dinner, of course.'

Hugh bowed. 'I should like to, Mr Benton. Thank you very much. I'm afraid the hour of my call was a little informal, but being round in these parts, I felt I must come and look Miss Benton up.'

His host smiled absent-mindedly, and walking to the window, stared through the gathering dusk at the house opposite, half hidden in the trees. And Hugh, who was watching him from under lowered lids, saw him suddenly clench both hands in a gesture of despair.

It cannot be said that dinner was a meal of sparkling gaiety. Mr Benton was palpably ill at ease, and beyond a few desultory remarks spoke hardly at all: while the girl, who sat opposite Hugh, though she made one or two valiant attempts to break the long silence, spent most of the meal in covertly watching her father. If anything more had been required to convince Drummond of the genuineness of his interview with her at the Carlton the preceding day, the atmosphere at this strained and silent party supplied it.

As if unconscious of anything peculiar, he rambled on in his usual inconsequent method, heedless of whether he was answered or not; but all the time his mind was busily working. He had already decided that a Rolls-Royce was not the only car on the market which could break down mysteriously, and with the town so far away, his host could hardly fail to ask him to stop the night. And then – he had not yet quite settled how – he proposed to have a closer look at The Elms.

At length the meal was over, and the maid, placing the decanter in front of Mr Benton, withdrew from the room.

'You'll have a glass of port, Captain Drummond,' remarked his host, removing the stopper and pushing the bottle towards him. 'An old pre-war wine which I can vouch for.'

Hugh smiled, and even as he lifted the heavy old cut glass, he stiffened suddenly in his chair. A cry – half shout, half scream, and stifled at once – had come echoing through the open windows. With a crash the stopper fell from Mr Benton's nerveless fingers, breaking the finger-bowl in front of him, while every vestige of colour left his face.

'It's something these days to be able to say that,' remarked Hugh, pouring himself out a glass. 'Wine, Miss Benton?' He looked at the girl, who was staring fearfully out of the window, and forced her to meet his eye. 'It will do you good.'

His tone was compelling, and after a moment's hesitation she pushed the glass over to him. 'Will you pour it out?' she said, and he saw that she was trembling all over.

'Did you – did you hear – anything?' With a vain endeavour to speak calmly, his host looked at Hugh.

'That night-bird?' he answered easily. 'Eerie noises they make, don't they? Sometimes in France, when everything was still, and only the ghostly green flares went hissing up, one used to hear 'em. Startled nervous sentries out of their lives.' He talked on, and gradually the colour came back to the other man's face. But Hugh noticed that he drained his port at a gulp, and immediately refilled his glass . . .

Outside everything was still; no repetition of that short, strangled cry again disturbed the silence. With the training bred of many hours in No Man's Land, Drummond was listening, even while he was speaking, for the faintest suspicious sound – but he heard nothing. The soft whispering night-noises came gently through the window; but the man who had screamed once did not even whimper again. He remembered hearing a similar cry near the brickstacks at Guinchy, and two nights later he had found the giver of it, at the ledge of a mine-crater, with glazed eyes that still held in them the horror of the final second. And more persistently than ever, his thoughts centred on the fifth occupant of the Rolls-Royce . . .

It was with almost a look of relief that Mr Benton listened to his tale of woe about his car.

'Of course you must stop here for the night,' he cried. 'Phyllis, my dear, will you tell them to get a room ready?'

With an inscrutable look at Hugh, in which thankfulness and apprehension seemed mingled, the girl left the room. There was an unnatural glitter in her father's eyes – a flush on his cheeks hardly to be accounted for by the warmth of the evening; and it struck Drummond that, during the time he had been pretending to look at his car, Mr Benton had been fortifying himself. It was obvious, even to the soldier's unprofessional eye, that the man's nerves had gone to pieces; and that unless something was done soon, his daughter's worst forebodings were likely to be fulfilled. He talked disjointedly and fast; his hands were not steady, and he seemed to be always waiting for something to happen.

Hugh had not been in the room ten minutes before his host produced the whisky, and during the time that he took to drink a mild nightcap, Mr Benton succeeded in lowering three extremely strong glasses of spirit. And what made it the more sad was that the man was obviously not a heavy drinker by preference.

At eleven o'clock Hugh rose and said good-night.

'You'll ring if you want anything, won't you?' said his host. 'We don't have very many visitors here, but I hope you'll find everything you require. Breakfast at nine.'

Drummond closed the door behind him, and stood for a moment in silence, looking round the hall. It was deserted, but he wanted to get the geography of the house firmly imprinted on his mind. Then a noise from the room he had just left made him frown sharply – his host was continuing the process of fortification – and he stepped across towards the drawing-room. Inside, as he hoped, he found the girl.

She rose the instant he came in, and stood by the mantelpiece with her hands locked.

'What was it?' she half whispered – 'that awful noise at dinner?'

He looked at her gravely for a while, and then he shook his head. 'Shall we leave it as a night-bird for the present?' he said quietly. Then he leaned towards her, and took her hands in his own. 'Go to bed, little girl,' he ordered; 'this is my show. And, may I say, I think you're just wonderful. Thank God you saw my advertisement!'

Gently he released her hands, and walking to the door, held it open for her. 'If by any chance you should hear things in the night – turn over and go to sleep again.'

'But what are you going to do?' she cried.

Hugh grinned. 'I haven't the remotest idea,' he answered. 'Doubtless the Lord will provide.'

The instant the girl had left the room Hugh switched off the lights and stepped across to the curtains which covered the long windows. He pulled them aside, letting them come together behind him; then, cautiously, he unbolted one side of the big centre window. The night was dark, and the moon was not due to rise for two or three hours, but he was too old a soldier to neglect any precautions. He wanted to see more of The Elms and its inhabitants; but he did not want them to see more of him.

Silently he dodged across the lawn towards the big trees at the end, and leaning up against one of them, he proceeded to make a more detailed survey of his objective. It was the same type of house as the one he had just left, and the grounds seemed about the same size. A wire fence separated the two places, and in the darkness Hugh could just make out a small wicket-gate, closing a path which connected both houses. He tried it, and found to his satisfaction that it opened silently.

Passing through, he took cover behind some bushes from which he could command a better view of Mr Lakington's abode. Save for one room on the ground floor the house was in darkness, and Hugh determined to have a look at that room. There was a chink in the curtains, through which the light was streaming out, which struck him as having possibilities.

Keeping under cover, he edged towards it, and at length, he got into a position from which he could see inside. And what he saw made him decide to chance it, and go even closer.

Seated at the table was a man he did not recognize; while on either side of him sat Lakington and Peterson. Lying on a sofa smoking a cigarette and reading a novel was a tall, dark girl, who seemed completely uninterested in the proceedings of the other three. Hugh placed her at once as the doubtful daughter Irma, and resumed his watch on the group at the table.

A paper was in front of the man, and Peterson, who was smoking a large cigar, was apparently suggesting that he should make use of the pen which Lakington was obligingly holding in readiness. In all respects a harmless tableau, save for one small thing – the expression on the man's face. Hugh had seen it before often – only then it had been called shell-shock. The man was dazed, semi-unconscious. Every now and then he stared round the room, as if bewildered; then he would shake his head and pass his hand wearily over his forehead. For a quarter of an hour the scene continued; then Lakington produced an instrument from his pocket. Hugh saw the man shrink back in terror, and reach for the pen. He saw the girl lie back on the sofa as if disappointed and pick up her novel again; and he saw Lakington's face set in a cold sneer. But what impressed him most in that momentary flash of action was Peterson. There was something inhuman in his complete passivity. By not the fraction of a second did he alter the rate at which he was smoking – the slow, leisurely rate of the connoisseur; by not the twitch of an eyelid did his expression change. Even as he watched the man signing his name, no trace of emotion showed on his face – whereas on Lakington's there shone a fiendish satisfaction.

The document was still lying on the table, when Hugh produced his revolver. He knew there was foul play about, and the madness of what he had suddenly made up his mind to do never struck him: being that manner of fool, he was made that way. But he breathed a pious prayer that he would shoot straight – and then he held his breath. The crack of the shot and the bursting of the only electric light bulb in the room were almost simultaneous; and the next second, with a roar of 'Come on, boys,' he burst through the window. At an immense advantage over the others, who could see nothing for the moment, he blundered round the room. He timed the blow at Lakington to a nicety; he hit him straight on the point of the jaw and he felt the man go down like a log. Then he grabbed at the paper on the table, which tore in his hand, and picking the dazed signer up bodily, he rushed through the window on to the lawn. There was not an instant to be lost; only the impossibility of seeing when suddenly plunged into darkness had enabled him to pull the thing off so far. And before that advantage disappeared he had to be back at The Larches with his burden, no lightweight for even a man of his strength to carry.

But there seemed to be no pursuit, no hue and cry. As he reached the little gate he paused and looked back, and he fancied he saw outside the window a gleam of white, such as a shirt-front. He lingered for an instant, peering into the darkness and recovering his breath, when with a vicious phut something buried itself in the tree beside him. Drummond lingered no more; long years of experience left no doubt in his mind as to what that something was.

'Compressed-air rifle – or electric,' he muttered to himself, stumbling on, and half dragging, half carrying his dazed companion.

He was not very clear in his own mind what to do next, but the matter was settled for him unexpectedly. Barely had he got into the drawing-room, when the door opened and the girl rushed in.

'Get him away at once,' she cried. 'In your car . . . Don't waste a second. I've started her up.'

'Good girl,' he cried enthusiastically. 'But what about you?'

She stamped her foot impatiently. 'I'm all right – absolutely all right. Get him away – that's all that matters.'

Drummond grinned. 'The humorous thing is that I haven't an idea who the bird is – except that –' He paused, with his eyes fixed on the man's left thumb. The top joint was crushed into a red, shapeless pulp, and suddenly the meaning of the instrument Lakington had produced from his pocket became clear. Also the reason of that dreadful cry at dinner . . .

'By God!' whispered Drummond, half to himself, while his jaws set like a steel vice. 'A thumbscrew. The devils . . . the bloody swine . . .'

'Oh! quick, quick,' the girl urged in an agony. 'They may be here at any moment.' She dragged him to the door, and together they forced the man into the car.

'Lakington won't,' said Hugh, with a grin. 'And if you

see him tomorrow – don't ask after his jaw . . . Good night, Phyllis.'

With a quick movement he raised her hand to his lips; then he slipped in the clutch and the car disappeared down the drive . . .

He felt a sense of elation and of triumph at having won the first round, and as the car whirled back to London through the cool night air his heart was singing with the joy of action. And it was perhaps as well for his peace of mind that he did not witness the scene in the room at The Elms.

Lakington still lay motionless on the floor; Peterson's cigar still glowed steadily in the darkness. It was hard to believe that he had ever moved from the table; only the bullet imbedded in a tree proved that somebody must have got busy. Of course, it might have been the girl, who was just lighting another cigarette from the stump of the old one.

At length Peterson spoke. 'A young man of dash and temperament,' he said genially. 'It will be a pity to lose him.'

'Why not keep him and lose the girl?' yawned Irma. 'I think he might amuse me –'

'We have always our dear Henry to consider,' answered Peterson. 'Apparently the girl appeals to him. I'm afraid, Irma, he'll have to go . . . and at once . . .'

The speaker was tapping his left knee softly with his hand; save for that slight movement he sat as if nothing had happened. And yet ten minutes before a carefully planned coup had failed at the instant of success. Even his most fearless accomplices had been known to confess that Peterson's inhuman calmness sent cold shivers down their backs.

CHAPTER 3

In Which Things Happen in
Half Moon Street

I

Hugh Drummond folded up the piece of paper he was studying and rose to his feet as the doctor came into the room. He then pushed a silver box of cigarettes across the table and waited.

'Your friend,' said the doctor, 'is in a very peculiar condition, Captain Drummond – very peculiar.' He sat down and, putting the tips of his fingers together, gazed at Drummond in his most professional manner. He paused for a moment, as if expecting an awed agreement with this profound utterance, but the soldier was calmly lighting a cigarette. 'Can you,' resumed the doctor, 'enlighten me at all as to what he has been doing during the last few days?'

Drummond shook his head. 'Haven't an earthly, doctor.'

'There is, for instance, that very unpleasant wound in his thumb,' pursued the other. 'The top joint is crushed to a pulp.'

'I noticed that last night,' answered Hugh non-committally. 'Looks as if it had been mixed up between a hammer and an anvil, don't it?'

'But you have no idea how it occurred?'

'I'm full of ideas,' said the soldier. 'In fact, if it's any help to you in your diagnosis, that wound was caused by the application of an unpleasant medieval instrument known as a thumbscrew.'

The worthy doctor looked at him in amazement. 'A thumbscrew! You must be joking, Captain Drummond.'

'Very far from it,' answered Hugh briefly. 'If you want to know, it was touch and go whether the other thumb didn't share the same fate.' He blew out a cloud of smoke, and smiled inwardly as he noticed the look of scandalized horror on his companion's face. 'It isn't his thumb that concerns me,' he continued; 'it's his general condition. What's the matter with him?'

The doctor pursed his lips and looked wise, while Drummond wondered that no one had ever passed a law allowing men of his type to be murdered on sight.

'His heart seems sound,' he answered after a weighty pause, 'and I found nothing wrong with him constitutionally. In fact, I may say, Captain Drummond, he is in every respect a most healthy man. Except – er – except for this peculiar condition.'

Drummond exploded. 'Damnation take it, and what on earth do you suppose I asked you to come round for? It's of no interest to me to hear that his liver is working properly.' Then he controlled himself. 'I beg your pardon, doctor: I had rather a trying evening last night. Can you give me any idea as to what has caused this peculiar condition?'

His companion accepted the apology with an acid bow. 'Some form of drug,' he answered.

Drummond heaved a sigh of relief. 'Now we're getting on,' he cried. 'Have you any idea what drug?'

'It is, at the moment, hard to say,' returned the other. 'It seems to have produced a dazed condition mentally, without having affected him physically. In a day or two, perhaps, I might be able to – er – arrive at some conclusion . . .'

'Which, at present, you have not. Right! Now we know where we are.' A pained expression flitted over the doctor's face: this young man was very direct. 'To continue,' Hugh went on, 'as you don't know what the drug is, presumably you don't know either how long it will take for the effect to wear off.'

'That – er – is, within limits, correct,' conceded the doctor.

'Right! Once again we know where we are. What about diet?'

'Oh! light . . . Not too much meat . . . No alcohol . . .' He rose to his feet as Hugh opened the door; really the war seemed to have produced a distressing effect on people's manners. Diet was the one question on which he always let himself go . . .

'Not much meat – no alcohol. Right! Good morning, doctor. Down the stairs and straight on. Good morning.' The door closed behind him, and he descended to his waiting car with cold disapproval on his face. The whole affair struck him as most suspicious – thumbscrews, strange drugs . . . Possibly it was his duty to communicate with the police . . .

'Excuse me, sir.' The doctor paused and eyed a well-dressed man who had spoken to him uncompromisingly.

'What can I do for you, sir?' he said.

'Am I right in assuming that you are a doctor?'

'You are perfectly correct, sir, in your assumption.'

The man smiled: obviously a gentleman, thought the practitioner, with his hand on the door of his car.

'It's about a great pal of mine, Captain Drummond,

who lives in here,' went on the other. 'I hope you won't think it unprofessional, but I thought I'd ask you privately how you find him.'

The doctor looked surprised. 'I wasn't aware that he was ill,' he answered.

'But I heard he'd had a bad accident,' said the man, amazed.

The doctor smiled. 'Reassure yourself, my dear sir,' he murmured in his best professional manner. 'Captain Drummond, so far as I am aware, has never been better. I – er – cannot say the same of his friend.' He stepped into his car. 'Why not go up and see for yourself?'

The car rolled smoothly into Piccadilly, but the man showed no signs of availing himself of the doctor's suggestion. He turned and walked rapidly away, and a few moments later – in an exclusive West End club – a trunk call was put through to Godalming – a call which caused the recipient to nod his head in satisfaction and order the Rolls-Royce.

Meanwhile, unconscious of this sudden solicitude for his health, Hugh Drummond was once more occupied with the piece of paper he had been studying on the doctor's entrance. Every now and then he ran his fingers through his crisp brown hair and shook his head in perplexity. Beyond establishing the fact that the man in the peculiar condition was Hiram C. Potts, the American multi-millionaire, he could make nothing out of it.

'If only I'd managed to get the whole of it,' he muttered to himself for the twentieth time. 'That dam' fellah Peterson was too quick.' The scrap he had torn off was typewritten, save for the American's scrawled signature, and Hugh knew the words by heart.

plete paralysis
ade of Britain
months I do
the holder of
of five million
do desire and
earl necklace and the
are at present
chess of Lamp-
k no questions
btained.

AM C. POTTS.

At length he replaced the scrap in his pocket-book and rang the bell.

'James,' he remarked as his servant came in, 'will you whisper "very little meat and no alcohol" in your wife's ear, so far as the bird next door is concerned? Fancy paying a doctor to come round and tell one that!'

'Did he say anything more, sir?'

'Oh! a lot. But that was the only thing of the slightest practical use, and I knew that already.' He stared thoughtfully out of the window. 'You'd better know,' he continued at length, 'that as far as I can see we're up against a remarkably tough proposition.'

'Indeed, sir,' murmured his servant. 'Then perhaps I had better stop any further insertion of that advertisement. It works out at six shillings a time.'

Drummond burst out laughing. 'What would I do without you, oh! my James,' he cried. 'But you may as well stop it. Our hands will be quite full for some time to come, and I hate disappointing hopeful applicants for my services.'

'The gentleman is asking for you, sir.' Mrs Denny's voice from the door made them look round, and Hugh rose.

'Is he talking sensibly, Mrs Denny?' he asked eagerly, but she shook her head.

'Just the same, sir,' she announced. 'Looking round the room all dazed like. And he keeps on saying "Danger".'

Hugh walked quickly along the passage to the room where the millionaire lay in bed.

'How are you feeling?' said Drummond cheerfully.

The man stared at him uncomprehendingly, and shook his head.

'Do you remember last night?' Hugh continued, speaking very slowly and distinctly. Then a sudden idea struck him and he pulled the scrap of paper out of his case. 'Do you remember signing that?' he asked, holding it out to him.

For a while the man looked at it; then with a sudden cry of fear he shrank away. 'No, no,' he muttered, 'not again.'

Hugh hurriedly replaced the paper. 'Bad break on my part, old bean; you evidently remember rather too well. It's quite all right,' he continued reassuringly; 'no one will hurt you.' Then after a pause: 'Is your name Hiram C. Potts?'

The man nodded his head doubtfully and muttered 'Hiram Potts' once or twice, as if the words sounded familiar.

'Do you remember driving in a motor car last night?' persisted Hugh.

But what little flash of remembrance had pierced the drug-clouded brain seemed to have passed; the man only stared dazedly at the speaker. Drummond tried him with a few more questions, but it was no use, and after a while he got up and moved towards the door.

'Don't you worry, old son,' he said with a smile. 'We'll have you jumping about like a two-year-old in a couple of days.'

Then he paused: the man was evidently trying to say something. 'What is it you want?' Hugh leant over the bed.

'Danger, danger.' Faintly the words came, and then, with a sigh, he lay back exhausted.

With a grim smile Drummond watched the motionless figure.

'I'm afraid,' he said half aloud, 'that you're rather like your medical attendant. Your only contribution to the sphere of pure knowledge is something I know already.'

He went out and quietly closed the door. And as he re-entered his sitting-room he found his servant standing motionless behind one of the curtains watching the street below.

'There's a man, sir,' he remarked without turning round, 'watching the house.'

For a moment Hugh stood still, frowning. Then he gave a short laugh. 'The devil there is!' he remarked. 'The game has begun in earnest, my worthy warrior, with the first nine points to us. For possession, even of a semi-dazed lunatic, is nine points of the law, is it not, James?'

His servant retreated cautiously from the curtain, and came back into the room. 'Of the law – yes, sir,' he repeated enigmatically. 'It is time, sir, for your morning glass of beer.'

II

At twelve o'clock precisely the bell rang, announcing a visitor, and Drummond looked up from the columns of the *Sportsman* as his servant came into the room.

'Yes, James,' he remarked. 'I think we are at home. I want you to remain within call, and under no circumstances let our sick visitor out of your sight for more than a minute. In fact, I think you'd better sit in his room.'

He resumed his study of the paper, and James, with a curt 'Very good, sir,' left the room. Almost at once he returned, and flinging open the door announced Mr Peterson.

Drummond looked up quickly and rose with a smile.

'Good morning,' he cried. 'This is a very pleasant surprise, Mr Peterson.' He waved his visitor to a chair. 'Hope you've had no more trouble with your car.'

Mr Peterson drew off his gloves, smiling amiably. 'None at all, thank you, Captain Drummond. The chauffeur appears to have mastered the defect.'

'It was your eye on him that did it. Wonderful thing – the human optic, as I said to your friend, Mr – Mr Laking. I hope that he's quite well and taking nourishment.'

'Soft food only,' said the other genially. 'Mr Lakington had a most unpleasant accident last night – most unpleasant.'

Hugh's face expressed his sympathy. 'How very unfortunate!' he murmured. 'I trust nothing serious.'

'I fear his lower jaw was fractured in two places.' Peterson helped himself to a cigarette from the box beside him. 'The man who hit him must have been a boxer.'

'Mixed up in a brawl, was he?' said Drummond, shaking his head. 'I should never have thought, from what little I've seen of Mr Lakington, that he went in for painting the town red. I'd have put him down as a most abstemious man – but one never can tell, can one? I once knew a fellah who used to get fighting drunk on three whiskies, and to look at him you'd have put him down as a Methodist parson. Wonderful the amount of cheap fun that chap got out of life.'

Peterson flicked the ash from his cigarette into the grate. 'Shall we come to the point, Captain Drummond?' he remarked affably.

Hugh looked bewildered. 'The point, Mr Peterson? Er – by all manner of means.'

Peterson smiled even more affably. 'I felt certain that you were a young man of discernment,' he remarked, 'and I wouldn't like to keep you from your paper a minute longer than necessary.'

'Not a bit,' cried Hugh. 'My time is yours – though I'd very much like to know your real opinion of The Juggernaut for the Chester Cup: It seems to me that he cannot afford to give Sumatra seven pounds on their form up to date.'

'Are you interested in gambling?' asked Peterson politely.

'A mild flutter, Mr Peterson, every now and then,' returned Drummond. 'Strictly limited stakes.'

'If you confine yourself to that you will come to no harm,' said Peterson. 'It is when the stakes become unlimited that the danger of a crash becomes unlimited too.'

'That is what my mother always told me,' remarked Hugh. 'She even went farther, dear good woman that she was. "Never bet except on a certainty, my boy," was her constant advice, "and then put your shirt on!" I can hear her saying it now, Mr Peterson, with the golden rays of the setting sun lighting up her sweet face.'

Suddenly Peterson leant forward in his chair. 'Young man,' he remarked, 'we've got to understand one another. Last night you butted in on my plans, and I do not like people who do that. By an act which, I must admit, appealed to me greatly, you removed something I require – something, moreover, which I intend to have. Breaking the electric bulb with a revolver-shot shows resource and initiative. The blow which smashed Henry Lakington's jaw in two places shows strength. All qualities which I admire, Captain Drummond – admire greatly. I should dislike having to deprive the world of those qualities.'

Drummond gazed at the speaker open-mouthed. 'My dear sir,' he protested feebly, 'you overwhelm me. Are you really accusing me of being a sort of Wild West show?' He waggled a finger at Peterson. 'You know you've been to the movies too much, like my fellah, James. He's got revolvers and things on the brain.'

Peterson's face was absolutely impassive; save for a slightly tired smile it was expressionless. 'Finally, Captain Drummond, you tore in half a piece of paper which I require – and removed a very dear old friend of my family, who is now in this house. I want them both back, please, and if you like I'll take them now.'

Drummond shrugged his shoulders resignedly. 'There is something about you, Mr Peterson,' he murmured, 'which I like. You strike me as being the type of man to whom a young girl would turn and pour out her maidenly secrets. So masterful, so compelling, so unruffled. I feel sure – when you have finally disabused your mind of this absurd hallucination – that we shall become real friends.'

Peterson still sat motionless save for a ceaseless tapping with his hand on his knee.

'Tell me,' continued Hugh, 'why did you allow this scoundrel to treat you in such an off-hand manner? It doesn't seem to me to be the sort of thing that ought to happen at all, and I suggest your going to the police at once.'

'Unfortunately a bullet intended for him just missed,' answered Peterson casually. 'A pity – because there would have been no trace of him by now.'

'Might be awkward for you,' murmured Hugh. 'Such methods, Mr Peterson, are illegal, you know. It's a dangerous thing to take the law into your own hands. May I offer you a drink?'

Peterson declined courteously. 'Thank you – not at this hour.' Then he rose. 'I take it, then, that you will not return me my property here and now.'

'Still the same delusion, I see!' remarked Hugh with a smile.

'Still the same delusion,' repeated Peterson. 'I shall be ready to receive both the paper and the man up till six o'clock tonight at 32A, Berners Street; and it is possible, I might even say probable, should they turn up by then, that I shall not find it necessary to kill you.'

Hugh grinned. 'Your forbearance amazes me,' he cried. 'Won't you really change your mind and have a drink?'

'Should they not arrive by then, I shall be put to the inconvenience of taking them, and in that case – much as I regret it – you may have to be killed. You're such an aggressive young man, Captain Drummond – and, I fear, not very tactful.' He spoke regretfully, drawing on his gloves; then as he got to the door he paused. 'I'm afraid that my words will not have much effect,' he remarked, 'but the episode last night *did* appeal to me. I would like to spare you – I would really. It's a sign of weakness, my young friend, which I view with amazement – but never-theless, it is there. So be warned in time. Return my property to Berners Street, and leave England for a few months.' His eyes seemed to burn into the soldier's brain. 'You are meddling in affairs,' he went on gently, 'of the danger of which you have no conception. A fly in the gear-box of a motor car would be a sounder prop-osition for a life insurance than you will be – if you continue on your present course.'

There was something so incredibly menacing in the soft, quiet voice, that Drummond looked at the speaker fascinated. He had a sudden feeling that he must be dreaming – that in a moment or two he would wake up and find that they had really been talking about the weather the whole time. Then the cynical gleam of triumph in Peterson's eyes acted on him like a cold douche; quite clearly that gentleman had misinterpreted his silence.

'Your candour is as refreshing,' he answered genially, 'as your similes are apt. I shudder to think of that poor little fly, Mr Peterson, especially with your chauffeur grinding his gears to pieces.' He held open the door for his visitor, and followed him into the passage. At the other end stood Denny, ostentatiously dusting a book-shelf, and Peterson glanced at him casually. It was char-acteristic of the man that no trace of annoyance showed on his face. He might have been any ordinary visitor taking his leave.

And then suddenly from the room outside which Denny was dusting there came a low moaning and an incoherent babble. A quick frown passed over Drum-mond's face, and Peterson regarded him thoughtfully.

'An invalid in the house?' he remarked. 'How inconven-ient for you!' He laid his hand for a moment on the soldier's arm. 'I sadly fear you're going to make a fool of yourself. And it will be such a pity.' He turned towards the stairs. 'Don't bother, please; I can find my own way out.'

III

Hugh turned back into his own room, and lighting a particularly noisy pipe, sat down in his own special chair, where James Denny found him five minutes later, with his hands deep in his pockets, and his legs crossed, staring out of the window. He asked him about lunch twice without result, and having finally been requested to go to hell, he removed himself aggrievedly to the kitchen. Drummond was under no delusions as to the risks he was running. Underrating his opponent had never been a fault of his, either in the ring or in France, and he had no intention of beginning now. The man who could abduct an American millionaire, and drug him till he was little better than a baby, and then use a thumb-screw to enforce his wishes, was not likely to prove over-scrupulous in the future. In fact, the phut of that bullet still rang unpleasantly in his ears.

After a while he began half unconsciously to talk aloud to himself. It was an old trick of his when he wanted to make up his mind on a situation, and he found that it helped him to concentrate his thoughts.

'Two alternatives, old buck,' he remarked, stabbing the air with his pipe. 'One – give the Potts bird up at Berners Street; two – do not. Number one – out of court at once. Preposterous – absurd. Therefore – number two holds the field.' He recrossed his legs, and ejected a large wineglassful of nicotine juice from the stem of his pipe on to the carpet. Then he sank back exhausted, and rang the bell.

'James,' he said, as the door opened, 'take a piece of paper and a pencil – if there's one with a point – and sit down at the table. I'm going to think, and I'd hate to miss out anything.'

His servant complied, and for a while silence reigned.

'First,' remarked Drummond, 'put down – "They know where Potts is."'

'Is, sir, or are?' murmured Denny, sucking his pencil.

'Is, you fool. It's a man, not a collection. And don't interrupt , for Heaven's sake. Two – "They will try to get Potts."'

'Yes, sir,' answered Denny, writing busily.

'Three – "They will not get Potts." That is as far as I've got at the moment, James – but every word of it stands. Not bad for a quarter of an hour, my trusty fellah – what?'

'That's the stuff to give the troops, sir,' agreed his audience, sucking his teeth.

Hugh looked at him in displeasure. 'That noise is not, James,' he remarked severely. 'Now you've got to do something else. Rise and with your well-known stealth approach the window, and see if the watcher still watcheth without.'

The servant took a prolonged survey, and finally announced that he failed to see him.

'Then that proves conclusively that he's there,' said Hugh. 'Write it down, James: four – "Owing to the watcher without, Potts cannot leave the house without being seen."'

'That's two withouts, sir,' ventured James tentatively; but Hugh, with a sudden light dawning in his eyes, was staring at the fireplace.

'I've got it, James,' he cried. 'I've got it . . . Five – "Potts must leave the house without being seen." I want him, James, I want him all to myself. I want to make much of him and listen to his childish prattle. He shall go to my cottage on the river, and you shall look after him.'

'Yes, sir,' returned James dutifully.

'And in order to get him there, we must get rid of the watcher without. How can we get rid of the bird — how can we, James, I ask you? Why, by giving him nothing further to watch for. Once let him think that Potts is no longer within, unless he's an imbecile he will no longer remain without.'

'I see, sir,' said James.

'No, you don't – you don't see anything. Now trot along over, James, and give my compliments to Mr Darrell. Ask him to come in and see me for a moment. Say I'm thinking and daren't move.'

James rose obediently, and Drummond heard him cross over the passage to the other suite of rooms that lay on the same floor. Then he heard the murmur of voices, and shortly afterwards his servant returned.

'He is in his bath, sir, but he'll come over as soon as he's finished.' He delivered the message and stood waiting. 'Anything more, sir?'

'Yes, James. I feel certain that there's a lot. But just to carry on with, I'll have another glass of beer.'

As the door closed, Drummond rose and started to pace up and down the room. The plan he had in mind was simple, but he was a man who believed in simplicity.

'Peterson will not come himself – nor will our one and only Henry. Potts has not been long in the country, which is all to the good. And if it fails – we shan't be any worse off than we are now. Luck – that's all; and the more you tempt her, the kinder she is.' He was still talking gently to himself when Peter Darrell strolled into the room.

'Can this thing be true, old boy,' remarked the newcomer. 'I hear you're in the throes of a brain-storm.'

'I am, Peter – and not even that repulsive dressing-gown of yours can stop it. I want you to help me.'

'All that I have, dear old flick, is yours for the asking. What can I do?'

'Well, first of all, I want you to come along and see the household pet.' He piloted Darrell along the passage to the American's room, and opened the door. The millionaire looked at them dazedly from the pillows, and Darrell stared back in startled surprise.

'My God! What's the matter with him?' he cried.

'I would give a good deal to know,' said Hugh grimly. Then he smiled reassuringly at the motionless man, and led the way back to the sitting-room.

'Sit down, Peter,' he said. 'Get outside that beer and listen to me carefully.'

For ten minutes he spoke, while his companion listened in silence. Gone completely was the rather vacuous-faced youth clad in a gorgeous dressing-gown; in his place there sat a keen-faced man nodding from time to time as a fresh point was made clear. Even so had both listened in the years that were past to their battalion commander's orders before an attack.

At length Hugh finished. 'Will you do it, old man?' he asked.

'Of course,' returned the other. 'But wouldn't it be better, Hugh,' he said pleadingly, 'to whip up two or three of the boys and have a real scrap? I don't seem to have anything to do.'

Drummond shook his head decidedly. 'No, Peter, my boy – not this show. We're up against a big thing; and if you like to come in with me, I think you'll have all you want in the scrapping line before you've finished. But this time, low cunning is the order.'

Darrell rose. 'Right you are, dearie. Your instructions shall be carried out to the letter. Come and feed your face with me. Got a couple of birds from the Gaiety lunching at the Cri.'

'Not today,' said Hugh. 'I've got quite a bit to get through this afternoon.'

As soon as Darrell had gone, Drummond again rang the bell for his servant.

'This afternoon, James, you and Mrs Denny will leave here and go to Paddington. Go out by the front door, and should you find yourselves being followed – as you probably will be – consume a jujube and keep your heads. Having arrived at the booking-office – take a ticket to Cheltenham, say goodbye to Mrs Denny in an impassioned tone, and exhort her not to miss the next train to that delectable inland resort. You might even speak slightingly about her sick aunt at Westbourne Grove, who alone prevents your admirable wife from accompanying you. Then, James, you will board the train for Cheltenham and go there. You will remain there for two days, during which period you must remember that you're a married man – even if you do go to the movies. You will then return here, and await further orders. Do you get me?'

'Yes, sir.' James stood to attention with a smart heel-click.

'Your wife – she has a sister or something, hasn't she, knocking about somewhere?'

'She 'as a palsied cousin in Camberwell, sir,' remarked James with justifiable pride.

'Magnificent,' murmured Hugh. 'She will dally until

eventide with her palsied cousin – if she can bear it – and then she must go by Underground to Ealing, where she will take a ticket to Goring. I don't think there will be any chance of her being followed – you'll have drawn them off. When she gets to Goring I want the cottage got ready at once, for two visitors.' He paused and lit a cigarette. 'Above all, James – mum's the word. As I told you a little while ago, the game has begun. Now just repeat what I've told you.'

He listened while his servant ran through his instructions, and nodded approvingly.

He dismissed Denny, and sat down at his desk. First he took the half-torn sheet out of his pocket, and putting it in an envelope, sealed it carefully. Then he placed it in another envelope, with a covering letter to his bank, requesting them to keep the enclosure intact.

Then he took a sheet of notepaper, and with much deliberation proceeded to pen a document which accorded him considerable amusement, judging by the grin which appeared from time to time on his face. This effusion he also enclosed in a sealed envelope, which he again addressed to his bank. Finally, he stamped the first, but not the second – and placed them both in his pocket.

For the next two hours he apparently found nothing better to do than eat a perfectly grilled chop prepared by Mrs Denny, and superintend his visitor unwillingly consuming a sago pudding. Then, with the departure of the Dennys for Paddington, which coincided most aptly with the return of Peter Darrell, a period of activity commenced in Half Moon Street. But being interior activity, interfering in no way with the placid warmth of the street outside, the gentleman without, whom a keen observer might have thought strangely interested in the beauties of that well-known thoroughfare – seeing that he had been there for three hours – remained serenely unconscious of it. His pal had followed the Dennys to Paddington. Drummond had not come out – and the watcher who watched without was beginning to get bored.

About 4.30 he sat up and took notice again as someone left the house; but it was only the superbly dressed young man whom he had discovered already was merely a clothes-peg calling himself Darrell.

The sun was getting low and the shadows were lengthening when a taxi drove up to the door. Immediately the watcher drew closer, only to stop with a faint smile as he saw two men get out of it. One was the immaculate Darrell; the other was a stranger, and both were quite obviously what in the vernacular is known as 'oiled'.

'You prisheless ole bean,' he heard Darrell say affectionately, 'this blinking cabsh my show.'

The other man hiccuped assent, and leant wearily against the palings.

'Right,' he remarked, 'ole friend of me youth. It shall be ash you wish.'

With a tolerant eye he watched them tack up the stairs, singing lustily in chorus. Then the door above closed, and the melody continued to float out through the open window.

Ten minutes later he was relieved. It was quite an unostentatious relief: another man merely strolled past him. And since there was nothing to report, he merely strolled away. He could hardly be expected to know that up in Peter Darrell's sitting-room two perfectly sober men were contemplating with professional eyes an extremely drunk gentleman singing in a chair, and that one of those two sober young men was Peter Darrell.

Then further interior activity took place in Half Moon Street, and as the darkness fell, silence gradually settled on the house.

Ten o'clock struck, then eleven – and the silence remained unbroken. It was not till eleven-thirty that a sudden small sound made Hugh Drummond sit up in his chair, with every nerve alert. It came from the direction of the kitchen – and it was the sound he had been awaiting for.

Swiftly he opened his door and passed along the passage to where the motionless man lay still in bed. Then he switched on a small reading-lamp, and with a plate of semolina in his hand he turned to the recumbent figure.

'Hiram C. Potts,' he said in a low, coaxing tone, 'sit up and take your semolina. Force yourself, laddie, force yourself. I know it's nauseating, but the doctor said no alcohol and very little meat.'

In the silence that followed, a board creaked outside, and again he tempted the sick man with food.

'Semolina, Hiram – semolina. Makes bouncing babies. I'd just love to see you bounce, my Potts.'

His voice died away, and he rose slowly to his feet. In the open door four men were standing, each with a peculiar-shaped revolver in his hand.

'What the devil,' cried Drummond furiously, 'is the meaning of this?'

'Cut it out,' cried the leader contemptuously. 'These guns are silent. If you utter – you die. Do you get me?'

The veins stood out on Drummond's forehead, and he controlled himself with an immense effort.

'Are you aware that this man is a guest of mine, and sick?' he said, his voice shaking with rage.

'You don't say,' remarked the leader, and one of the

others laughed. 'Rip the bed-clothes off, boys, and gag the young cock-sparrow.'

Before he could resist, a gag was thrust in Drummond's mouth and his hands were tied behind his back. Then, helpless and impotent, he watched three of them lift up the man from the bed, and, putting a gag in his mouth also, carry him out of the room.

'Move,' said the fourth to Hugh. 'You join the picnic.'

With fury gathering in his eyes he preceded his captor along the passage and downstairs. A large car drove up as they reached the street, and in less time than it takes to tell, the two helpless men were pushed in, followed by the leader; the door was shut and the car drove off.

'Don't forget,' he said to Drummond suavely, 'this gun *is* silent. You had better be the same.'

At one o'clock the car swung up to The Elms. For the last ten minutes Hugh had been watching the invalid in the corner, who was making frantic efforts to loosen his gag. His eyes were rolling horribly, and he swayed from side to side in his seat, but the bandages round his hands held firm and at last he gave it up.

Even when he was lifted out and carried indoors he did not struggle; he seemed to have sunk into a sort of apathy. Drummond followed with dignified calmness, and was led into a room off the hall.

In a moment or two Peterson entered, followed by his daughter. 'Ah! my young friend,' cried Peterson affably. 'I hardly thought you'd give me such an easy run as this.' He put his hand into Drummond's pockets, and pulled out his revolver and a bundle of letters. 'To your bank,' he murmured. 'Oh! surely, surely not that as well. Not even stamped. Ungag him, Irma – and untie his hands. My very dear young friend – you pain me.'

'I wish to know, Mr Peterson,' said Hugh quietly, 'by

what right this dastardly outrage has been committed. A friend of mine, sick in bed – removed; abducted in the middle of the night: to say nothing of me.'

With a gentle laugh Irma offered him a cigarette. '*Mon Dieu!*' she remarked, 'but you are most gloriously ugly, my Hugh!' Drummond looked at her coldly, while Peterson, with a faint smile, opened the envelope in his hand. And, even as he pulled out the contents, he paused suddenly and the smile faded from his face. From the landing upstairs came a heavy crash, followed by a flood of the most appalling language.

'What the – hell do you think you're doing, you flat-faced son of a Maltese goat? And where the – am I, anyway?'

'I must apologize for my friend's language,' murmured Hugh gently, 'but you must admit he has some justification. Besides, he was, I regret to state, quite wonderfully drunk earlier this evening, and just as he was sleeping it off these desperadoes abducted him.'

The next moment the door burst open, and an infuriated object rushed in. His face was wild, and his hand was bandaged, showing a great red stain on the thumb.

'What's this – jest?' he howled furiously. 'And this damned bandage all covered with red ink?'

'You must ask our friend here, Mullings,' said Hugh. 'He's got a peculiar sense of humour. Anyway, he's got the bill in his hand.'

In silence they watched Peterson open the paper and read the contents, while the girl leant over his shoulder.

To Mr Peterson, The Elms, Godalming.

	£.	s.	d.
To hire one demobilized soldier	5	0	0

	£.	s.	d.
To making him drunk (in this item present strength and cost of drink and said soldier's capacity must be allowed for)	5	0	0
To bottle of red ink	0	0	1
To shock to system	10	0	0
TOTAL	£20	0	1

It was Irma who laughed.

'Oh! but, my Hugh,' she gurgled, *'que vous êtes adorable!'*

But he did not look at her. His eyes were on Peterson, who with a perfectly impassive face was staring at him fixedly.

CHAPTER 4

In Which He Spends a Quiet Night at The Elms

I

'It is a little difficult to know what to do with you, young man,' said Peterson gently, after a long silence. 'I knew you had no tact.'

Drummond leaned back in his chair and regarded his host with a faint smile.

'I must come to you for lessons, Mr Peterson. Though I frankly admit,' he added genially, 'that I have never been brought up to regard the forcible abduction of a harmless individual and a friend who is sleeping off the effects of what low people call a jag as being exactly typical of that admirable quality.'

Peterson's glance rested on the dishevelled man still standing by the door, and after a moment's thought he leaned forward and pressed a bell.

'Take that man away,' he said abruptly to the servant who came into the room, 'and put him to bed. I will consider what to do with him in the morning.'

'Consider be damned,' howled Mullings, starting forward angrily. 'You'll consider a thick ear, Mr Blooming Knowall. What I wants to know –'

The words died away in his mouth, and he gazed at Peterson like a bird looks at a snake. There was something so ruthlessly malignant in the stare of the grey-blue

eyes, that the ex-soldier who had viewed going over the
top with comparative equanimity, as being part of his
job, quailed and looked apprehensively at Drummond.

'Do what the kind gentleman tells you, Mullings,' said
Hugh, 'and go to bed.' He smiled at the man reassuringly. 'And if you're very, very good, perhaps, as a great
treat, he'll come and kiss you good-night.'

'Now *that*,' he remarked as the door closed behind
them, 'is what I call tact.'

He lit a cigarette, and thoughtfully blew out a cloud of
smoke.

'Stop this fooling,' snarled Peterson. 'Where have you
hidden Potts?'

'Tush, tush,' murmured Hugh. 'You surprise me. I had
formed such a charming mental picture of you, Mr Peterson, as the strong, silent man who never lost his temper,
and here you are disappointing me at the beginning of
our acquaintance.'

For a moment he thought that Peterson was going
to strike him, and his own fist clenched under the
table.

'I wouldn't, my friend,' he said quietly; 'indeed I
wouldn't. Because if you hit me, I shall most certainly hit
you. And it will not improve your beauty.'

Slowly Peterson sank back in his chair, and the veins
which had been standing out on his forehead became
normal again. He even smiled; only the ceaseless tapping
of his hand on his left knee betrayed his momentary loss
of composure. Drummond's fist unclenched, and he
stole a look at the girl. She was in her favourite attitude on
the sofa, and had not even looked up.

'I suppose that it is quite useless for me to argue with
you,' said Peterson after a while.

'I was a member of my school debating society,'

remarked Hugh reminiscently. 'But I was never much good. I'm too obvious for argument, I'm afraid.'

'You probably realize from what has happened tonight,' continued Peterson, 'that I am in earnest.'

'I should be sorry to think so,' answered Hugh. 'If that is the best you can do, I'd cut it right out and start a tomato farm.'

The girl gave a little gurgle of laughter and lit another cigarette.

'Will you come and do the dangerous part of the work for us, Monsieur Hugh?' she asked.

'If you promise to restrain the little fellows, I'll water them with pleasure,' returned Hugh lightly.

Peterson rose and walked over to the window, where he stood motionless staring out into the darkness. For all his assumed flippancy, Hugh realized that the situation was what in military phraseology might be termed critical. There were in the house probably half a dozen men who, like their master, were absolutely unscrupulous. If it suited Peterson's book to kill him, he would not hesitate to do so for a single second. And Hugh realized, when he put it that way in his own mind, that it was no exaggeration, no *façon de parler*, but a plain, unvarnished statement of fact. Peterson would no more think twice of killing a man if he wished to, than the normal human being would of crushing a wasp.

For a moment the thought crossed his mind that he would take no chances by remaining in the house; that he would rush Peterson from behind and escape into the darkness of the garden. But it was only momentary – gone almost before it had come, for Hugh Drummond was not that manner of man – gone even before he noticed that Peterson was standing in such a position that he could see every detail of the room behind him reflected in the glass through which he stared.

A fixed determination to know what lay in that sinister brain replaced his temporary indecision. Events up to date had moved so quickly that he had hardly had time to get his bearings; even now the last twenty-four hours seemed almost a dream. And as he looked at the broad back and massive head of the man at the window, and from him to the girl idly smoking on the sofa, he smiled a little grimly. He had just remembered the thumbscrew of the preceding evening. Assuredly the demobilized officer who found peace dull was getting his money's worth; and Drummond had a shrewd suspicion that the entertainment was only just beginning.

A sudden sound outside in the garden made him look up quickly. He saw the white gleam of a shirt front, and the next moment a man pushed open the window and came unsteadily into the room. It was Mr Benton, and quite obviously he had been seeking consolation in the bottle.

'Have you got him?' he demanded thickly, steadying himself with a hand on Peterson's arm.

'I have not,' said Peterson shortly, eyeing the swaying figure in front of him contemptuously.

'Where is he?'

'Perhaps if you ask your daughter's friend Captain Drummond, he might tell you. For Heaven's sake sit down, man, before you fall down.' He pushed Benton roughly into a chair, and resumed his impassive stare into the darkness.

The girl took not the slightest notice of the new arrival who gazed stupidly at Drummond across the table.

'We seem to be moving in an atmosphere of cross-purposes, Mr Benton,' said the soldier affably. 'Our host will not get rid of the idea that I am a species of bandit. I hope your daughter is quite well.'

'Er – quite, thank you,' muttered the other.

'Tell her, will you, that I propose to call on her before returning to London tomorrow. That is, if she won't object to my coming early.'

With his hands in his pockets, Peterson was regarding Drummond from the window.

'You propose leaving us tomorrow, do you?' he said quietly.

Drummond stood up.

'I ordered my car for ten o'clock,' he answered. 'I hope that will not upset the household arrangements,' he continued, turning to the girl, who was laughing softly and polishing her nails.

'*Vraiment*!' But you grow on one, my Hugh,' she smiled. 'Are we really losing you so soon?'

'I am quite sure that I shall be more useful to Mr Peterson at large, than I am cooped up here,' said Hugh. 'I might even lead him to this hidden treasure which he thinks I've got.'

'You will do that all right,' remarked Peterson. 'But at the moment I was wondering whether a little persuasion now – might not give me all the information I require more quickly and with less trouble.'

A fleeting vision of a mangled, pulp-like thumb flashed across Hugh's mind; once again he heard that hideous cry, half animal, half human, which had echoed through the darkness the preceding night, and for an instant his breath came a little faster. Then he smiled, and shook his head.

'I think you are rather too good a judge of human nature to try anything so foolish,' he said thoughtfully. 'You see, unless you kill me, which I don't think would suit your book, you might find explanations a little difficult tomorrow.'

For a while there was silence in the room, broken at length by a short laugh from Peterson.

'For a young man truly your perspicacity is great,' he remarked. 'Irma, is the blue room ready? If so, tell Luigi to show Captain Drummond to it.'

'I will show him myself,' she answered, rising. 'And then I shall go to bed. *Mon Dieu!* my Hugh, but I find your country *très ennuyeux*.' She stood in front of him for a moment, and then led the way to the door, glancing at him over her shoulder.

Hugh saw a quick look of annoyance pass over Peterson's face as he turned to follow the girl, and it struck him that that gentleman was not best pleased at the turn of events. It vanished almost as soon as it came, and Peterson waved a friendly hand at him, as if the doings of the night had been the most ordinary thing in the world. Then the door closed, and he followed his guide up the stairs.

The house was beautifully furnished. Hugh was no judge of art, but even his inexperienced eye could see that the prints on the walls were rare and valuable. The carpets were thick, and his feet sank into them noiselessly; the furniture was solid and in exquisite taste. And it was as he reached the top of the stairs that a single deep-noted clock rang a wonderful chime and then struck the hour. The time was just three o'clock.

The girl opened the door of a room and switched on the light. Then she faced him smiling, and Hugh looked at her steadily. He had no wish whatever for any conversation, but as she was standing in the centre of the doorway it was impossible for him to get past her without being rude.

'Tell me, you ugly man,' she murmured, 'why you are such a fool.'

Hugh smiled, and, as has been said before, Hugh's smile transformed his face.

'I must remember that opening,' he said. 'So many people, I feel convinced, would like to say it on first acquaintance, but confine themselves to merely thinking it. It establishes a basis of intimacy at once, doesn't it?'

She swayed a little towards him, and then, before he realized her intention, she put a hand on his shoulder.

'Don't you understand,' she whispered fiercely, 'that they'll kill you?' She peered past him half fearfully, and then turned to him again. 'Go, you idiot, go – while there's time. Oh! if I could only make you understand; if you'd only believe me! Get out of it – go abroad; do anything – but don't fool around here.'

In her agitation she was shaking him to and fro.

'It seems a cheerful household,' remarked Hugh, with a smile. 'May I ask why you're all so concerned about me? Your estimable father gave me the same advice yesterday morning.'

'Don't ask why,' she answered feverishly, 'because I can't tell you. Only you must believe that what I say is the truth – you must. It's just possible that if you go now and tell them where you've hidden the American you'll be all right. But if you don't –' Her hand dropped to her side suddenly. 'Breakfast will be at nine, my Hugh: until then, *au revoir*.'

He turned as she left the room, a little puzzled by her change of tone. Standing at the top of the stairs was Peterson, watching them both in silence . . .

II

In the days when Drummond had been a platoon commander, he had done many dangerous things. The ordinary joys of the infantry subaltern's life – such as going over the top, and carrying out raids – had not proved sufficient for his appetite. He had specialized in peculiar stunts of his own: stunts over which he was singularly reticent; stunts over which his men formed their own conclusions, and worshipped him accordingly.

But Drummond was no fool, and he had realized the vital importance of fitting himself for these stunts to the best of his ability. Enormous physical strength is a great asset, but it carries with it certain natural disadvantages. In the first place, its possessor is frequently clumsy: Hugh had practised in France till he could move over ground without a single blade of grass rustling. Van Dyck – a Dutch trapper – had first shown him the trick, by which a man goes forward on his elbows like a snake, and is here one moment and gone the next, with no one the wiser.

Again, its possessor is frequently slow: Hugh had practised in France till he could kill a man with his bare hands in a second. Olaki – a Japanese – had first taught him two or three of the secrets of his trade, and in the intervals of resting behind the lines he had perfected them until it was even money whether the Jap or he would win in a practice bout.

And there were nights in No Man's Land when his men would hear strange sounds, and knowing that Drummond was abroad on his wanderings, would peer eagerly over the parapet into the desolate torn-up waste in front. But they never saw anything, even when the green ghostly flares went hissing up into the darkness and the shadows danced fantastically. All was silent and still; the sudden shrill whimper was not repeated.

Perhaps a patrol coming back would report a German, lying huddled in a shell-hole, with no trace of a wound, but only a broken neck; perhaps the patrol never found anything. But whatever the report, Hugh Drummond only grinned and saw to his men's breakfasts. Which is why there are in England today quite a number of civilians who acknowledge only two rulers – the King and Hugh Drummond. And they would willingly die for either.

The result on Drummond was not surprising: as nearly as a man may be he was without fear. And when the idea came to him as he sat on the edge of his bed thoughtfully pulling off his boots, no question of the possible risk entered into his mind. To explore the house seemed the most natural thing in the world, and with characteristic brevity he summed up the situation as it struck him.

'They suspect me anyhow: in fact, they know I took Potts. Therefore even if they catch me passage-creeping, I'm no worse off than I am now. And I might find something of interest. Therefore, carry on, brave heart.'

The matter was settled; the complete bench of bishops headed by their attendant satellites would not have stopped him, nor the fact that the German front-line trench was a far safer place for a stranger than The Elms at night. But he didn't know that fact, and it would have cut no more ice than the episcopal dignitaries, if he had . . .

It was dark in the passage outside as he opened the door of his room and crept towards the top of the stairs. The collar of his brown lounge coat was turned up, and his stockinged feet made no sound on the heavy pile carpet. Like a huge shadow he vanished into the blackness, feeling his way forward with the uncanny instinct that comes from much practice. Every now and then he paused and listened intently, but the measured ticking of the clock below and the occasional creak of a board alone broke the stillness.

For a moment his outline showed up against the faint grey light which was coming through a window half-way down the stairs; then he was gone again, swallowed up in the gloom of the hall. To the left lay the room in which he had spent the evening, and Drummond turned to the right. As he had gone up to bed he had noticed a door screened by a heavy curtain which he thought might be the room Phyllis Benton had spoken of – the room where Henry Lakington kept his ill-gotten treasures. He felt his way along the hall, and at length his hand touched the curtain – only to drop it again at once. From close behind him had come a sharp, angry hiss . . .

He stepped back a pace and stood rigid, staring at the spot from which the sound had seemed to come – but he could see nothing. Then he leaned forward and once more moved the curtain. Instantly it came again, sharper and angrier than before.

Hugh passed a hand over his forehead and found it damp. Germans he knew, and things on two legs, but what was this that hissed so viciously in the darkness? At length he determined to risk it, and drew from his pocket a tiny electric torch. Holding it well away from his body, he switched on the light. In the centre of the beam, swaying gracefully to and fro, was a snake. For a moment he watched it fascinated as it spat at the light angrily; he saw the flat hood where the vicious head was set on the upright body; then he switched off the torch and retreated rather faster than he had come.

'A convivial household,' he muttered to himself

through lips that were a little dry. 'A hooded cobra is an unpleasing pet.'

He stood leaning against the banisters regaining his self-control. There was no further sound from the cobra; seemingly it only got annoyed when its own particular domain was approached. In fact, Hugh had just determined to reconnoitre the curtained doorway again to see if it was possible to circumvent the snake, when a low chuckle came distinctly to his ears from the landing above.

He flushed angrily in the darkness. There was no doubt whatever as to the human origin of that laugh, and Hugh suddenly realized that he was making the most profound fool of himself. And such a realization, though possibly salutary to all of us at times, is most unpleasant.

For Hugh Drummond, who, with all his lack of conceit, had a very good idea of Hugh Drummond's capabilities, to be at an absolute disadvantage – to be laughed at by some dirty swine whom he could strangle in half a minute – was impossible! His fists clenched, and he swore softly under his breath. Then as silently as he had come down, he commenced to climb the stairs again. He had a hazy idea that he would like to hit something – hard.

There were nine stairs in the first half of the flight, and it was as he stood on the fifth that he again heard the low chuckle. At the same instant something whizzed past his head so low that it almost touched his hair, and there was a clang on the wall beside him. He ducked instinctively, and regardless of noise raced up the remaining stairs on all fours. His jaw was set like a vice, his eyes were blazing; in fact, Hugh Drummond was seeing red.

He paused when he reached the top, crouching in the darkness. Close to him he could feel someone else, and holding his breath, he listened. Then he heard the man move – only the very faintest sound – but it was enough. Without a second's thought he sprang, and his hands closed on human flesh. He laughed gently; then he fought in silence.

His opponent was strong above the average, but after a minute he was like a child in Hugh's grasp. He choked once or twice and muttered something; then Hugh slipped his right hand gently on to the man's throat. His fingers moved slowly round, his thumb adjusted itself lovingly, and the man felt his head being forced back irresistibly. He gave one strangled cry, and then the pressure relaxed . . .

'One half-inch more, my gentle humorist,' Hugh whispered in his ear, 'and your neck would have been broken. As it is, it will be very stiff for some days. Another time – don't laugh. It's dangerous.'

Then, like a ghost, he vanished along the passage in the direction of his own room.

'I wonder who the bird was,' he murmured thoughtfully to himself. 'Somehow I don't think he'll laugh quite so much in future – damn him.'

III

At eight o'clock the next morning a burly-looking ruffian brought in some hot water and a cup of tea. Hugh watched him through half-closed eyes, and eliminated him from the competition. His bullet head moved freely on a pair of massive shoulders; his neck showed no traces of nocturnal trouble. As he pulled up the blinds the light fell full on his battered, rugged face, and suddenly Hugh sat up in bed and stared at him.

'Good Lord!' he cried, 'aren't you Jem Smith?'

The man swung round like a flash and glared at the bed.

'Wot the 'ell 'as that got to do wiv you?' he snarled, and then his face changed. 'Why, strike me pink, if it ain't young Drummond.'

Hugh grinned.

'Right in one, Jem. What in the name of fortune are you doing in this outfit?'

But the man was not to be drawn.

'Never you mind, sir,' he said grimly. 'I reckons that's my own business.'

'Given up the game, Jem?' asked Hugh.

'It give me up, when that cross-eyed son of a gun Young Baxter fought that cross down at 'Oxton. Gawd! if I could get the swine – just once again – s'welp me, I'd –' Words failed the ex-bruiser; he could only mutter. And Hugh, who remembered the real reason why the game had given Jem up, and a period of detention at His Majesty's expense had taken its place, preserved a discreet silence.

The pug paused as he got to the door, and looked at Drummond doubtfully. Then he seemed to make up his mind, and advanced to the side of the bed.

'It ain't none o' my business,' he muttered hoarsely, 'but seeing as 'ow you're one of the boys, if I was you I wouldn't get looking too close at things in this 'ere 'ouse. It ain't 'ealthy: only don't say as I said so.'

Hugh smiled.

'Thank you, Jem. By the way, has anyone got a stiff neck in the house this morning?'

'Stiff neck!' echoed the man. 'Strike me pink if that ain't

funny – you're asking, I mean. The bloke's sitting up in 'is bed swearing awful. Can't move 'is 'ead at all.'

'And who, might I ask, is the bloke?' said Drummond, stirring his tea.

'Why, Peterson, o' course. 'Oo else? Breakfast at nine.'

The door closed behind him, and Hugh lit a cigarette thoughtfully. Most assuredly he was starting in style: Lakington's jaw one night, Peterson's neck the second, seemed a sufficiently energetic opening to the game for the veriest glutton. Then that cheerful optimism which was the envy of his friends asserted itself.

'Supposin' I'd killed 'em,' he murmured, aghast. 'Just supposin'. Why, the bally show would have been over, and I'd have had to advertise again.'

Only Peterson was in the dining-room when Hugh came down. He had examined the stairs on his way, but he could see nothing unusual which would account for the thing which had whizzed past his head and clanged sullenly against the wall. Nor was there any sign of the cobra by the curtained door; merely Peterson standing in a sunny room behind a bubbling coffee-machine.

'Good morning,' remarked Hugh affably. 'How are we all today? By Jove! that coffee smells good.'

'Help yourself,' said Peterson. 'My daughter is never down as early as this.'

'Rarely conscious before eleven – what!' murmured Hugh. 'Deuced wise of her. May I press you to a kidney?' He returned politely towards his host, and paused in dismay. 'Good heavens! Mr Peterson, is your neck hurting you?'

'It is,' answered Peterson grimly.

'A nuisance, having a stiff neck. Makes everyone laugh, and one gets no sympathy. Bad thing – laughter

. . . At times, anyway.' He sat down and commenced to eat his breakfast.

'Curiosity is a great deal worse, Captain Drummond. It was touch and go whether I killed you last night.'

The two men were staring at one another steadily.

'I think I might say the same,' returned Drummond.

'Yes and no,' said Peterson. 'From the moment you left the bottom of the stairs, I had your life in the palm of my hand. Had I chosen to take it, my young friend, I should not have had this stiff neck.'

Hugh returned to his breakfast unconcernedly.

'Granted, laddie, granted. But had I not been of such a kindly and forbearing nature, you wouldn't have had it, either.' He looked at Peterson critically. 'I'm inclined to think it's a great pity I didn't break your neck, while I was about it.' Hugh sighed, and drank some coffee. 'I see that I shall have to do it some day, and probably Lakington's as well . . . By the way, how is our Henry? I trust his jaw is not unduly inconveniencing him.'

Peterson, with his coffee cup in his hand, was staring down the drive.

'Your car is a little early, Captain Drummond,' he said at length. 'However, perhaps it can wait two or three minutes, while we get matters perfectly clear. I should dislike you not knowing where you stand.' He turned round and faced the soldier. 'You have deliberately, against my advice, elected to fight me and the interests I represent. So be it. From now on, the gloves are off. You embarked on this course from a spirit of adventure, at the instigation of the girl next door. She, poor little fool, is concerned over that drunken waster – her father. She asked you to help her – you agreed; and, amazing though it may seem, up to now you have scored a certain measure of success. I admit it, and I admire you for it. I apologize now for having played the fool with you last night; you're the type of man whom one should kill outright – or leave alone.'

He set down his coffee cup, and carefully snipped the end off a cigar.

'You are also the type of man who will continue on the path he has started. You are completely in the dark; you have no idea whatever what you are up against.' He smiled grimly, and turned abruptly on Hugh. 'You fool – you stupid young fool. Do you *really* imagine that you can beat me?'

The soldier rose and stood in front of him.

'I have a few remarks of my own to make,' he answered, 'and then we might consider the interview closed. I ask nothing better than that the gloves should be off – though with your filthy methods of fighting, anything you touch will get very dirty. As you say, I am completely in the dark as to your plans; but I have a pretty shrewd idea what I'm up against. Men who can employ the thumbscrew on a poor defenceless brute seem to me to be several degrees worse than cannibals, and therefore if I put you down as one of the lowest types of degraded criminal I shall not be very wide of the mark. There's no good you snarling at me, you swine; it does everybody good to hear some home truths – and don't forget it was you who pulled off the gloves.'

Drummond lit a cigarette; then his merciless eyes fixed themselves again on Peterson.

'There is only one thing more,' he continued. 'You have kindly warned me of my danger: let me give you a word of advice in my turn. I'm going to fight you; if I can, I'm going to beat you. Anything that may happen to me is part of the game. But if anything happens to Miss Benton during the course of operations, then, as surely as there is a God above, Peterson, I'll get at you somehow and murder you with my own hands.'

For a few moments there was silence, and then with a short laugh Drummond turned away.

'Quite melodramatic,' he remarked lightly. 'And very bad for the digestion so early in the morning. My regards to your charming daughter, also to him of the broken jaw. Shall we meet again soon?' He paused at the door and looked back.

Peterson was still standing by the table, his face expressionless.

'Very soon indeed, young man,' he said quietly. 'Very soon indeed . . .'

Hugh stepped out into the warm sunshine and spoke to his chauffeur.

'Take her out into the main road, Jenkins,' he said, 'and wait for me outside the entrance to the next house. I shan't be long.'

Then he strolled through the garden towards the little wicket-gate that led to The Larches. Phyllis! The thought of her was singing in his heart to the exclusion of everything else. Just a few minutes with her; just the touch of her hand, the faint smell of the scent she used – and then back to the game.

He had almost reached the gate, when, with a sudden crashing in the undergrowth, Jem Smith blundered out into the path. His naturally ruddy face was white, and he stared round fearfully.

'Gawd! sir,' he cried, 'mind you. 'Ave yer seen it?'

'Seen what, Jem?' asked Drummond.

'That there brute. 'E's escaped; and if 'e meets a stranger –' He left the sentence unfinished, and stood listening. From somewhere behind the house came a deep-throated, snarling roar; then the clang of a padlock shooting home in metal, followed by a series of heavy thuds as if some big animal was hurling itself against the bars of a cage.

'They've got it,' muttered Jem, mopping his brow.

'You seem to have a nice little crowd of pets about the house,' remarked Drummond, putting a hand on the man's arm as he was about to move off. 'What was that docile creature we've just heard calling to its young?'

The ex-pugilist looked at him sullenly.

'Never you mind, sir; it ain't no business of yours. An' if I was you, I wouldn't make it your business to find out.'

A moment later he had disappeared into the bushes, and Drummond was left alone. Assuredly a cheerful household, he reflected; just the spot for a rest-cure. Then he saw a figure on the lawn of the next house which banished everything else from his mind; and opening the gate, he walked eagerly towards Phyllis Benton.

IV

'I heard you were down here,' she said gravely, holding out her hand to him. 'I've been sick with anxiety ever since father told me he'd seen you.'

Hugh imprisoned the little hand in his own huge ones, and smiled at the girl.

'I call that just sweet of you,' he answered. 'Just sweet . . . Having people worry about me is not much in my line, but I think I rather like it.'

'You're the most impossible person,' she remarked, releasing her hand. 'What sort of a night did you have?'

'Somewhat parti-coloured,' returned Hugh lightly. 'Like the hoary old curate's egg – calm in parts.'

'But why did you go at all?' she cried, beating her

hands together. 'Don't you realize that if anything happens to you, I shall never forgive myself?'

The soldier smiled reassuringly.

'Don't worry, little girl,' he said. 'Years ago I was told by an old gipsy that I should die in my bed of old age and excessive consumption of invalid port . . . As a matter of fact, the cause of my visit was rather humorous. They abducted me in the middle of the night, with an ex-soldier of my old battalion, who was, I regret to state, sleeping off the effects of much indifferent liquor in my rooms.'

'What are you talking about?' she demanded.

'They thought he was your American millionaire cove, and the wretched Mullings was too drunk to deny it. In fact, I don't think they ever asked his opinion at all.' Hugh grinned reminiscently. 'A pathetic spectacle.'

'Oh! but splendid,' cried the girl a little breathlessly. 'And where was the American?'

'Next door – safe with a very dear old friend of mine. Peter Darrell. You must meet Peter some day – you'll like him.' He looked at her thoughtfully. 'No,' he added, 'on second thoughts, I'm not at all sure that I shall let you meet Peter. You might like him too much; and he's a dirty dog.'

'Don't be ridiculous,' she cried with a faint blush. 'Tell me, where is the American now?'

'Many miles out of London,' answered Hugh. 'I think we'll leave it at that. The less you know, Miss Benton, at the moment – the better.'

'Have you found out anything?' she demanded eagerly.

Hugh shook his head.

'Not a thing. Except that your neighbours are as pretty a bunch of scoundrels as I ever want to meet.'

'But you'll let me know if you do.' She laid a hand beseechingly on his arm. 'You know what's at stake for me, don't you? Father, and – oh! but you know.'

'I know,' he answered gravely. 'I know, old thing. I promise I'll let you know anything I find out. And in the meantime I want you to keep an eye fixed on what goes on next door, and let me know anything of importance by letter to the Junior Sports Club.' He lit a cigarette thoughtfully. 'I have an idea that they feel so absolutely confident in their own power, that they are going to make the fatal mistake of underrating their opponents. We shall see.' He turned to her with a twinkle in his eyes. 'Anyway, our Mr Lakington will see that you don't come to any harm.'

'The brute!' she cried, very low. 'How I hate him!' Then – with a sudden change of tone, she looked up at Drummond. 'I don't know whether it's worth mentioning,' she said slowly, 'but yesterday afternoon four men came at different times to The Elms. They were the sort of type one sees tub-thumping in Hyde Park, all except one, who looked like a respectable working-man.'

Hugh shook his head.

'Don't seem to help much, does it? Still, one never knows. Let me know anything like that in future at the club.'

'Good morning, Miss Benton.' Peterson's voice behind them made Drummond swing round with a smothered curse. 'Our inestimable friend, Captain Drummond, brought such a nice young fellow to see me last night, and then left him lying about the house this morning.'

Hugh bit his lip with annoyance; until that moment he had clean forgotten that Mullings was still in The Elms.

'I have sent him along to your car,' continued Peterson

suavely, 'which I trust was the correct procedure. Or did you want to give him to me as a pet?'

'From a rapid survey, Mr Peterson, I should think you have quite enough already,' said Hugh. 'I trust you paid him the money you owe him.'

'I will allot it to him in my will,' remarked Peterson. 'If you do the same in yours, doubtless he will get it from one of us sooner or later. In the meantime, Miss Benton, is your father up?'

The girl frowned.

'No – not yet.'

'Then I will go and see him in bed. For the present, *au revoir*.' He walked towards the house, and they watched him go in silence. It was as he opened the drawing-room window that Hugh called after him:

'Do you like the horse Elliman's or the ordinary brand?' he asked. 'I'll send you a bottle for that stiff neck of yours.'

Very deliberately Peterson turned round.

'Don't trouble, thank you, Captain Drummond. I have my own remedies, which are far more efficacious.'

CHAPTER 5

In Which There is Trouble at Goring

I

'Did you have a good night, Mullings?' remarked Hugh as he got into his car.

The man grinned sheepishly.

'I dunno what the game was, sir, but I ain't for many more of them. They're about the ugliest crowd of blackguards in that there 'ouse that I ever wants to see again.'

'How many did you see altogether?' asked Drummond.

'I saw six actual like, sir; but I 'eard others talking.'

The car slowed up before the post office and Hugh got out. There were one or two things he proposed to do in London before going to Goring, and it struck him that a wire to Peter Darrell might allay that gentleman's uneasiness if he was late in getting down. So new was he to the tortuous ways of crime, that the foolishness of the proceeding never entered his head: up to date in his life, if he had wished to send a wire he had sent one. And so it may be deemed a sheer fluke on his part, that a man dawdling by the counter aroused his suspicions. He was a perfectly ordinary man, chatting casually with the girl on the other side; but it chanced that, just as Hugh was holding the post office pencil up, and gazing at its so-called point with an air of resigned anguish, the perfectly ordinary man ceased chatting and looked at him. Hugh caught his eye for a fleeting second; then the conversation continued. And as he turned to pull out the pad of forms, it struck him that the man had looked away just a trifle too quickly . . .

A grin spread slowly over his face, and after a moment's hesitation he proceeded to compose a short wire. He wrote it in block letters for additional clearness; he also pressed his hardest as befitted a blunt pencil. Then with the form in his hand he advanced to the counter.

'How long will it take to deliver in London?' he asked the girl . . .

The girl was not helpful. It depended, he gathered, on a variety of circumstances, of which not the least was the perfectly ordinary man who talked so charmingly. She did not say so, in so many words, but Hugh respected her none the less for her maidenly reticence.

'I don't think I'll bother, then,' he said, thrusting the wire into his pocket. 'Good morning . . .'

He walked to the door, and shortly afterwards his car rolled down the street. He would have liked to remain and see the finish of his little jest, but, as is so often the case, imagination is better than reality. Certain it is that he chuckled consumedly the whole way up to London, whereas the actual finish was tame.

With what the girl considered peculiar abruptness, the perfectly ordinary man concluded his conversation with her, and decided that he too would send a wire. And then, after a long and thoughtful pause at the writing-bench, she distinctly heard an unmistakable 'Damn!' Then he walked out, and she saw him no more.

Moreover, it is to be regretted that the perfectly ordinary man told a lie a little later in the day, when giving his report to someone whose neck apparently inconvenienced him greatly. But then a lie is frequently more tactful than the truth, and to have announced that the sole result of his morning's labours had been to decipher a wire addressed to The Elms, which contained the cryptic remark, 'Stung again, stiff neck, stung again,' would not have been tactful. So he lied, as has been stated, thereby showing his wisdom . . .

But though Drummond chuckled to himself as the car rushed through the fresh morning air, once or twice a gleam that was not altogether amusement shone in his eyes. For four years he had played one game where no mistakes were allowed; the little incident of the post office had helped to bring to his mind the certainty that he had now embarked on another where the conditions were much the same. That he had scored up to date was luck rather than good management, and he was far too shrewd not to realize it. Now he was marked, and luck with a marked man cannot be tempted too far.

Alone and practically unguarded he had challenged a gang of international criminals: a gang not only utterly unscrupulous, but controlled by a master-mind. Of its power as yet he had no clear idea; of its size and immediate object he had even less. Perhaps it was as well. Had he realized even dimly the immensity of the issues he was up against, had he had but an inkling of the magnitude of the plot conceived in the sinister brain of his host of the previous evening, then, cheery optimist though he was, even Hugh Drummond might have wavered. But he had no such inkling, and so the gleam in his eyes was but transitory, the chuckle that succeeded it more wholehearted than before. Was it not sport in a land flowing with strikes and profiteers; sport such as his soul loved?

'I am afraid, Mullings,' he said as the car stopped in

front of his club, 'that the kindly gentleman with whom we spent last night has repudiated his obligations. He refuses to meet the bill I gave him for your services. Just wait here a moment.'

He went inside, returning in a few moments with a folded cheque.

'Round the corner, Mullings, and an obliging fellah in a black coat will shove you out the necessary Bradburys.'

The man glanced at the cheque.

'Fifty quid, sir!' he gasped. 'Why – it's too much, sir . . . I . . .'

'The labourer, Mullings, is worthy of his hire. You have been of the very greatest assistance to me; and, incidentally, it is more than likely that I may want you again. Now, where can I get hold of you?'

'13, Green Street, 'Oxton, sir, 'll always find me. And any time, sir, as you wants me, I'd like to come just for the sport of the thing.'

Hugh grinned.

'Good lad. And it may be sooner than you think.'

With a cheery laugh he turned back into his club, and for a moment or two the ex-soldier stood looking after him. Then with great deliberation he turned to the chauffeur, and spat reflectively.

'If there was more like 'im, and less like '*im*' – he indicated a stout vulgarian rolling past in a large car and dreadful clothes – 'things wouldn't 'appen such as is 'appening today. Ho! no . . .'

With which weighty dictum Mr Mullings, late private of the Royal Loamshires, turned his steps in the direction of the 'obliging fellah in a black coat'.

II

Inside the Junior Sports Club, Hugh Drummond was burying his nose in a large tankard of the ale for which that cheery pothouse was still famous. And in the intervals of this most delightful pastime he was trying to make up his mind on a peculiarly knotty point. Should he or should he not communicate with the police on the matter? He felt that as a respectable citizen of the country it was undoubtedly his duty to tell somebody something. The point was who to tell and what to tell him. On the subject of Scotland Yard his ideas were nebulous; he had a vague impression that one filled in a form and waited – tedious operations, both.

'Besides, dear old flick,' he murmured abstractedly to the portrait of the founder of the club, who had drunk the cellar dry and then died, 'am I a respectable citizen? Can it be said with any certainty, that if I filled in a form saying all that had happened in the last two days, I shouldn't be put in quod myself?'

He sighed profoundly and gazed out into the sunny square. A waiter was arranging the first editions of the evening papers on a table, and Hugh beckoned to him to bring one. His mind was still occupied with his problem, and almost mechanically he glanced over the columns. Cricket, racing, the latest divorce case and the latest strike – all the usual headings were there. And he was just putting down the paper, to again concentrate on his problem, when a paragraph caught his eye.

STRANGE MURDER IN BELFAST

The man whose body was discovered in such peculiar circumstances near the docks has been identified as Mr James Granger, the confidential secretary to Mr Hiram Potts, the American multi-millionaire, at present in this country. The unfortunate victim of this dastardly outrage – his head, as we reported in our last night's issue, was nearly severed from his body – had apparently been sent over on business by Mr Potts, and had arrived the preceding day. What he was doing in the locality in which he was found is a mystery.

We understand that Mr Potts, who has recently been indisposed, has returned to the Carlton, and is greatly upset at the sudden tragedy.

The police are confident that they will shortly obtain a clue, though the rough element in the locality where the murder was committed presents great difficulties. It seems clear that the motive was robbery, as all the murdered man's pockets were rifled. But the most peculiar thing about the case is the extraordinary care taken by the murderer to prevent the identification of the body. Every article of clothing, even down to the murdered man's socks, had had the name torn out, and it was only through the criminal overlooking the tailor's tab inside the inner breast-pocket of Mr Granger's coat that the police were enabled to identify the body.

Drummond laid down the paper on his knees, and stared a little dazedly at the club's immoral founder.

'Holy smoke! Laddie,' he murmured, 'that man Peterson ought to be on the committee here. Verily, I believe, he could galvanize the staff into some semblance of activity.'

'Did you order anything, sir?' A waiter paused beside him.

'No,' murmured Drummond, 'but I will rectify the omission. Another large tankard of ale.'

The waiter departed, and Hugh picked up the paper again.

'We understand,' he murmured gently to himself, 'that Mr Potts, who has recently been indisposed, has returned to the Carlton . . . Now that's very interesting . . .' He lit a cigarette and lay back in his chair. 'I was under the impression that Mr Potts was safely tucked up in bed, consuming semolina pudding, at Goring. It requires elucidation.'

'I beg your pardon, sir,' remarked the waiter, placing the beer on the table beside him.

'You needn't,' returned Hugh. 'Up to date you have justified my fondest expectations. And as a further proof of my goodwill, I would like you to get me a trunk call – 2 X Goring.'

A few minutes later he was in the telephone box.

'Peter, I have seldom been so glad to hear your voice. Is all well? Good! Don't mention any names. Our guest is there, is he? Gone on strike against more milk puddings, you say. Coax him, Peter. Make a noise like a sturgeon, and he'll think it's caviare. Have you seen the papers? There are interesting doings in Belfast, which concern us rather intimately. I'll be down later, and we'll have a powwow.'

He hung up the receiver and stepped out of the box.

'If, Algy,' he remarked to a man who was looking at the tape machine outside, 'the paper says a blighter's somewhere and you know he's somewhere else – what do you do?'

'Up to date in such cases I have always shot the editor,' murmured Algy Longworth. 'Come and feed.'

'You're so helpful, Algy. A perfect rock of strength. Do you want a job?'

'What sort of a job?' demanded the other suspiciously.

'Oh! not work, dear old boy. Damn it, man – you know me better than that, surely!'

'People are so funny nowadays,' returned Longworth gloomily. 'The most unlikely souls seem to be doing things and trying to look as if they were necessary. What is this job?'

Together the two men strolled into the luncheon-room, and long after the cheese had been finished, Algy Longworth was still listening in silence to his companion.

'My dear old bean,' he murmured ecstatically as Hugh finished, 'my *very* dear old bean. I think it's the most priceless thing I ever heard. Enrol me as a member of the band. And, incidentally, Toby Sinclair is running round in circles asking for trouble. Let's rope him in.'

'Go and find him this afternoon, Algy,' said Hugh, rising. 'And tell him to keep his mouth shut. I'd come with you, but it occurs to me that the wretched Potts, bathed in tears at the Carlton, is in need of sympathy. I would have him weep on my shoulder awhile. So long, old dear. You'll hear from me in a day or two.'

It was as he reached the pavement that Algy dashed out after him, with genuine alarm written all over his face.

'Hugh,' he spluttered, 'there's only one stipulation. An armistice must be declared during Ascot week.'

With a thoughtful smile on his face Drummond saun-tered along Pall Mall. He had told Longworth more or less on the spur of the moment, knowing that gentle-man's capabilities to a nicety. Under a cloak of assumed flippancy he concealed an iron nerve which had never yet failed him; and, in spite of the fact that he wore an entirely unnecessary eyeglass, he could see further into a brick wall than most of the people who called him a fool.

It was his suggestion of telling Toby Sinclair that caused the smile. For it had started a train of thought in Drummond's mind which seemed to him to be good. If Sinclair – why not two or three more equally trusty sportsmen? Why not a gang of the boys?

Toby possessed a V C, and a good one – for there are grades of the V C, and those grades are appreciated to a nicety by the recipient's brother officers if not by the general public. The show would fit Toby like a glove . . . Then there was Ted Jerningham, who combined the roles of an amateur actor of more than average merit with an ability to hit anything at any range with every conceivable type of firearm. And Jerry Seymour in the Flying Corps . . . Not a bad thing to have a flying man – up one's sleeve . . . And possibly someone versed in the ways of tanks might come in handy . . .

The smile broadened to a grin; surely life was very good. And then the grin faded, and something suspiciously like a frown took its place. For he had arrived at the Carlton, and reality had come back to him. He seemed to see the almost headless body of a man lying in a Belfast slum . . .

'Mr Potts will see no one, sir,' remarked the man to whom he addressed his question. 'You are about the twentieth gentleman who has been here already today.'

Hugh had expected this, and smiled genially.

'Precisely, my stout fellow,' he remarked, 'but I'll lay a small amount of money that they were newspaper men. Now, I'm not. And I think that if you will have this note delivered to Mr Potts, he will see me.'

He sat down at a table, and drew a sheet of paper towards him. Two facts were certain: first, that the man upstairs was not the real Potts; second, that he was one of Peterson's gang. The difficulty was to know exactly how to word the note. There might be some mystic password, the omission of which would prove him an impostor at once. At length he took a pen and wrote rapidly; he would have to chance it.

Urgent. A message from headquarters.

He sealed the envelope and handed it with the necessary five shillings for postage to the man. Then he sat down to wait. It was going to be a ticklish interview if he was to learn anything, but the thrill of the game had fairly got him by now, and he watched eagerly for the messenger's return. After what seemed an interminable delay he saw him crossing the lounge.

'Mr Potts will see you, sir. Will you come this way?'

'Is he alone?' said Hugh, as they were whirled up in the lift.

'Yes, sir. I think he was expecting you.'

'Indeed,' murmured Hugh. 'How nice it is to have one's expectations realized.'

He followed his guide along a corridor, and paused outside a door while he went into a room. He heard a murmur of voices, and then the man reappeared.

'This way, sir,' he said, and Hugh stepped inside, to stop with an involuntary gasp of surprise. The man seated in the chair *was* Potts, to all intents and purposes. The likeness was extraordinary, and had he not known that the real article was at Goring he would have been completely deceived himself.

The man waited till the door was closed: then he rose and stepped forward suspiciously.

'I don't know you,' he said. 'Who are you?'

'Since when has everyone employed by headquarters known one another?' Drummond returned guardedly. 'And, incidentally, your likeness to our lamented friend is wonderful. It very nearly deceived even me.'

The man, not ill-pleased, gave a short laugh.

'It'll pass, I think. But it's risky. These cursed reporters have been badgering the whole morning . . . And if his wife or somebody comes over, what then?'

Drummond nodded in agreement.

'Quite so. But what can you do?'

'It wasn't like Rosca to bungle in Belfast. He's never left a clue before, and he had plenty of time to do the job properly.'

'A name inside a breast-pocket might easily be overlooked,' remarked Hugh, seizing the obvious clue.

'Are you making excuses for him?' snarled the other. 'He's failed, and failure is death. Such is our rule. Would you have it altered?'

'Most certainly not. The issues are far too great for any weakness . . .'

'You're right, my friend – you're right. Long live the Brotherhood.' He stared out of the window with smouldering eyes, and Hugh preserved a discreet silence. Then suddenly the other broke out again . . . 'Have they killed that insolent puppy of a soldier yet?'

'Er – not yet,' murmured Hugh mildly.

'They must find the American at once.' The man thumped the table emphatically. 'It was important before – at least his money was. Now with this blunder – it's vital.'

'Precisely,' said Hugh. 'Precisely.'

'I've already interviewed one man from Scotland Yard, but every hour increases the danger. However, you have a message for me. What is it?'

Hugh rose and casually picked up his hat. He had got more out of the interview than he had hoped for, and there was nothing to be gained by prolonging it. But it struck him that Mr Potts's impersonator was a man of unpleasant disposition, and that tactically a flanking movement to the door was indicated. And, being of an open nature himself, it is possible that the real state of affairs showed for a moment on his face. Be that as it may, something suddenly aroused the other's suspicions, and with a snarl of fury he sprang past Hugh to the door.

'Who are you?' He spat the words out venomously, at the same time whipping an ugly-looking knife out of his pocket.

Hugh replaced his hat and stick on the table and grinned gently.

'I am the insolent puppy of a soldier, dear old bird,' he remarked, watching the other warily. 'And if I were you I'd put the toothpick away . . . You might hurt yourself –'

As he spoke he was edging, little by little, towards the other man, who crouched, snarling by the door. His eyes, grim and determined, never left the other's face; his hands, apparently hanging listless by his sides, were tingling with the joy of what he knew was coming.

'And the penalty of failure is death, isn't it, dear one?' He spoke almost dreamily; but not for an instant did his attention relax. The words of Olaki, his Japanese instructor, were ringing through his brain: 'Distract his attention if you can; but, as you value your life, don't let him distract yours.'

And so, almost imperceptibly, he crept towards the other man, talking gently.

'Such is your rule. And I think you have failed, haven't

you, you unpleasant specimen of humanity? How will they kill you, I wonder?'

It was at that moment that the man made his mistake. It is a mistake that has nipped the life of many a promising pussy in the bud, at the hands, or rather the teeth, of a dog that knows. He looked away; only for a moment – but he looked away. Just as a cat's nerves give after a while and it looks round for an avenue of escape, so did the crouching man takes his eyes from Hugh. And quick as any dog, Hugh sprang.

With his left hand he seized the man's right wrist, with his right he seized his throat. Then he forced him upright against the door and held him there. Little by little the grip of his right hand tightened, till the other's eyes were starting from his head, and he plucked at Hugh's face with an impotent left arm, an arm not long enough by three inches to do any damage. And all the while the soldier smiled gently, and stared into the other's eyes. Even when inch by inch he shifted his grip on the man's knife hand he never took his eyes from his opponent's face; even when with a sudden gasp of agony the man dropped his knife from fingers which, of a sudden, had become numb, the steady merciless glance still bored into his brain.

'You're not very clever at it, are you?' said Hugh softly. 'It would be so easy to kill you now, and, except for the inconvenience I should undoubtedly suffer, it mightn't be a bad idea. But they know me downstairs, and it would make it so awkward when I wanted to dine here again . . . So, taking everything into account, I think –'

There was a sudden lightning movement, a heave and a quick jerk. The impersonator of Potts was dimly conscious of flying through the air, and of hitting the floor some yards from the door. He then became acutely conscious that the floor was hard, and that being winded is a most painful experience. Doubled up and groaning, he watched Hugh pick up his hat and stick, and make for the door. He made a frantic effort to rise, but the pain was too great, and he rolled over cursing, while the soldier, his hand on the door-knob, laughed gently.

'I'll keep the toothpick,' he remarked, 'as a memento.'

The next moment he was striding along the corridor towards the lift. As a fight it had been a poor one, but his brain was busy with the information he had heard. True, it had been scrappy in the extreme, and, in part, had only confirmed what he had suspected all along. The wretched Granger had been foully done to death, for no other reason than that he was the millionaire's secretary. Hugh's jaw tightened; it revolted his sense of sport. It wasn't as if the poor blighter had done anything; merely because he existed and might ask inconvenient questions he had been removed. And as the lift shot downwards, and the remembrance of the grim struggle he had had in the darkness of The Elms the night before came back to his mind, he wondered once again if he had done wisely in not breaking Peterson's neck while he had had the chance.

He was still debating the question in his mind as he crossed the tea-lounge. And almost unconsciously he glanced toward the table where three days before he had had tea with Phyllis Benton, and had been more than half inclined to believe that the whole thing was an elaborate leg-pull.

'Why, Captain Drummond, you look pensive.' A well-known voice from a table at his side made him look down, and he bowed a little grimly. Irma Peterson was regarding him with a mocking smile.

He glanced at her companion, a young man whose face

seemed vaguely familiar to him, and then his eyes rested once more on the girl. Even his masculine intelligence could appreciate the perfection – in a slightly foreign style – of her clothes; and, as to her beauty, he had never been under any delusions. Nor, apparently, was her escort, whose expression was not one of unalloyed pleasure at the interruption of his tête-à-tête.

'The Carlton seems rather a favourite resort of yours,' she continued, watching him through half-closed eyes. 'I think you're wise to make the most of it while you can.'

'While I can?' said Hugh. 'That sounds rather depressing.'

'I've done my best,' continued the girl, 'but matters have passed out of my hands, I'm afraid.'

Again Hugh glanced at her companion, but he had risen and was talking to some people who had just come in.

'Is he one of the firm?' he remarked. 'His face seems familiar.'

'Oh, no!' said the girl. 'He is – just a friend. What have you been doing this afternoon?'

'That, at any rate, is straight and to the point,' laughed Hugh. 'If you want to know, I've just had a most depressing interview.'

'You're a very busy person, aren't you, my ugly one?' she murmured.

'The poor fellow, when I left him, was quite prostrated with grief, and – er pain,' he went on mildly.

'Would it be indiscreet to ask who the poor fellow is?' she asked.

'A friend of your father's, I think,' said Hugh, with a profound sigh. 'So sad. I hope Mr Peterson's neck is less stiff by now?'

The girl began to laugh softly.

'Not very much, I'm afraid. And it's made him a little irritable. Won't you wait and see him?'

'Is he here now?' said Hugh quickly.

'Yes,' answered the girl. 'With his friend whom you've just left. You're quick, *mon ami* – quite quick.' She leaned forward suddenly. 'Now, why don't you join us instead of so foolishly trying to fight us? Believe me, Monsieur Hugh, it is the only thing that can possibly save you. You know too much.'

'Is the invitation to amalgamate official, or from your own charming brain?' murmured Hugh.

'Made on the spur of the moment,' she said lightly. 'But it may be regarded as official.'

'I'm afraid it must be declined on the spur of the moment,' he answered in the same tone. 'And equally to be regarded as official. Well, *au revoir*. Please tell Mr Peterson how sorry I am to have missed him.'

'I will most certainly,' answered the girl. 'But then, *mon ami*, you will be seeing him again soon, without doubt . . .'

She waved a charming hand in farewell, and turned to her companion, who was beginning to manifest symptoms of impatience. But Drummond, though he went into the hall outside, did not immediately leave the hotel. Instead, he buttonholed an exquisite being arrayed in gorgeous apparel, and led him to a point of vantage.

'You see that girl,' he remarked, 'having tea with a man at the third table from the big palm? Now, can you tell me who the man is? I seem to know his face, but I can't put a name to it.'

'That, sir,' murmured the exquisite being, with the faintest perceptible scorn of such ignorance, 'is the Marquis of Laidley. His lordship is frequently here.'

'Laidley!' cried Hugh, in sudden excitement. 'Laidley!

The Duke of Lampshire's son! You priceless old stuffed tomato – the plot thickens.'

Completely regardless of the scandalized horror on the exquisite being's face, he smote him heavily in the stomach and stepped into Pall Mall. For clean before his memory had come three lines on the scrap of paper he had torn from the table at The Elms, that first night, when he had grabbed the dazed millionaire from under Peterson's nose.

> earl necklace and the
> are at present
> chess of Lamp-

The Duchess of Lampshire's pearls were world-famous; the Marquis of Laidley was apparently enjoying his tea. And between the two there seemed to be a connection rather too obvious to be missed.

III

'I'm glad you two fellows came down,' said Hugh thoughtfully, as he entered the sitting-room of his bunga-low at Goring. Dinner was over, and stretched in three chairs were Peter Darrell, Algy Longworth, and Toby Sinclair. The air was thick with smoke, and two dogs lay curled up on the mat, asleep. 'Did you know that a man came here this afternoon, Peter?'

Darrell yawned and stretched himself.

'I did not. Who was it?'

'Mrs Denny has just told me.' Hugh reached out a hand for his pipe, and proceeded to stuff it with tobacco. 'He came about the water.'

'Seems a very righteous proceeding, dear old thing,' said Algy lazily.

'And he told her that I had told him to come. Unfortunately, I'd done nothing of the sort.'

His three listeners sat up and stared at him.

'What do you mean, Hugh?' asked Toby Sinclair at length.

'It's pretty obvious, old boy,' said Hugh grimly. 'He no more came about the water than he came about my aunt. I should say that about five hours ago Peterson found out that our one and only Hiram C. Potts was upstairs.'

'Good Lord!' spluttered Darrell, by now very wide awake. 'How the devil has he done it?'

'There are no flies on the gentleman,' remarked Hugh. 'I didn't expect he'd do it quite so quick, I must admit. But it wasn't very difficult for him to find out that I had a bungalow here, and so he drew the covert.'

'And he's found the bally fox,' said Algy. 'What do we do, sergeant-major?'

'We take it in turns – two at a time – to sit up with Potts.' Hugh glanced at the other three. 'Damn it – you blighters – wake up!'

Darrel struggled to his feet and walked up and down the room.

'I don't know what it is,' he said, rubbing his eyes, 'I feel most infernally sleepy.'

'Well, listen to me – confound you . . . Toby!' Hugh hurled a tobacco-pouch at the offender's head.

'Sorry, old man.' With a start Sinclair sat up in his chair and blinked at Hugh.

'They're almost certain to try and get him tonight,' went on Hugh. 'Having given the show away by leaving a clue on the wretched secretary, they must get the real man as soon as possible. It's far too dangerous to leave the – leave the –' His head dropped forward on his chest: a short, half-strangled snore came from his lips. It had the effect of waking him for the moment, and he staggered to his feet.

The other three, sprawling in their chairs, were openly and unashamedly asleep; even the dogs lay in fantastic attitudes, breathing heavily, inert like logs.

'Wake up!' shouted Hugh wildly. 'For God's sake – wake up! We've been drugged!'

An iron weight seemed to be pressing down on his eyelids: the desire for sleep grew stronger and stronger. For a few moments more he fought against it, hopelessly, despairingly; while his legs seemed not to belong to him, and there was a roaring noise in his ears. And then, just before unconsciousness overcame him, there came to his bemused brain the sound of a whistle thrice repeated from outside the window. With a last stupendous effort he fought his way towards it, and for a moment he stared into the darkness. There were dim figures moving through the shrubs, and suddenly one seemed to detach itself. It came nearer, and the light fell on the man's face. His nose and mouth were covered with a sort of pad, but the cold, sneering eyes were unmistakable.

'Lakington!' gasped Hugh, and then the roaring noise increased in his head; his legs struck work altogether. He collapsed on the floor and lay sprawling, while Lakington, his face pressed against the glass outside, watched in silence.

'Draw the curtains.' Lakington was speaking, his voice muffled behind the pad, and one of the men did as he said. There were four in all, each with a similar pad over his mouth and nose. 'Where did you put the generator, Brownlow?'

'In the coal-scuttle.' A man whom Mrs Denny would have had no difficulty in recognizing, even with the mask on his face, carefully lifted a small black box out of the scuttle from behind some coal, and shook it gently, holding it to his ear. 'It's finished,' he remarked, and Lakington nodded.

'An ingenious invention is gas,' he said, addressing another of the men. 'We owe your nation quite a debt of gratitude for the idea.'

A guttural grunt left no doubt as to what that nation was, and Lakington dropped the box into his pocket.

'Go and get him,' he ordered briefly, and the others left the room.

Contemptuously Lakington kicked one of the dogs; it rolled over and lay motionless in its new position. Then he went in turn to each of the three men sprawling in the chairs. With no attempt at gentleness he turned their faces up to the light, and studied them deliberately; then he let their heads roll back again with a thud. Finally he went to the window and stared down at Drummond. In his eyes was a look of cold fury, and he kicked the unconscious man savagely in the ribs.

'You young swine,' he muttered. 'Do you think I'll forget that blow on the jaw!'

He took another box out of his pocket and looked at it lovingly.

'Shall I?' With a short laugh he replaced it. 'It's too good a death for you, Captain Drummond, DSO, MC. Just to snuff out in your sleep. No, my friend, I think I can devise something better than that; something really artistic.'

Two other men came in as he turned away, and Lakington looked at them.

'Well,' he asked, 'have you got the old woman?'

'Bound and gagged in the kitchen,' answered one of them laconically. 'Are you going to do this crow in?'

The speaker looked at the unconcious men with hatred in his eyes.

'They encumber the earth – this breed of puppy.'

'They will not encumber it for long,' said Lakington softly. 'But the one in the window there is not going to die quite so easily: I have a small unsettled score with him . . .'

'All right; he's in the car.' A voice came from outside the window, and with a last look at Hugh Drummond, Lakington turned away.

'Then we'll go,' he remarked. '*Au revoir*, my blundering young bull. Before I've finished with you, you'll scream for mercy. And you won't get it . . .'

Through the still night air there came the thrumming of the engine of a powerful car. Gradually it died away and there was silence. Only the murmur of the river over the weir broke the silence, save for an owl which hooted mournfully in a tree nearby. And then, with a sudden crack, Peter Darrell's head rolled over and hit the arm of his chair.

CHAPTER 6

In Which a Very Old Game Takes Place on The Hog's Back

I

A thick grey mist lay over the Thames. It covered the water and the low fields to the west like a thick white carpet; it drifted sluggishly under the old bridge which spans the river between Goring and Streatley. It was the hour before dawn, and sleepy passengers, rubbing the windows of their carriages as the Plymouth boat express rushed on towards London, shivered and drew their rugs closer around them. It looked cold . . . cold and dead.

Slowly, almost imperceptibly, the vapour rose, and spread outwards up the wooded hills by Basildon. It drifted through the shrubs and rose-bushes of a little garden, which stretched from a bungalow down to the water's edge, until at length wisps of it brushed gently round the bungalow itself. It was a daily performance in the summer, and generally the windows of the lower rooms remained shut till long after the mist had gone and the sun was glinting through the trees on to the river below. But on this morning there was a change in the usual programme. Suddenly the window of one of the downstair rooms was flung open, and a man with a white haggard face leant out drawing great gulps of fresh air into his lungs. Softly the white wraiths eddied past him into the room behind – a room in which a queer, faintly sweet smell still hung – a room in which three other men lay sprawling uncouthly in chairs, and two dogs lay motionless on the hearthrug.

After a moment or two the man withdrew, only to appear again with one of the others in his arms. And then, having dropped his burden through the window on to the lawn outside, he repeated his performance with the remaining two. Finally he pitched the two dogs after them, and then, with his hand to his forehead, staggered down to the water's edge.

'Holy smoke!' he muttered to himself, as he plunged his head into the cold water; 'talk about the morning after! . . . Never have I thought of such a head.'

After a while, with the water still dripping from his face, he returned to the bungalow and found the other three in varying stages of partial insensibility.

'Wake up, my heroes,' he remarked, 'and go and put your great fat heads in the river.'

Peter Darrell scrambled unsteadily to his feet. 'Great Scott! Hugh,' he muttered thickly, 'what's happened?'

'We've been had for mugs,' said Drummond grimly.

Algy Longworth blinked at him foolishly from his position in the middle of a flower-bed.

'Dear old soul,' he murmured at length, 'you'll have to change your wine merchants. Merciful Heavens! is the top of my head still on?'

'Don't be a fool, Algy,' grunted Hugh. 'You weren't drunk last night. Pull yourself together, man; we were all of us drugged or doped somehow. And now,' he added bitterly, 'we've all got heads, and we have not got Potts.'

'I don't remember anything,' said Toby Sinclair, 'except falling asleep. Have they taken him?'

'Of course they have,' said Hugh. 'Just before I went

off I saw 'em all in the garden and that swine Lakington was with them. However, while you go and put your nuts in the river, I'll go up and make certain.'

With a grim smile he watched the three men lurch down to the water; then he turned and went upstairs to the room which had been occupied by the American millionaire. It was empty, as he had known it would be, and with a smothered curse he made his way downstairs again. And it was as he stood in the little hall saying things gently under his breath that he heard a muffled moaning noise coming from the kitchen. For a moment he was nonplussed; then, with an oath at his stupidity, he dashed through the door. Bound tightly to the table, with a gag in her mouth, the wretched Mrs Denny was sitting on the floor, blinking at him wrathfully . . .

'What on earth will Denny say to me when he hears about this!' said Hugh, feverishly cutting the cords. He helped her to her feet, and then forced her gently into a chair. 'Mrs Denny, have those swine hurt you?'

Five minutes served to convince him that the damage, if any, was mental rather than bodily, and that her vocal powers were not in the least impaired. Like a dam bursting, the flood of the worthy woman's wrath surged over him; she breathed a hideous vengeance on every one impartially. Then she drove Hugh from the kitchen, and slammed the door in his face.

'Breakfast in half an hour,' she cried from inside – 'not that one of you deserves it.'

'We are forgiven,' remarked Drummond, as he joined the other three on the lawn. 'Do any of you feel like breakfast? Fat sausages and crinkly bacon.'

'Shut up,' groaned Algy, 'or we'll throw you into the river. What I want is a brandy and soda – half a dozen of 'em.'

'I wish I knew what they did to us,' said Darrell. 'Because, if I remember straight, I drank bottled beer at dinner, and I'm damned if I see how they could have doped that.'

'I'm only interested in one thing, Peter,' remarked Drummond grimly, 'and that isn't what they did to us. It's what we're going to do to them.'

'Count me out,' said Algy. 'For the next year I shall be fully occupied resting my head against a cold stone. Hugh, I positively detest your friends . . .'

It was a few hours later that a motor car drew up outside that celebrated chemist in Piccadilly whose pick-me-ups are known from Singapore to Alaska. From it there descended four young men, who ranged themselves in a row before the counter and spoke no word. Speech was unnecessary. Four foaming drinks were consumed, four acid-drops were eaten, and then, still in silence, the four young men got back into the car and drove away. It was a solemn rite, and on arrival at the Junior Sports Club the four performers sank into four large chairs, and pondered gently on the vileness of the morning after. Especially when there hadn't been a night before. An unprofitable meditation evidently, for suddenly, as if actuated by a single thought, the four young men rose from their four large chairs and again entered the motor car.

The celebrated chemist whose pick-me-ups are known from Singapore to Alaska gazed at them severely.

'A very considerable bend, gentlemen,' he remarked.

'Quite wrong,' answered the whitest and most haggard of the row. 'We are all confirmed Pussyfoots, and have been consuming non-alcoholic beer.'

Once more to the scrunch of acid-drops the four young

men entered the car outside; once more, after a brief and silent drive, four large chairs in the smoking-room of the Junior Sports Club received an occupant. And it was so, even until luncheon time . . .

'Are we better?' said Hugh, getting to his feet, and regarding the other three with a discerning eye.

'No,' murmured Toby, 'but I am beginning to hope that I may live. Four Martinis and then we will gnaw a cutlet.'

II

'Has it struck you fellows,' remarked Hugh, at the conclusion of lunch, 'that seated round this table are four officers who fought with some distinction and much discomfort in the recent historic struggle?'

'How beautifully you put it, old flick!' said Darrell.

'Has it further struck you fellows,' continued Hugh, 'that last night we were done down, trampled on, had for mugs by a crowd of dirty blackguards composed largely of the dregs of the universe?'

'A veritable Solomon,' said Algy, gazing at him admiringly through his eyeglass. 'I told you this morning I detested your friends.'

'Has it still further struck you,' went on Hugh, a trifle grimly, 'that we aren't standing for it? At any rate, I'm not. It's my palaver this, you fellows, and if you like . . . Well, there's no call on you to remain in the game. I mean – er –'

'Yes, we're waiting to hear what the devil you do mean,' said Toby uncompromisingly.

'Well – er,' stammered Hugh, 'there's a big element of risk – er – don't you know, and there's no earthly reason

why you fellows should get roped in and all that. I mean –
er – I'm sort of pledged to see the thing through, don't
you know, and –' He relapsed into silence, and stared at
the tablecloth, uncomfortably aware of three pairs of eyes
fixed on him.

'Well – er –' mimicked Algy, 'there's a big element of
risk – er – don't you know, and I mean – er – we're sort of
pledged to bung you through the window, old bean, if
you talk such consolidated drivel.'

Hugh grinned sheepishly.

'Well, I had to put it to you fellows. Not that I ever
thought for a moment you wouldn't see the thing
through – but last evening is enough to show you that
we're up against a tough crowd. A damned tough
crowd,' he added thoughtfully. 'That being so,' he went
on briskly, after a moment or two, 'I propose that we
should tackle the blighters tonight.'

'Tonight!' echoed Darrell. 'Where?'

'At The Elms, of course. That's where the wretched
Potts is for a certainty.'

'And how do you propose that we should set about it?'
demanded Sinclair.

Drummond drained his port and grinned gently.

'By stealth, dear old beans – by stealth. You – and I
thought we might rake in Ted Jerningham, and perhaps
Jerry Seymour, to join the happy throng – will make a
demonstration in force, with the idea of drawing off the
enemy, thereby leaving the coast clear for me to explore
the house for the unfortunate Potts.'

'Sounds very nice in theory,' said Darrell dubiously,
'but . . .'

'And what do you mean by a demonstration?' said
Longworth. 'You don't propose we should sing carols
outside the drawing-room window, do you?'

'My dear people,' Hugh murmured protestingly, 'surely you know me well enough by now to realize that I can't possibly have another idea for at least ten minutes. That is just the general scheme; doubtless the mere vulgar details will occur to us in time. Besides it's someone else's turn now.' He looked round the table hopefully.

'We might dress up or something,' remarked Toby Sinclair, after a lengthy silence.

'What in the name of Heaven is the use of that?' said Darrell witheringly. 'It's not private theatricals, nor a beauty competition.'

'Cease wrangling, you two,' said Hugh suddenly, a few moment later. 'I've got a perfect cerebral hurricane raging. An accident . . . A car . . . What is the connecting link . . . Why, drink. Write it down, Algy, or we might forget. Now, can you beat that?'

'We might have some chance,' said Darrell kindly, 'if we had the slightest idea what you were talking about.'

'I should have thought it was perfectly obvious,' returned Hugh coldly. 'You know, Peter, your worry is that you're too quick on the uptake. Your brain is too sharp.'

'How do you spell connecting?' demanded Algy, looking up from his labours. 'And, anyway, the damn pencil won't write.'

'Pay attention, all of you,' said Hugh. 'Tonight, some time about ten of the clock, Algy's motor will proceed along the Godalming-Guildford road. It will contain you three – also Ted and Jerry Seymour, if we can get 'em. On approaching the gate of The Elms, you will render the night hideous with your vocal efforts. Stray passers-by will think that you are tight. Then will come the dramatic moment, when, with a heavy crash, you ram the gate.'

'How awfully jolly!' spluttered Algy. 'I beg to move that your car be used for the event.'

'Can't be done, old son,' laughed Hugh. 'Mine's faster than yours, and I'll be wanting it myself. Now – to proceed. Horrified at this wanton damage to property, you will leave the car and proceed in mass formation up the drive.'

'Still giving tongue?' queried Darrell.

'Still giving tongue. Either Ted or Jerry or both of 'em will approach the house and inform the owner in heart-broken accents that they have damaged his gate-post. You three will remain in the garden – you might be recognized. Then it will be up to you. You'll have several men all round you. Keep 'em occupied – somehow. They won't hurt you; they'll only be concerned with seeing that you don't go where you're not wanted. You see, as far as the world is concerned, it's just an ordinary country residence. The last thing they want to do is to draw any suspicion on themselves – and, on the face of it, you are merely five convivial wanderers who have looked on the wine when it was red. I think,' he added thoughtfully, 'that ten minutes will be enough for me . . .'

'What will you be doing?' said Toby.

'I shall be looking for Potts. Don't worry about me. I may find him; I may not. But when you have given me ten minutes – you clear off. I'll look after myself. Now is that clear?'

'Perfectly,' said Darrell, after a short silence. 'But I don't know that I like it, Hugh. It seems to me, old son, that you're running an unnecessary lot of risk.'

'Got any alternative?' demanded Drummond.

'If we're all going down,' said Darrell. 'Why not stick together and rush the house in a gang?'

'No go, old bean,' said Hugh decisively. 'Too many of

'em to hope to pull it off. No, low cunning is the only thing that's got an earthly of succeeding.'

'There is one other possible suggestion,' remarked Toby slowly. 'What about the police? From what you say, Hugh, there's enough in that house to jug the whole bunch.'

'Toby!' gasped Hugh. 'I thought better of you. You seriously suggest that we should call in the police! And then return to a life of toping and ease! Besides,' he continued, removing his eyes from the abashed author of this hideous suggestion, 'there's a very good reason for keeping the police out of it. You'd land the girl's father in the cart, along with the rest of them. And it makes it so devilish awkward if one's father-in-law is in prison!'

'When are we going to see this fairy?' demanded Algy.

'You, personally, never. You're far too immoral. I might let the others look at her from a distance in a year or two.' With a grin he rose, and then strolled towards the door. 'Now go and rope in Ted and Jerry, and for the love of Heaven don't ram the wrong gate.'

'What are you going to do yourself?' demanded Peter, suspiciously.

'I'm going to look at her from close to. Go away, all of you, and don't listen outside the telephone box.'

III

Hugh stopped his car at Guildford station and, lighting a cigarette, strolled restlessly up and down. He looked at his watch a dozen times in two minutes; he threw away his smoke before it was half finished. In short he manifested every symptom usually displayed by the male of the species when awaiting the arrival of the opposite sex. Over the telephone he had arranged that SHE should come by train from Godalming to confer with him on a matter of great importance; SHE had said she would, but what was it? He, having no suitable answer ready, had made a loud buzzing noise indicative of a telephone exchange in pain, and then rung off. And now he was waiting in that peculiar condition of mind which reveals itself outwardly in hands that are rather too warm, and feet that are rather too cold.

'When is this bally train likely to arrive?' He accosted a phlegmatic official, who regarded him coldly and doubted the likelihood of its being more than a quarter of an hour early.

At length it was signalled, and Hugh got back into his car. Feverishly he scanned the faces of the passengers as they came out into the street, until, with a sudden quick jump of his heart, he saw her, cool and fresh, coming towards him with a faint smile on her lips.

'What is this very important matter you want to talk to me about?' she demanded, as he adjusted the rug round her.

'I'll tell you when we get out on the Hog's Back,' he said, slipping in his clutch. 'It's absolutely vital.'

He stole a glance at her, but she was looking straight in front of her, and her face seemed expressionless.

'You must stand a long way off when you do,' she said demurely. 'At least if it's the same thing as you told me over the phone.'

Hugh grinned sheepishly.

'The Exchange went wrong,' he remarked at length. 'Astonishing how rotten the telephones are in Town these days.'

'Quite remarkable,' she returned. 'I thought you

weren't feeling very well or something. Of course, if it was the Exchange . . .'

'They sort of buzz and blow, don't you know,' he explained helpfully.

'That must be most fearfully jolly for them,' she agreed. And there was silence for the next two miles . . .

Once or twice he looked at her out of the corner of his eye, taking in every detail of the sweet profile so near to him. Except for their first meeting at the Carlton, it was the only time he had ever had her completely to himself, and Hugh was determined to make the most of it. He felt as if he could go on driving for ever, just he and she alone. He had an overwhelming longing to put out his hand and touch a soft tendril of hair which was blowing loose just behind her ear; he had an overwhelming longing to take her in his arms, and . . . It was then that the girl turned and looked at him. The car swerved dangerously . . .

'Let's stop,' she said, with the suspicion of a smile. 'Then you can tell me.'

Hugh drew into the side of the road, and switched off the engine.

'You're not fair,' he remarked, and if the girl saw his hand trembling a little as he opened the door, she gave no sign. Only her breath came a shade faster, but a mere man could hardly be expected to notice such a trifle as that . . .

He came and stood beside her, and his right arm lay along the seat just behind her shoulders.

'You're not fair,' he repeated gravely. 'I haven't swerved like that since I first started to drive.'

'Tell me about this important thing,' she said a little nervously.

He smiled, and no woman yet born could see Hugh Drummond smile without smiling too.

'You darling!' he whispered, under his breath – 'you adorable darling!' His arm closed around her, and almost before she realized it, she felt his lips on hers. For a moment she sat motionless, while the wonder of it surged over her, and the sky seemed more gloriously blue, and the woods a richer green. Then, with a little gasp, she pushed him away.

'You mustn't . . . oh! you mustn't, Hugh,' she whispered.

'And why not, little girl?' he said exultingly. 'Don't you know I love you?'

'But look, there's a man over there, and he'll see.'

Hugh glanced at the stolid labourer in question, and smiled.

'Go an absolute mucker over the cabbages, what! Plant carrots by mistake.' His face was still very close to hers. 'Well?'

'Well, what?' she murmured.

'It's your turn,' he whispered. 'I love you, Phyllis – just love you.'

'But it's only two or three days since we met,' she said feebly.

'And phwat the divil has that got to do with it, at all?' he demanded. 'Would I be wanting longer to decide such an obvious fact? Tell me,' he went on, and she felt his arm round her again forcing her to look at him – 'tell me, don't you care . . . a little?'

'What's the use?' She still struggled, but, even to her, it wasn't very convincing. 'We've got other things to do . . . We can't think of . . .'

And then this very determined young man settled matters in his usual straightforward fashion. She felt herself lifted bodily out of the car as if she had been a child: she found herself lying in his arms, with Hugh's eyes looking very tenderly into her own and a whimsical grin round his mouth.

'Cars pass here,' he remarked, 'with great regularity. I know you'd hate to be discovered in this position.'

'Would I?' she whispered. 'I wonder . . .'

She felt his heart pound madly against her; and with a sudden quick movement she put both her arms round his neck and kissed him on the mouth.

'Is that good enough?' she asked, very low: and just for a few moments, Time stood still . . . Then, very gently, he put her back in the car.

'I suppose,' he remarked resignedly, 'that we had better descend to trivialities. We've had lots of fun and games since I last saw you a year or two ago.'

'Idiot boy,' she said happily. 'It was yesterday morning.'

'The interruption is considered trivial. Mere facts don't count when it's you and me.' There was a further interlude of uncertain duration, followed rapidly by another because the first was so nice.

'To resume,' continued Hugh. 'I regret to state that they've got Potts.'

The girl sat up quickly and stared at him.

'Got him? Oh, Hugh! How did they manage it?'

'I'm damned if I know,' he answered grimly. 'They found out that he was in my bungalow at Goring during the afternoon by sending round a man to see about the water. Somehow or other he must have doped the drink or the food, because after dinner we all fell asleep. I can just remember seeing Lakington's face outside in the garden, pressed against the window, and then everything went out. I don't remember anything more till I woke this morning with the most appalling head. Of course, Potts had gone.'

'I heard the car drive up in the middle of the night,' said the girl thoughtfully. 'Do you think he's at The Elms now?'

'That is what I propose to find out tonight,' answered Hugh. 'We have staged a little comedy for Peterson's especial benefit, and we are hoping for the best.'

'Oh, boy, do be careful!' She looked at him anxiously. 'I'd never forgive myself if anything happened to you. I'd feel it was all due to me, and I just couldn't bear it.'

'Dear little girl,' he whispered tenderly, 'you're simply adorable when you look like that. But not even for you would I back out of this show now.' His mouth set in a grim line. 'It's gone altogether too far, and they've shown themselves to be so completely beyond the pale that it's got to be fought out. And when it has been,' he caught both her hands in his . . . 'and we've won . . . why, then girl o' mine, we'll get Peter Darrell to be best man.'

Which was the cue for the commencement of the last and longest interlude, terminated only by the sudden and unwelcome appearance of a motor bus covered within and without by unromantic sightseers, and paper bags containing bananas.

They drove slowly back to Guildford, and on the way he told her briefly of the murder of the American's secretary in Belfast, and his interview the preceding afternoon with the impostor at the Carlton.

'It's a tough proposition,' he remarked quietly. 'They're absolutely without scruple, and their power seems unlimited. I know they are after the Duchess of Lampshire's pearls: I found the beautiful Irma consuming tea with young Laidley yesterday – you know, the Duke's eldest son. But there's something more in the wind than that, Phyllis – something which, unless I'm a mug of the first water, is an infinitely larger proposition than that.'

The car drew up at the station, and he strolled with her on to the platform. Trivialities were once more banished: vital questions concerning when it had first happened – by both; whether he was quite sure it would last for ever – by her; what she could possibly see in him – by him; and wasn't everything just too wonderful for words – mutual and carried *nem. con.*

Then the train came in, and he put her into a carriage. And two minutes later, with the touch of her lips warm on his, and her anxious little cry, 'Take care, my darling! – take care!' still ringing in his ears, he got into his car and drove off to a hotel to get an early dinner. Love for the time was over; the next round of the other game was due. And it struck Drummond that it was going to be a round where a mistake would not be advisable.

IV

At a quarter to ten he backed his car into the shadow of some trees not far from the gate of The Elms. The sky was overcast, which suited his purpose, and through the gloom of the bushes he dodged rapidly towards the house. Save for a light in the sitting-room and one in a bedroom upstairs, the front of the house was in darkness, and, treading noiselessly on the turf, he explored all round it. From a downstairs room on one side came the hoarse sound of men's voices, and he placed that as the smoking-room of the gang of ex-convicts and black-guards who formed Peterson's staff. There was one bedroom light at the back of the house, and thrown on the blind he could see the shadow of a man. As he watched, the man got up and moved away, only to return in a moment or two and take up his old position.

'It's one of those two bedrooms,' he muttered to himself, 'if he's here at all.'

Then he crouched in the shadow of some shrubs and waited. Through the trees to his right he could see The Larches, and once, with a sudden quickening of his heart, he thought he saw the outline of the girl show up in the light from the drawing-room. But it was only for a second, and then it was gone . . .

He peered at his watch: it was just ten o'clock. The trees were creaking gently in the faint wind; all around him the strange night noises – noises which play pranks with a man's nerves – were whispering and muttering. Bushes seemed suddenly to come to life, and move; eerie shapes crawled over the ground towards him – figures which existed only in his imagination. And once again the thrill of the night stalker gripped him.

He remembered the German who had lain motionless for an hour in a little gully by Hebuterne, while he from behind a stunted bush had tried to locate him. And then that one creak as the Boche had moved his leg. And then . . . the end. On that night, too, the little hummocks had moved and taken themselves strange shapes: fifty times he had imagined he saw him; fifty times he knew he was wrong – in time. He was used to it; the night held no terrors for him, only a fierce excitement. And thus it was that as he crouched in the bushes, waiting for the game to start, his pulse was as normal, and his nerves as steady, as if he had been sitting down to supper. The only difference was that in his hand he held something tight-gripped.

At last faintly in the distance he heard the hum of a car.

Rapidly it grew louder, and he smiled grimly to himself as the sound of five unmelodious voices singing lustily struck his ear. They passed along the road in front of the house. There was a sudden crash – then silence; but only for a moment.

Peter's voice came first:

'You priceless old ass, you've rammed the blinking gate.'

It was Jerry Seymour who then took up the ball. His voice was intensely solemn – also extremely loud.

'Preposhterous. Perfectly preposhterous. We must go and apologize to the owner . . . I . . . I . . . absholutely . . . musht apologize . . . Quite unpardonable . . . You can't go about country . . . knocking down gates . . . Out of queshtion . . .'

Half consciously Hugh listened, but, now that the moment for action had come, every faculty was concentrated on his own job. He saw half a dozen men go rushing out into the garden through a side door, and then two more ran out and came straight towards him. They crashed past him and went on into the darkness, and for an instant he wondered what they were doing. A little later he was destined to find out . . .

Then came a peal at the front-door bell, and he determined to wait no longer. He darted through the garden door, to find a flight of back stairs in front of him, and in another moment he was on the first floor. He walked rapidly along the landing, trying to find his bearings, and, turning a corner, he found himself at the top of the main staircase – the spot where he had fought Peterson two nights previously.

From below Jerry Seymour's voice came clearly.

'Are you the pro-propri-tor, ole friend? Because there's been . . . accident . . .'

He waited to hear no more, but walked quickly on to the room which he calculated was the one where he had seen the shadow on the blind. Without a second's hesitation he flung the door open and walked in. There, lying in the bed, was the American, while crouched beside him, with a revolver in his hand, was a man . . .

For a few seconds they watched one another in silence, and then the man straightened up.

'The soldier!' he snarled. 'You young pup!'

Deliberately, almost casually, he raised his revolver, and then the unexpected happened. A jet of liquid ammonia struck him full in the face, and with a short laugh Hugh dropped his water-pistol in his pocket, and turned his attention to the bed. Wrapping the millionaire in a blanket, he picked him up, and, paying no more attention to the man gasping and choking in a corner, he raced for the back stairs.

Below he could still hear Jerry hiccuping gently, and explaining to the pro . . . pro . . . pritor that he pershonally would repair . . . inshisted on repairing . . . any and every gateposht he posshessed . . . And then he reached the garden . . .

Everything had fallen out exactly as he had hoped, but had hardly dared to expect. He heard Peterson's voice, calm and suave as usual, answering Jerry. From the garden in front came the dreadful sound of a duet by Algy and Peter. Not a soul was in sight; the back of the house was clear. All that he had to do was to walk quietly through the wicket-gate to The Larches with his semiconscious burden, get to his car and drive off. It all seemed so easy that he laughed . . .

But there were one or two factors that he had forgotten, and the first and most important one was the man upstairs. The window was thrown up suddenly, and the man leaned out waving his arms. He was still gasping with the strength of the ammonia, but Hugh saw him clearly in the light from the room behind. And as he cursed himself for a fool in not having tied him up, from the trees close by there came the sharp clang of metal.

With a quick catch in his breath he began to run. The two men who had rushed past him before he had entered the house, and whom, save for a passing thought, he had disregarded, had become the principal danger. For he had heard that clang before; he remembered Jem Smith's white horror-struck face, and then his sigh of relief as the thing – whatever it was – was shut in its cage. And now it was out, dodging through the trees, let loose by the two men.

Turning his head from side to side, peering into the gloom, he ran on. What an interminable distance it seemed to the gate . . . and even then . . . He heard something crash into a bush on his right, and give a snarl of anger. Like a flash he swerved into the undergrowth on the left.

Then began a dreadful game. He was still some way from the fence, and he was hampered at every step by the man slung over his back. He could hear the thing blundering about searching for him, and suddenly, with a cold feeling of fear, he realized that the animal was in front of him – that his way to the gate was barred. The next moment he saw it.

Shadowy, indistinct, in the darkness, he saw something glide between two bushes. Then it came out into the open and he knew it had seen him, though as yet he could not make out what it was. Grotesque and horrible it crouched on the ground, and he could hear its heavy breathing, as it waited for him to move.

Cautiously he lowered the millionaire to the ground,

and took a step forward. It was enough; with a snarl of fury the crouching form rose and shambled towards him. Two hairy arms shot towards his throat, he smelt the brute's fetid breath, hot and loathsome, and he realized what he was up against. It was a partially grown gorilla.

For a full minute they fought in silence, save for the hoarse grunts of the animal as it tried to tear away the man's hand from its throat, and then encircle him with its powerful arms. And with his brain cold as ice Hugh saw his danger and kept his head. It couldn't go on: no human being could last the pace, whatever his strength. And there was only one chance of finishing it quickly, the possibility that the grip taught him by Olaki would serve with a monkey as it did with a man.

He shifted his left thumb an inch or two on the brute's throat, and the gorilla, thinking he was weakening, redoubled his efforts. But still those powerful hands clutched its throat; try as it would, it failed to make them budge. And then, little by little, the fingers moved, and the grip which had been tight before grew tighter still.

Back went its head; something was snapping in its neck. With a scream of fear and rage it wrapped its legs round Drummond, squeezing and writhing. And then suddenly there was a tearing snap, and the great limbs relaxed and grew limp.

For a moment the man stood watching the still quivering brute lying at his feet; then, with a gasp of utter exhaustion, he dropped on the ground himself. He was done – utterly cooked; even Peterson's voice close behind scarcely roused him.

'Quite one of the most amusing entertainments I've seen for a long time.' The calm, expressionless voice made him look up wearily, and he saw that he was surrounded by men. The inevitable cigar glowed red in the darkness, and after a moment or two he scrambled unsteadily to his feet.

'I'd forgotten your damned menagerie, I must frankly confess,' he remarked. 'What's the party for?' He glanced at the men who had closed in round him.

'A guard of honour, my young friend,' said Peterson suavely, 'to lead you to the house. I wouldn't hesitate . . . it's very foolish. Your friends have gone, and, strong as you are, I don't think you can manage ten.'

Hugh commenced to stroll towards the house.

'Well, don't leave the wretched Potts lying about. I dropped him over there.' For a moment the idea of making a dash for it occurred to him, but he dismissed it at once. The odds were too great to make the risk worthwhile, and in the centre of the group he and Peterson walked side by side.

'The last man whom poor Sam had words with,' said Peterson reminiscently, 'was found next day with his throat torn completely out.'

'A lovable little thing,' murmured Hugh. 'I feel quite sorry at having spoilt his record.'

Peterson paused with his hand on the sitting-room door, and looked at him benevolently.

'Don't be despondent, Captain Drummond. We have ample time at our disposal to ensure a similar find tomorrow morning.'

CHAPTER 7

In Which He Spends an Hour or Two on a Roof

I

Drummond paused for a moment at the door of the sitting-room, then with a slight shrug he stepped past Peterson. During the last few days he had grown to look on this particular room as the private den of the principals of the gang. He associated it in his mind with Peterson himself, suave, impassive, ruthless; with the girl Irma, perfectly gowned, lying on the sofa, smoking innumerable cigarettes, and manicuring her already faultless nails; and in a lesser degree, with Henry Lakington's thin, cruel face, and blue, staring eyes.

But tonight a different scene confronted him. The girl was not there: her accustomed place on the sofa was occupied by an unkempt-looking man with a ragged beard. At the end of the table was a vacant chair, on the right of which sat Lakington regarding him with malevolent fury. Along the table on each side there were half a dozen men, and he glanced at their faces. Some were obviously foreigners; some might have been anything from murderers to Sunday-school teachers. There was one with spectacles and the general appearance of an intimidated rabbit, while his neighbour, helped by a large red scar right across his cheek, and two bloodshot eyes, struck Hugh as being the sort of man with whom one would not share a luncheon basket.

'I know he'd snatch both drumsticks and gnaw them simultaneously,' he reflected, staring at him fascinated; 'and then he'd throw the bones in your face.'

Peterson's voice from just behind his shoulder roused him from his distressing reverie.

'Permit me, gentlemen, to introduce to you Captain Drummond, DSO, MC, the originator of the little entertainment we have just had.'

Hugh bowed gravely.

'My only regret is that it failed to function,' he remarked. 'As I told you outside, I'd quite forgotten your menagerie. In fact' – his glance wandered slowly and somewhat pointedly from face to face at the table – 'I had no idea it was such a large one.'

'So this is the insolent young swine, is it?' The blood-shot eyes of the man with the scarred face turned on him morosely. 'What I cannot understand is why he hasn't been killed by now.'

Hugh waggled an accusing finger at him.

'I knew you were a nasty man as soon as I saw you. Now look at Henry up at the end of the table; he doesn't say that sort of thing. And you do hate me, don't you, Henry? How's the jaw?'

'Captain Drummond,' said Lakington, ignoring Hugh and addressing the first speaker, 'was very nearly killed last night. I thought for some time as to whether I would or not, but I finally decided it would be much too easy a death. So it can be remedied tonight.'

If Hugh felt a momentary twinge of fear at the calm, expressionless tone, and the half-satisfied grunt which greeted the words, no trace of it showed on his face. Already the realization had come to him that if he got through the night alive he would be more than passing lucky, but he was too much of a fatalist to let that worry him unduly. So he merely stifled a yawn, and again turned to Lakington.

'So it was you, my little one, whose fairy face I saw pressed against the window. Would it be indiscreet to ask how you got the dope into us?'

Lakington looked at him with an expression of grim satisfaction on his face.

'You were gassed, if you want to know. An admirable invention of my friend Kauffner's nation.'

A guttural chuckle came from one of the men, and Hugh looked at him grimly.

'The scum certainly would not be complete,' he remarked to Peterson, 'without a filthy Boche in it.'

The German pushed back his chair with an oath, his face purple with passion.

'A filthy Boche,' he muttered thickly, lurching towards Hugh. 'Hold him the arms of, and I will the throat tear out . . .'

The intimidated rabbit rose protestingly at this prospect of violence; the scarred sportsman shot out of his chair eagerly, the lust of battle in his blood-shot eyes. The only person save Hugh who made no movement was Peterson, and he, very distinctly, chuckled. Whatever his failings, Peterson had a sense of humour . . .

It all happened so quickly. At one moment Hugh was apparently intent upon selecting a cigarette, the next instant the case had fallen to the floor; there was a dull, heavy thud, and the Boche crashed back, overturned a chair, and fell like a log to the floor, his head hitting the wall with a vicious crack. The bloodshot being resumed his seat a little limply; the intimidated bunny gave a stifled gasp and breathed heavily; Hugh resumed his search for a cigarette.

'After which breezy interlude,' remarked Peterson, 'let us to business get.'

Hugh paused in the act of striking a match, and for the first time a genuine smile spread over his face.

'There are moments, Peterson,' he murmured, 'when you really appeal to me.'

Peterson took the empty chair next to Lakington.

'Sit down,' he said shortly. 'I can only hope that I shall appeal to you still more before we kill you.'

Hugh bowed and sat down.

'Consideration,' he murmured, 'was always your strong point. May I ask how long I have to live?'

Peterson smiled genially.

'At the very earnest request of Mr Lakington you are to be spared until tomorrow morning. At least, that is our present intention. Of course, there might be an accident in the night: in a house like this one can never tell. Or' – he carefully cut the end off a cigar – 'you might go mad, in which case we shouldn't bother to kill you. In fact, it would really suit our book better if you did: the disposal of corpses, even in these days of advanced science, presents certain difficulties – not insuperable – but a nuisance. And so, if you go mad, we shall not be displeased.'

Once again he smiled genially.

'As I said before, in a house like this, you never can tell . . .'

The intimidated rabbit, still breathing heavily, was staring at Hugh, fascinated; and after a moment Hugh turned on him with a courteous bow.

'Laddie,' he remarked, 'you've been eating onions. Do you mind deflecting the blast in the opposite direction?'

His calm imperturbability seemed to madden Lakington, who with a sudden movement rose from his chair and leaned across the table, while the veins stood out like whipcord on his usually expressionless face.

'You wait,' he snarled thickly; 'you wait till I've finished with you. You won't be so damned humorous then . . .'

Hugh regarded the speaker languidly.

'Your supposition is more than probable,' he remarked, in a bored voice. 'I shall be too intent on getting into a Turkish bath to remove the contamination to think of laughing.'

Slowly Lakington sank back in his chair, a hard, merciless smile on his lips; and for a moment or two there was silence in the room. It was broken by the unkempt man on the sofa, who, without warning, exploded unexpectedly.

'A truce to all this fooling,' he burst forth in a deep rumble; 'I confess I do not understand it. Are we assembled here tonight, comrades, to listen to private quarrels and stupid talk?'

A murmur of approval came from the others, and the speaker stood up waving his arms.

'I know not what this young man has done: I care less. In Russia such trifles matter not. He has the appearance of a bourgeois, therefore he must die. Did we not kill thousands – aye, tens of thousands of his kidney, before we obtained the great freedom? Are we not going to do the same in this accursed country?' His voice rose to the shrill, strident note of the typical tub-thumper. 'What is this wretched man,' he continued, waving a hand wildly at Hugh, 'that he should interrupt the great work for one brief second? Kill him now – throw him in a corner, and let us proceed.'

He sat down again, amidst a further murmur of approval in which Hugh joined heartily.

'Splendid,' he murmured. 'A magnificent peroration. Am I right, sir, in assuming that you are what is vulgarly known as a Bolshevist?'

The man turned his sunken eyes, glowing with the burning fires of fanaticism, on Drummond.

'I am one of those who are fighting for the freedom of the world,' he cried harshly, 'for the right to live of the proletariat. The workers were the bottom dogs in Russia till they killed the rulers. Now – they rule, and the money they earn goes into their own pockets, not those of incompetent snobs.' He flung out his arms. He seemed to shrivel up suddenly, as if exhausted with the violence of his passion. Only his eyes still gleamed with the smouldering madness of his soul.

Hugh looked at him with genuine curiosity; it was the first time he had actually met one of these wild visionaries in the flesh. And then the curiosity was succeeded by a very definite amazement; what had Peterson to do with such as he?

He glanced casually at his principal enemy, but his face showed nothing. He was quietly turning over some papers; his cigar glowed as evenly as ever. He seemed to be no whit surprised by the unkempt one's outburst: in fact, it appeared to be quite in order. And once again Hugh stared at the man on the sofa with puzzled eyes.

For the moment his own deadly risk was forgotten; a growing excitement filled his mind. Could it be possible that here, at last, was the real object of the gang; could it be possible that Peterson was organizing a deliberate plot to try and Bolshevize England? If so, where did the Duchess of Lampshire's pearls come in? What of the American, Hiram Potts? Above all, what did Peterson hope to make out of it himself? And it was as he arrived at that point in his deliberation that he looked up to find Peterson regarding him with a faint smile.

'It is a little difficult to understand, isn't it, Captain Drummond?' he said, carefully flicking the ash off his cigar. 'I told you you'd find yourself in deep water.' Then he resumed the contemplation of the papers in front of him, as the Russian burst out again.

'Have you ever seen a woman skinned alive?' he howled wildly, thrusting his face forward at Hugh. 'Have you ever seen men killed with the knotted rope; burned almost to death and then set free, charred and mutilated wrecks? But what does it matter provided only freedom comes, as it has in Russia. Tomorrow it will be England: in a week the world . . . Even if we have to wade through rivers of blood up to our throats, nevertheless it will come. And in the end we shall have a new earth.'

Hugh lit a cigarette and leaned back in his chair.

'It seems a most alluring programme,' he murmured. 'And I shall have much pleasure in recommending you as manager of a babies' crèche. I feel certain the little ones would take to you instinctively.'

He half closed his eyes, while a general buzz of conversation broke out round the table. Tongues had been loosened, wonderful ideals conjured up by the Russian's inspiring words; and for the moment he was forgotten. Again and again the question hammered at his brain – what in the name of Buddha had Peterson and Lakington to do with this crowd? Two intensely brilliant, practical criminals mixed up with a bunch of ragged-trousered visionaries, who, to all intents and purposes, were insane . . .

Fragments of conversation struck his ears from time to time. The intimidated rabbit, with the light of battle in his watery eye, was declaiming on the glories of Workmen's Councils; a bullet-headed man who looked like a down-at-heels racing tout was shouting an inspiring battle-cry about no starvation wages and work for all.

'Can it be possible,' thought Hugh grimly, 'that such as these have the power to control big destinies?' And then, because he had some experience of what one unbalanced brain, whose owner could talk, was capable of achieving; because he knew something about mob psychology, his half-contemptuous amusement changed to a bitter foreboding.

'You fool,' he cried suddenly to the Russian and everyone ceased talking. 'You poor damned boob! You – and your new earth! In Petrograd today bread is two pounds four shillings a pound; tea, fifteen pounds a pound. Do you call that freedom? Do you suggest that we should wade to *that*, through rivers of blood?' He gave a contemptuous laugh. 'I don't know which distresses me most, your maggoty brain or your insanitary appearance.'

Too surprised to speak, the Russian sat staring at him; and it was Peterson who broke the silence with his suave voice.

'Your distress, I am glad to say, is not likely to be one of long duration,' he remarked. 'In fact, the time has come for you to retire for the night, my young friend.'

He stood up smiling; then walked over to the bell behind Hugh and rang it.

'Dead or mad – I wonder which.' He threw the end of his cigar into the grate as Hugh rose. 'While we deliberate down here on various matters of importance we shall be thinking of you upstairs – that is to say, if you get there. I see that Lakington is even now beginning to gloat in pleasant anticipation.'

Not a muscle on the soldier's face twitched; not by the hint of a look did he show the keenly watching audience that he realized his danger. He might have been an ordinary guest preparing to go to bed; and in Peterson's face there shone for a moment a certain unwilling admiration. Only Lakington's was merciless, with its fiendish look of anticipation, and Hugh stared at him with level eyes for a while before he turned towards the door.

'Then I will say good-night,' he remarked casually. 'Is it the same room that I had last time?'

'No,' said Peterson. 'A different one – specially prepared for you. If you get to the top of the stairs a man will show you where it is.' He opened the door and stood there smiling. And at that moment all the lights went out.

II

The darkness could be felt, as real darkness inside a house always can be felt. Not the faintest glimmer even of greyness showed anywhere, and Hugh remained motionless, wondering what the next move was going to be. Now that the night's ordeal had commenced, all his nerve had returned to him. He felt ice cold; and as his powerful hands clenched and unclenched by his sides, he grinned faintly to himself.

Behind him in the room he could hear an occasional movement in one of the chairs, and once from the hall outside he caught the sound of whispering. He felt that he was surrounded by men, thronging in on him from all sides, and suddenly he gave a short laugh. Instantly silence settled – strain as he would he could not hear a sound. Then very cautiously he commenced to feel his way towards the door.

Outside a car went by honking discordantly, and with a sort of cynical amusement he wondered what its occupants would think if they knew what was happening in the house so near them. And at that moment someone brushed past him. Like a flash Hugh's hand shot out and gripped him by the arm. The man wriggled and twisted, but he was powerless as a child, and with another short laugh Hugh found his throat with his other hand. And again silence settled on the room . . .

Still holding the unknown man in front of him, he reached the foot of the stairs, and there he paused. He had suddenly remembered the mysterious thing which had whizzed past his head that other night, and then clanged sullenly into the wall beside him. He had gone up five stairs when it had happened, and now with his foot on the first he started to do some rapid thinking.

If, as Peterson had kindly assured him, they proposed to try and send him mad, it was unlikely that they would kill him on the stairs. At the same time it was obviously an implement capable of accurate adjustment, and therefore it was more than likely that they would use it to frighten him. And if they did – if they did . . . The unknown man wriggled feebly in his hands, and a sudden unholy look came on to Hugh's face.

'It's the only possible chance,' he said to himself, 'and if it's you or me, laddie, I guess it's got to be you.'

With a quick heave he jerked the man off his feet, and lifted him up till his head was above the level of his own. Then clutching him tight, he commenced to climb. His own head was bent down, somewhere in the regions of the man's back, and he took no notice of the feebly kicking legs.

Then at last he reached the fourth step, and gave a final adjustment to his semi-conscious burden. He felt that the hall below was full of men, and suddenly Peterson's voice came to him out of the darkness.

'That is four, Captain Drummond. What about the fifth step?'

'A very good-looking one as far as I remember,' answered Hugh. 'I'm just going to get on to it.'

'That should prove entertaining,' remarked Peterson. 'I'm just going to switch on the current.'

Hugh pressed his head even lower in the man's back and lifted him up another three inches.

'How awfully jolly!' he murmured. 'I hope the result will please you.'

'I'd stand quite still if I were you,' said Peterson suavely. 'Just listen.'

As Hugh had gambled on, the performance was designed to frighten. Instead of that, something hit the neck of the man he was holding with such force that it wrenched him clean out of his arms. Then came the clang beside him, and with a series of ominous thuds a body rolled down the stairs into the hall below.

'You fool.' He heard Lakington's voice, shrill with anger. 'You've killed him. Switch on the light . . .'

But before the order could be carried out Hugh had disappeared, like a great cat, into the darkness of the passage above. It was neck or nothing; he had at the most a minute to get clear. As luck would have it the first room he darted into was empty, and he flung up the window and peered out.

A faint, watery moon showed him a twenty-foot drop on to the grass, and without hesitation he flung his legs over the sill. Below a furious hubbub was going on; steps were already rushing up the stairs. He heard Peterson's calm voice, and Lakington's hoarse with rage, shouting inarticulate orders. And at that moment something prompted him to look upwards.

It was enough – that one look; he had always been mad, he always would be. It was a dormer window, and to an active man access to the roof was easy. Without an instant's hesitation he abandoned all thoughts of retreat; and when two excited men rushed into the room he was firmly ensconced, with his legs astride of the ridge of the window, not a yard from their heads.

Securely hidden in the shadow he watched the subsequent proceedings with genial toleration. A raucous bellow from the two men announced that they had discovered his line of escape; and in half a minute the garden was full of hurrying figures. One, calm and impassive, his identity betrayed only by the inevitable cigar, stood by the garden door, apparently taking no part in the game; Lakington, blind with fury, was running round in small circles, cursing everyone impartially.

'The car is still there.' A man came up to Peterson, and Hugh heard the words distinctly.

'Then he's probably over at Benton's house. I will go and see.'

Hugh watched the thick-set, massive figure stroll down towards the wicket-gate, and he laughed gently to himself. Then he grew serious again, and with a slight frown he pulled out his watch and peered at it. Half-past one . . . two more hours before dawn. And in those two hours he wanted to explore the house from on top; especially he wanted to have a look at the mysterious central room of which Phyllis had spoken to him – the room where Lakington kept his treasures. But until the excited throng below went indoors, it was unsafe to move. Once out of the shadow, anyone would be able to see him crawling over the roof in the moonlight.

At times the thought of the helpless man for whose death he had in one way been responsible recurred to him, and he shook his head angrily. It had been necessary, he realized: you can carry someone upstairs in a normal house without him having his neck broken – but still . . . And then he wondered who he was. It had been one of the men who sat round the table – of that he was tolerably certain. But which . . . ? Was it the frightened bunny, or the Russian, or the gentleman with the bloodshot eye? The only comfort was that whoever it had been, the world would not be appreciably the poorer for his sudden decease. The only regret was that it hadn't been dear Henry . . . He had a distaste for Henry which far exceeded his dislike of Peterson.

'He's not over there.' Peterson's voice came to him from below. 'And we've wasted time enough as it is.'

The men had gathered together in a group, just below where Hugh was sitting, evidently awaiting further orders.

'Do you mean to say we've lost the young swine again?' said Lakington angrily.

'Not lost – merely mislaid,' murmured Peterson. 'The more I see of him, the more do I admire his initiative.'

Lakington snorted.

'It was that damned fool Ivolsky's own fault,' he snarled; 'why didn't he keep still as he was told to do?'

'Why, indeed?' returned Peterson, his cigar glowing red. 'And I'm afraid we shall never know. He is very dead.' He turned towards the house. 'That concludes the entertainment, gentlemen, for tonight. I think you can all go to bed.'

'There are two of you watching the car, aren't there?' demanded Lakington.

'Rossiter and Le Grange,' answered a voice.

Peterson paused by the door.

'My dear Lakington, it's quite unnecessary. You underrate that young man . . .'

He disappeared into the house, and the others followed slowly. For the time being Hugh was safe, and with a sigh of relief he stretched his cramped limbs and lay back against the sloping roof. If only he had dared to light a cigarette . . .

III

It was half an hour before Drummond decided that it was safe to start exploring. The moon still shone fitfully through the trees, but since the two car watchers were near the road on the other side of the house, there was but little danger to be apprehended from them. First he took off his shoes, and tying the laces together, he slung them round his neck. Then, as silently as he could, he commenced to scramble upwards.

It was not an easy operation; one slip and nothing could have stopped him slithering down and finally crashing into the garden below, with a broken leg, at the very least, for his pains. In addition, there was the risk of dislodging a slate, an unwise proceeding in a house where most of the occupants slept with one eye open. But at last he got his hands over the ridge of the roof, and in another moment he was sitting straddle-wise across it.

The house, he discovered, was built on a peculiar design. The ridge on which he sat continued at the same height all round the top of the roof, and formed, roughly, the four sides of a square. In the middle the roof sloped down to a flat space from which stuck up a glass structure, the top of which was some five or six feet below his level. Around it was a space quite large enough to walk in comfort; in fact, on two sides there was plenty of room for a deck chair. The whole area was completely screened from view, except to anyone in an aeroplane. And what struck him still further was that there was no window that he could see anywhere on the inside of the roof. In fact, it was absolutely concealed and private. Incidentally, the house had originally been built by a gentleman of doubtful sanity, who spent his life observing the spots in Jupiter through a telescope, and having plunged himself and his family into complete penury, sold the house and observatory complete for what he could get. Lakington, struck with its possibilities for his own hobby, bought it on the spot; and from that time Jupiter spotted undisturbed.

With the utmost caution Hugh lowered himself to the full extent of his arms; then he let himself slip the last two or three feet on to the level space around the glass roof. He had no doubt in his mind that he was actually above the secret room, and, on tiptoe, he stole round looking for some spot from which he could get a glimpse below. At the first inspection he thought his time had been wasted; every pane of glass was frosted, and in addition there seemed to be a thick blind of some sort drawn across from underneath, of the same type as is used by photographers for altering the light.

A sudden rattle close to him made him start violently, only to curse himself for a nervous ass the next moment, and lean forward eagerly. One of the blinds had been released from inside the room, and a pale, diffused light came filtering out into the night from the side of the glass roof. He was still craning backwards and forwards to try and find some chink through which he could see, when, with a kind of uncanny deliberation, one of the panes of glass slowly opened. It was worked on a ratchet from inside, and Hugh bowed his thanks to the unseen operator below. Then he leant forward cautiously, and peered in . . .

The whole room was visible to him, and his jaw tightened as he took in the scene. In an armchair, smoking as unconcernedly as ever, sat Peterson. He was reading a letter, and occasionally underlining some point with a pencil. Beside him on a table was a big ledger, and every now and then he would turn over a few pages and make an entry. But it was not Peterson on whom the watcher above was concentrating his attention; it was Lakington – and the thing beside him on the sofa.

Lakington was bending over a long bath full of some light-brown liquid from which a faint vapour was rising. He was in his shirt sleeves, and on his hands he wore what looked like rubber gloves, stretching right up to his elbows. After a while he dipped a test-tube into the liquid, and going over to a shelf he selected a bottle and added a few drops to the contents of the tube. Apparently satisfied with the result, he returned to the bath and shook in some white powder. Immediately the liquid commenced to froth and bubble, and at the same moment Peterson stood up.

'Are you ready?' he said, taking off his coat and picking up a pair of gloves similar to those the other was wearing.

'Quite,' answered Lakington abruptly. 'We'll get him in.'

They approached the sofa; and Hugh, with a kind of fascinated horror, forced himself to look. For the thing that lay there was the body of the dead Russian, Ivolsky.

The two men picked him up and, having carried the body to the bath, they dropped it into the fuming liquid. Then, as if it was the most normal thing in the world, they peeled off their long gloves and stood watching. For a minute or so nothing happened, and then gradually the body commenced to disappear. A faint, sickly smell came through the open window, and Hugh wiped the sweat off his forehead. It was too horrible, the hideous delibera-tion of it all. And whatever vile tortures the wretched man had inflicted on others in Russia, yet it was through him that his dead body lay there in the bath, disappear-ing slowly and relentlessly . . .

Lakington lit a cigarette and strolled over to the fire-place.

'Another five minutes should be enough,' he remarked. 'Damn that cursed soldier!'

Peterson laughed gently, and resumed the study of his ledger.

'To lose one's temper with a man, my dear Henry, is a sign of inferiority. But it certainly is a nuisance that Ivolsky is dead. He could talk more unmitigated drivel to the minute than all the rest of 'em put together . . . I really don't know who to put in the Midland area.'

He leaned back in his chair and blew out a cloud of smoke. The light shone on the calm, impassive face; and with a feeling of wonder that was never far absent from his mind when he was with Peterson, Hugh noted the high, clever forehead, the firmly moulded nose and chin, the sensitive, humorous mouth. The man lying back in the chair watching the blue smoke curling up from his cigar might have been a great lawyer or an eminent divine; some well-known statesman, perhaps, or a Napoleon of finance. There was power in every line of his figure, in every movement of his hands. He might have reached to the top of any profession he had cared to follow . . . Just as he had reached the top in his present one . . . Some kink in the brain, some little cog wrong in the wonderful mechanism, and a great man had become a great criminal. Hugh looked at the bath: the liquid was almost clear.

'You know my feelings on the subject,' remarked Lakington, taking a red velvet box out of a drawer in the desk. He opened it lovingly, and Hugh saw the flash of diamonds. Lakington let the stones run through his hands, glittering with a thousand flames, while Peterson watched him contemptuously.

'Baubles,' he said scornfully. 'Pretty baubles. What will you get for them?'

'Ten, perhaps fifteen thousand,' returned the other. 'But it's not the money I care about; it's the delight in having them, and the skill required to get them.'

Peterson shrugged his shoulders.

'Skill which would give you hundreds of thousands if you turned it into proper channels.'

Lakington replaced the stones, and threw the end of his cigarette into the grate.

'Possibly, Carl, quite possibly. But it boils down to this, my friend, that you like the big canvas with broad effects; I like the miniature and the well-drawn etching.'

'Which makes us a very happy combination,' said Peterson, rising and walking over to the bath. 'The pearls, don't forget, are your job. The big thing' – he turned to the other, and a trace of excitement came into his voice – 'the big thing is mine.' Then with his hands in his pockets he stood staring at the brown liquid. 'Our friend is nearly cooked, I think.'

'Another two or three minutes,' said Lakington, joining him. 'I must confess I pride myself on the discovery of that mixture. Its only drawback is that it makes murder too easy . . .'

The sound of the door opening made both men swing round instantly; then Peterson stepped forward with a smile.

'Back, my dear? I hardly expected you so soon.'

Irma came a little way into the room, and stopped with a sniff of disgust.

'What a horrible smell!' she remarked. 'What on earth have you been doing?'

'Disposing of a corpse,' said Lakington. 'It's nearly finished.'

The girl threw off her opera cloak, and coming forward, peered over the edge of the bath.

'It's not my ugly soldier?' she cried.

'Unfortunately not,' returned Lakington grimly; and Peterson laughed.

'Henry is most annoyed, Irma. The irrepressible Drummond has scored again.'

In a few words he told the girl what had happened, and she clapped her hands together delightedly.

'Assuredly I shall have to marry that man,' she cried. 'He is quite the least boring individual I have met in this atrocious country.' She sat down and lit a cigarette. 'I saw Walter tonight.'

'Where?' demanded Peterson quickly. 'I thought he was in Paris.'

'He was this morning. He came over especially to see you. They want you there for a meeting at the Ritz.'

Peterson frowned.

'It's most inconvenient,' he remarked with a shade of annoyance in his voice. 'Did he say why?'

'Amongst other things I think they're uneasy about the

American,' she answered. 'My dear man, you can easily slip over for a day.'

'Of course I can,' said Peterson irritably; 'but that doesn't alter the fact that it's inconvenient. Things will be shortly coming to a head here, and I want to be on the spot. However –' He started to walk up and down the room, frowning thoughtfully.

'Your fish is hooked, *mon ami*,' continued the girl to Lakington. 'He has already proposed three times; and he has introduced me to a dreadful-looking woman of extreme virtue, who has adopted me as her niece for the great occasion.'

'What great occasion?' asked Lakington, looking up from the bath.

'Why, his coming of age,' cried the girl. 'I am to go to Laidley Towers as an honoured guest of the Duchess of Lampshire. What do you think of that, my friend? The old lady will be wearing pearls and all complete, in honour of the great day, and I shall be one of the admiring house party.'

'How do you know she'll have them in the house?' said Lakington.

'Because dear Freddie has told me so,' answered the girl. 'I don't think you're very bright tonight, Henry. When the young Pooh-ba comes of age, naturally his devoted maternal parent will sport her glad rags. Incidentally, the tenants are going to present him with a loving cup, or a baby giraffe, or something. You might like to annex that too.' She blew two smoke rings and then laughed.

'Freddie is really rather a dear at times. I don't think I've ever met anyone who is so nearly an idiot without being one. Still,' she repeated thoughtfully, 'he's rather a dear.'

Lakington turned a handle underneath the bath, and the liquid, now clear and still, commenced to sink rapidly. Fascinated, Hugh watched the process; in two minutes the bath was empty – a human body had completely disappeared without leaving a trace. It seemed to him as if he must have been dreaming, as if the events of the whole night had been part of some strange jumbled nightmare. And then, having pinched himself to make sure he was awake, he once more glued his eyes to the open space of the window.

Lakington was swabbing out the bath with some liquid on the end of a mop; Peterson, his chin sunk on his chest, was still pacing slowly up and down; the girl, her neck and shoulders gleaming white in the electric light, was lighting a second cigarette from the stump of the first. After a while Lakington finished his cleaning operations and put on his coat.

'What,' he asked curiously, 'does he think you are?'

'A charming young girl,' answered Irma demurely, 'whose father lost his life in the war, and who at present ekes out a precarious existence in a government office. At least, that's what he told Lady Frumpley – she's the woman of unassailable virtue. She was profoundly sentimental and scents a romance, in addition to being a snob and scenting a future duke, to say nothing of a future duchess. By the mercy of Allah she's on a committee with his mother for distributing brown-paper underclothes to destitute Belgians, and so Freddie wangled an invite for her. *Voilà tout.*'

'Splendid!' said Lakington slowly. 'Splendid! Young Laidley comes of age in about a week, doesn't he?'

'Monday, to be exact, and so I go down with my dear aunt on Saturday.'

Lakington nodded his head as if satisfied, and then glanced at his watch.

'What about bed?' he remarked.

'Not yet,' said Peterson, halting suddenly in his walk. 'I must see the Yank before I go to Paris. We'll have him down here now.'

'My dear Carl, at this hour?' Lakington stifled a yawn.

'Yes. Give him an injection, Henry – and, by God, we'll make the fool sign. Then I can actually take it over to the meeting with me.'

He strode to the door, followed by Lakington; and the girl in the chair stood up and stretched her arms above her head. For a moment or two Hugh watched her; then he too stood upright and eased his cramped limbs.

'Make the fool sign.' The words echoed through his brain, and he stared thoughtfully at the grey light which showed the approach of dawn. What was the best thing to do? 'Make' with Peterson generally implied torture if other means failed, and Hugh had no intention of watching any man tortured. At the same time something of the nature of the diabolical plot conceived by Peterson was beginning to take a definite shape in his mind, though many of the most important links were still missing. And with this knowledge had come the realization that he was no longer a free agent. The thing had ceased to be a mere sporting gamble with himself and a few other chosen spirits matched against a gang of criminals; it had become – if his surmise was correct – a national affair. England herself – her very existence – was threatened by one of the vilest plots ever dreamed of in the brain of man. And then, with a sudden rage at his own impotence, he realized that even now he had nothing definite to go on. He *must* know more; somehow or other he must get to Paris; he must attend that meeting at the Ritz. How he was going to do it he hadn't the faintest idea; the furthest he could get as he stood on the roof, watching the first faint streaks of orange in the east, was the definite decision that if Peterson went to Paris, he would go too. And then a sound from the room below brought him back to his vantage point. The American was sitting in a chair, and Lakington, with a hypodermic syringe in his hand, was holding his arm.

He made the injection, and Hugh watched the millionaire. He was still undecided as to how to act, but for the moment, at any rate, there was nothing to be done. And he was very curious to hear what Peterson had to say to the wretched man, who, up to date, had figured so largely in every round.

After a while the American ceased staring vacantly in front of him, and passed his hand dazedly over his forehead. Then he half rose from his chair and stared at the two men sitting facing him. His eyes came round to the girl, and with a groan he sank back again, plucking feebly with his hands at his dressing-gown.

'Better, Mr Potts?' said Peterson suavely.

'I – I –' stammered the other. 'Where am I?'

'At The Elms, Godalming, if you wish to know.'

'I thought – I thought –' He rose swaying. 'What do you want with me? Damn you!'

'Tush, tush,' murmured Peterson. 'There is a lady present, Mr Potts. And our wants are so simple. Just your signature to a little agreement, by which in return for certain services you promise to join us in our – er – labours, in the near future.'

'I remember,' cried the millionaire. 'Now I remember. You swine – you filthy swine, I refuse . . . absolutely.'

'The trouble is, my friend, that you are altogether too big an employer of labour to be allowed to refuse, as I pointed out to you before. You must be in with us, otherwise you might wreck the scheme. Therefore I require your signature. I lost it once, unfortunately – but it wasn't a very good signature; so perhaps it was all for the best.'

'And when you've got it,' cried the American, 'what good will it be to you? I shall repudiate it.'

'Oh, no! Mr Potts,' said Peterson with a thoughtful smile; 'I can assure you, you won't. The distressing malady from which you have recently been suffering will again have you in its grip. My friend, Mr Lakington, is an expert on that particular illness. It renders you quite unfit for business.'

For a while there was silence, and the millionaire stared round the room like a trapped animal.

'I refuse!' he cried at last. 'It's an outrage against humanity. You can do what you like.'

'Then we'll start with a little more thumbscrew,' remarked Peterson, strolling over to the desk and opening a drawer. 'An astonishingly effective implement, as you can see if you look at your thumb.' He stood in front of the quivering man, balancing the instrument in his hands. 'It was under its influence you gave us the first signature, which we so regrettably lost. I think we'll try it again . . .'

The American gave a strangled cry of terror, and then the unexpected happened. There was a crash as a pane of glass splintered and fell to the floor close beside Lakington; and with an oath he sprang asid and looked up.

'Peep-bo,' came a well-known voice from the skylight. 'Clip him one over the jaw, Potts, my boy, but don't you sign.'

CHAPTER 8

In Which He Goes to Paris
for a Night

I

Drummond had acted on the spur of the moment. It would have been manifestly impossible for any man, certainly of his calibre, to have watched the American being tortured without doing something to try to help him. At the same time the last thing he had wanted to do was to give away his presence on the roof. The information he had obtained that night was of such vital importance that it was absolutely essential for him to get away with it somehow; and, at the moment, his chances of so doing did not appear particularly bright. It looked as if it was only a question of time before they must get him.

But as usual with Drummond, the tighter the corner, the cooler his head. He watched Lakington dart from the room, followed more slowly by Peterson, and then occurred one of those strokes of luck on which the incorrigible soldier always depended. The girl left the room as well.

She kissed her hand towards him, and then she smiled.

'You intrigue me, ugly one,' she remarked, looking up, 'intrigue me vastly. I am now going out to get a really good view of the Kill.'

And the next moment Potts was alone. He was staring

up at the skylight, apparently bewildered by the sudden turn of events, and then he heard the voice of the man above speaking clearly and insistently.

'Go out of the room. Turn to the right. Open the front door. You'll see a house through some trees. Go to it. When you get there, stand on the lawn and call "Phyllis". Do you get me?'

The American nodded dazedly; then he made a great effort to pull himself together, as the voice continued:

'Go at once. It's your only chance. Tell her I'm on the roof here.'

With a sigh of relief he saw the millionaire leave the room; then he straightened himself up, and proceeded to reconnoitre his own position. There was a bare chance that the American would get through, and if he did, everything might yet be well. If he didn't – Hugh shrugged his shoulders grimly and laughed.

It had become quite light, and after a moment's indecision Drummond took a running jump, and caught the ridge of the sloping roof on the side nearest the road. To stop by the skylight was to be caught like a rat in a trap, and he would have to take his chance of being shot. After all, there was a considerable risk in using firearms so near a main road, where at any time some labourer or other early riser might pass along. Notoriety was the last thing which Peterson desired, and if it got about that one of the pastimes at The Elms was potting stray human beings on the roof, the inquiries might become somewhat embarrassing.

It was as Hugh threw his leg over the top of the roof, and sat straddle-ways, leaning against a chimney-stack, that he got an idea. From where he was he could not see The Larches, and so he did not know what luck the American had had. But he realized that it was long odds against his getting through, and that his chief hope lay in himself. Wherefore, as has just been said, he got an idea – simple and direct; his ideas always were. It occurred to him that far too few unbiased people knew where he was; it further occurred to him that it was a state of affairs which was likely to continue unless he remedied it himself. And so, just as Peterson came strolling round a corner of the house, followed by several men and a long ladder, Hugh commenced to sing. He shouted, he roared at the top of his very powerful voice and all the time he watched the men below with a wary eye. He saw Peterson look nervously over his shoulder towards the road, and urge the men on to greater efforts, and the gorgeous simplicity of his manœuvre made Hugh burst out laughing. Then, once again, his voice rose to its full pitch, as he greeted the sun with a bellow which scared every rook in the neighbourhood.

It was just as two labourers came to investigate the hideous din that Peterson's party discovered the ladder was too short by several yards.

Then with great rapidity the audience grew. A passing milkman; two commercial travellers who had risen with the lark and entrusted themselves and their samples to a Ford car; a gentleman of slightly inebriated aspect, whose trousers left much to the imagination; and finally more farm labourers. Never had such a titbit of gossip for the local pub been seen before in the neighbourhood; it would furnish a topic of conversation for weeks to come. And still Hugh sang and Peterson cursed; and still the audience grew. Then, at last, there came the police with notebook all complete, and the singer stopped singing to laugh.

The next moment the laugh froze on his lips. Standing by the skylight, with his revolver raised, was Lakington, and Hugh knew by the expression on his face that his finger was trembling on the trigger. Out of view of the crowd below he did not know of its existence, and, in a flash, Hugh realized his danger. Somehow Lakington had got up on the roof while the soldier's attention had been elsewhere; and now, his face gleaming with an unholy fury, Lakington was advancing step by step towards him with the evident intention of shooting him.

'Good morrow, Henry,' said Hugh quietly. 'I wouldn't fire if I were you. We are observed, as they say in melodrama. If you don't believe me,' his voice grew a little tense, 'just wait while I talk to Peterson, who is at present deep in converse with the village constable and several farm labourers.'

He saw doubt dawn in Lakington's eyes, and instantly followed up his advantage.

'I'm sure you wouldn't like the notoriety attendant upon a funeral, Henry dear; I'm sure Peterson would just hate it. So, to set your mind at rest, I'll tell him you're here.'

It is doubtful whether any action in Hugh Drummond's life ever cost him such an effort of will as the turning of his back on the man standing two yards below him, but he did it apparently without thought. He gave one last glance at the face convulsed with rage, and then with a smile he looked down at the crowd below.

'Peterson,' he called out affably, 'there's a pal of yours up here – dear old Henry. And he's very annoyed at my concert. Would you just speak to him, or would you like me to be more explicit? He is so annoyed that there might be an accident at any moment, and I see that the police have arrived. So – er –'

Even at that distance he could see Peterson's eyes of fury, and he chuckled softly to himself. He had the whole gang absolutely at his mercy, and the situation appealed irresistibly to his sense of humour.

But when the leader spoke, his voice was as sauve as ever: the eternal cigar glowed evenly at its normal rate.

'Are you up on the roof, Lakington?' The words came clearly through the still summer air.

'Your turn, Henry,' said Drummond. 'Prompter's voice off – "Yes, dear Peterson, I am here, even upon the roof, with a liver of hideous aspect."'

For one moment he thought he had gone too far, and that Lakington, in his blind fury, would shoot him then and there and chance the consequences. But with a mighty effort the man controlled himself, and his voice, when he answered, was calm.

'Yes, I'm here. What's the matter?'

'Nothing,' cried Peterson, 'but we've got quite a large and appreciative audience down here, attracted by our friend's charming concert, and I've just sent for a large ladder by which he can come down and join us. So there is nothing that you can do – nothing.' He repeated the word with a faint emphasis, and Hugh smiled genially.

'Isn't he wonderful, Henry?' he murmured. 'Thinks of everything; staff work marvellous. But you nearly had a bad lapse then, didn't you? It really would have been embarrassing for you if my corpse had deposited itself with a dull thud on the corns of the police.'

'I'm interested in quite a number of things, Captain Drummond,' said Lakington slowly, 'but they all count as nothing beside one – getting even with you. And when I do . . .' He dropped the revolver into his coat pocket, and stood motionless, staring at the soldier.

'Ah! when!' mocked Drummond. 'There have been so many "whens", Henry dear. Somehow I don't think you can be very clever. Don't go – I'm so enjoying my heart-to-heart talk. Besides, I wanted to tell you the story about the girl, the soap, and the bath. That's to say, if the question of baths isn't too delicate.'

Lakington paused as he got to the skylight.

'I have a variety of liquids for bathing people in,' he remarked. 'The best are those I use when the patient is alive.'

The next instant he opened a door in the skylight which Hugh had failed to discover during the night, and, climbing down a ladder inside the room, disappeared from view.

'Hullo, old bean!' A cheerful shout from the ground made Hugh look down. There, ranged round Peterson, in an effective group, were Peter Darrell, Algy Longworth, and Jerry Seymour. 'Birds'-nestin'?'

'Peter, old soul,' cried Hugh joyfully, 'I never thought the day would come when I should be pleased to see your face, but it has! For Heaven's sake get a move on with that blinking ladder; I'm getting cramp.'

'Ted and his pal, Hugh, have toddled off in your car,' said Peter, 'so that only leaves us four and Toby.'

For a moment Hugh stared at him blankly, while he did some rapid mental arithmetic. He even neglected to descend at once by the ladder which had at last been placed in position. 'Ted and us four and Toby' made six – and six was the strength of the party as it had arrived. Adding the pal made seven; so who the deuce was the pal?

The matter was settled just as he reached the ground. Lakington, wild-eyed and almost incoherent, rushed from the house, and, drawing Peterson on one side, spoke rapidly in a whisper.

'It's all right,' muttered Algy rapidly. 'They're half-way to London by now, and going like hell if I know Ted.'

It was then that Hugh started to laugh. He laughed till the tears poured down his face, and Peterson's livid face of fury made him laugh still more.

'Oh, you priceless pair!' he sobbed. 'Right under your bally noses. Stole away. Yoicks!' There was another interlude for further hilarity. 'Give it up, you two old dears, and take to knitting. Miss one and purl three, Henry my boy, and Carl in a nightcap can pick up the stitches you drop.' He took out his cigarette-case. 'Well, *au revoir*. Doubtless we shall meet again quite soon. And, above all, Carl, don't do anything in Paris which you would be ashamed of my knowing.'

With a friendly wave he turned on his heel and strolled off, followed by the other three. The humour of the situation was irresistible; the absolute powerlessness of the whole assembled gang to lift a finger to stop them in front of the audience, which as yet showed no sign of departing, tickled him to death. In fact, the last thing Hugh saw, before a corner of the house hid them from sight, was the majesty of the law moistening his indelible pencil in the time-honoured method, and advancing on Peterson with his notebook at the ready.

'One brief interlude, my dear old warriors,' announced Hugh, 'and then we must get gay. Where's Toby?'

'Having his breakfast with your girl,' chuckled Algy. 'We thought we'd better leave someone on guard, and she seemed to love him best.'

'Repulsive hound!' cried Hugh. 'Incidentally, boys, how did you manage to roll up this morning?'

'We all bedded down at your girl's place last night,' said Peter, 'and then this morning, who should come and sing carols but our one and only Potts. Then we heard your deafening din on the roof, and blew along.'

'Splendid!' remarked Hugh, rubbing his hands

together, 'simply splendid! Though I wish you'd been there to help with that damned gorilla.'

'Help with what?' spluttered Jerry Seymour.

'Gorilla, old dear,' returned Hugh, unmoved. 'A docile little creature I had to kill.'

'The man,' murmured Algy, 'is indubitably mad. I'm going to crank the car.'

II

'Go away,' said Toby, looking up as the door opened and Hugh strolled in. 'Your presence is unnecessary and uncalled for, and we're not pleased. Are we, Miss Benton?'

'Can you bear him, Phyllis?' remarked Hugh with a grin. 'I mean, lying about the house all day?'

'What's the notion, old son?' Toby Sinclair stood up, looking slightly puzzled.

'I want you to stop here, Toby,' said Hugh, 'and not let Miss Benton out of your sight. Also keep your eyes skinned on The Elms, and let me know by phone to Half Moon Street anything that happens. Do you get me?'

'I get you,' answered the other, 'but I say, Hugh, can't I do something a bit more active? I mean, of course, there's nothing I'd like better than to . . .' He broke off in mild confusion as Phyllis Benton laughed merrily.

'Do something more active!' echoed Hugh. 'You bet your life, old boy. A rapid one-step out of the room. You're far too young for what's coming now.'

With a resigned sigh Toby rose and walked to the door.

'I shall have to listen at the keyhole,' he announced, 'and thereby get earache. You people have no consideration whatever.'

'I've got five minutes, little girl,' whispered Hugh, taking her into his arms as the door closed. 'Five minutes of Heaven . . . By Jove! But you look great – simply great.'

The girl smiled up at him.

'It strikes me, Master Hugh, that you have failed to remove your beard this morning.'

Hugh grinned.

'Quite right, kid. They omitted to bring me my shaving water on to the roof.'

After a considerable interval, in which trifles such as beards mattered not, she smoothed her hair and sat down on the arm of a chair.

'Tell me what's happened, boy,' she said eagerly.

'Quite a crowded night.' With a reminiscent smile he lit a cigarette. And then quite briefly he told her of the events of the past twelve hours, being, as is the manner of a man, more interested in watching the sweet colour which stained her cheeks from time to time, and noticing her quickened breathing when he told her of his fight with the gorilla, and his ascent of the murderous staircase. To him it was all over and now finished, but to the girl who sat listening to the short, half-clipped sentences, each one spoken with a laugh and a jest, there came suddenly the full realization of what this man was doing for her. It was she who had been the cause of his running all these risks; it was her letter that he had answered. Now she felt that if one hair of his head was touched, she would never forgive herself.

And so when he had finished, and pitched the stump of his cigarette into the grate, falteringly she tried to dissuade him. With her hands on his coat, and her big eyes misty with her fears for him, she begged him to give it all up. And even as she spoke, she gloried in the fact that she knew it was quite useless. Which made her plead all the harder, as is the way of a woman with her man.

And then, after a while, her voice died away, and she fell silent. He was smiling, and so, perforce, she had to smile too. Only their eyes spoke those things which no human being may put into words. And so, for a time, they stood . . .

Then, quite suddenly, he bent and kissed her.

'I must go, little girl,' he whispered. 'I've got to be in Paris tonight. Take care of yourself.'

The next moment he was gone.

'For God's sake take care of her, Toby!' he remarked to that worthy, whom he found sitting disconsolately by the front door. 'Those blighters are the limit.'

'That's all right, old man,' said Sinclair gruffly. 'Good huntin'!'

He watched the tall figure stride rapidly to the waiting car, the occupants of which were simulating sleep as a mild protest at the delay; then, with a smile, he rose and joined the girl.

'Some lad,' he remarked. 'And if you don't mind my saying so, Miss Benton, I wouldn't change him if I was you. Unless, of course,' he added, as an afterthought, 'you'd prefer me!'

III

'Have you got him all right, Ted?' Hugh flung the question eagerly at Ted Jerningham, who was lounging in a chair at Half Moon Street, with his feet on the mantelpiece.

'I've got him right enough,' answered that worthy, 'but he don't strike me as being Number One value. He's gone off the boil. Become quite gaga again.' He stood up and stretched himself. 'Your worthy servant is with him, making hoarse noises to comfort him.'

'Hell!' said Hugh, 'I thought we might get something out of him. I'll go and have a look at the bird. Beer in the corner, boys, if you want it.'

He left the room, and went along the passage to inspect the American. Unfortunately Jerningham was only too right: the effects of last night's injection had worn off completely, and the wretched man was sitting motion-less in a chair, staring dazedly in front of him.

''Opeless, sir,' remarked Denny, rising to his feet as Hugh came into the room. 'He thinks this 'ere meat juice is poison, and he won't touch it.'

'All right, Denny,' said Drummond. 'Leave the poor blighter alone. We've got him back, and that's some-thing. Has your wife told you about her little adventure?'

His servant coughed deprecatingly.

'She has, sir. But, Lor' bless you, she don't bear no malice.'

'Then she's one up on me, Denny, for I bear lots of it towards that gang of swine.' Thoughtfully he stood in front of the millionaire, trying in vain to catch some gleam of sense in the vacant eyes. 'Look at that poor devil; isn't that enough by itself to make you want to kill the whole crowd?' He turned on his heel abruptly, and opened the door. 'Try and get him to eat if you can.'

'What luck?' Jerningham looked up as he came back into the other room.

'Dam' all, as they say in the vernacular. Have you blighters finished the beer?'

'Probably,' remarked Peter Darrell. 'What's the programme now?'

Hugh examined the head of his glass with a professional eye before replying.

'Two things,' he murmured at length, 'fairly leap to the eye. The first is to get Potts away to a place of safety; the second is to get over to Paris.'

'Well, let's get gay over the first, as a kick-off,' said Jerningham, rising. 'There's a car outside the door; there is England at our disposal. We'll take him away; you pad the hoof to Victoria and catch the boat train.'

'It sounds too easy,' remarked Hugh. 'Have a look out of the window, Ted, and you'll see a man frightfully busy doing nothing not far from the door. You will also see a racing-car just across the street. Put a wet compress on your head, and connect the two.'

A gloomy silence settled on the assembly, to be broken by Jerry Seymour suddenly waking up with a start.

'I've got the Stomach-ache,' he announced proudly.

His listeners gazed at him unmoved.

'You shouldn't eat so fast,' remarked Algy severely. 'And you certainly oughtn't to drink that beer.'

To avert the disaster he immediately consumed it himself, but Jerry was too engrossed with his brain-storm to notice.

'I've got the Stomach-ache,' he repeated, 'and she ought to be ready by now. In fact I know she is. My last crash wasn't a bad one. What about it?'

'You mean? . . .' said Hugh, staring at him.

'I mean,' answered Jerry, 'that I'll go off to the aerodrome now, and get her ready. Bring Potts along in half an hour, and I'll take him to the Governor's place in Norfolk. Then I'll take you over to Paris.'

'Great! – simply great!' With a report like a gun Hugh hit the speaker on the back, inadvertently knocking him down. Then an idea struck him. 'Not your place, Jerry;

they'll draw that at once. Take him to Ted's; Lady Jerningham won't mind, will she, old boy?'

'The mater mind?' Ted laughed. 'Good Lord, no; she gave up minding anything years ago.'

'Right!' said Hugh. 'Off you go, Jerry. By the way, how many will she hold?'

'Two beside me,' spluttered the proud proprietor of the Stomach-ache. 'And I wish you'd reserve your endearments for people of your own size, you great, fat, hulking monstrosity.'

He reached the door with a moment to spare, and Hugh came back laughing.

'Verily – an upheaval in the grey matter,' he cried, carefully refilling his glass. 'Now, boy, what about Paris?'

'Is it necessary to go at all?' asked Peter.

'It wouldn't have been if the Yank had been sane,' answered Drummond. 'As it is, I guess I've got to. There's something going on, young fellahs, which is big; and I can't help thinking one might get some useful information from the meeting at the Ritz tonight. Why is Peterson hand-in-glove with a wild-eyed, ragged-trousered crowd of revolutionaries? Can you tell me that? If so, I won't go.'

'The great point is whether you'll find out, even if you do,' returned Peter. 'The man's not going to stand in the hall and shout it through a megaphone.'

'Which is where Ted comes in,' said Hugh affably. 'Does not the Stomach-ache hold two?'

'My dear man,' cried Jerningham, 'I'm dining with a perfectly priceless she tonight!'

'Oh, no, you're not, my lad. You're going to do some amateur acting in Paris. Disguised as a waiter, or a chambermaid, or a coffee machine or something – you will discover secrets.'

'But good heavens, Hugh!' Jerningham waved both hands in feeble protest.

'Don't worry me,' cried Drummond, 'don't worry me; it's only a vague outline, and you'll look great as a bath-sponge. There's the telephone . . . Hallo!' He picked off the receiver. 'Speaking. Is that you, Toby? Oh! the Rolls has gone, has it? With Peterson inside. Good! So long, old dear.'

He turned to the others.

'There you are, you see. He's left for Paris. That settles it.'

'Conclusively,' murmured Algy mildly. 'Any man who leaves a house in a motor car always goes to Paris.'

'Dry up!' roared Hugh. 'Was your late military education so utterly lacking that you have forgotten the elementary precept of putting yourself in the enemy's place? If I was Peterson, and I wanted to go to Paris, do you suppose that fifty people knowing about it would prevent me? You're a fool, Algy – and leave me some more beer.'

Resignedly Algy sat down, and after a pause for breath, Drummond continued.

'Now listen – all of you. Ted – off you go, and raise a complete waiter's outfit, dicky and all complete. Peter – you come with me to the aerodrome, and afterwards look up Mullings, at 13, Green Street, Hoxton, and tell him to get in touch with at least fifty demobilized soldiers who are on for a scrap. Algy – you hold the fort here, and don't get drunk on my ale. Peter will join you, when he's finished with Mullings, and he's not to get drunk either. Are you all on?'

'On,' muttered Darrell weakly. 'My head is playing an anthem.'

'It'll play an oratorio before we're through with this

job, old son,' laughed Hugh. 'Let's get gay with Potts.'

Ten minutes later he was at the wheel of his car with Darrell and the millionaire behind. Algy, protesting vigorously at being, as he said, left out of it, was endeavouring to console himself by making out how much money he would have won if he'd followed his infallible system of making money on the turf; Jerningham was wandering along Piccadilly anxiously wondering at what shop he could possibly ask for a dicky, and preserve his hitherto blameless reputation. But Hugh seemed in no great hurry to start. A whimsical smile was on his face, as out of the corner of his eye he watched the man who had been busy doing nothing feverishly trying to crank his car, which, after the manner of the brutes, had seized that moment to jib.

'Get away, man – get away,' cried Peter. 'What are you waiting for?'

Hugh laughed.

'Peter,' he remarked, 'the refinements of this game are lost on you.'

Still smiling, he got out and walked up to the perspiring driver.

'A warm day,' he murmured. 'Don't hurry; we'll wait for you.' Then, while the man, utterly taken aback, stared at him speechlessly, he strolled back to his own car.

'Hugh – you're mad, quite mad,' said Peter resignedly, as with a spluttering roar the other car started, but Hugh still smiled. On the way to the aerodrome, he stopped twice after a block in the traffic to make quite sure that the pursuer should have no chance of losing him, and, by the time they were clear of the traffic and spinning towards their destination, the gentleman in the car behind fully agreed with Darrell.

At first he had expected some trick, being a person of tortuous brain; but as time went on, and nothing unexpected happened, he became reassured. His orders were to follow the millionaire, and inform headquarters where he was taken to. And assuredly at the moment it seemed easy money. In fact, he even went so far as to hum gently to himself, after he had put a hand in his pocket to make sure his automatic revolver was still there.

Then, quite suddenly, the humming stopped and he frowned. The car in front had swung off the road, and turned through the entrance of a small aerodrome. It was a complication which had not entered his mind, and with a curse he pulled up his car just short of the gates. What the devil was he to do now? Most assuredly he could not pursue an aeroplane in a motor – even a racer. Blindly, without thinking, he did the first thing that came into his head. He left his car standing where it was, and followed the others into the aerodrome on foot. Perhaps he could find out something from one of the mechanics; someone might be able to tell him where the plane was going.

There she was with the car beside her, and already the millionaire was being strapped into his seat. Drummond was talking to the pilot, and the sleuth, full of eagerness, accosted a passing mechanic.

'Can you tell me where that aeroplane is going to?' he asked ingratiatingly.

It was perhaps unfortunate that the said mechanic had just had a large spanner dropped on his toe, and his answer was not helpful. It was an education in one way, and at any other time the pursuer would have treated it with the respect it deserved. But, as it was, it was not of great value, which made it the more unfortunate that Peter Darrell should have chosen that moment to look round. And all he saw was the mechanic talking

earnestly to the sleuth . . . Whereupon he talked earnestly to Drummond . . .

In thinking it over after, that unhappy man, whose job
had seemed so easy, found it difficult to say exactly what
happened. All of a sudden he found himself surrounded
by people – all very affable and most conversational. It
took him quite five minutes to get back to his car, and by
that time the plane was a speck in the west. Drummond
was standing by the gates when he got there, with a look
of profound surprise on his face.

'One I have seen often,' remarked the soldier; 'two
sometimes; three rarely; four never. Fancy four punc-
tures – all at the same time! Dear, dear! I positively insist
on giving you a lift.'

He felt himself irresistibly propelled towards Drummond's car, with only time for a fleeting glimpse at his
own four flat tyres, and almost before he realized it they
were away. After a few minutes, when he had recovered
from his surprise, his hand went instinctively to his
pocket, to find the revolver had gone. And it was then
that the man he had thought mad laughed gently.

'Didn't know I was once a pickpocket, did you?' he
remarked affably. 'A handy little gun, too. Is it all right,
Peter?'

'All safe,' came a voice from behind.

'Then dot him one.'

The sleuth had a fleeting vision of stars of all colours
which danced before his eyes, coupled with a stunning
blow on the back of the head. Vaguely he realized the car
was pulling up – then blackness. It was not till four hours
later that a passing labourer, having pulled him out from
a not over-dry ditch, laid him out to cool. And, incidentally, with his further sphere of usefulness we are not
concerned . . .

IV

'My dear fellow, I told you we'd get here somehow.' Hugh Drummond stretched his legs luxuriously. 'The fact that it was necessary to crash your blinking bus in a stray field in order to avoid their footling passport regulations is absolutely immaterial. The only damage is a dent in Ted's dicky, but all the best waiters have that. They smear it with soup to show their energy . . . My God! Here's another of them.'

A Frenchman was advancing towards them down the stately vestibule of the Ritz waving protesting hands. He addressed himself in a voluble crescendo to Drummond, who rose and bowed deeply. His knowledge of French was microscopic, but such trifles were made to be overcome.

'*Mais oui, Monsieur mon Colonel,*' he remarked affably, when the gendarme paused for lack of breath, '*vous comprenez que nôtre machine avait crashé dans un field des turnipes. Nouse avons lost nôtre direction. Nous sommes hittés dans l'estomacs . . . Comme ci, comme ça . . . Vous comprenez, n'est-ce-pas, mon Colonel?*' He turned fiercely on Jerry, 'Shut up, you damn fool; don't laugh!'

'*Mais, messieurs, vous n'avez pas des passeports.*' The little man, torn between gratification at his rapid promotion and horror at such an appalling breach of regulations, shot up and down like an agitated semaphore. '*Vous comprenez; c'est defendu d'arriver en Paris sans des passeports?*'

'*Parfaitement, mon Colonel,*' continued Hugh, unmoved. '*Mais vous comprenez que nous avons crashé dans un field des turnipes – non; des rognons . . .* What the hell are you laughing at, Jerry?'

'*Oignons*, old boy,' spluttered the latter. '*Rognons* are kidneys.'

'What the dickens does that matter?' demanded Hugh. '*Vous comprenez, mon Colonel, n'est-ce-pas? Vive la France! En-bas les Boches! Nous avons crashé.*'

The gendarme shrugged his shoulders with a hopeless gesture, and seemed on the point of bursting into tears. Of course this large Englishman was mad; why otherwise should he spit in the kidneys? And that is what he continued to state was his form of amusement. Truly an insane race, and yet he had fought in the brigade next to them near Montauban in July '16 – and he had liked them – those mad Tommies. Moreover, this large, imperturbable man, with the charming smile, showed a proper appreciation of his merits – an appreciation not shared up to the present, regrettable to state, by his own superiors. Colonel – *parbleu; eh bien!* Pourquoi non? . . .

At last he produced a notebook; he felt unable to cope further with the situation himself.

'*Vôtre nom, M'sieur, s'il vous plait?*'

'Undoubtedly, *mon Colonel*,' remarked Hugh vaguely. '*Nous crashons dans –*'

'Ah! *Mais oui, mais oui, M'sieur.*' The little man danced in his agitation. '*Vous m'avez déjâ dit que vous avez craché dans le rognons, mais je désire vôtre nom.*'

'He wants your name, old dear,' murmured Jerry, weakly.

'Oh, does he?' Hugh beamed on the gendarme. 'You priceless little bird! My name is Captain Hugh Drummond.'

And as he spoke, a man sitting close by, who had been an amused onlooker of the whole scene, stiffened suddenly in his chair, and stared hard at Hugh. It was only for a second, and then he was once more merely the politely interested spectator. But Hugh had seen that quick look, though he gave no sign; and when at last the Frenchman departed, apparently satisfied, he leaned over and spoke to Jerry.

'See that man with the suit of reach-me-downs and the cigar,' he remarked. 'He's in this game; I'm just wondering on which side.'

He was not left long in doubt, for barely had the swing doors closed behind the gendarme, when the man in question rose and came over to him.

'Excuse me, sir,' he said, in a pronounced nasal twang, 'but I heard you say you were Captain Hugh Drummond. I guess you're one of the men I've come across the water to see. My card.'

Hugh glanced at the pasteboard languidly.

'Mr Jerome K. Green,' he murmured. 'What a jolly sort of name.'

'See here, Captain,' went on the other, suddenly displaying a badge hidden under his coat. 'That'll put you wise.'

'Far from it, Mr Green. What's it the prize for – throwing cards into a hat?'

The American laughed.

'I guess I've sort of taken to you,' he remarked. 'You're real fresh. That badge is the badge of the police force of the United States of America; and that same force is humming some at the moment.' He sat down beside Hugh, and bent forward confidentially. 'There's a prominent citizen of New York City been mislaid, Captain; and, from information we've got, we reckon you know quite a lot about his whereabouts.'

Hugh pulled out his cigarette-case.

'Turkish this side – Virginian that. Ah! But I see you're

smoking.' With great deliberation he selected one himself, and lit it. 'You were saying, Mr Green?'

The detective stared at him thoughtfully; at the moment he was not quite certain how to tackle this large and self-possessed young man.

'Might I ask why you're over here?' he asked at length, deciding to feel his way.

'The air is free to everyone, Mr Green. As long as you get your share to breathe, you can ask anything you like.'

The American laughed again.

'I guess I'll put my cards down,' he said, with sudden decision. 'What about Hiram C. Potts?'

'What, indeed?' remarked Hugh. 'Sounds like a riddle, don't it?'

'You've heard of him, Captain?'

'Few people have not.'

'Yes – but you've met him recently,' said the detective, leaning forward. 'You know where he is, and' – he tapped Hugh on the knee impressively – 'I want him. I want Hiram C. Potts like a man wants a drink in a dry state. I want to take him back in cotton-wool to his wife and daughters. That's why I'm over this side, Captain, just for that one purpose.'

'There seems to me to be a considerable number of people wandering around who share your opinion about Mr Potts,' drawled Hugh. 'He must be a popular sort of cove.'

'Popular ain't the word for it, Captain,' said the other. 'Have you got him now??'

'In a manner of speaking, yes,' answered Hugh, beckoning to a passing waiter. 'Three Martinis.'

'Where is he?' snapped the detective eagerly.

Hugh laughed.

'Being wrapped up in cotton-wool by somebody else's

wife and daughters. You were a little too quick, Mr Green; you may be all you say – on the other hand, you may not. And these days I trust no one.'

The American nodded his head in approval.

'Quite right,' he remarked. 'My motto – and yet I'm going to trust you. Weeks ago we heard things on the other side, through certain channels, as to a show which was on the rails over here. It was a bit vague, and there were big men in it; but at the time it was no concern of ours. You run your own worries, Captain, over this side.'

Hugh nodded.

'Go on,' he said curtly.

'Then Hiram Potts got mixed up in it; exactly how, we weren't wise to. But it was enough to bring me over here. Two days ago I got this cable.' He produced a bundle of papers, and handed one to Drummond. 'It's in cipher, as you see; I've put the translation underneath.'

Hugh took the cablegram and glanced at it. It was short and to the point:

> Captain Hugh Drummond, of Half Moon Street, London, is your man.

He glanced up at the American, who drained his cocktail with the air of a man who is satisfied with life.

'Captain Hugh Drummond, of Half Moon Street, London, is my man,' he chuckled. 'Well, Captain, what about it now. Will you tell me why you've come to Paris? I guess it's something to do with the business I'm on.'

For a few moments Hugh did not reply, and the American seemed in no hurry for an answer. Some early arrivals for dinner sauntered through the lounge, and Drummond watched them idly as they passed. The American detective certainly seemed all right, but . . .

Casually, his glance rested on a man sitting just opposite, reading the paper. He took in the short, dark beard – the immaculate, though slightly foreign evening clothes; evidently a wealthy Frenchman giving a dinner party in the restaurant, by the way the head waiter was hovering around. And then suddenly his eyes narrowed, and he sat motionless.

'Are you interested in the psychology of gambling, Mr Green?' he remarked, turning to the somewhat astonished American. 'Some people cannot control their eyes or their mouth if the stakes are big; others cannot control their hands. For instance, the gentleman opposite. Does anything strike you particularly with regard to him?'

The detective glanced across the lounge.

'He seems to like hitting his knee with his left hand,' he said, after a short inspection.

'Precisely,' murmured Hugh. 'That is why I came to Paris.'

CHAPTER 9

In Which He Has a Near Shave

I

'Captain, you have me guessing.' The American bit the end off another cigar, and leaned back in his chair. 'You say that swell Frenchman with the waiters hovering about like fleas round a dog's tail is the reason you came to Paris. Is he kind of friendly with Hiram C. Potts?'

Drummond laughed.

'The first time I met Mr Potts,' he remarked, 'that swell Frenchman was just preparing to put a thumbscrew on his second thumb.'

'Second?' The detective looked up quickly.

'The first had been treated earlier in the evening,' answered Drummond quietly. 'It was then that I removed your millionaire pal.'

The other lit his cigar deliberately.

'Say, Captain,' he murmured, 'you ain't pulling my leg by any chance, are you?'

'I am not,' said Drummond shortly. 'I was told, before I met him, that the gentleman over there was one of the boys . . . He is, most distinctly. In fact, though up to date such matters have not been much in my line, I should put him down as a sort of super-criminal. I wonder what name he is passing under here?'

The American ceased pulling at his cigar.

'Do they vary?'

'In England he is clean-shaven, possesses a daughter, and answers to Carl Peterson. As he is at present I should never have known him, but for that little trick of his.'

'Possesses a daughter!' For the first time the detective displayed traces of excitement. 'Holy Smoke! It can't be him!'

'Who?' demanded Drummond.

But the other did not answer. Out of the corner of his eye he was watching three men who had just joined the subject of their talk, and on his face was a dawning amazement. He waited till the whole party had gone into the restaurant, then, throwing aside his caution, he turned excitedly to Drummond.

'Are you certain,' he cried, 'that that's the man who has been monkeying with Potts?'

'Absolutely,' said Hugh. 'He recognized me; whether he thinks I recognized him or not, I don't know.'

'Then what,' remarked the detective, 'is he doing here dining with Hocking, our cotton trust man; with Steinemann, the German coal man; and with that other guy whose face is familiar, but whose name I can't place? Two of 'em at any rate, Captain, have got more millions than we're ever likely to have thousands.'

Hugh stared at the American.

'Last night,' he said slowly, 'he was forgathering with a crowd of the most atrocious ragged-trousered revolutionaries it's ever been my luck to run up against.'

'We're in it, Captain, right in the middle of it,' cried the detective, slapping his leg. 'I'll eat my hat if that Frenchman isn't Franklyn – or Libstein – or Baron Darott – or any other of the blamed names he calls himself. He's the biggest proposition we've ever been up against on this little old earth, and he's done us every time. He never commits himself, and if he does, he always covers his tracks. He's a genius; he's the goods. Gee!' he whistled gently under his breath. 'If we could only lay him by the heels.'

For a while he stared in front of him, lost in his dream of pleasant anticipation; then, with a short laugh, he pulled himself together.

'Quite a few people have thought the same, Captain,' he remarked, 'and there he is – still drinking highballs. You say he was with a crowd of revolutionaries last night. What do you mean exactly?'

'Bolshevists, Anarchists, members of the Do-no-work-and-have-all-the-money Brigade,' answered Hugh. 'But excuse me a moment. Waiter.'

A man who had been hovering round came up promptly.

'Four of 'em, Ted,' said Hugh in a rapid undertone. 'Frenchman with a beard, a Yank, and two Boches. Do your best.'

'Right-o, old bean!' returned the waiter, 'but don't hope for too much.'

He disappeared unobtrusively into the restaurant, and Hugh turned with a laugh to the American, who was staring at him in amazement.

'Who the devil is that guy?' asked the detective at length.

'Ted Jerningham – son of Sir Patrick Jerningham, Bt., and Lady Jerningham, of Jerningham Hall, Rutland, England,' answered Hugh, still grinning. 'We may be crude in our methods, Mr Green, but you must admit we do our best. Incidentally, if you want to know, your friend Mr Potts is at present tucked between the sheets at that very house. He went there by aeroplane this morning.' He waved a hand towards Jerry. 'He was the pilot.'

'Travelled like a bird, and sucked up a plate of meat-juice at the end,' announced that worthy, removing his eyes with difficulty from a recently arrived fairy opposite. 'Who says that's nothing, Hugh: the filly across the road there, with that bangle affair round her knee?'

'I must apologize for him, Mr Green,' remarked Hugh. 'He has only recently left school, and knows no better.'

But the American was shaking his head a little dazedly.

'Crude!' he murmured, 'crude! If you and your pals, Captain, are ever out of a job, the New York police is yours for the asking.' He smoked for a few moments in silence, and then, with a quick hunch of his shoulders, he turned to Drummond. 'I guess there'll be time to throw bouquets after,' he remarked. 'We've got to get busy on what your friend Peterson's little worry is; we've then got to stop it – some old how. Now, does nothing sort of strike you?' He looked keenly at the soldier. 'Revolutionaries, Bolshevists, paid agitators last night: international financiers this evening. Why, the broad outline of the plan is as plain as the nose on your face; and it's just the sort of game that man would love . . .' The detective stared thoughtfully at the end of his cigar, and a look of comprehension began to dawn on Hugh's face.

'Great Scott! Mr Green,' he said, 'I'm beginning to get you. What was defeating me was, why two men like Peterson and Lakington should be mixed up with last night's crowd.'

'Lakington! Who's Lakington?' asked the other quickly.

'Number Two in the combine,' answered Hugh, 'and a nasty man.'

'Well, we'll leave him out for the moment,' said the American. 'Doesn't it strike you that there are quite a number of people in this world who would benefit if England became a sort of second Russia? That such a thing would be worth money – big money? That such a thing would be worth paying through the nose for? It would have to be done properly; your small strike here, your small strike there, ain't no manner of use. One gigantic syndicalist strike all over your country – that's what Peterson's playing for, I'll stake my bottom dollar. How he's doing it is another matter. But he's in with the big financiers: and he's using the tub-thumping Bolshies as tools. Gad! It's a big scheme' – he puffed twice at his cigar – 'a durned big scheme. Your little old country, Captain, is, saving one, the finest on God's earth; but she's in a funny mood. She's sick, like most of us are; maybe she's a little sicker than a good many people think. But I reckon Peterson's cure won't do any manner of good, excepting to himself and those blamed capitalists who are putting up the dollars.'

'Then where the devil does Potts come in?' said Hugh, who had listened intently to every word the American had said. 'And the Duchess of Lampshire's pearls?'

'Pearls!' began the American, when the restaurant door opened suddenly and Ted Jerningham emerged. He seemed to be in a hurry, and Hugh half rose in his chair. Then he sat back again, as with miraculous rapidity a crowd of infuriated head waiters and other great ones appeared from nowhere and surrounded Jerningham.

Undoubtedly this was not the way for a waiter to leave the hotel – even if he had just been discovered as an imposter and sacked on the spot. And undoubtedly if he had been a waiter, this large body of scandalized beings would have removed him expeditiously through some secret buttery-hatch, and dropped him on the pavement out of a back entrance.

But not being a waiter, he continued to advance, while

his *entourage*, torn between rage at his effrontery and horror at the thought of a scene, followed in his wake.

Just opposite Hugh he halted, and in a clear voice addressed no one in particular:

'You're spotted. Look out. Ledger at Godalming.'

Then, engulfed once more in the crowd, he continued his majestic progress, and finally disappeared a little abruptly from view.

'Cryptic,' murmured the American, 'but some lad. Gee! He had that bunch guessing.'

'The ledger at Godalming,' said Hugh thoughtfully. 'I watched Peterson, through the skylight last night, getting gay with that ledger. I'm thinking we'll have to look inside it, Mr Green.'

He glanced up as one of the chucking-out party came back, and asked what had happened.

'*Mon Dieu, m'sieur*,' cried the waiter despairingly. ''E vas an imposter, *n'est-ce-pas – un scélerat*; 'e upset ze fish all over ze shirtfront of Monsieur le Comte.'

'Was that the gentleman with the short beard, dining with three others?' asked Drummond gravely.

'*Mais oui, m'sieur*. He dine here always if 'e is in Paris – does le Comte de Guy. Oh! *Mon Dieu! C'est terrible!*'

Wringing his hands, the waiter went back into the restaurant, and Hugh shook silently.

'Dear old Ted,' he murmured, wiping the tears from his eyes. 'I knew he'd keep his end up.' Then he stood up. 'What about a little dinner at Maxim's? I'm thinking we've found out all we're likely to find, until we can get to that ledger. And thanks to your knowing those birds, Mr Green, our trip to Paris has been of considerable value.'

The American nodded.

'I guess I'm on,' he remarked slowly; 'but, if you take my advice, Captain, you'll look nippy tonight. I wouldn't linger around corners admiring the mud. Things kind o' happen at corners.'

II

But on that particular evening the detective proved wrong. They reached Maxim's without mishap, they enjoyed an excellent dinner, during which the American showed himself to be a born conversationalist as well as a shrewd man of the world. And over the coffee and liqueurs Hugh gave him a brief outline of what had taken place since he first got mixed up in the affair. The American listened in silence, though amazement shone on his face as the story proceeded. The episode of the disappearing body especially seemed to tickle his fancy, but even over that he made no remark. Only when Hugh had finished, and early arrivals for supper were beginning to fill the restaurant, did he sum up the matter as he saw it.

'A tough proposition, Captain – damned tough. Potts is our biggest shipping man, but where he comes on the picture at that moment has me beat. As for the old girl's jewels, they don't seem to fit in at all. All we can do is to put our noses inside that ledger, and see the book of the words. It'll sure help some.'

And as Hugh switched off the electric light in his bedroom, having first seen that his torch was ready to hand in case of emergency, he was thinking of the detective's words. Getting hold of the ledger was not going to be easy – far from it; but the excitement of the case had fairly obsessed him by now. He lay in bed, turning over in his mind every possible and impossible scheme by which he could get into the secret centre room at The Elms. He knew the safe the ledger was kept in: but safes are awkward propositions for the ordinary mortal to tackle. Anyway, it wasn't a thing which could be done in a minute's visit; he would have to manage at least a quarter or half an hour's undisturbed search, the thought of which, with his knowledge of the habits of the household, almost made him laugh out loud. And, at that moment, a fly pinged past his head . . .

He felt singularly wide-awake, and, after a while, he gave up attempting to go to sleep. The new development which had come to light that evening was uppermost in his thoughts; and, as he lay there, covered only with a sheet, for the night was hot, the whole vile scheme unfolded itself before his imagination. The American was right in his main idea – of that he had no doubt; and in his mind's eye he saw the great crowds of idle, foolish men led by a few hot-headed visionaries and paid blackguards to their so-called Utopia. Starvation, misery, ruin, utter and complete, lurked in his mental picture; spectres disguised as great ideals, but grinning sardonically under their masks. And once again he seemed to hear the toc-toc of machine guns, as he had heard them night after night during the years gone by. But this time they were mounted on the pavements of the towns of England, and the swish of the bullets, which had swept like swarms of cockchafers over No Man's Land, now whistled down the streets between rows of squalid houses . . . And once again a fly pinged past his head.

With a gesture of annoyance he waved his arm. It was hot – insufferably hot, and he was beginning to regret that he had followed the earnest advice of the American to sleep with his windows shut and bolted. What on earth could Peterson do to him in a room at the Ritz? But he had promised the detective, and there it was – curtains drawn, window bolted, door locked. Moreover, and he smiled grimly to himself as he remembered it, he had even gone so far as to emulate the hysterical maiden lady of fiction and peer under the bed . . .

The next moment the smile ceased abruptly, and he lay rigid, with every nerve alert. Something had moved in the room . . .

It had only been a tiny movement, more like the sudden creak of a piece of furniture than anything else – but it was not quite like it. A gentle, slithering sound had preceded the creak; the sound such as a man would make who, with infinite precaution against making a noise, was moving in a dark room; a stealthy, uncanny noise. Hugh peered into the blackness tensely. After the first moment of surprise his brain was quite cool. He had looked under the bed, he had hung his coat in the cupboard, and save for those two obvious places there was no cover for a cat. And yet, with a sort of sixth sense that four years of war had given him, he knew that noise had been made by some human agency. Human! The thought of the cobra at The Elms flashed into his mind, and his mouth set more grimly. What if Peterson had introduced some of his abominable menagerie into the room? . . . Then, once more, the thing like a fly sounded loud in his ear. And was it his imagination, or had he heard a faint sibilant hiss just before?

Suddenly it struck him that he was at a terrible disadvantage. The thing, whatever it was, knew, at any rate approximately, his position: he had not the slightest notion where it was. And a blind man boxing a man who could see, would have felt just about as safe. With Hugh, such a conclusion meant instant action. It might be dangerous on the floor: it most certainly was far more so in bed. He felt for his torch, and then, with one convulsive bound, he was standing by the door, with his hand on the electric-light switch.

Then he paused and listened intently. Not a sound could he hear; the thing, whatever it was, had become motionless at his sudden movement. For an appreciable time he stood there, his eyes searching the darkness – but even he could see nothing, and he cursed the American comprehensively under his breath. He would have given anything for even the faintest grey light, so that he could have some idea of what it was and where it was. Now he felt utterly helpless, while every moment he imagined some slimy, crawling brute touching his bare feet – creeping up him . . .

He pulled himself together sharply. Light was essential and at once. But, if he switched on, there would be a moment when the thing would see him before he could see the thing – and such moments are not helpful. There only remained his torch; and on the Ancre, on one occasion, he had saved his life by judicious use. The man behind one of those useful implements is in blackness far more impenetrable than the blackest night, for the man in front is dazzled. He can only shoot at the torch: therefore, hold it to one side and in front of you . . .

The light flashed out, darting round the room. Ping! Something hit the sleeve of his pyjamas, but still he could see nothing. The bed, with the clothes thrown back; the washstand; the chair with his trousers and shirt – everything was as it had been when he turned in. And then he heard a second sound – distinct and clear. It came from high up, near the ceiling, and the beam caught the big cupboard and travelled up. It reached the top, and rested there, fixed and steady. Framed in the middle of it, peering over the edge, was a little hairless, brown face, holding what looked like a tube in its mouth. Hugh had one glimpse of a dark, skinny hand putting something in the tube, and then he switched off the torch and ducked, just as another fly pinged over his head and hit the wall behind.

One thing, at any rate, was certain: the other occupant of the room was human, and with that realization all his nerve returned. There would be time enough later on to find out how he got there, and what those strange pinging noises had been caused by. Just at that moment only one thing was on the programme; and without a sound he crept round the bed towards the cupboard, to put that one thing into effect in his usual direct manner.

Twice did he hear the little whistling hiss from above, but nothing sang past his head. Evidently the man had lost him, and was probably still aiming at the door. And then, with hands that barely touched it, he felt the outlines of the cupboard.

It was standing an inch or two from the wall, and he slipped his fingers behind the back on one side. He listened for a moment, but no movement came from above; then, half facing the wall, he put one leg against it. There was one quick, tremendous heave; a crash which sounded deafening; then silence. And once again he switched on his torch . . .

Lying on the floor by the window was one of the smallest men he had ever seen. He was a native of sorts, and Hugh turned him over with his foot. He was quite unconscious, and the bump on his head, where it had hit the floor, was rapidly swelling to the size of a large orange. In his hand he still clutched the little tube, and Hugh gingerly removed it. Placed in position at one end was a long splinter of wood, with a sharpened point; and by the light of his torch Hugh saw that it was faintly discoloured with some brown stain.

He was still examining it with interest when a thunderous knock came on the door. He strolled over and switched on the electric light; then he opened the door.

An excited night-porter rushed in, followed by two or three other people in varying stages of undress, and stopped in amazement at the scene. The heavy cupboard, with a great crack across the back, lay face downwards on the floor; the native still lay curled up and motionless.

'One of the hotel pets?' queried Hugh pleasantly, lighting a cigarette. 'If it's all the same to you, I wish you'd remove him. He was – ah – finding it uncomfortable on the top of the cupboard.'

It appeared that the night-porter could speak English; it also appeared that the lady occupying the room below had rushed forth demanding to be led to the basement, under the misapprehension that war had again been declared and the Germans were bombing Paris. It still further appeared that there was something most irregular about the whole proceeding – the best people at the Ritz did not do these things. And then, to crown everything, while the uproar was at its height, the native on the floor, opening one beady and somewhat dazed eye, realized that things looked unhealthy. Unnoticed, he lay 'doggo' for a while; then, like a rabbit which has almost been trodden on, he dodged between the legs of the men in the room, and vanished through the open door. Taken by surprise, for a moment no one moved: then, simultaneously, they dashed into the passage. It was empty, save for one scandalized old gentleman in a nightcap, who was peering out of a room opposite angrily demanding the cause of the hideous din.

Had he seen a native – a black man? He had seen no

native, and if other people only drank water, they wouldn't either. In fact, the whole affair was scandalous, and he should write to the papers about it. Still muttering, he withdrew, banging his door, and Hugh, glancing up, saw the American detective advancing towards them along the corridor.

'What's the trouble, Captain?' he asked, as he joined the group.

'A friend of the management elected to spend the night on the top of my cupboard, Mr Green,' answered Drummond, 'and got cramp half-way through.'

The American gazed at the wreckage in silence. Then he looked at Hugh, and what he saw on that worthy's face apparently decided him to maintain that policy. In fact, it was not till the night-porter and his attendant minions had at last, and very dubiously, withdrawn, that he again opened his mouth.

'Looks like a hectic night,' he murmured. 'What happened?' Briefly Hugh told him what had occurred, and the detective whistled softly.

'Blowpipe and poisoned darts,' he said shortly, returning the tube to Dummond. 'Narrow escape – damned narrow! Look at your pillow.'

Hugh looked: embedded in the linen were four pointed splinters similar to the one he held in his hand; by the door were three more, lying on the floor.

'An engaging little bird,' he laughed; 'but nasty to look at.'

He extracted the little pieces of wood and carefully placed them in an empty matchbox: the tube he put into his cigarette-case.

'Mighty come in handy: you never know,' he remarked casually.

'They might if you stand quite still,' said the American,

with a sudden, sharp command in his voice. 'Don't move.'

Hugh stood motionless, staring at the speaker who, with eyes fixed on his right forearm, had stepped forward. From the loose sleeve of his pyjama coat the detective gently pulled another dart and dropped it into the matchbox.

'Not far off getting you that time, Captain,' he cried cheerfully. 'Now you've got the whole blamed outfit.'

III

It was the Comte de Guy who boarded the boat express at the Gare du Nord the next day; it was Carl Peterson who stepped off the boat express at Boulogne. And it was only Drummond's positive assurance which convinced the American that the two characters were the same man.

He was leaning over the side of the boat reading a telegram when he first saw Hugh ten minutes after the boat had left the harbour; and if he had hoped for a different result to the incident of the night before, no sign of it showed on his face. Instead he waved a cheerful greeting to Drummond.

'This is a pleasant surprise,' he remarked affably. 'Have you been to Paris, too?'

For a moment Drummond looked at him narrowly. Was it a stupid bluff, or was the man so sure of his power of disguise that he assumed with certainty he had not been recognized? And it suddenly struck Hugh that, save for that one tell-tale habit – a habit which, in all probability, Peterson himself was unconscious of – he would *not* have recognized him.

'Yes,' he answered lightly. 'I came over to see how you behaved yourself!'

'What a pity I didn't know!' said Peterson, with a good-humoured chuckle. He seemed in excellent spirits, as he carefully tore the telegram into tiny pieces and dropped them overboard. 'We might have had another of our homely little chats over some supper. Where did you stay?'

'At the Ritz. And you?'

'I always stop at the Bristol,' answered Peterson. 'Quieter than the Ritz, I think.'

'Yes, it was quite dreadful last night,' murmured Hugh. 'A pal of mine – quite incorrigible – that bird over there' – he pointed to Ted Jerningham, who was strolling up and down the deck with the American – 'insisted on dressing up as a waiter.' He laughed shortly at the sudden gleam in the other's eye, as he watched Jerningham go past. 'Not content with that, he went and dropped the fish over some warrior's boiled shirt, and had to leave in disgrace.' He carefully selected a cigarette. 'No accountin' for this dressing-up craze, is there, Carl? You'd never be anything but your own sweet self, would you, little one? Always the girls' own friend – tender and true.' He laughed softly; from previous experience he knew that this particular form of baiting invariably infuriated Peterson. 'Some day, my Carl, you must tell me of your life, and your early struggles, amidst all the bitter temptations of this wicked world.'

'Some day,' snarled Peterson, 'I'll –'

'Stop.' Drummond held up a protesting hand. 'Not that, my Carl – anything but that.'

'Anything but what?' said the other savagely.

'I felt it in my bones,' answered Drummond, 'that you were once more on the point of mentioning my decease. I couldn't bear it, Carl: on this beautiful morning I should burst into tears. It would be the seventeenth time that that sad event has been alluded to either by you or our Henry: and I'm reluctantly beginning to think that you'll have to hire an assassin, and take lessons from him.' He looked thoughtfully at the other, and an unholy joy began to dawn on his face. 'I see you have thrown away your cigar, Carl. May I offer you a cigarette? No? . . . But why so brusque? Can it be – oh no! surely not – can it be that my little pet is feeling icky-boo? Face going green – slight perspiration – collar tight – only the yawning stage between him and his breakfast! Some people have all the fun of the fair. And I thought of asking you to join me below at lunch. There's some excellent fat pork . . .'

A few minutes later, Jerningham and the American found him leaning by himself against the rail, still laughing weakly.

'I ask no more of life,' he remarked when he could speak. 'Anything else that may come will be an anti-climax.'

'What's happened?' asked Jerningham.

'It's happening,' said Drummond joyfully. 'It couldn't possibly be over yet. Peterson, our one and only Carl, has been overcome by the waves. And when he's feeling a little better I'll take him a bit of crackling . . .' Once again he gave way to unrestrained mirth, which finally sub-sided sufficiently to allow him to stagger below and feed.

At the top of the stairs leading to the luncheon saloon, he paused, and glanced into the secret place reserved for those who have from early childhood voted for a Channel tunnel.

'There he is,' he whispered ecstatically, 'our little Carl, busy recalling his past. It may be vulgar, Ted: doubtless it is. I don't care. Such trifles matter not in the supreme moments of one's life; and I can imagine of only one more supreme than this.'

'What's that?' asked Ted, firmly piloting him down the stairs.

'The moment when he and Henry sit side by side and recall their pasts together,' murmured Hugh solemnly. 'Think of it, man – think of it! Each cursin' the other between spasms. My hat! What a wonderful, lovely dream to treasure through the weary years!' He gazed abstractedly at the waiter. 'Roast beef – underdone,' he remarked, 'and take a plate of cold fat up to the silence room above. The third gentleman from the door would like to look at it.'

But third gentleman from the door, even in the midst of his agony, was consoled by one reflection.

'Should it be necessary, letter awaits him.' So had run the telegram, which he had scattered to the winds right under Drummond's nose. And it *was* necessary. The mutton-headed young sweep had managed to escape once again: though Petro had assured him that the wretched native had never yet failed. And he personally had seen the man clamber on to the top of the cupboard . . .

For a moment his furious rage overcame his sufferings . . . Next time . . . next time . . . and then the seventh wave of several seventh waves arrived. He had a fleeting glimpse of the scoundrel Drummond, apparently on the other side of a see-saw, watching him delightedly from outside; then, with a dreadful groan, he snatched his new basin, just supplied by a phlegmatic steward, from the scoundrel next him, who had endeavoured to appropriate it.

IV

'Walk right in, Mr Green,' said Hugh, as, three hours later, they got out of a taxi in Half Moon Street. 'This is my little rabbit-hutch.'

He followed the American up the stairs, and produced his latchkey. But before he could even insert it in the hole the door was flung open, and Peter Darrell stood facing him with evident relief in his face.

'Thank the Lord you've come, old son,' he cried, with a brief look at the detective. 'There's something doing down at Godalming I don't like.'

He followed Hugh into the sitting-room.

'At twelve o'clock today Toby rang up. He was talking quite ordinarily – you know the sort of rot he usually gets off his chest – when suddenly he stopped quite short and said, "My God! What do you want?" I could tell he'd looked up, because his voice was muffled. Then there was the sound of a scuffle, I heard Toby curse, then nothing more. I rang and rang and rang – no answer.'

'What did you do?' Drummond, with a letter in his hand which he had taken off the mantelpiece, was listening grimly.

'Algy was here. He motored straight off to see if he could find out what was wrong. I stopped here to tell you.'

'Anything through from him?'

'Not a word. There's foul play, or I'll eat my hat.'

But Hugh did not answer. With a look on his face which even Peter had never seen before, he was reading the letter. It was short and to the point, but he read it three times before he spoke.

'When did this come?' he asked.

'An hour ago,' answered the other. 'I very nearly opened it.'

'Read it,' said Hugh. He handed it to Peter and went to the door.

'Denny,' he shouted, 'I want my car round at once.' Then he came back into the room. 'If they've hurt one hair of her head,' he said, his voice full of a smouldering fury, 'I'll murder that gang one by one with my bare hands.'

'Say, Captain, may I see this letter?' said the American; and Hugh nodded.

'"For pity's sake, come at once,"' read the detective aloud. '"The bearer of this is trustworthy."' He thoughtfully picked his teeth. 'Girl's writing. Do you know her?'

'My fiancée,' said Hugh shortly.

'Certain?' snapped the American.

'Certain!' cried Hugh. 'Of course I am, I know every curl of every letter.'

'There is such a thing as forgery,' remarked the detective dispassionately.

'Damn it, man!' exploded Hugh. 'Do you imagine I don't know my own girl's writing?'

'A good many bank cashiers have mistaken their customers' writing before now,' said the other, unmoved. 'I don't like it, Captain. A girl in *real* trouble wouldn't put in that bit about the bearer.'

'You go to hell,' remarked Hugh briefly. 'I'm going to Godalming.'

'Well,' drawled the American, 'not knowing Godalming, I don't know who scores. But, if you go there – I come too.'

'And me,' said Peter, brightening up.

Hugh grinned.

'Not you, old son. If Mr Green will come, I'll be delighted; but I want you here at headquarters.'

He turned round as his servant put his head in at the door.

'Car here, sir. Do you want a bag packed?'

'No – only my revolver. Are you ready, Mr Green?'

'Sure thing,' said the American. 'I always am.'

'Then we'll move.' And Peter, watching the car resignedly from the window, saw the American grip his seat with both hands, and then raise them suddenly in silent prayer, while an elderly charlady fled with a scream to the safety of the area below.

They did the trip in well under the hour, and the detective got out of the car with a faint sigh of relief.

'You've missed your vocation, Captain,' he murmured. 'If you pushed a bath-chair it would be safer for all parties. I bolted two bits of gum in that excursion.'

But Drummond was already out of earshot, dodging rapidly through the bushes on his way to The Larches; and when the American finally overtook him, he was standing by a side-door knocking hard on the panels.

'Seems kind of empty,' said the detective thoughtfully, as the minutes went by and no one came. 'Why not try the front door?'

'Because it's in sight of the other house,' said Hugh briefly. 'I'm going to break in.'

He retreated a yard from the door, then, bracing his shoulder, he charged it once. And the door, as a door, was not . . . Rapidly the two men went from room to room – bedrooms, servants' quarters, even the bath-room. Every one was empty: not a sound could be heard in the house. Finally, only the dining-room remained, and as they stood by the door looking round, the

American shifted his third piece of gum to a new point of vantage.

'Somebody has been rough-housing by the look of things,' he remarked judicially. 'Looks like a boozing den after a thick night.'

'It does,' remarked Hugh grimly, taking in the disorder of the room. The tablecloth was pulled off, the telephone lay on the floor. China and glass, smashed to pieces, littered the carpet; but what caught his eye, and caused him suddenly to step forward and pick it up, was a plain circle of glass with a black cord attached to it through a small hole.

'Algy Longworth's eyeglass,' he muttered. 'So he's been caught too.'

And it was at that moment that, clear and distinct through the still evening air, they heard a woman's agonized scream. It came from the house next door, and the American, for a brief space, even forgot to chew his gum.

The next instant he darted forward.

'Stop, you young fool!' he shouted, but he was too late.

He watched Drummond, running like a stag, cross the lawn and disappear in the trees. For a second he hesitated; then, with a shrug of square shoulders, he rapidly left the house by the way they had entered. And a few minutes later, Drummond's car was skimming back towards London, with a grim-faced man at the wheel, who had apparently felt the seriousness of the occasion so acutely as to deposit his third piece of spearmint on the underneath side of the steering-wheel for greater safety.

But, seeing that the owner of the car was lying in blissful unconsciousness in the hall of The Elms, surrounded by half a dozen men, this hideous vandalism hurt him not.

CHAPTER 10

In Which the Hun Nation Decreases by One

I

Drummond had yielded to impulse – the blind, all-powerful impulse of any man who is a man to get to the woman he loves if she wants him. As he had dashed across the lawn to The Elms, with the American's warning cry echoing in his ears, he had been incapable of serious thought. Subconsciously he had known that, from every point of view, it was the act of a madman; that he was deliberately putting his head into what, in all probability, was a carefully prepared noose; that, from every point of view, he could help Phyllis better by remaining a free agent outside. But when a girl shrieks, and the man who loves her hears it, arguments begin to look tired. And what little caution might have remained to Hugh completely vanished as he saw the girl watching him with agonized terror in her face, from an upstair window, as he dashed up to the house. It was only for a brief second that he saw her; then she disappeared suddenly, as if snatched away by some invisible person.

'I'm coming, darling.' He had given one wild shout, and hurled himself through the door which led into the house from the garden. A dazzling light of intense brilliance had shone in his face, momentarily blinding him; then had come a crushing blow on the back of his head. One groping, wild step forward, and Hugh Drummond, dimly conscious of men all round him, had pitched forward on his face into utter oblivion.

'It's too easy,' Lakington's sneering voice broke the silence, as he looked vindictively at the unconscious man.

'So you have thought before, Henry,' chuckled Peterson, whose complete recovery from his recent unfortunate indisposition was shown by the steady glow of the inevitable cigar. 'And he always bobs up somehow. If you take my advice you'll finish him off here and now, and run no further risks.'

'Kill him while he's unconscious?' Lakington laughed evilly. 'No, Carl, not under any circumstances, whatever. He has quite a lengthy score to pay and by God! he's going to pay it this time.' He stepped forward and kicked Drummond twice in the ribs with a cold, animal fury.

'Well, don't kick him when he's down, guv'nor. You'll 'ave plenty o' time after.' A hoarse voice from the circle of men made Lakington look up.

'You cut it out, Jem Smith,' he snarled, 'or I might find plenty of time after for others beside this young swine.' The ex-pugilist muttered uneasily under his breath, but said no more, and it was Peterson who broke the silence.

'What are you going to do with him?'

'Lash him up like the other two,' returned Lakington, 'and leave him to cool until I get back tomorrow. But I'll bring him round before I go, and just talk to him for a little. I wouldn't like him not to know what was going to happen to him. Anticipation is always delightful.' He turned to two of the men standing near. 'Carry him into my room,' he ordered, 'and another of you get the rope.'

And so it was that Algy Longworth and Toby Sinclair, with black rage and fury in their hearts, watched the limp form of their leader being carried into the central room.

Swathed in rope, they sat motionless and impotent, in their respective chairs, while they watched the same process being performed on Drummond. He was no amateur at the game, was the rope-winder, and by the time he had finished, Hugh resembled nothing so much as a lifeless brown mummy. Only his head was free, and that lolled forward helplessly.

Lakington watched the performance for a time; then, wearying of it, he strolled over to Algy's chair.

'Well, you puppy,' he remarked, 'are you going to try shouting again?' He picked up the rhinoceros-hide riding-whip lying on the floor, and bent it between his hands. 'That weal on your face greatly improves your beauty, and next time you'll get two, and a gag as well.'

'How's the jaw, you horrible bit of dreg?' remarked Algy insultingly, and Toby laughed.

'Don't shake his nerve, Algy,' he implored. 'For the first time in his filthy life he feels safe in the same room as Hugh.'

The taunt seemed to madden Lakington, who sprang across the room and lashed Sinclair over the face. But even after the sixth cut no sound came from the helpless man, though the blood was streaming down inside his collar. His eyes, calm and sneering, met those of the raving man in front of him without a quiver, and, at last, Peterson himself intervened.

'Stop it, Lakington.' His voice was stern as he caught the other's upraised arm. 'That's enough for the time.'

For a moment it seemed as if Lakington would have struck Peterson himself; then he controlled himself, and, with an ugly laugh, flung the whip into a corner.

'I forgot,' he said slowly. 'It's the leading dog we want – not the puppies that run after him yapping.' He spun round on his heel. 'Have you finished?'

The rope-artist bestowed a final touch to the last knot, and surveyed his handiwork with justifiable pride.

'Cold mutton,' he remarked tersely, 'would be lively compared to him when he wakes up.'

'Good! Then we'll bring him to.'

Lakington took some crystals from a jar on one of the shelves, and placed them in a tumbler. Then he added a few drops of liquid and held the glass directly under the unconscious man's nose. Almost at once the liquid began to effervesce, and in less than a minute Drummond opened his eyes and stared dazedly round the room. He blinked foolishly as he saw Longworth and Sinclair; then he looked down and found he was similarly bound himself. Finally he glanced up at the man bending over him, and full realization returned.

'Feeling better, my friend?' With a mocking smile, Lakington laid the tumbler on a table close by.

'Much, thank you, Henry,' murmured Hugh. 'Ah! and there's Carl. How's the tummy, Carl? I hope for your sake that it's feeling stronger than the back of my head.'

He grinned cheerfully, and Lakington struck him on the mouth.

'You can stop that style of conversation, Captain Drummond,' he remarked. 'I dislike it.'

Hugh stared at the striker in silence.

'Accept my congratulations,' he said at length, in a low voice which, despite himself, shook a little. 'You are the first man who has ever done that, and I shall treasure the memory of that blow.'

'I'd hate it to be a lonely memory,' remarked Lakington. 'So here's another, to keep it company.' Again he struck him, then with a laugh he turned on his heel. 'My compliments to Miss Benton,' he said to a man standing near the door, 'and ask her to be good enough to come down for a few minutes.'

The veins stood out on Drummond's forehead at the mention of the girl, but otherwise he gave no sign; and, in silence, they waited for her arrival.

She came almost at once, a villainous-looking black-guard with her, and as she saw Hugh she gave a pitiful little moan and held out her hand to him.

'Why did you come, boy?' she cried. 'Didn't you know it was only a forgery – that note?'

'Ah! was it?' said Hugh softly. 'Was it, indeed?'

'An interesting point,' murmured Lakington. 'Surely if a charming girl is unable – or unwilling – to write to her fiancé, her father is a very suitable person to supply the deficiency. Especially if he has been kindly endowed by Nature with a special aptitude for – er – imitating writing.'

Mr Benton, who had been standing outside the door, came lurching into the room.

'Quite ri', Laking – Laking – ton,' he announced solemnly. 'Dreadful thing to sep – separate two young people.' Then he saw Drummond, and paused, blinking foolishly. 'Whash he all tied up for li' that?'

Lakington smiled evilly.

'It would be a pity to lose him, now he's come, wouldn't it?'

The drunken man nodded two or three times; then a thought seemed to strike him, and he advanced slowly towards Hugh, wagging a finger foolishly.

'Thash reminds me, young fellah,' he hiccuped grave-ly, 'you never asked my consent. You should have asked father's consent. Mosh incon – inconshiderate. Don't you agree with me, Mishter Peterson?'

'You will find the tantalus in the dining-room,' said Peterson coldly. 'I should say you require one more drink to produce complete insensibility, and the sooner you have it the better.'

'Inshensibility!' With outraged dignity the wretched man appealed to his daughter. 'Phyllis, did you hear? Thish man says I'sh in – inebri . . . says I'sh drunk. Gratui . . . tous inshult . . .'

'Oh, father, father,' cried the girl, covering her face with her hands. 'For pity's sake go away! You've done enough harm as it is.'

Mr Benton backed towards the door, where he paused, swaying.

'Disgraceful,' he remarked solemnly. 'Rising generation no reshpect for elders and bettersh! Teach 'em lesson, Lakington. Do 'em all good. One – two – three, all ranged in a – in a row. Do 'em good –' His voice tailed off, and, after a valiant attempt to lean against a door which was not there, he collapsed gracefully in a heap on the floor.

'You vile hound,' said Phyllis, turning like a young tigress on Lakington. 'It's your doing entirely, that he's in that condition.'

But Lakington merely laughed.

'When we're married,' he answered lightly, 'we'll put him into a really good home for inebriates.'

'Married!' she whispered tensely. 'Married! Why, you loathsome reptile, I'd kill myself before I married you.'

'An excellent curtain,' remarked Lakington suavely, 'for the third act of a melodrama. Doubtless we can elaborate it later. In the meantime, however' – he glanced at his watch – 'time presses. And I don't want to go without telling you a little about the programme, Captain Drummond. Unfortunately both Mr Peterson and I have to leave you for tonight; but we shall be returning tomorrow morning – or, at any rate, I shall. You will be left in charge of Heinrich – you remember the filthy Boche? – with whom you had words the other night. As you may expect, he entertains feelings of great friendship and affection for you, so you should not lack for any bodily comforts, such as may be possible in your present some-what cramped position. Then tomorrow, when I return, I propose to try a few experiments on you, and, though I fear you will find them painful, it's a great thing to suffer in the cause of science . . . You will always have the satisfaction of knowing that dear little Phyllis will be well cared for.' With a sudden, quick movement, he seized the girl and kissed her before she realized his intention. The rope round Drummond creaked as he struggled impotently, and Lakington's sneering face seemed to swim in a red glow.

'That is quite in keeping, is it not,' he snarled 'to kiss the lady, and to strike the man like this – and this – and this? . . .' A rain of blows came down on Drummond's face, till, with a gasping sigh, the girl slipped fainting to the floor.

'That'll do, Lakington,' said Peterson, intervening once again. 'Have the girl carried upstairs, and send for Heinrich. It's time we were off.'

With an effort Lakington let his hand fall to his side, and stood back from his victim.

'Perhaps for the present, it will,' he said slowly. 'But tomorrow – tomorrow, Captain Drummond, you shall scream to Heaven for mercy, until I take out your tongue and you can scream no more.' He turned as the German came into the room. 'I leave them to you, Heinrich,' he remarked shortly. 'Use the dog-whip if they shout, and gag them.'

The German's eyes were fixed on Hugh gloatingly.

'They will not shout twice,' he said in his guttural voice. 'The dirty Boche to it himself will see.'

II

'We appear,' remarked Hugh quietly, a few minutes later, 'to be in for a cheery night.'

For a moment the German had left the room, and the three motionless, bound figures, sitting grotesquely in their chairs, were alone.

'How did they get you, Toby?'

'Half a dozen of 'em suddenly appeared,' answered Sinclair shortly, 'knocked me on the head, and the next thing I knew I was here in this damned chair.'

'Is that when you got your face?' asked Hugh.

'No,' said Toby, and his voice was grim. 'We share in the matter of faces, old man.'

'Lakington again, was it?' said Hugh softly. 'Dear Heavens! if I could get one hand on that . . .' He broke off and laughed. 'What about you, Algy?'

'I went blundering in over the way, old bean,' returned that worthy, 'and some dam' fellow knocked my eye-glass off. So, as I couldn't see to kill him, I had to join the picnic here.'

Hugh laughed, and then suddenly grew serious.

'By the way, you didn't see a man chewing gum on the horizon, did you, when I made my entrance? Dog-robber suit, and face like a motor-mascot.'

'Thank God, I was spared that!' remarked Algy.

'Good!' returned Hugh. 'He's probably away with it by now, and he's no fool. For I'm thinking it's only Peter and him between us and –' He left his remark unfinished, and for a while there was silence. 'Jerry is over in France still, putting stamp-paper on his machine; Ted's gone up to see that Potts is taking nourishment.'

'And here we sit like three well-preserved specimens in a bally museum,' broke in Algy, with a rueful laugh. 'What'll they do to us, Hugh?'

But Drummond did not answer, and the speaker, seeing the look on his face, did not press the question.

Slowly the hours dragged on, until the last gleams of daylight had faded from the skylight above, and a solitary electric light, hung centrally, gave the only illumination. Periodically Heinrich had come in to see that they were still secure; but from the sounds of hoarse laughter which came at frequent intervals through the half-open door, it was evident that the German had found other and more congenial company. At length he appeared carrying a tray with bread and water on it, which he placed on a table near Hugh.

'Food for you, you English swine,' he remarked, looking gloatingly at each in turn. 'Herr Lakington the order gave, so that you will be fit tomorrow morning. Fit for the torture.' He thrust his flushed face close to Drummond's and then deliberately spat at him.

Algy Longworth gave a strangled grunt, but Drummond took no notice. For the past half-hour he had been sunk in thought, so much so that the others had believed him asleep. Now, with a quiet smile, he looked up at the German.

'How much, my friend,' he remarked, 'are you getting for this?'

The German leered at him.

'Enough to see that you tomorrow are here,' he said.

'And I always believed that yours was a business nation,' laughed Hugh. 'Why, you poor fool, I've got a thousand pounds in notes in my cigarette-case.' For a moment the German stared at him; then a look of greed came into his pig-eyes.

'You hof, hof you?' he grunted. 'Then the filthy Boche will for you of them take care.'

Hugh looked at him angrily.

'If you do,' he cried, 'you must let me go.'

The German leered still more.

'*Natürlich*. You shall out of the house at once walk.'

He stepped up to Drummond and ran his hands over his coat, while the others stared at one another in amazement. Surely Hugh didn't imagine the swine would really let him go; he would merely take the money and probably spit in his face again. Then they heard him speaking, and a sudden gleam of comprehension dawned on their faces.

'You'll have to undo one of the ropes, my friend, before you can get at it,' said Hugh quietly.

For a moment the German hesitated. He looked at the ropes carefully; the one that bound the arms and the upper part of the body was separate from the rope round the legs. Even if he did undo it the fool Englishman was still helpless, and he knew that he was unarmed. Had he not himself removed his revolver, as he lay unconscious in the hall? What risk was there, after all? Besides, if he called someone else in he would have to share the money.

And, as he watched the German's indecision, Hugh's forehead grew damp with sweat . . . Would he undo the rope? Would greed conquer caution?

At last the Boche made up his mind, and went behind the chair. Hugh felt him fumbling with the rope, and flashed an urgent look of caution at the other two.

'You'd better be careful, Heinrich,' he remarked, 'that none of the others see, or you might have to share.'

The German ceased undoing the knot, and grunted. The English swine had moments of brightness, and he went over and closed the door. Then he resumed the operation of untying the rope; and, since it was performed behind the chair, he was in no position to see the look on Drummond's face. Only the two spectators could see that, and they had almost ceased breathing in their excitement. That he had a plan they knew; what it was they could not even guess.

At last the rope fell clear, and the German sprang back.

'Put the case on the table,' he cried, having not the slightest intention of coming within range of those formidable arms.

'Certainly not,' said Hugh, 'until you undo my legs. Then you shall have it.'

Quite loosely he was holding the case in one hand; but the others, watching his face, saw that it was strained and tense.

'First I the notes must have.' The German strove to speak conversationally, but all the time he was creeping nearer and nearer to the back of the chair. 'Then I your legs undo, and you may go.'

Algy's warning cry rang out simultaneously with the lightning dart of the Boche's hand as he snatched at the cigarette-case over Drummond's shoulder. And then Drummond laughed a low, triumphant laugh. It was the move he had been hoping for, and the German's wrist was held fast in his vicelike grip. His plan had succeeded.

And Longworth and Sinclair, who had seen many things in their lives, the remembrance of which will be with them till their dying day, had never seen and are never likely to see anything within measurable distance of what they saw in the next few minutes. Slowly, inexorably, the German's arm was being twisted, while he uttered hoarse, gasping cries, and beat impotently at Drummond's head with his free hand. Then at last there was a dull crack as the arm broke, and a scream of pain, as he lurched round the chair and stood helpless in front of the soldier, who still held the cigarette-case in his left hand.

They saw Drummond open the cigarette-case and take

from it what looked like a tube of wood. Then he felt in his pocket and took out a matchbox, containing a number of long thin splinters. And, having fitted one of the splinters into the tube, he put the other end in his mouth.

With a quick heave they saw him jerk the German round and catch his unbroken arm with his free left hand. And the two bound watchers looked at Hugh's eyes as he stared at the moaning Boche, and saw that they were hard and merciless.

There was a sharp, whistling hiss, and the splinter flew from the tube into the German's face. It hung from his cheek, and even the ceaseless movement of his head failed to dislodge it.

'I have broken your arm, Boche,' said Drummond at length, 'and now I have killed you. I'm sorry about it; I wasn't particularly anxious to end your life. But it had to be done.'

The German, hardly conscious of what he had said owing to the pain in his arm, was frantically kicking the Englishman's legs, still bound to the chair; but the iron grip on his wrists never slackened. And then quite suddenly came the end. With one dreadful, convulsive heave the German jerked himself free, and fell doubled up on the floor. Fascinated, they watched him writhing and twisting, until at last, he lay still . . . The Boche was dead . . .

'My God!' muttered Hugh, wiping his forehead. 'Poor brute.'

'What was that blow-pipe affair?' cried Sinclair hoarsely.

'The thing they tried to finish me with in Paris last night,' answered Hugh grimly, taking a knife out of his waistcoat pocket. 'Let us trust that none of his pals come in to look for him.'

A minute later he stood up, only to sit down again

abruptly, as his legs gave way. They were numbed and stiff with the hours he had spent in the same position, and for a while he could do nothing but rub them with his hands, till the blood returned and he could feel once more.

Then, slowly and painfully, he tottered across to the others and set them free as well. They were in an even worse condition than he had been; and it seemed as if Algy would never be able to stand again, so completely dead was his body from the waist downwards. But, at length, after what seemed an eternity to Drummond, who realized only too well that should the gang come in they were almost as helpless in their present condition as if they were still bound in their chairs, the other two recovered. They were still stiff and cramped – all three of them – but at any rate they could move; which was more than could be said of the German, who lay twisted and rigid on the floor with his eyes staring up at them – a glassy, horrible stare.

'Poor brute!' said Hugh again, looking at him with a certain amount of compunction. 'He was a miserable specimen – but still . . .' He shrugged his shoulders. 'And the contents of my cigarette-case are half a dozen gaspers, and a ten-bob Bradbury patched together with stamp paper!'

He swung round on his heel as if dismissing the matter, and looked at the other two.

'All fit now? Good! We've got to think what we're going to do, for we're not out of the wood yet by two or three miles.'

'Let's get the door open,' remarked Algy, 'and explore.'

Cautiously they swung it open, and stood motionless. The house was in absolute silence; the hall was deserted.

'Switch out the light,' whispered Hugh. 'We'll wander round.'

They crept forward stealthily in the darkness, stopping every now and then to listen. But no sound came to their ears; it might have been a house of the dead.

Suddenly Drummond, who was in front of the other two, stopped with a warning hiss. A light was streaming out from under a door at the end of a passage, and, as they stood watching it, they heard a man's voice coming from the same room. Someone else answered him, and then there was silence once more.

At length Hugh moved forward again, and the others followed. And it was not until they got quite close to the door that a strange, continuous noise began to be noticeable – a noise which came most distinctly from the lighted room. It rose and fell with monotonous regularity; at times it resembled a brass band – at others it died away to a gentle murmur. And occasionally it was punctuated with a strangled snort . . .

'Great Scott!' muttered Hugh excitedly, 'the whole boiling bunch are asleep, or I'll eat my hat.'

'Then who was it that spoke?' said Algy. 'At least two of 'em are awake right enough.'

And, as if in answer to his question, there came the voice again from inside the room.

'Wal, Mr Darrell, I guess we can pass on, and leave this bunch.'

With one laugh of joyful amazement Hugh flung open the door, and found himself looking from the range of a yard into two revolvers.

'I don't know how you've done it, boys,' he remarked, 'but you can put those guns away. I hate looking at them from that end.'

'What the devil have they done to all your dials?' said Darrell, slowly lowering his arm.

'We'll leave that for the time,' returned Hugh grimly,

as he shut the door. 'There are other more pressing matters to be discussed.'

He glanced round the room, and a slow grin spread over his face. There were some twenty of the gang, all of them fast asleep. They sprawled grotesquely over the table, they lolled in chairs; they lay on the floor, they huddled in corners. And, without exception, they snored and snorted.

'A dandy bunch,' remarked the American, gazing at them with satisfaction. 'That fat one in the corner took enough dope to kill a bull, but he seems quite happy.' Then he turned to Drummond. 'Say now, Captain, we've got a lorryload of the boys outside; your friend here thought we'd better bring 'em along. So it's up to you to get busy.'

'Mullings and his crowd,' said Darrell, seeing the look of mystification on Hugh's face. 'When Mr Green got back and told me you'd shoved your great mutton-head in it again, I thought I'd better bring the whole outfit.'

'Oh, you daisy!' cried Hugh, rubbing his hands together, 'you pair of priceless beans! The Philistines are delivered into our hands, even up to the neck.' For a few moments he stood, deep in thought; then once again the grin spread slowly over his face. 'Right up to their necks,' he repeated, 'so that it washes round their back teeth. Get the boys in, Peter; and get these lumps of meat carted out to the lorry. And, while you do that, we'll go upstairs and mop up.'

III

Even in his wildest dreams Hugh had never imagined such a wonderful opportunity. To be in complete possession of the house, with strong forces at his beck and call, was a state of affairs which rendered him almost speechless.

'Up the stairs on your hands and knees,' he ordered, as they stood in the hall. 'There are peculiarities about this staircase which require elucidation at a later date.'

But the murderous implement which acted in conjunction with the fifth step was not in use, and they passed up the stairs in safety.

'Keep your guns handy,' whispered Hugh. 'We'll draw each room in turn till we find the girl.'

But they were not to be put to so much trouble. Suddenly a door opposite opened, and the man who had been guarding Phyllis Benton peered out suspiciously. His jaw fell, and a look of aghast surprise spread over his face as he saw the four men in front of him. Then he made a quick movement as if to shut the door, but before he realized what had happened the American's foot was against it, and the American's revolver was within an inch of his head.

'Keep quite still, son,' he drawled, 'or I guess it might sort of go off.'

But Hugh had stepped past him, and was smiling at the girl who, with a little cry of joyful wonder, had risen from her chair.

'Your face, boy,' she whispered, as he took her in his arms, regardless of the other; 'your poor old face! Oh! that brute, Lakington!'

Hugh grinned.

'It's something to know, old thing,' he remarked cheerily, 'that anything could damage it. Personally I have always thought that any change on it must be for the better.'

He laughed gently, and for a moment she clung to him,

unmindful of how he had got to her, glorying only in the fact that he had. It seemed to her that there was nothing which this wonderful man of hers couldn't manage; and now, blindly trusting, she waited to be told what to do. The nightmare was over; Hugh was with her . . .

'Where's your father, dear?' he asked her after a little pause.

'In the dining-room, I think,' she answered with a shiver, and Hugh nodded gravely.

'Are there any cars outside?' He turned to the American.

'Yours,' answered that worthy, still keeping his eyes fixed on his prisoner's face, which had now turned a sickly green.

'And mine is hidden behind Miss Benton's greenhouse unless they've moved it,' remarked Algy.

'Good!' said Hugh. 'Algy, take Miss Benton and her father up to Half Moon Street – at once. Then come back here.'

'But Hugh —' began the girl appealingly.

'At once, dear, please.' He smiled at her tenderly, but his tone was decided. 'This is going to be no place for you in the near future.' He turned to Longworth and drew him aside. 'You'll have a bit of a job with the old man,' he whispered. 'He's probably paralytic by now. But get on with it, will you? Get a couple of the boys to give you a hand.'

With no further word of protest the girl followed Algy, and Hugh drew a breath of relief.

'Now, you ugly-looking blighter,' he remarked to the cowering ruffian, who was by this time shaking with fright, 'we come to you. How many of these rooms up here are occupied – and which?'

It appeared that only one was occupied – everyone else

was below . . . The one opposite . . . In his anxiety to please, he moved towards it; and with a quickness that would have done even Hugh credit, the American tripped him up.

'Not so blamed fast, you son of a gun,' he snapped, 'or there sure will be an accident.'

But the noise he made as he fell served a good purpose. The door of the occupied room was flung open, and a thin, weedy object clad in a flannel night-gown stood on the threshold blinking foolishly.

'Holy smoke!' spluttered the detective, after he had gazed at the apparition in stunned silence for a time. 'What, under the sun, is it?'

Hugh laughed.

'Why, it's the onion-eater; the intimidated rabbit,' he said delightedly. 'How are you, little man?'

He extended an arm, and pulled him into the passage, where he stood spluttering indignantly.

'This is an outrage, sir,' he remarked; 'a positive outrage.'

'Your legs undoubtedly are,' remarked Hugh, gazing at them dispassionately. 'Put on some trousers – and get a move on. Now you' – he jerked the other man to his feet – 'when does Lakington return?'

'Termorrow, sir,' stammered the other.

'Where is he now?'

The man hesitated for a moment, but the look in Hugh's eyes galvanized him into speech.

'He's after the old woman's pearls, sir – the Duchess of Lampshire's.'

'Ah!' returned Hugh softly. 'Of course he is. I forgot.'

'Strike me dead, guv'nor,' cringed the man, 'I never meant no 'arm – I didn't really. I'll tell you all I know, sir. I will, strite.'

'I'm quite certain you will,' said Hugh. 'And if you don't, you swine, I'll make you. When does Peterson come back?'

'Termorrow, too, sir, as far as I knows,' answered the man, and at that moment the intimidated rabbit shot rapidly out of his room, propelled by an accurate and forcible kick from Toby, who had followed him in to ensure rapidity of toilet.

'And what's he doing?' demanded Drummond.

'On the level, guv'nor, I can't tell yer. Strite, I can't; 'e can.' The man pointed to the latest arrival, who, with his nightdress tucked into his trousers, stood gasping painfully after the manner of a recently landed fish.

'I repeat, sir,' he sputtered angrily, 'that this is an outrage. By what right . . .'

'Dry up,' remarked Hugh briefly. Then he turned to the American. 'This is one of the ragged-trousered brigade I spoke to you about.'

For a while the three men studied him in silence; then the American thoughtfully transferred his chewing-gum to a fresh place.

'Wal,' he said, 'he looks like some kind o' disease; but I guess he's got a tongue. Say, flop-ears, what are you, anyway?'

'I am the secretary of a social organization which aims at the amelioration of the conditions under which the workers of the world slave,' returned the other with dignity.

'You don't say,' remarked the American unmoved. 'Do the workers of the world know about it?'

'And I again demand to know,' said the other, turning to Drummond, 'the reason for this monstrous indignity.'

'What do you know about Peterson, little man?' said Hugh, paying not the slightest attention to his protests.

'Nothing, save that he is the man whom we have been looking for, for years,' cried the other. 'The man of stupendous organizing power, who has brought together and welded into one the hundreds of societies similar to mine, who before this have each, on their own, been feebly struggling towards the light. Now we are combined, and our strength is due to him.'

Hugh exchanged glances with the American.

'Things become clearer,' he murmured. 'Tell me, little man,' he continued, 'now that you're all welded together, what do you propose to do?'

'That you shall see in good time,' cried the other triumphantly. 'Constitutional methods have failed – and, besides, we've got no time to wait for them. Millions are groaning under the intolerable bonds of the capitalist: those millions we shall free, to a life that is worthy of a man. And it will all be due to our leader – Carl Peterson.'

A look of rapt adoration came into his face, and the American laughed in genuine delight.

'Didn't I tell you, Captain, that that guy was the goods?' But there was no answering smile on Hugh's face.

'He's the goods right enough,' he answered grimly. 'But what worries me is how to stop their delivery.'

At that moment Darrell's voice came up from the hall.

'The whole bunch are stowed away, Hugh. What's the next item?'

Hugh walked to the top of the stairs.

'Bring 'em both below,' he cried over his shoulder, as he went down. A grin spread over his face as he saw half a dozen familiar faces in the hall, and he hailed them cheerily.

'Like old times, boys,' he laughed. 'Where's the driver of the lorry?'

'That's me, sir.' One of the men stepped forward. 'My mate's outside.'

'Good!' said Hugh. 'Take your bus ten miles from here: then drop that crowd one by one on the road as you go along. You can take it from me that none of 'em will say anything about it, even when they wake up. Then take her back to your garage; I'll see you later.'

'Now,' went on Hugh, as they heard the sound of the departing lorry, 'we've got to set the scene for tomorrow morning.' He glanced at his watch. 'Just eleven. How long will it take me to get the old buzz-box to Laidley Towers?'

'Laidley Towers,' echoed Darrell. 'What the devil are you going there for?'

'I just can't bear to be parted from Henry for one moment longer than necessary,' said Hugh quietly. 'And Henry is there, in a praiseworthy endeavour to lift the Duchess's pearls . . . Dear Henry!' His two fists clenched, and the American, looking at his face, laughed softly.

But it was only for a moment that Drummond indulged in the pleasures of anticipation; all that could come after. And just now there were other things to be done – many others, if events next morning were to go as they should.

'Take those two into the centre room,' he cried. 'Incidentally there's a dead Boche on the floor, but he'll come in very handy in my little scheme.'

'A dead Boche!' The intimidated rabbit gave a frightened squeak. 'Good heavens! You ruffian, this is beyond a joke.'

Hugh looked at him coldly.

'You'll find it beyond a joke, you miserable little rat,' he said quietly, 'if you speak to me like that.' He laughed as the other shrank past him. 'Three of you boys in there,' he ordered briskly, 'and if either of them gives the slightest trouble clip him over the head. Now let's have the rest of the crowd in here, Peter.'

They came filing in, and Hugh waved a cheery hand in greeting.

'How goes it, you fellows?' he cried with his infectious grin. 'Like a company powwow before popping the parapet. What! And it's a bigger show this time, boys, than any you've had over the water.' His face set grimly for a moment; then he grinned again, as he sat down on the foot of the stairs. 'Gather round, and listen to me.'

For five minutes he spoke, and his audience nodded delightedly. Apart from their love for Drummond – and three out of every four of them knew him personally – it was a scheme which tickled them to death. And he was careful to tell them just enough of the sinister design of the master-criminal to make them realize the bigness of the issue.

'That's all clear, then,' said Drummond, rising. 'Now I'm off. Toby, I want you to come, too. We ought to be there by midnight.'

'There's only one point, Captain,' remarked the American, as the group began to disperse. 'That safe – and the ledger.' He fumbled in his pocket, and produced a small india-rubber bottle. 'I've got the soup here – gelignite,' he explained, as he saw the mystified look on the other's face. 'I reckoned it might come in handy. Also a fuse and detonator.'

'Splendid!' said Hugh, 'splendid! You're an acquisition, Mr Green, to any gathering. But I think – I *think* – Lakington first. Oh! yes – most undoubtedly – Henry first!'

And once again the American laughed softly at the look on his face.

CHAPTER 11

In Which Lakington Plays
his Last 'Coup'

I

'Toby, I've got a sort of horrid feeling that the hunt is nearly over.'

With a regretful sigh Hugh swung the car out of the sleeping town of Godalming in the direction of Laidley Towers. Mile after mile dropped smoothly behind the powerful two-seater, and still Drummond's eyes wore a look of resigned sadness.

'Very nearly over,' he remarked again. 'And then once more the tedium of respectability positively stares us in the face.'

'You'll be getting married, old bean,' murmured Toby Sinclair hopefully.

For a moment his companion brightened up.

'True, O King,' he answered. 'It will ease the situation somewhat; at least I suppose so. But think of it Toby; no Lakington, no Peterson – nothing at all to play about with and keep one amused.'

'You're very certain, Hugh.' With a feeling almost of wonder Sinclair glanced at the square-jawed, ugly profile beside him. 'There's many a slip . . .'

'My dear old man,' interrupted Drummond, 'there's only one cure for the proverb-quoting disease – a dose of salts in the morning.' For a while they raced on through the warm summer's night in silence, and it was not till they were within a mile of their destination that Sinclair spoke again.

'What are you going to do with them, Hugh?'

'Who – our Carl and little Henry?' Drummond grinned gently. 'Why, I think that Carl and I will part amicably – unless, of course, he gives me any trouble. And as for Lakington – we'll have to see about Lakington.' The grin faded from his face as he spoke. 'We'll have to see about our little Henry,' he repeated softly. 'And I can't help feeling, Toby, that between us we shall find a method of ridding the earth of such a thoroughly unpleasing fellow.'

'You mean to kill him?' grunted the other non-committally.

'Just that, and no more,' responded Hugh. 'Tomorrow morning as ever is. But he's going to get the shock of his young life before it happens.'

He pulled the car up silently in the deep shadows of some trees, and the two men got out.

'Now, old boy, you take her back to The Elms. The ducal abode is close to – I remember in my extreme youth being worse than passing sick by those bushes over there after a juvenile bun-worry . . .'

'But confound it all,' spluttered Toby Sinclair. 'Don't you want me to help you?'

'I do: by taking the buzz-box back. This little show is my shout.'

Grumbling disconsolately, Sinclair stepped back into the car.

'You make me tired,' he remarked peevishly. 'I'll be damned if you get any wedding present out of me. In fact,' and he fired a Parthian shot at his leader, 'you won't have any wedding. I shall marry her myself!'

For a moment or two Hugh stood watching the car as it disappeared down the road along which they had just come, while his thoughts turned to the girl now safely asleep in his flat in London. Another week – perhaps a fortnight – but no more. Not a day more . . . And he had a pleasant conviction that Phyllis would not require much persuasion to come round to his way of thinking – even if she hadn't arrived there already . . . And so delightful was the train of thought thus conjured up, that for a while Peterson and Lakington were forgotten. The roseate dreams of the young about to wed have been known to act similarly before.

Wherefore to the soldier's instinctive second nature, trained in the war and sharpened by his grim duel with the gang, must be given the credit of preventing the ringing of the wedding-bells being postponed for good. The sudden snap of a twig close by, the sharp hiss of a compressed-air rifle, seemed simultaneous with Hugh hurling himself flat on his face behind a sheltering bush. In reality there was that fraction of a second between the actions which allowed the bullet to pass harmlessly over his body instead of finishing his career there and then. He heard it go zipping through the undergrowth as he lay motionless on the ground; then very cautiously he turned his head and peered about. A man with an ordinary revolver is at a disadvantage against someone armed with a silent gun, especially when he is not desirous of alarming the neighbourhood.

A shrub was shaking a few yards away, and on it Hugh fixed his half-closed eyes. If he lay quite still the man, whoever he was, would probably assume the shot had taken effect, and come and investigate. Then things would be easier, as two or three Boches had discovered to their cost in days gone by.

For two minutes he saw no one; then very slowly the branches parted and the white face of a man peered through. It was the chauffeur who usually drove the Rolls-Royce, and he seemed unduly anxious to satisfy himself that all was well before coming nearer. The fame of Hugh Drummond had spread abroad amongst the satellites of Peterson.

At last he seemed to make up his mind, and came out into the open. Step by step he advanced towards the motionless figure, his weapon held in readiness to shoot at the faintest movement. But the soldier lay sprawling and inert, and by the time the chauffeur had reached him there was no doubt in that worthy's mind that, at last, this wretched meddler with things that concerned him not had been laid by the heels. Which was as unfortunate for the chauffeur as it had been for unwary Huns in the past.

Contemptuously he rolled Drummond over; then noting the relaxed muscles and inert limbs, he laid his gun on the ground preparatory to running through his victim's pockets. And the fact that such an action was a little more foolish than offering a man-eating tiger a peppermint lozenge did not trouble the chauffeur. In fact, nothing troubled him again.

He got out one gasping cry of terror as he realized his mistake; then he had a blurred consciousness of the world upside down, and everything was over. It was Olaki's most dangerous throw, carried out by gripping the victim's wrists and hurling his body over by a heave of the legs. And nine times out of ten the result was a broken neck. This was one of the nine.

For a while the soldier stared at the body, frowning thoughtfully. To have killed the chauffeur was inconvenient, but since it had happened it necessitated a little

rearrangement of his plans. The moon was setting and
the night would become darker, so there was a good
chance that Lakington would not recognize that the
driver of his car had changed. And if he did – well, it
would be necessary to forgo the somewhat theatrical
entertainment he had staged for his benefit at The Elms.
Bending over the dead man, he removed his long
grey driving-coat and cap; then, without a sound, he
threaded his way through the bushes in search of the
car.

He found it about a hundred yards nearer the house, so
well hidden in a small space off the road that he was
almost on top of it before he realized the fact. To his relief
it was empty, and placing his own cap in a pocket under
the seat he put on the driving-coat of his predecessor.
Then, with a quick glance to ensure that everything was
in readiness for the immediate and rapid departure such
as he imagined Lakington would desire, he turned and
crept stealthily towards the house.

II

Laidley Towers was *en fête*. The Duchess, determined
that every conceivable stunt should be carried out which
would make for the entertainment of her guests, had
spared no pains to make the evening a success. The
Duke, bored to extinction, had been five times routed out
of his study by his indefatigable spouse, and was now, at
the moment Hugh first came in sight of the house,
engaged in shaking hands with a tall, aristocratic-looking
Indian . . .

'How-d'ye-do,' he murmured vacantly. 'What did you
say the dam' fellah's name was, my dear?' he whispered

in a hoarse undertone to the Duchess, who stood beside
him welcoming the distinguished foreigner.

'We're so glad you could come, Mr Ram Dar,' remarked the Duchess affably. 'Everyone is so looking
forward to your wonderful entertainment.' Round her
neck were the historic pearls, and as the Indian bowed
low over her outstretched hand, his eyes gleamed for a
second.

'Your Grace is too kind.' His voice was low and deep,
and he glanced thoughtfully around the circle of faces
near him. 'Maybe the sands that come from the mountains that lie beyond the everlasting snows will speak the
truth; maybe the gods will be silent. Who knows . . . who
knows?'

As if unconsciously his gaze rested on the Duke, who
manfully rose to the occasion.

'Precisely, Mr Rum Rum,' he murmured helpfully;
'who indeed? If they let you down, don't you know,
perhaps you could show us a card trick?'

He retired in confusion, abashed by the baleful stare of
the Duchess, and the rest of the guests drew closer. The
jazz band was having supper; the last of the perspiring
tenants had departed, and now the bonne-bouche of the
evening was about to begin.

It had been the Marquis of Laidley himself who had
suggested getting hold of this most celebrated performer,
who had apparently never been in England before. And
since the Marquis of Laidley's coming-of-age was the
cause of the whole evening's entertainment, his suggestion had been hailed with acclamation. How he had
heard about the Indian, and from whom, were points
about which he was very vague; but since he was a very
vague young man, the fact elicited no comment. The
main thing was that here, in the flesh, was a dark,

mysterious performer of the occult, and what more could a house party require? And in the general excitement Hugh Drummond crept closer to the open window. It was the Duchess he was concerned with and her pearls, and the arrival of the Indian was not going to put him off his guard . . . Then suddenly his jaw tightened: Irma Peterson had entered the room with young Laidley.

'Do you want anything done, Mr Ram Dar?' asked the Duchess – 'the lights down or the window shut?'

'No, I thank you,' returned the Indian. 'The night is still; there is no wind. And the night is dark – dark with strange thoughts, that thronged upon me as I drew nigh to the house – whispering through the trees.' Again he fixed his eyes on the Duke. 'What is your pleasure, Protector of the Poor?'

'Mine?' cried that pillar of the House of Lords, hurriedly stifling a yawn. 'Any old thing, my dear fellow . . . You'd much better ask one of the ladies.'

'As you will,' returned the other gravely; 'but if the gods speak the truth, and the sand does not lie, I can but say what is written.'

From a pocket in his robe he took a bag and two small bronze dishes, and placing them on a table stood waiting.

'I am ready,' he announced. 'Who first will learn of the things that are written on the scroll of Fate?'

'I say, hadn't you better do it in private, Mr Rum?' murmured the Duke apprehensively. 'I mean, don't you know, it might be a little embarrassing if the jolly old gods really did give tongue; and I don't see anybody getting killed in the rush.'

'Is there so much to conceal?' demanded the Indian, glancing round the group, contempt in his brooding eyes. 'In the lands that lie beyond the snows we have nothing to conceal. There is nothing that can be concealed, because all is known.'

And it was at that moment that the intent watcher outside the window began to shake with silent mirth. For the face was the face of the Indian, Ram Dar, but the voice was the voice of Lakington. It struck him that the next ten minutes or so might be well worthwhile. The problem of removing the pearls from the Duchess's neck before such an assembly seemed to present a certain amount of difficulty even to such an expert as Henry. And Hugh crept a little nearer the window, so as to miss nothing. He crept near enough, in fact, to steal a look at Irma, and in doing so saw something which made him rub his eyes and then grin once more. She was standing on the outskirts of the group, an evening wrap thrown loosely over her arm. She edged a step or two towards a table containing bric-à-brac, the centre of which was occupied, as the place of honour, by a small inlaid Chinese cabinet – a box standing on four grotesquely carved legs. It was a beautiful ornament, and he dimly remembered having heard its history – a story which reflected considerable glory on the predatory nature of a previous Duke. At the moment, however, he was not concerned with its past history, but with its present fate; and it was the consummate quickness of the girl that made him rub his eyes.

She took one lightning glance at the other guests who were craning eagerly forward round the Indian; then she half dropped her wrap on the table and picked it up again. It was done so rapidly, so naturally, that for a while Hugh thought he had made a mistake. And then a slight rearrangement of her wrap to conceal a hard outline beneath, as she joined the others, dispelled any doubts. The small inlaid Chinese cabinet now standing on the table was not the one that had been there previously. The original was under Irma Peterson's cloak . . .

Evidently the scene was now set – the necessary props were in position – and Hugh waited with growing impatience for the principal event. But the principal performer seemed in no hurry. In fact, in his dry way Lakington was thoroughly enjoying himself. An intimate inside knowledge of the skeletons that rattled their bones in the cupboards of most of those present enabled the gods to speak with disconcerting accuracy; and as each victim insisted on somebody new facing the sands that came from beyond the mountains, the performance seemed likely to last indefinitely.

At last a sudden delighted burst of applause came from the group, announcing the discomfiture of yet another guest, and with it Lakington seemed to tire of the amusement. Engrossed though he was in the anticipation of the main item which was still to be staged, Drummond could not but admire the extraordinary accuracy of the character study. Not a detail had been overlooked; not a single flaw in Lakington's acting could he notice. It *was* an Indian who stood there, and when a few days later Hugh returned her pearls to the Duchess, for a long time neither she nor her husband would believe that Ram Dar had been an Englishman disguised. And when they had at last been persuaded of that fact, and had been shown the two cabinets side by side, it was the consummate boldness of the crime, coupled with its extreme simplicity, that staggered them. For it was only in the reconstruction of it that the principal beauty of the scheme became apparent. The element of luck was reduced to a minimum, and at no stage of the proceedings was it impossible, should things go amiss, for Lakington to go as he had come, a mere Indian entertainer. Without the necklace, true, in such an event; but unsuspected, and free to try again. As befitted his last, it was perhaps his greatest effort . . . And this was what happened as seen by the fascinated onlooker crouching near the window outside.

Superbly disdainful, the Indian tipped back his sand into the little bag, and replacing it in his pocket, stalked to the open window. With arms outstretched he stared into the darkness, seeming to gather strength from the gods whom he served.

'Do your ears not hear the whisperings of the night?' he demanded. 'Life rustling in the leaves; death moaning through the grasses.' And suddenly he threw back his head and laughed, a fierce, mocking laugh; then he swung round and faced the room. For a while he stood motionless, and Hugh, from the shelter of the bushes, wondered whether the two quick flashes that had come from his robe as he spoke – flashes such as a small electric torch will give, and which were unseen by anyone else – were a signal to the defunct chauffeur.

Then a peculiar look came over the Indian's face, as his eyes fell on the Chinese cabinet.

'Where did the Protector of the Poor obtain the sacred cabinet of the Chow Kings?' He peered at it reverently, and the Duke coughed.

'One of my ancestors picked it up somewhere,' he answered apologetically.

'Fashioned with the blood of men, guarded with their lives, and one of your ancestors picked it up!' The Duke withered completely under the biting scorn of the words, and seemed about to say something, but the Indian had turned away, and his long, delicate fingers were hovering over the box. 'There is power in this box,' he continued, and his voice was low and thoughtful. 'Years ago a man who came from the land where dwells the Great Brooding Spirit told me of this thing. I wonder . . . I wonder . . .'

With gleaming eyes he stared in front of him, and a woman shuddered audibly.

'What is it supposed to do?' she ventured timidly.

'In that box lies the power unknown to mortal man though the priests of the Temple City have sometimes discovered it before they pass beyond. Length you know, and height, and breadth – but in that box lies more.'

'You don't mean the fourth dimension, do you?' demanded a man incredulously.

'I know not what you call it, sahib,' said the Indian quietly. 'But it is the power which renders visible or invisible at will.'

For a moment Hugh felt an irresistible temptation to shout the truth through the window, and give Lakington away; then his curiosity to see the next move in the game conquered the wish, and he remained silent. So perfect was the man's acting that, in spite of having seen the substitution of the boxes, in spite of knowing the whole thing was bunkum, he felt he could almost believe it himself. And as for the others – without exception – they were craning forward eagerly, staring first at the Indian and then at the box.

'I say, that's a bit of a tall order, isn't it, Mr Rum Bar?' protested the Duke a little feebly. 'Do you mean to say you can put something into that box, and it disappears?'

'From mortal eye, Protector of the Poor, though it is still there,' answered the Indian. 'And that only too for a time. Then it reappears again. So runs the legend.'

'Well, stuff something in and let's see,' cried young Laidley, starting forward, only to pause before the Indian's outstretched arm.

'Stop, sahib,' he ordered sternly. 'To you that box is nothing; to others – of whom I am one of the least – it is sacred beyond words.' He stalked away from the table, and the guests' disappointment showed on their faces.

'Oh, but Mr Ram Dar,' pleaded the Duchess, 'can't you satisfy our curiosity after all you've said?'

For a moment he seemed on the point of refusing outright; then he bowed, a deep oriental bow.

'Your Grace,' he said with dignity, 'for centuries that box contained the jewels – precious beyond words – of the reigning Queens of the Chow Dynasty. They were wrapped in silver and gold tissue – of which this is a feeble, modern substitute.'

From a cummerbund under his robe he drew a piece of shining material, the appearance of which was greeted with cries of feminine delight.

'You would not ask me to commit sacrilege?' Quietly he replaced the material in his belt and turned away, and Hugh's eyes glistened at the cleverness with which the man was acting. Whether they believed it or not, there was not a soul in the room by this time who was not consumed with eagerness to put the Chinese cabinet to the test.

'Supposing you took my pearls, Mr Ram Dar,' said the Duchess diffidently. 'I know that compared to such historic jewels they are poor, but perhaps it would not be sacrilege.'

Not a muscle on Lakington's face twitched, though it was the thing he had been playing for. Instead he seemed to be sunk in thought, while the Duchess continued pleading, and the rest of the party added their entreaties. At length she undid the fastening and held the necklace out, but he only shook his head.

'You ask a great thing of me, your Grace,' he said.

'Only by the exercise of my power can I show you this secret – even if I can show you at all. And you are unbelievers.' He paced slowly to the window, ostensibly to commune with the gods on the subject; more materially to flash once again the signal into the darkness. Then, as if he had decided suddenly, he swung round.

'I will try,' he announced briefly, and the Duchess headed the chorus of delight. 'Will the Presences stand back, and you, your Grace, take that?' He handed her the piece of material. 'No hand but yours must touch the pearls. Wrap them up inside the silver and gold.' Aloofly he watched the process. 'Now advance alone, and open the box. Place the pearls inside. Now shut and lock it.' Obediently the Duchess did as she was bid; then she stood waiting for further instructions.

But apparently by this time the Great Brooding Spirit was beginning to take effect. Singing a monotonous, harsh chant, the Indian knelt on the floor, and poured some powder into a little brazier. He was still close to the open window, and finally he sat down with his elbows on his knees, and his head rocking to and fro in his hands.

'Less light – less light!' The words seemed to come from a great distance – ventriloquism in a mild way was one of Lakington's accomplishments; and as the lights went out a greenish, spluttering flame rose from the brazier. A heavy, odorous smoke filled the room, but framed and motionless in the eerie light sat the Indian, staring fixedly in front of him. After a time the chant began again: it grew and swelled in volume till the singer grew frenzied and beat his head with his hands. Then abruptly it stopped.

'Place the box upon the floor,' he ordered, 'in the light of the Sacred fire.' Hugh saw the Duchess kneel down on the opposite side of the brazier, and place the box on the floor, while the faces of the guests – strange and ghostly in the green light – peered like spectres out of the heavy smoke. This was undoubtedly a show worth watching.

'Open the box!' Harshly the words rang through the silent room, and with fingers that trembled a little the Duchess turned the key and threw back the lid.

'Why, it's empty!' she cried in amazement, and the guests craned forward to look.

'Put not your hand inside,' cried the Indian in sudden warning, 'or perchance it will remain empty.'

The Duchess rapidly withdrew her hand, and stared incredulously through the smoke at his impassive face.

'Did I not say that there was power in the box?' he said dreamily. 'The power to render invisible – the power to render visible. Thus came protection to the jewels of the Chow Queens.'

'That's all right, Mr Ram Dar,' said the Duchess a little apprehensively. 'There may be power in the box, but my pearls don't seem to be.'

The Indian laughed.

'None but you has touched the cabinet, your Grace; none but you must touch it till the pearls return. They are there now; but not for mortal eyes to see.'

Which, incidentally, was no more than the truth.

'Look, oh! sahibs, look; but do not touch. See that to your vision the box is empty . . .' He waited motionless, while the guests thronged round, with expressions of amazement; and Hugh, safe from view in the thick, sweet-smelling smoke, came even nearer in his excitement.

'It is enough,' cried the Indian suddenly. 'Shut the box, your Grace, and lock it as before. Now place it on the table whence it came. Is it there?'

'Yes.' The Duchess's voice came out of the green fog.

'Go not too near,' he continued warningly. 'The gods must have space – the gods must have space.'

Again the harsh chant began, at times swelling to a shout, at times dying away to a whisper. And it was during one of these latter periods that a low laugh, instantly checked, disturbed the room. It was plainly audible, and someone irritably said, 'Be quiet!' It was not repeated, which afforded Hugh, at any rate, no surprise. For it had been Irma Peterson who had laughed, and it might have been hilarity, or it might have been a signal.

The chanting grew frenzied and more frenzied; more and more powder was thrown on the brazier till dense clouds of the thick vapour were rolling through the room, completely obscuring everything save the small space round the brazier, and the Indian's tense face poised above it.

'Bring the box, your Grace,' he cried harshly, and once more the Duchess knelt in the circle of light, with a row of dimly seen faces above her.

'Open; but as you value your pearls – touch them not.' Excitedly she threw back the lid, and a chorus of cries greeted the appearance of the gold and silver tissue at the bottom of the box.

'They're here, Mr Ram Dar.'

In the green light the Indian's sombre eyes stared round the group of dim faces.

'Did I not say,' he answered, 'that there was power in the box? But in the name of that power – unknown to you – I warn you: do not touch those pearls till the light has burned low in the brazier. If you do they will disappear – never to return. Watch, but do not touch!'

Slowly he backed towards the window, unperceived in the general excitement; and Hugh dodged rapidly towards the car. It struck him that the seance was over, and he just had time to see Lakington snatch something which appeared to have been let down by a string from above, before turning into the bushes and racing for the car. As it was, he was only a second or two in front of the other, and the last vision he had through a break in the trees, before they were spinning smoothly down the deserted road, was an open window in Laidley Towers from which dense volumes of vapour poured steadily out. Of the house party behind, waiting for the light to burn low in the brazier, he could see no sign through the opaque wall of green fog.

It took five minutes, so he gathered afterwards from a member of the house party, before the light had burned sufficiently low for the Duchess to consider it safe to touch the pearls. In various stages of asphyxiation the assembled guests had peered at the box, while the cynical comments of the men were rightly treated by the ladies with the contempt they deserved. Was the necklace not there, wrapped in its gold and silver tissue, where a few minutes before there had been nothing?

'Some trick of that beastly light,' remarked the Duke peevishly. 'For Heaven's sake throw the dam' thing out of the window.'

'Don't be a fool, John,' retorted his spouse. 'If you could do this sort of thing, the House of Lords might be some use to somebody.'

And when two minutes later they stared horror-struck at a row of ordinary marbles laboriously unwrapped from a piece of gold and silver tissue, the Duke's pungent agreement with his wife's sentiment passed uncontradicted. In fact, it is to be understood that over the scene which followed it was best to draw a decent veil.

III

Drummond, hunched low over the wheel, in his endeavour to conceal his identity from the man behind, knew nothing of that at the time. Every nerve was centred on eluding the pursuit he thought was a certainty; for the thought of Lakington, when everything was prepared for his reception, being snatched from his clutches even by the majesty of the law was more than he could bear. And for much the same reason he did not want to have to deal with him until The Elms was reached; the staging there was so much more effective.

But Lakington was far too busy to bother with the chauffeur.

One snarling curse as they had entered, for not having done as he had been told, was the total of their conversation during the trip. During the rest of the time the transformation to the normal kept Lakington busy, and Hugh could see him reflected in the windscreen removing the make-up from his face, and changing his clothes.

Even now he was not quite clear how the trick had been worked. That there had been two cabinets, that was clear – one false, the other the real one. That they had been changed at the crucial moment by the girl Irma was also obvious. But how had the pearls disappeared in the first case, and then apparently reappeared again? For of one thing he was quite certain. Whatever was inside the parcel of gold and silver tissue which, for all he knew, they might be still staring at, it was not the historic necklace.

And he was still puzzling it over in his mind when the car swung into the drive at The Elms.

'Change the wheels as usual,' snapped Lakington as he got out, and Hugh bent forward to conceal his face. 'Then report to me in the central room.'

And out of the corner of his eye Hugh watched him enter the house with one of the Chinese cabinets clasped in his hand . . .

'Toby,' he remarked to that worthy, whom he found mournfully eating a ham sandwich in the garage, 'I feel sort of sorry for our Henry. He's just had the whole complete ducal outfit guessing, dressed up as an Indian; he's come back here with a box containing the Duchess's pearls or I'll eat my hat, and feeling real good with himself; and now instead of enjoying life he's got to have a little chat with me.'

'Did you drive him back?' demanded Sinclair, producing a bottle of Bass.

'Owing to the sudden decease of his chauffeur I had to,' murmured Hugh. 'And he's very angry over something. Let's go on the roof.'

Silently they both climbed the ladder which had been placed in readiness, to find Peter Darrell and the American detective already in position. A brilliant light streamed out through the glass dome, and the inside of the central room was clearly visible.

'He's already talked to what he thinks is you,' whispered Peter ecstatically, 'and he is not in the best of tempers.'

Hugh glanced down, and a grim smile flickered round his lips. In the three chairs sat the motionless, bound figures, so swathed in rope that only the tops of their heads were visible, just as Lakington had left him and Toby and Algy earlier in the evening. The only moving thing in the room was the criminal himself, and at the moment he was seated at the table with the Chinese cabinet in front of him. He seemed to be doing something inside with a penknife, and all the time he kept up a running commentary to the three bound figures.

'Well, you young swine, have you enjoyed your night?' A feeble moan came from one of the chairs. 'Spirit broken at last, is it?' With a quick turn of his wrist he prised open two flaps of wood, and folded them back against the side. Then he lifted out a parcel of gold and silver tissue from underneath.

'My hat!' muttered Hugh. 'What a fool I was not to think of it! Just a false bottom actuated by closing the lid. And a similar parcel in the other cabinet.'

But the American, whistling gently to himself, had his eyes fixed on the rope of wonderful pearls which Lakington was holding lovingly in his hands.

'So easy, you scum,' continued Lakington, 'and you thought to pit yourself against me. Though if it hadn't been for Irma' – he rose and stood in front of the chair where he had last left Drummond – 'it might have been awkward. She was quick, Captain Drummond, and that fool of a chauffeur failed to carry out my orders, and create a diversion. You will see what happens to people who failed to carry out my orders in a minute. And after that you'll never see anything again.'

'Say, he's a dream – that guy,' muttered the American. 'What pearls are those he's got?'

'The Duchess of Lampshire's,' whispered Hugh. 'Lifted right under the noses of the whole bally house party.'

With a grunt the detective rearranged his chewing-gum; then once more the four watchers on the roof glued their eyes to the glass. And the sight they saw a moment or two afterwards stirred even the phlegmatic Mr Green.

A heavy door was swinging slowly open, apparently of its own volition, though Hugh, stealing a quick glance at Lakington, saw that he was pressing some small studs in a niche in one of the walls. Then he looked back at the door, and stared dumbfounded. It was the mysterious cupboard of which Phyllis had spoken to him, but nothing he had imagined from her words had prepared him for the reality. It seemed to be literally crammed to overflowing with the most priceless loot. Gold vessels of fantastic and beautiful shapes littered the floor; while on the shelves were arranged the most wonderful collection of precious stones, which shone and scintillated in the electric light till their glitter almost blinded the watchers.

'Shades of Chu Chin Chow, Ali Baba and the forty pundits!' muttered Toby. 'The dam' man's a genius.'

The pearls were carefully placed in a position of honour, and for a few moments Lakington stood gloating over his collection.

'Do you see them, Captain Drummond?' he asked quietly. 'Each thing obtained by my brain – my hands. All mine – mine!' His voice rose to a shout. 'And you pit your puny wits against me.' With a laugh he crossed the room, and once more pressed the studs. The door swung slowly to and closed without a sound, while Lakington still shook with silent mirth.

'And now,' he resumed, rubbing his hands, 'we will prepare your bath, Captain Drummond.' He walked over to the shelves where the bottles were ranged, and busied himself with some preparations. 'And while it is getting ready, we will just deal with the chauffeur who neglected his orders.'

For a few minutes he bent over the chemicals, and then he poured the mixture into the water which half filled the long bath at the end of the room. A faintly acid smell rose to the four men above, and the liquid turned a pale green.

'I told you I had all sorts of baths, didn't I?' continued Lakington; 'some for those who are dead, and some for those who are alive. This is the latter sort, and has the great advantage of making the bather wish it was one of the former.' He stirred the liquid gently with a long glass rod. 'About five minutes before we're quite ready,' he announced. 'Just time for the chauffeur.'

He went to a speaking-tube, down which he blew. Somewhat naturally there was no answer, and Lakington frowned.

'A stupid fellow,' he remarked softly. 'But there is no hurry; I will deal with him later.'

'You certainly will,' muttered Hugh on the roof. 'And perhaps not quite so much later as you think, friend Henry.'

But Lakington had returned to the chair which contained, as he thought, his chief enemy, and was standing beside it with an unholy joy shining on his face.

'And since I have to deal with him later, Captain Drummond, DSO, MC, I may as well deal with you now. Then it will be your friend's turn. I am going to cut the ropes, and carry you, while you're so numbed that you can't move, to the bath. Then I shall drop you in, Captain Drummond, and when afterwards, you pray for death, I shall mercifully spare your life – for a while.'

He slashed at the ropes behind the chair, and the four men craned forward expectantly.

'There,' snarled Lakington. 'I'm ready for you, you young swine.'

And even as he spoke, the words died away on his lips, and with a dreadful cry he sprang back. For with a dull, heavy thud the body of the dead German Heinrich rolled off the chair and sprawled at his feet.

'My God!' screamed Lakington. 'What has happened? I – I –'

He rushed to the bell and pealed it frantically, and with a smile of joy Hugh watched his frenzied terror. No one came in answer to the ring, and Lakington dashed to the door, only to recoil into the room with a choking noise in his throat. Outside in the hall stood four masked men, each with a revolver pointing at his heart.

'My cue,' muttered Hugh. 'And you understand, fellows, don't you? – he's my meat.'

The next moment he had disappeared down the ladder, and the three remaining watchers stared motionless at the grim scene. For Lakington had shut the door and was crouching by the table, his nerve utterly gone. And all the while the puffed, bloated body of the German sprawled on the floor . . .

Slowly the door into the hall opened, and with a scream of fear Lakington sprang back. Standing in the doorway was Hugh Drummond, and his face was grim and merciless.

'You sent for your chauffeur, Henry Lakington,' he remarked quietly. 'I am here.'

'What do you mean?' muttered Lakington thickly.

'I drove you back from Laidley Towers tonight,' said Hugh with a slight smile. 'The proper man was foolish and had to be killed.' He advanced a few steps into the room, and the other shrank back. 'You look frightened, Henry. Can it be that the young swine's wits are, after all, better than yours?'

'What do you want?' gasped Lakington, through dry lips.

'I want you, Henry – just you. Hitherto, you've always used gangs of your ruffians against me. Now my gang occupies this house. But I'm not going to use them. It's going to be just – you and I. Stand up, Henry, stand up – as I have always stood up to you.' He crossed the room and stood in front of the cowering man.

'Take half – take half,' he screamed. 'I've got treasure – I've . . .'

And Drummond hit him a fearful blow on the mouth.

'I shall take all, Henry, to return to their rightful owners. Boys' – he raised his voice – 'carry out these other two, and undo them.'

The four masked men came in, and carried out the two chairs.

'The intimidated rabbit, Henry, and the kindly gentleman you put to guard Miss Benton,' he remarked as the door closed. 'So now we may regard ourselves as being alone. Just you and I. And one of us, Lakington – you devil in human form – is going into that bath.'

'But the bath means death,' shrieked Lakington – 'death in agony.'

'That will be unfortunate for the one who goes in,' said Drummond, taking a step towards him.

'You would murder me?' half sobbed the terrified man.

'No, Lakington; I'm not going to murder you.' A gleam of hope came into the other's eyes. 'But I'm going to fight you in order to decide which of us two ceases to adorn the earth; that is, if your diagnosis of the contents of the bath is correct. What little gleam of pity I might have possessed for you has been completely extinguished by your present exhibition of nauseating cowardice. Fight, you worm, fight; or I'll throw you in!'

And Lakington fought. The sudden complete turning of the tables had for the moment destroyed his nerve; now, at Drummond's words, he recovered himself. There was no mercy on the soldier's face, and in his inmost heart Lakington knew that the end had come. For strong and wiry though he was, he was no match for the other.

Relentlessly he felt himself being forced towards the deadly liquid he had prepared for Drummond, and as the irony of the thing struck him, the sweat broke out on his forehead and he cursed aloud. At last he backed into the edge of the bath, and his struggles redoubled. But still there was no mercy on the soldier's face, and he felt himself being forced further and further over the liquid until he was only held from falling into it by Drummond's grip on his throat.

Then, just before the grip relaxed and he went under, the soldier spoke once:

'Henry Lakington,' he said, 'the retribution is just.'

Drummond sprang back, and the liquid closed over the wretched man's head. But only for a second. With a dreadful cry, Lakington leapt out, and even Drummond felt a momentary qualm of pity. For the criminal's clothes were already burnt through to the skin, and his face – or what was left of it – was a shining copper colour. Mad with agony, he dashed to the door, and flung it open. The four men outside, aghast at the spectacle, recoiled and let him through. And the kindly mercy which Lakington had never shown to anyone in his life was given to him at the last.

Blindly he groped his way up the stairs, and as Drummond got to the door the end came. Someone must have put in gear the machinery which worked on the fifth step, or perhaps it was automatic. For suddenly a heavy steel weight revolving on an arm whizzed out from the wall and struck Lakington behind the neck. Without a sound he fell forward, and the weight unchecked, clanged sullenly home. And thus did the invention of which he was proudest break the inventor's own neck. Truly, the retribution was just . . .

'That only leaves Peterson,' remarked the American coming into the hall at that moment, and lighting a cigar.

'That only leaves Peterson,' agreed Drummond. 'And the girl,' he added as an afterthought.

CHAPTER 12

In Which the Last Round
Takes Place

I

It was during the next hour or two that the full value of
Mr Jerome K. Green as an acquisition to the party became
apparent. Certain other preparations in honour of Peterson's arrival were duly carried out, and then arose the
question of the safe in which the all-important ledger was
kept.

'There it is,' said Drummond, pointing to a heavy steel
door flush with the wall, on the opposite side of the room
to the big one containing Lakington's ill-gotten treasure.
'And it doesn't seem to me that you're going to open that
one by pressing any buttons in the wall.'

'Then, Captain,' drawled the American, 'I guess we'll
open it otherwise. It's sure plumb easy. I've been getting
gay with some of the household effects, and this bar of
soap sort of caught my eye.'

From his pocket he produced some ordinary yellow
soap, and the others glanced at him curiously.

'I'll just give you a little demonstration,' he continued,
'of how our swell cracksmen over the water open safes
when the owners have been so tactless as to remove the
keys.'

Dexterously he proceeded to seal up every crack in the
safe door with the soap, leaving a small gap at the top

unsealed. Then round that gap he built what was to all intents and purposes a soap dam.

'If any of you boys,' he remarked to the intent group around him, 'think of taking this up as a means of livelihood, be careful of this stuff.' From another pocket he produced an india-rubber bottle. 'Don't drop it on the floor if you want to be measured for your coffin. There'll just be a boot and some bits to bury.'

The group faded away, and the American laughed.

'Might I ask what it is?' murmured Hugh politely from the neighbourhood of the door.

'Sure thing, Captain,' returned the detective, carefully pouring some of the liquid into the soap dam. 'This is what I told you I'd got – gelignite; or, as the boys call it, the oil. It runs right round the cracks of the door inside the soap.' He added a little more, and carefully replaced the stopper in the bottle. 'Now a detonator and a bit of fuse, and I guess we'll leave the room.'

'It reminds one of those dreadful barbarians the Sappers, trying to blow up things,' remarked Toby, stepping with some agility into the garden; and a moment or two later the American joined them.

'It may be necessary to do it again,' he announced, and as he spoke the sound of a dull explosion came from inside the house. 'On the other hand,' he continued, going back into the room and quietly pulling the safe door open, 'it may not. There's your book, Captain.'

He calmly relit his cigar as if safe opening was the most normal undertaking, and Drummond lifted out the heavy ledger and placed it on the table.

'Go out in relays, boys,' he said to the group of men by the door, 'And get your breakfasts. I'm going to be busy for a bit.'

He sat down at the table and began to turn the pages.

The American was amusing himself with the faked Chinese cabinet; Toby and Peter sprawled in two chairs, unashamedly snoring. And after a while the detective put down the cabinet, and coming over, sat at Drummond's side.

Every page contained an entry – sometimes half a dozen – of the same type, and as the immensity of the project dawned on the two men their faces grew serious.

'I told you he was a big man, Captain,' remarked the American, leaning back in his chair and looking at the open book through half-closed eyes.

'One can only hope to heaven that we're in time,' returned Hugh. 'Damn it, man,' he exploded, 'surely the police must know of this!'

The American closed his eyes still more.

'Your English police know most things,' he drawled, 'but you've sort of got some peculiar laws in your country. With us, if we don't like a man – something happens. He kind o' ceases to sit up and take nourishment. But over here, the more scurrilous he is, the more he talks bloodshed and riot, the more constables does he get to guard him from catching cold.'

The soldier frowned.

'Look at this entry here,' he grunted. 'That blighter is a Member of Parliament. What's he getting four payments of a thousand pounds for?'

'Why, surely, to buy some nice warm underclothes with,' grinned the detective. Then he leaned forward and glanced at the name. 'But isn't he some pot in one of your big trade unions?'

'Heaven knows,' grunted Hugh. 'I only saw the blighter once, and then his shirt was dirty.' He turned over a few more pages thoughtfully. 'Why, if these are the sums of money Peterson has blown, the man must have spent a fortune. Two thousand pounds to Ivolsky. Incidentally, that's the bloke who had words with the whatnot on the stairs.'

In silence they continued their study of the book. The whole of England and Scotland had been split up into districts, regulated by population rather than area, and each district appeared to be in the charge of one director. A varying number of sub-districts in every main division had each their sub-director and staff, and at some of the names Drummond rubbed his eyes in amazement. Briefly, the duties of every man were outlined: the local-ity in which his work lay, his exact responsibilities, so that overlapping was reduced to a minimum. In each case the staff was small, the work largely that of organization. But in each district there appeared ten or a dozen names of men who were euphemistically described as lecturers; while at the end of the book there appeared nearly fifty names – both of men and women – who were proudly denoted as first-class general lecturers. And if Drum-mond had rubbed his eyes at some of the names on the organizing staffs, the first-class general lecturers dep-rived him of speech.

'Why,' he spluttered after a moment, 'a lot of these people's names are absolute household words in the country. They may be swine – they probably are. Thank God! I've very rarely met any; but they ain't criminals.'

'No more is Peterson,' grinned the American; 'at least not on that book. See here, Captain, it's pretty clear what's happening. In any country today you've got all sorts and conditions of people with more wind than brain. They just can't stop talking, and as yet it's not a criminal offence. Some of 'em believe what they say, like Spindleshanks upstairs; some of 'em don't. And if they don't, it makes 'em worse: they start writing as well.

You've got clever men, intellectual men – look at some of those guys in the first-class general lecturers – and they're the worst of the lot. Then you've got another class – the men with the business brain, who think they're getting the sticky end of it, and use the talkers to pull the chestnuts out of the fire for them. And the chestnuts, who are the poor blamed decent working-men, are promptly dropped in the ash-pit to keep 'em quiet. They all want something for nothing, and I guess it can't be done. They all think they're fooling one another, and what's really going at the moment is that Peterson is fooling the whole bunch. He wants all the strings in his hands, and it looks to me as if he'd got 'em there. He's got the money – and we know where he got it from; he's got the organization – all either red-hot revolutionaries, or intellectual windstorms, or calculating knaves. He's amalgamated 'em, Captain; and the whole blamed lot, whatever they may think, are really working for him.'

Drummond, thoughtfully, lit a cigarette.

'Working towards a revolution in this country,' he remarked quietly.

'Sure thing,' answered the American. 'And when he brings it off, I guess you won't catch Peterson for dust. He'll pocket the boodle, and the boobs will stew in their own juice. I guessed it in Paris; that book makes it a certainty. But it ain't criminal. In a Court of Law he could swear it was an organization for selling birdseed.'

For a while Drummond smoked in silence, while the two sleepers shifted uneasily in their chairs. It all seemed so simple in spite of the immensity of the scheme. Like most normal Englishmen, politics and labour disputes had left him cold in the past; but no one who ever glanced at a newspaper could be ignorant of the volcano that had been simmering just beneath the surface for years past.

'Not one in a hundred' – the American's voice broke into his train of thought – 'of the so-called revolutionary leaders in this country are disinterested, Captain. They're out for Number One, and when they've talked the boys into bloody murder, and your existing social system is down-and-out, they'll be the leaders in the new one. That's what they're playing for – power; and when they've got it, God help the men who gave it to 'em.'

Drummond nodded, and lit another cigarette. Odd things he had read recurred to him: trade unions refusing to allow discharged soldiers to join them; the reiterated threats of direct action. And to what end?

A passage in a part of the ledger evidently devoted to extracts from the speeches of the first-class general lecturers caught his eye:

'To me, the big fact of modern life is the war between classes . . . People declare that the method of direct action inside a country will produce a revolution. I agree . . . it involves the creation of an army.'

And beside the cutting was a note by Peterson in red ink:

'An excellent man! Send for protracted tour.'

The note of exclamation appealed to Hugh; he could see the writer's tongue in his cheek as he put it in.

'It involves the creation of an army . . .' The words of the intimidated rabbit came back to his mind. 'The man of stupendous organizing power, who has brought together and welded into one the hundreds of societies similar to mine, who before this have each, on their own, been feebly struggling towards the light. Now we are combined, and our strength is due to him.'

In other words, the army was on the road to completion, an army where ninety per cent of the fighters – duped by the remaining ten – would struggle blindly towards a dim, half-understood goal, only to find out too late that the whip of Solomon had been exchanged for the scorpion of his son . . .

'Why can't they be made to understand, Mr Green?' he cried bitterly. 'The working-man – the decent fellow –'

The American thoughtfully picked his teeth.

'Has anyone tried to make 'em understand, Captain? I guess I'm no intellectual guy, but there was a French writer fellow – Victor Hugo – who wrote something that sure hit the nail in the head. I copied it out, for it seemed good to me.' From his pocket-book he produced a slip of paper. '"The faults of women, children, servants, the weak, the indigent, and the ignorant are the faults of husbands, father, masters, the strong, the rich, and the learned." Wal!' he leaned back in his chair, 'there you are. Their proper leaders have sure failed them, so they're running after that bunch of cross-eyed skaters. And sitting here, watching 'em run, and laughing fit to beat the band, is your pal, Peterson!'

It was at that moment that the telephone bell rang, after a slight hesitation Hugh picked up the receiver.

'Very well,' he grunted, after listening for a while. 'I will tell him.'

He replaced the receiver and turned to the American.

'Mr Ditchling will be here for the meeting at two, and Peterson will be late,' he announced slowly.

'What's Ditchling when he's at home?' asked the other.

'One of the so-called leaders,' answered Hugh briefly turning over the pages of the ledger. 'Here's his dossier, according to Peterson. "Ditchling, Charles. Good speaker; clever; unscrupulous. Requires big money; worth it. Drinks."'

For a while they stared at the brief summary, and then the American burst into a guffaw of laughter.

'The mistake you've made, Captain, in this county is not giving Peterson a seat in your Cabinet. He'd have the whole caboose eating out of his hand; and if you paid him a few hundred thousands a year, he might run straight and grow pigs as a hobby . . .'

II

It was a couple of hours later that Hugh rang up his rooms in Half Moon Street. From Algy, who spoke to him, he gathered that Phyllis and her father were quite safe, though the latter was suffering in the manner common to the morning after. But he also found out another thing – that Ted Jerningham had just arrived with the hapless Potts in tow, who was apparently sufficiently recovered to talk sense. He was still weak and dazed, but no longer imbecile.

'Tell Ted to bring him down to The Elms at once,' ordered Hugh. 'There's a compatriot of his here, waiting to welcome him with open arms.'

'Potts is coming, Mr Green,' he said, putting down the receiver. 'Our Hiram C. And he's talking sense. It seems to me that we may get a little light thrown on the activities of Mr Hocking and Herr Steinemann, and the other bloke.'

The American nodded slowly.

'Von Gratz,' he said. 'I remember his name now. Steel man. Maybe you're right, Captain, and that he knows something; anyway, I guess Hiram C. Potts and I stick closer than brothers till I restore him to the bosom of his family.'

But Mr Potts, when he did arrive, exhibited no great inclination to stick close to the detective; in fact, he showed the greatest reluctance to enter the house at all. As Algy had said, he was still weak and dazed, and the sight of the place where he had suffered so much produced such an effect on him that for a while Hugh feared he was going to have a relapse. At length, however, he seemed to get back his confidence, and was persuaded to come into the central room.

'It's all right, Mr Potts,' Drummond assured him over and over again. 'Their gang is dispersed, and Lakington is dead. We're all friends here now. You're quite safe. This is Mr Green, who has come over from New York especially to find you and take you back to your family.'

The millionaire stared in silence at the detective, who rolled his cigar round in his mouth.

'That's right, Mr Potts. There's the little old sign.' He threw back his coat, showing the police badge, and the millionaire nodded. 'I guess you've had things humming on the other side, and if it hadn't been for the Captain here and his friends they'd be humming still.'

'I am obliged to you, sir,' said the American, speaking for the first time to Hugh. The words were slow and hesitating, as if he was not quite sure of his speech. 'I seem to remember your face,' he continued, 'as part of the awful nightmare I've suffered the last few days – or is it weeks? I seem to remember having seen you, and you were always kind.'

'That's all over now, Mr Potts,' said Hugh gently. 'You got into the clutches of the most infernal gang of swine, and we've been trying to get you out again.' He looked at him quietly. 'Do you think you can remember enough to tell us what happened at the beginning? Take your time,' he urged. 'There's no hurry.'

The others drew nearer eagerly, and the millionaire passed his hand dazedly over his forehead.

'I was stopping at the Carlton,' he began, 'with Granger, my secretary. I sent him over to Belfast on a shipping deal and –' He paused and looked round the group. 'Where is Granger?' he asked.

'Mr Granger was murdered in Belfast, Mr Potts,' said Drummond quietly, 'by a member of the gang that kidnapped you.'

'Murdered! Jimmy Granger murdered!' He almost cried in his weakness. 'What did the swine want to murder him for?'

'Because they wanted you alone,' explained Hugh. 'Private secretaries ask awkward questions.'

After a while the millionaire recovered his composure, and with many breaks and pauses the slow, disjointed story continued.

'Lakington! That was the name of the man I met at the Carlton. And then there was another . . . Peter . . . Peterson. That's it. We all dined together, I remember, and it was after dinner, in my private sitting-room, that Peterson put up his proposition to me . . . It was a suggestion that he thought would appeal to me as a business man. He said – what was it? – that he could produce a gigantic syndicalist strike in England – revolution, in fact; and that as one of the biggest ship-owners – the biggest, in fact – outside this country, I should be able to capture a lot of the British carrying trade. He wanted two hundred and fifty thousand pounds to do it, paid one month after the result was obtained . . . Said there were others in it . . .'

'On that valuation,' interrupted the detective thoughtfully, 'it makes one million pounds sterling,' and Drummond nodded. 'Yes, Mr Potts; and then?'

'I told him,' said the millionaire, 'that he was an infernal scoundrel, and that I'd have nothing whatever to do with such a villainous scheme. And then – almost the last thing I can remember – I saw Peterson look at Lakington. Then they both sprang on me, and I felt something prick my arm. And after that I can't remember anything clearly. Your face, sir' – he turned to Drummond – 'comes to me out of a kind of dream; and yours, too,' he added to Darrell. 'But it was like a long, dreadful nightmare, in which vague things, over which I had no power, kept happening, until I woke up late last night in this gentleman's house.' He bowed to Ted Jerningham, who grinned cheerfully.

'And mighty glad I was to hear you talking sense again, sir,' he remarked. 'Do you mean to say you have no recollection of how you got there?'

'None, sir; none,' answered the millionaire. 'It was just part of a dream.'

'It shows the strength of the drug those swine used on you,' said Drummond grimly. 'You went there in an aeroplane, Mr Potts.'

'An aeroplane!' cried the other in amazement. 'I don't remember it. I've got no recollection of it whatever. There's only one other thing that I can lay hold of, and that's all dim and muzzy . . . Pearls . . . A great rope of pearls . . . I was to sign a paper; and I wouldn't . . . I did once, and then there was a shot, and the light went out, and the paper disappeared . . .'

'It's at my bank at this moment, Mr Potts,' said Hugh; 'I took that paper, or part of it, that night.'

'Did you?' The millionaire looked at him vaguely. 'It was to promise them a million dollars when they had done what they said . . . I remember that . . . And the pearl necklace . . . The Duchess of . . .' He paused and shook his head wearily.

'The Duchess of Lampshire's?' prompted Hugh.

'That's it,' said the other. 'The Duchess of Lampshire's. It was saying that I wanted her pearls, I think, and would ask no questions as to how they were got.'

The detective grunted.

'Wanted to incriminate you properly, did they? Though it seems to me that it was a blamed risky game. There should have been enough money from the other three to run the show without worrying you, when they found you weren't for it.'

'Wait,' said the millionaire, 'that reminds me. Before they assaulted me at the Carlton, they told me the others wouldn't come in unless I did.'

For a while there was silence, broken at length by Hugh.

'Well, Mr Potts, you've had a mouldy time, and I'm very glad it's over. But the person you've got to thank for putting us fellows on to your tracks is a girl. If it hadn't been for her, I'm afraid you'd still be having nightmares.'

'I would like to see her and thank her,' said the millionaire quickly.

'You shall,' grinned Hugh. 'Come to the wedding; it will be in a fortnight or thereabouts.'

'Wedding!' Mr Potts looked a little vague.

'Yes! Mine and hers. Ghastly proposition, isn't it?'

'The last straw,' remarked Ted Jerningham. 'A more impossible man as a bridegroom would be hard to think of. But in the meantime I pinched half a dozen of the old man's Perrier Jouet 1911 and put 'em in the car. What say you?'

'Say!' snorted Hugh. 'Idiot boy! Does one speak on such occasions?'

And it was so . . .

III

'What's troubling me,' remarked Hugh later, 'is what to do with Carl and that sweet girl Irma.'

The hour for the meeting was drawing near, and though no one had any idea as to what sort of a meeting it was going to be, it was obvious that Peterson would be one of the happy throng.

'I should say the police might now be allowed a look in,' murmured Darrell mildly. 'You can't have the man lying about the place after you're married.'

'I suppose not,' answered Drummond regretfully. 'And yet it's a dreadful thing to finish a little show like this with the police – if you'll forgive my saying so, Mr Green.'

'Sure thing,' drawled the American. 'But we have our uses, Captain, and I'm inclined to agree with your friend's suggestion. Hand him over along with his book, and they'll sweep up the mess.'

'It would be an outrage to let the scoundrel go,' said the millionaire fiercely. 'The man Lakington you say is dead; there's enough evidence to hang this brute as well. What about my secretary in Belfast?'

But Drummond shook his head.

'I have my doubts, Mr Potts, if you'd be able to bring that home to him. Still, I can quite understand your feeling rattled with the bird.' He rose and stretched himself; then he glanced at his watch. 'It's time you all retired, boys; the party ought to be starting soon. Drift in again with the lads, the instant I ring the bell.'

Left alone Hugh made certain once again that he knew the right combination of studs on the wall to open the big door which concealed the stolen store of treasure – and other things as well; then, lighting a cigarette, he sat down and waited.

The end of the chase was in sight, and he had determined it should be a fitting end, worthy of the chase itself
– theatrical, perhaps, but at the same time impressive.
Something for the Ditchlings of the party to ponder on in
the silent watches of the night . . . Then the police – it
would have to be the police, he admitted sorrowfully –
and after that, Phyllis.

And he was just on the point of ringing up his flat to tell
her that he loved her, when the door opened and a man
came in. Hugh recognized him at once as Vallance
Nestor, an author of great brilliance – in his own eyes –
who had lately devoted himself to the advancement of
revolutionary labour.

'Good afternoon,' murmured Drummond affably.
'Mr Peterson will be a little late. I am his private
secretary.'

The other nodded and sat down languidly.

'What did you think of my last little effort in the
Midlands?' he asked, drawing off his gloves.

'Quite wonderful,' said Hugh. 'A marvellous help to
the great Cause.'

Vallance Nestor yawned slightly and closed his eyes,
only to open them again as Hugh turned the pages of the
ledger on the table.

'What's that?' he demanded.

'This is the book,' replied Drummond carelessly,
'where Mr Peterson records his opinions of the immense
value of all his fellow-workers. Most interesting
reading.'

'Am I in it?' Vallance Nestor rose with alacrity.

'Why, of course,' answered Drummond. 'Are you not
one of the leaders? Here you are.' He pointed with his
finger, and then drew back in dismay. 'Dear, dear! there
must be some mistake.'

But Vallance Nestor, with a frozen and glassy eye, was

staring fascinated at the following choice description of himself:

'Nestor, Vallance. Author – so-called. Hot-air factory, but useful up to a point. Inordinately conceited and a monumental ass. Not fit to be trusted far.'

'What,' he spluttered at length, 'is the meaning of this abominable insult?'

But Hugh, his shoulders shaking slightly, was welcoming the next arrival – a rugged, beetle-browed man, whose face seemed vaguely familiar, but whose name he was unable to place.

'Crofter,' shouted the infuriated author, 'look at this as a description of me.'

And Hugh watched the man, whom he now knew to be one of the extremist members of Parliament, walk over and glance at the book. He saw him conceal a smile, and then Vallance Nestor carried the good work on.

'We'll see what he says about you – impertinent blackguard.'

Rapidly he turned the pages, and Hugh glanced over Crofter's shoulder at the dossier.

He just had time to read: 'Crofter, John. A consummate blackguard. Playing entirely for his own hand. Needs careful watching,' when the subject of the remarks, his face convulsed with fury, spun round and faced him.

'Who wrote that?' he snarled.

'Must have been Mr Peterson,' answered Hugh placidly. 'I see you had five thousand out of him, so perhaps he considers himself privileged. A wonderful judge of character, too,' he murmured, turning away to greet Mr Ditchling, who arrived somewhat opportunely, in company with a thin pale man – little more than a youth – whose identity completely defeated Drummond.

'My God!' Crofter was livid with rage. 'Me and

Peterson will have words this afternoon. Look at this, Ditchling.' On second thoughts he turned over some pages. 'We'll see what this insolent devil has to say about you.'

'Drinks!' Ditchling thumped the table with a heavy fist. 'What the hell does he mean? Say you, Mr Secretary – what's the meaning of this?'

'They represent Mr Peterson's considered opinions of you all,' said Hugh genially. 'Perhaps this other gentle-man . . .'

He turned to the pale youth, who stepped forward with a surprised look. He seemed to be not quite clear what had upset the others, but already Nestor had turned up his name.

'Terrance, Victor. A wonderful speaker. Appears really to believe that what he says will benefit the working-man. Consequently very valuable; but indubit-ably mad.'

'Does he mean to insult us deliberately?' demanded Crofter, his voice still shaking with passion.

'But I don't understand,' said Victor Terrance dazedly. 'Does Mr Peterson not believe in our teachings, too?' He turned slowly and looked at Hugh, who shrugged his shoulders.

'He should be here at any moment,' he answered, and as he spoke the door opened and Carl Peterson came in.

'Good afternoon, gentlemen,' he began, and then he saw Hugh. With a look of speechless amazement he stared at the soldier, and for the first time since Hugh had known him his face blanched. Then his eyes fell on the open ledger, and with a dreadful curse he sprang for-ward. A glance at the faces of the men who stood watching told him what he wanted to know, and with another oath his hand went to his pocket.

'Take your hand out, Carl Peterson.' Drummond's voice rang through the room, and the arch-criminal, looking sullenly up, found himself staring into the muzzle of a revolver. 'Now, sit down at the table – all of you. The meeting is about to commence.'

'Look here,' blustered Crofter, 'I'll have the law on you . . .'

'By all manner of means, Mr John Crofter, consummate blackguard,' answered Hugh calmly. 'But that comes afterwards. Just now – sit down.'

'I'm damned if I will,' roared the other, springing at the soldier. And Peterson, sitting sullenly at the table trying to readjust his thoughts to the sudden blinding certainty that through some extraordinary accident everything had miscarried, never stirred as a half-stunned Member of Parliament crashed to the floor beside him.

'Sit down, I said,' remarked Drummond affably. 'But if you prefer to lie down, it's all the same to me. Are there any more to come, Peterson?'

'No, damn you. Get it over!'

'Right! Throw your gun on the floor.' Drummond picked the weapon up and put it in his pocket; then he rang the bell. 'I had hoped,' he murmured, 'for a larger gathering, but one cannot have everything, can one, Mr Monumental Ass?'

But Vallance Nestor was far too frightened to resent the insult; he could only stare foolishly at the soldier, while he plucked at his collar with a shaking hand. Save to Peterson, who understood, if only dimly, what had happened, the thing had come as such a complete surprise that even the sudden entrance of twenty masked men, who ranged themselves in single rank behind their chairs, failed to stir the meeting. It seemed merely in keeping with what had gone before.

'I shall not detain you long, gentlemen,' began Hugh suavely. 'Your general appearance and the warmth of the weather have combined to produce in me a desire for sleep. But before I hand you over to the care of the sportsmen who stand so patiently behind you, there are one or two remarks I wish to make. Let me say at once that on the subject of Capital and Labour I am supremely ignorant. You will therefore be spared any dissertation on the subject. But from an exhaustive study of the ledger which now lies upon the table, and a fairly intimate knowledge of its author's movements, I and my friends have been put to the inconvenience of treading on you.

'There are many things, we know, which are wrong in this jolly old country of ours; but given time and the right methods I am sufficiently optimistic to believe that they could be put right. That, however, would not suit your book. You dislike the right method, because it leaves all of you much where you were before. Every single one of you – with the sole possible exception of you, Mr Terrance, and you're mad – is playing with revolution for his own ends: to make money out of it – to gain power . . .

'Let us start with Peterson – your leader. How much did you say he demanded, Mr Potts, as the price of revolution?'

With a strangled cry Peterson sprang up as the American millionaire, removing his mask, stepped forward.

'Two hundred and fifty thousand pounds, you swine, was what you asked me.' The millionaire stood confronting his tormentor, who dropped back in his chair with a groan. 'And when I refused, you tortured me. Look at my thumb.'

With a cry of horror the others sitting at the table looked at the mangled flesh, and then at the man who had done it. This, even to their mind, was going too far.

'Then there was the same sum,' continued Drummond, 'to come from Hocking, the American cotton man – half German by birth; Steinemann, the German coal man; von Gratz, the German steel man. Is that not so, Peterson?' It was an arrow at a venture, but it hit the mark, and Peterson nodded.

'So one million pounds was the stake this benefactor of humanity was playing for,' sneered Drummond. 'One million pounds as the mere price of a nation's life-blood . . . But, at any rate, he had the merit of playing big, whereas the rest of you scum – and the other beauties so ably catalogued in that book – messed about at his beck and call for packets of bull's-eyes. Perhaps you laboured under the delusion that you were fooling him, but the whole lot of you are so damned crooked that you probably thought of nothing but your own filthy skins.

'Listen to me!' Hugh Drummond's voice took on a deep, commanding ring, and against their will the four men looked at the broad, powerful soldier, whose sincerity shone clear in his face. 'Not by revolutions and direct action will you make this island of ours right – though I am fully aware that this is the last thing you could wish to see happen. But with your brains, and for your own unscrupulous ends, you gull the working-man into believing it. And he, because you can talk with your tongues in your cheeks, is led away. He believes you will give him Utopia; whereas, in reality, you are leading him to hell. And you know it. Evolution is our only chance – not revolution; but you, and others like you, stand to gain more by the latter . . .'

His hand dropped to his side, and he grinned.

'Quite a break for me,' he remarked. 'I'm getting

hoarse. I'm now going to hand you four over to the boys. There's an admirable, but somewhat muddy pond outside, and I'm sure you'd like to look for newts. If any of you want to summon me for assault and battery, my name is Drummond – Captain Drummond, of Half Moon Street. But I warn you that that book will be handed into Scotland Yard tonight. Out with 'em, boys, and give 'em hell . . .

'And now, Carl Peterson,' he remarked, as the door closed behind the last of the struggling prophets of a new world, 'it's time that you and I settled our little account, isn't it?'

The master-criminal rose and stood facing him. Apparently he had completely recovered himself; the hand with which he lit his cigar was as steady as a rock.

'I congratulate you, Captain Drummond,' he remarked suavely. 'I confess I have no idea how you managed to escape from the cramped position I left you in last night, or how you have managed to install your own men in this house. But I have even less idea how you discovered about Hocking and the other two.'

Hugh laughed shortly.

'Another time, when you disguise yourself as the Comte de Guy, remember one thing, Carl. For effective concealment it is necessary to change other things beside your face and figure. You must change your mannerisms and unconscious little tricks. No – I won't tell you what it is that gave you away. You can ponder over it in prison.'

'So you mean to hand me over to the police, do you?' said Peterson slowly.

'I see no other course open to me,' replied Drummond. 'It will be quite a *cause célèbre*, and ought to do a lot to edify the public.'

The sudden opening of the door made both men look round. Then Drummond bowed, to conceal a smile.

'Just in time, Miss Irma,' he remarked, 'for settling day.'

The girl swept past him and confronted Peterson.

'What has happened?' she panted. 'The garden is full of people whom I've never seen. And there were two young men running down the drive covered with weeds and dripping with water.'

Peterson smiled grimly.

'A slight set-back has occurred, my dear. I have made a big mistake – a mistake which has proved fatal. I have underestimated the ability of Captain Drummond; and as long as I live I shall always regret that I did not kill him the night he went exploring in this house.'

Fearfully the girl faced Drummond; then she turned again to Peterson.

'Where's Henry?' she demanded.

'That again is a point on which I am profoundly ignorant,' answered Peterson. 'Perhaps Captain Drummond can enlighten us on that also?'

'Yes,' remarked Drummond, 'I can. Henry has had an accident. After I drove him back from the Duchess's last night' – the girl gave a cry, and Peterson steadied her with his arm – 'we had words – dreadful words. And for a long time, Carl, I thought it would be better if you and I had similar words. In fact, I'm not sure even now that it wouldn't be safer in the long run . . .'

'But where is he?' said the girl, through dry lips.

'Where you ought to be, Carl,' answered Hugh grimly. 'Where, sooner or later, you will be.'

He pressed the studs in the niche of the wall, and the door of the big safe swung open slowly. With a scream of terror the girl sank half-fainting on the floor, and even

Peterson's cigar dropped on the floor from his nerveless lips. For, hung from the ceiling by two ropes attached to his arms, was the dead body of Henry Lakington. And even as they watched, it sagged lower, and one of the feet hit sullenly against a beautiful old gold vase . . .

'My God!' muttered Peterson. 'Did you murder him?'

'Oh, no!' answered Drummond. 'He inadvertently fell in the bath he got ready for me, and then when he ran up the stairs in considerable pain, that interesting mechanical device broke his neck.'

'Shut the door,' screamed the girl; 'I can't stand it.'

She covered her face with her hands, shuddering, while the door slowly swung to again.

'Yes,' remarked Drummond thoughtfully, 'it should be an interesting trial. I shall have such a lot to tell them about the little entertainments here, and all your endearing ways.'

With the big ledger under his arm he crossed the room, and called to some men who were standing outside in the hall; and as the detectives, thoughtfully supplied by Mr Green, entered the central room, he glanced for the last time at Carl Peterson and his daughter. Never had the cigar glowed more evenly between the master-criminal's lips; never had the girl Irma selected a cigarette from her gold and tortoiseshell case with more supreme indifference.

'Goodbye, my ugly one!' she cried, with a charming smile, as two of the men stepped up to her.

'Goodbye,' Hugh bowed, and a tinge of regret showed for a moment in his eyes.

'Not goodbye, Irma.' Carl Peterson removed his cigar, and stared at Drummond steadily. 'Only *au revoir*, my friend; only *au revoir*.'

Epilogue

'I simply can't believe it, Hugh.' In the lengthening shadows Phyllis moved a little nearer to her husband, who, quite regardless of the publicity of their position, slipped an arm round her waist.

'Can't believe what, darling?' he demanded lazily.

'Why, that all that awful nightmare is over. Lakington dead, and the other two in prison, and us married.'

'They're not actually in jug yet, old thing,' said Hugh. 'And somehow . . .' he broke off and stared thoughtfully at a man sauntering past them. To all appearances he was a casual visitor taking his evening walk along the front of the well-known seaside resort so largely addicted to honeymoon couples. And yet . . . was he? Hugh laughed softly; he'd got suspicion on the brain.

'Don't you think they'll be sent to prison?' cried the girl.

'They may be sent right enough, but whether they arrive or not is a different matter. I don't somehow see Carl picking oakum. It's not his form.'

For a while they were silent, occupied with matters quite foreign to such trifles as Peterson and his daughter.

'Are you glad I answered your advertisement?' inquired Phyllis at length.

'The question is too frivolous to deserve an answer,' remarked her husband severely.

'But you aren't sorry it's over?' she demanded.

'It isn't over, kid; it's just begun.' He smiled at her tenderly. 'Your life and mine . . . isn't it just wonderful?'

And once again the man sauntered past them. But this time he dropped a piece of paper on the path, just at Hugh's feet, and the soldier, with a quick movement which he hardly stopped to analyse, covered it with his shoe. The girl hadn't seen the action; but then, as girls will do after such remarks, she was thinking of other things. Idly Hugh watched the saunterer disappear in the more crowded part of the esplanade, and for a moment there came on to his face a look which, happily for his wife's peace of mind, she failed to notice.

'No,' he said, *à propos* of nothing, 'I don't see the gentleman picking oakum. Let's go and eat, and after dinner I'll run you up to the top of the headland . . .'

With a happy sigh she rose. It *was* just wonderful! and together they strolled back to their hotel. In his pocket was the piece of paper; and who could be sending him messages in such a manner save one man – a man now awaiting his trial?

In the hall he stayed behind to inquire for letters, and a man nodded to him.

'Heard the news?' he inquired.

'No,' said Hugh. 'What's happened?'

'That man Peterson and the girl have got away. No trace of 'em.' Then he looked at Drummond curiously. 'By the way, you had something to do with that show, didn't you?'

'A little,' smiled Hugh. 'Just a little.'

'Police bound to catch 'em again,' continued the other. 'Can't hide yourself these days.'

And once again Hugh smiled, as he drew from his pocket the piece of paper:

'Only *au revoir*, my friend; only *au revoir*.'

He glanced at the words written in Peterson's neat writing, and the smile broadened. Assuredly life was still good; assuredly . . .

'Are you ready for dinner, darling?' Quickly he swung round, and looked at the sweet face of his wife.

'Sure thing, kid,' he grinned. 'Dead sure; I've had the best appetiser the old pot-house can produce.'

'Well, you're very greedy. Where's mine?'

'Effects of bachelordom, old thing. For the moment I forgot you. I'll have another. Waiter – two Martinis.'

And into an ashtray nearby, he dropped a piece of paper torn into a hundred tiny fragments.

'Was that a love-letter?' she demanded with assumed jealousy.

'Not exactly, sweetheart,' he laughed back. 'Not exactly.' And over the glasses their eyes met. 'Here's to hoping, kid; here's to hoping.'

THE END

Discarded

THE
TRUTH
DENTIST

A NOVEL BY

LINDSAY BARRETT

Alive to the jive. The drone of choppers up above. The interview where Annabel Chong, the current world record holder for fucks...Two hundred and fifty-one in ten hours...Have you got your two and a bit minutes ready...delicately fingers a courgette, running her heavily mascaraed eyes over the produce present for the benefit of the cameras and demurely states 'I love anal sex'.

Poor girl. I feel sorry for her. In ten years time she'll struggle to get out of bed. Haemorrhoids weighing her down even after the fifth operation. All that psychic energy poured into a hard-core porn star as the Big Bosses count the endless wedges of tainted money... We love you Annabel Chong and feel for you. What does the future hold...? Maybe she'll be lucky enough to marry an eighty year old Texas oil magnate and manage to fuck him to death with her magnetic arsehole, cooing and bellowing, having first established that he's had his lawyers redraft his will with Annabel the sole beneficiary...Perhaps she'll quite understandably tire of the male organ and develop a passion for young coffee-coloured ladies with willing tongues, the strongest organ in the body, or strapped-on vibrators that run on solar-powered energy. All doubtless done for the benefit of the omnipresent cameras...Her record will be long gone by then and her flesh will be starting to show wrinkles. Still in the marketplace though, still addicted to the cameras, to the sodomite gyrations of her hips and buttocks. To the adoration of celebrity status and her legion of masturbating fans. All savaged pricks and sticky fingertips. The GRRRLS walk on by with freshly coloured merkins to baffle us by. Venusian boy/girls interacting on Annabel's website. Leaving e-mail messages of anal love and queries like 'Has Peter Sellers contacted you yet from the after-life?'. Sex, drugs, rock and rap, anything to fill the widening gap. The daily void still growing like a gigantic chasm. Broader and deeper than Annabel Chong's arsehole. More diverse than the Taliban's definition of the law of Sharia.

Spirited away from our souls. Lost, dimensionless...You make money and succeed. Do anything to please. And I do mean anything! The spirit of Georgy calling me back to a time and a place of innocence. A sense of well being and hope in the air. Our childhood dream worlds where Georgy walked into the lounge and excitedly recounted the plot of 'Vera Cruz', ad-libbing all the Burt Lancaster impressions. Excitedly commandeering the radiogram with 'You've just got to listen to this' and playing my first hearing of Elvis's 'Heartbreak Hotel'...The firsts are endless, just like the best two examples. Yet the talk never drifted around to Nagasaki and Hiroshima. To the Ban the Bomb marches and the threat of nuclear extinction...They'd done their bit. Sacrificed their youth out there in the Western desert and watched their best friends mown down at the abortive landing at Monte Cassino...Intellectual wrangling wasn't high on the agenda, only the will to live, to enjoy the present and laugh at the Goons and Tony Hancock on the wireless. Gas ovens weren't mentioned and the only connection with them were the endless plays of the Diary of Anne Frank. Politics and the present future were lost in the lust for life. The catching up to be done. Yet you can never catch up. You can never get your youth back. As Annabel Chong will find out...

The lost innocence that never really existed. Only posed in childhood dreams and the sense of excitement that Georgy conveyed by his very presence...The numbing need to distance themselves from what they had seen and experienced...We can mock them today. Point to the failure of Suez and the dollar-forging instincts of the American Dream of the Fifties hot on the coattails of McCarthyism. It's easy to be snide. How many so-called respectable men will marry Annabel now...? Can you sit comfortably in a crowded room with your wife and know for sure that every adult in the room of every sexual persuasion has had her. Has widened that hole till she perpetually shits silver dollars...Our innocence is lost. We have reached the other side of Paradise and we don't like it because we can never go back. Never reclaim it. The Spirit of Georgy is encapsulated in a time warp which may have been false yet existed in the present. In the way that people were just happy to be alive. No G.I. Bills here for returning war heroes. No free college education and cheap housing. No chance to shun a youngish Jack Kerouac on the road hitch-hiking out from the Big Sur. Mum, Dad, Buddy and Sis oblivious, sucked in by the all-encompassing drive for wealth and peering behind every crevice for commie infiltrators.

"You were going to write about the spirit of Georgy..."

"I am... it's just ... well, daily reports have a way of taking over, commandeering one's thoughts."

"Give me an example then?"

"I'm going to, Sweet Pea, I'm going to... Yesterday a group of teenagers broke into Belfast Zoo using wire cutters to get through two perimeter fences and reach the penguin enclosure..."

"At night?"

"What do you think, Moonchild! Yes, of course, at bloody night. Anyway, having attained the penguin enclosure they attacked and beat several penguins with iron bars and rocks, killing a few. They stunned four and flung them into the lions' den. The attackers then drifted off into the night laughing, leaving piles of empty beer cans behind."

"That's really awful! Still, all those fingerprints on the cans..."

"The worrying aspect, Sweet Pea, is that these kids aren't stupid. They all wore gloves."

"What about DNA then? Fibres of clothing and strands of hair etc.?"

"Well, that's not going to help nine dead penguins. Though I suppose penguin revenge is a thought... I don't have that much faith in DNA as a detecting method. Over-rated at present. The Hitchcockian fear... There you are, Sweet Pea, a perfectly innocent hitchhiker passing through a small town in the Mid-West. The local Pigs seize you, do tests and declare that your DNA profile matches that of a killer who buggered and butchered two local teenage girls on the day you were stranded with your numb thumb. Juries place incredible store by DNA evidence. Convicted when innocent. Not a price. You might as well be the eternal stranger travelling a few leagues in the Middle Ages. The days of the Plague. Step foot in a new village and they will stone you to death before you even reach the church fountain for a drink..."

"You don't have much faith in scientific procedures, do you?"

"That's not true, Sweet Pea. It's the Human Race I don't trust."

"Were you always like that?"

"No. I lived under the influence of the Spirit of Georgy. I believed the best of people. I was conned in the Hippie Age and thought Enlightenment was with us with the dawning of the Age of Aquarius. Little did I believe that Aquarians are a communicating sign, blandly put. The Age beckoned in the microchip and the Net. Communication, not faith and belief. With greater communication and human numbers ever spiralling, I believe we will witness a modern age of the Witch Finder General. The old Chaka method that sought out and killed a million zula souls in no time. The smelling out method..."

"God, I wouldn't want to spend too much time in your company; I'd get really depressed. I have to believe the best of people. I don't want to reach your position in life and see nihilism and futility at every turn. Things have always been grim. What made you think because you'd been indoctrinated in the Spirit of Georgy that you had a right to expect a better, safer, more spiritual planet...? Collective communes. Isn't that how you spent most of your late youth? Living in Hippie communes and smoking everything!"

"Simplistic thoughts and ideas convey very little, Moonchild. I could... what's the point! We are all faceless today. Materialistic beyond our wildest dreams. We have uncovered the id and let loose most of the horrors lain seething in our collective unconscious..."

The light splintered across the frame of the bike, glinting on the redbrick flats that rose up like giant anthills all around us. All noise and activity. The rebirth of the nesting process.

On and on the bicycle whizzes through the ungrassed courtyards of concrete and football games. People smiling. Yes, it may come as a shock to you, but people used to smile and wave at absolute strangers. Pass the time of evening as the sun affords an orange backdrop to the hastily erected goals of jackets and jumpers. Twenty-a-side as the ball bounces against the gleaming spokes. Georgy kicks it away, smirks...Why be afraid when you've marched into Tobruk, charged maniacally up the hill at Monte Cassino. Stared at the drifting human smoke of the gas ovens at Dachau...Early evening football games during the summer nights on these council and Trust estates are heaven. Still this side of Paradise, having looked down the barrel of Hell. Lived with fear till it no longer mattered. Imagined your own death every night

for two years till you finally gave up worrying and went out hunting for that bullet with your name on it...Searched for it. Screamed for it but it wouldn't come. Wouldn't release this pain and ambivalence towards the self. The idea of self. Just a human carcass to kill and be killed. One of a million Desert Ants pretending to be Rats and heading for a nihilistic existence...No gin-slings and days of recovery for this boy. No singing and dancing on the Asian continent and drumming for a Ralph Reader Gang show.

You live with it and it's never going to end. You stop expecting anything. Any hopes or dreams have long since disappeared. Each day brings the totally unexpected and is the same. False reports. Little hinted-at canards to dupe the duplicitous...The sand eats into your young bones and you feel as old as the Universe. Nothing ever happened before this...no end in sight...Bravery isn't an act you even contemplate...Everyone shitting themselves before they go into action...You may not fear, but you are still afraid.

This nihilistic tidal march of men, trucks, jeeps; a human juggernaut of people perpetually moving, seething masses of displaced villagers. All the photographers and journos. The Broadcasting units mingling with braying donkeys, spitting and hissing camels, frightened horses: the streaming caravan and cavalcade of war making its way across the Western Desert...One person can instigate this and set into motion thirty million deaths, evoke carnage, cause world mayhem, one person...But you don't think any of these thoughts then. All your energies concentrated on the next meal, order, fresh water, jerry can of petrol, foot sores, bed sores, sand encrusted up the jacksy, mouth sores and termites. Rotting mosquito nets and the all-pervading smell of human sweat. Men's sweat. Everywhere, the rank smell. Life governed by smell and the next surge. The next front. Always gossip, news...That woman who placed an advert in the local newspaper last week. Seeking a man, a lover and a husband. She closed with 'must not be too smelly'... How did she know? Was she a nurse out there on the Western Front? The sheer volume of shit and sweat. Bully beef and chocolate. Everything covered in a blue haze by the incessant cigarette smoking. All the armies marching on forty untipped a day. Woodbines, Players and Senior Service. Just to disguise the never-ending smells...latrines and graves. Hospitals tents full of wounded veterans too weak to blow their own brains out...Oh, the unyielding glory of war. From Troy to Tobruk. The other side of Paradise....

Through it all the all-pervading, all-encompassing heat...Each morning waking with the sun-up. Diving naked into an icy-cold swimming pool. The temperature plummets at night, descending from Hell-fire to Arctic tundra in just a few short hours. Well before the sun even blinks its first new-day wink in imitation of Osiris, young brown-limbed boys drag canvas tarpaulins across the pool, just to maintain that icy freshness for a few extra minutes...Georgy plunging deep down. Plunging and rising, spray gushing above the surface as the boys laugh, wave and cavort...All thoughts gone. All desires sublimated. We are in the Army now. Thinking is frowned upon. In fact, actively discouraged. 'Think out here, Sonny, and you'll soon be dead!' Sure. Probably right. Thinking breeds carrion meat for vultures and rodents that patrol this inferno land. Gift-wrapped human meat on a skewer for the shifting desert sands…Plunging into that icy water. Yesterday, today, tomorrow. All the same…Fresh orders, whispers, music blaring from a Forces programme…We'll meet again…we'll never meet again anywhere again because we have all been destroyed. We may wander back home and be proclaimed as heroes…'He was one of the first on the scene at Dachau, you know!'… We may not have reached Berlin first, but we sure as hell got to Dachau…'Ashtrays, ashtrays. Genuine Nazi ashtrays made out of human skulls. Two cigarettes a piece. C'mon, take some home as mementoes'…Bags of human fertiliser to stick on the compost heap on the allotment when the triumphant hero returns…

"His life changed forever when he met his future wife, Jackie, then."

"How did you know that, Sweet Pea? I mean, I don't believe I've ever recounted that to you!"

"I'm clairvoyant, that's how. I can sense your inner thoughts, look into the wave patterns of your brain. Receive little messages and snippets of what you're thinking."

"Hell, that's unnerving, Moonchild…Stop winding me up! I've told you many things and you obviously remember them all!"

"Tell me again please."

"Well, Sweet Pea, it's hard recalling things through the eyes of a child. Little snatched moments that probably take on immense proportions out of all reasoning to the true cause and purpose…My maternal Grandmother had a Trust Estate flat a little way along from the Chelsea Swimming Baths. You can imagine the small estate with minor side roads encircling the entrances. Well, one of these side roads lay between the Baths and the back of my Gran's flat. Most of the street was taken up with the administrative offices of an auto company named Eustace Watkins. After the war was over Georgy returned to live with Gran and Pop. He was the youngest of their four children and the only one left unmarried. He had an old Army buddy called Roy who worked in the offices at Eustace Watkins. One day after work they met up for a drink and Roy bought along two girls from the typing pool. One of them was called Jackie and, without labouring the point, Georgy was smitten straight away. His experience and contact with women had been pretty limited. I heard tell of a liaison with a Sandra from Aston, but that was about it. You've got to remember the times and the fact that he'd spent the ages of eighteen to twenty-three surviving the theatre of war…"

"You're getting upset recalling this. Don't tell it in linear fashion, just recount the images that remain with you."

"Thank you, Sweet Pea. That's what I really like best about you, you're kind…I can't ever remember anybody reading to me as a child except Jackie. I can see her now, sat on the end of my bed reading a story. I don't remember what the story was, and I have no recall of her ever touching me or kissing me goodnight... Maybe she did it for Georgy. A dutiful new family chore. Making good with his favourite child and filling in a few blanks for future reference... Being a pageboy in a kilt at St. Luke's church in Sydney Street. A very grand church and a huge gathering. I was excruciatingly shy that day and must have tried to hide my head in the pleated folds of Jackie's white and cream wedding gown. Funny though, for all my shyness I held the train on my own and slowly walked along the aisle without any coaching. I suppose it was only when I stopped holding the train and the major part of the ceremony was over that I became aware of so many people watching me. Self-realisation bringing blushes. Also, I was determined not to let Georgy down... I overheard some of my aunts' chatterings a few weeks before the wedding about how they really should have bridesmaids. How the dressmakers were having to make the train out of a lighter material so as the little Scottish pageboy could carry it... I didn't know what that missing final sound was then, though I felt its menace. I know it better now as a snort of derision... Cold, wet and windy on holiday on the Norfolk Broads. I'd had an intense visit from the Dreamweaver and woke up suddenly in my tiny cabin in the fore of the boat. Slam! Ouch! Smashing my head on the roof of the bunk as I sat up, startled. I suppose I must have started howling and crying. I can remember sitting on a sort of sofa in the saloon. Jackie sitting opposite me, not saying anything. Dad and Georgy out on deck in the descending fog...The way she looked. Was I a little monster who'd unintentionally interrupted their early-morning lovemaking? Probably. Thinking back, that fits...picking up on whispers, complaints, murmurs of discontent. Small children are often forgotten, they were then. Safety in numbers for children, them and us. Complaints about dirt. How 'She' never cleans their flat. How 'She' can't cook properly. How 'She' is only interested in having a good time, whatever that was. I carried this information inside of me. Secretly taking on the air of disgust my Grandmother had conveyed. When we next went to dinner I tasted the food carefully, chewing each mouthful very slowly. It seemed okay to a young Epicurean like me. Later I deliberately made my brightly coloured spinning top disappear behind the settee in the lounge. Kneeling down to recover it, sure enough there were quite a few frail coils of dirt. Grey-black puffballs clinging around the back castors. Suspicions confirmed. Suddenly in my mind the idea of having a good time was reliant on you not cleaning your flat. 'She' was condemned...Whether I liked her or not I don't know. But up until then she had always been quite sweet and kind to me. Bringing presents and arriving with Georgy. I suppose I was always cosseted and defended my cluster of adult angels and avengers, but she had done nothing exceptional to impinge on my existence. That is until...In those days, Sweet Pea, the Football Pools were like the National Lottery today. Huge first dividend winners. It's hard to calculate money that far back, but I suppose a half a million pounds then was something like ten plus million today. Pop always did the Pools like everybody else. He had a method of always using the same numbers. Eight draws from ten. Of course, he'd never won a Bavarian sausage. The problem with that system is that you become stuck with it. Especially after a few years, you start fantasising that if you should change your special numbers, the very week that you do they'll come up. Stupid I know, but there you go. Pop had been ill for some time and was virtually confined to bed. Jackie was always very sweet to him and used to drop in on him in her lunch hour from Eustace Watkins. Anyway, this particular week she insisted on taking Pop's Pools coupon and posting it for him. Gran persisted that there really was no need. After all, why change a losing routine. It was only to humour Pop after all and give him something to look forward to. But no. Jackie wasn't having any of that. Her special relationship with Pop. She was bound to bring him luck and when he'd won we could all share in his good fortune. Gran scowled in my direction then and banged a few pots in the scullery. Pop liked Jackie's fleeting visits, they cheered him up. She was so kind and thoughtful. An attractive young lady married to his youngest, visiting an old man close to Death's door. The fateful Saturday came and Pop was ecstatic. The results were usually read out over the wireless at five o'clock on a Saturday evening. By half-past five I believe that any tenant of those Trust flats who didn't know that Pop had got eight draws up was lost to the world and permanently in limboland. Pop was out and about and dressed. The healing power of money. I don't know if it's money, probably more likely excitement. Like the time Alan Caddy's father went crazy when Telstar reached number one in the Hit parade. He came shouting and screaming for joy up our block. In fact he was so excited that he looked like heart attack material. Dad managed to get him into the lounge and sit him down, give him a glass of whisky and we all supported his excitement for Alan. Even the neighbours who used to complain about Alan scraping a violin when he was thirteen and disturbing their early evening peace... The excitement in our household was tremendous, we were all going to share in Pop's good fortune. Come the fateful Monday and Jackie's lunchtime visit. Surprised to be greeted at the door by Pop and kissed on the cheek. Over a cup of tea she calmly announced that she'd forgotten to post his coupon. She 'd never thought he was going to win anyway. She passed it off carelessly, with a casual wave of the hands, a glance at her wristwatch and an 'I must be going!' Pop got undressed and went back to bed. Took a few more watches apart that he couldn't mend and stared at the prison of his ceiling... No apologies, you understand. No 'I'm sorry.' Didn't she realise that she of all people would have shared in his good fortune? No! A careless wave of the hand and she was off. Gran quite coldly informed her next day that Pop had relapsed and wouldn't be having any more lunchtime visitations from her... Everybody round about knew. Circulated gossip and shock-horror stories courtesy of Pop's old mate Bob Shilling propping up the public bar of the Beehive pub. As a small child, of course, I didn't fully understand. Sure, I realised the loss, but not the off-hand manner. How she'd put her hand up, declared her interest and love for an old man then pissed on his fate and walked away totally unconcerned without a hair out of place."

"Did you grow to hate her?"

"Strangely, I didn't, Sweet Pea. She just sort of disappeared out of my thoughts. That's the lovely thing about being a child. Each day is a whole new universe of experience. You're in the present and that's all that matters... I mean Jackie must still have been around, but I can't for the life of me remember any other times or moments with her. Of course, in retrospect, her presence and name must have been mud after the Pools incident with

Pop. Simply confirmed the low opinion of her held by the family in general. Whether Georgy was happy or not I can't remember....

One winter I was very ill with influenza. An outbreak infecting its way across the Smoke. I was laid in one room with my mother in the next. This particular lunch-hour and Georgy came in on his break. He'd purchased some blue and silver balloons dancing on the end of a red piece of string. The laughing faces of Mickey Mouse, Minnie and Goofy. Though besides those balloons I've always found Mickey Mouse quite sinister...Georgy coming into my room and galvanising the very air. These balloons weaving a hello. Tying them to a knob on the side table drawer cupboard and flicking them with his fingers to make them move. Doing the different voices and sending me into crying hysterics in my heavy-headed, swollen-eyed state. He then left me these precious gifts and went next door to be with his sick 'Liz'. Later returning to give me some medicine...I used to hear family tales about him. How he'd been ridiculed in the late nineteen thirties for continually claiming that 'Man' would land on the moon. How in future centuries there would be space travel. He belonged to some galactic space club that used to meet twice a week near the Albert Hall. The homemade chemistry set when he'd blown out all of Gran's windows and nearly blown himself up with it. The gymnastic displays and entering the junior national championships where he came third on the rings. Most of these were told to me later on, you understand. The comparison and inherited characteristics of Pop... Playing the mandolin and the banjo. How the family used to meet up every Sunday morning before the war. All of them playing instruments. Mandolin, trumpet, banjo, trombone, ukulele, with Liz on the piano. Families on the Trust estate used to gather below in the courtyard to listen to them...The complicated construction of valve radio sets. I suppose just the joy of getting them to work ... empty wooden cotton reels fitted with miniature winding coils. Suddenly Georgy would be looking at you across a room and two of these cotton reels would start rolling at you over the floor. Waiting for that look of childish wonder on your puzzled face...but best of all the early morning crossbar rides on his bicycle. Every Tuesday and Thursday at seven, like clockwork during the summer. How far we travelled in reality I have no idea. Probably for no longer than an hour at most. The exhilaration of it. The warmth and fecundity of his presence sliced with danger and adventure...I suppose that once he was married these treats lessened though I have no remembrance of disappointment..."

"Do you spend a lot of time living in the past?"

"I didn't think you'd visit today, Sweet Pea...No homework? No, I don't think so. It doesn't feel like it to me. But you can never truly tell these things about yourself. In fact, until you started interrogating me with your probing questions, this particular period of my life had lain untouched...I suppose I'd rejected it, Moonchild. Left it in the attic of my childhood. Developed put-on airs and graces, became an intellectual snob and partly pretended it had never happened. We all do it. Correction, some of us do. Little Billy Liar attitudes. Disowning great chunks of ourselves because our early lives don't fit with the surreal identikit pictures we have of who we would have liked to have been. It's partly teenage rebellion where you take against everything around you which eventually gives you the energy to make a clean break. Become more yourself. In my case that particular time and place was drenched in snobbery. Only the British could have ruled India because they were the only nation who were as class-riddled as the Indians....It was in the air in my time. Relayed through the media. Reinforced in nearly every social exchange. Hit you twice a week as the cock crowed and the Pathe News emphasised it in the cinema. Definitely Them and Us. You were made to feel very aware of it, even as a small child...I was taken one day by 'Liz' on one of her upholstery jobs. A grand lady in a large house in Park Walk, Chelsea. I think it was just a cover job. Two or three armchairs...I seem to remember a velvet footstool. I just sat and watched...As we left and entered the high-ceilinged hallway, 'Liz' bent down to my face and put her forefinger to her lips. I turned around and stood perfectly still as she slipped off her high heels and tiptoed in stockinged feet back to the drawing-room door. She crouched down bending her ear to the keyhole and listened. Gradually her face became the colour of a vivid beetroot. She suddenly reared up and around with a face like thunder. Slipped her shoes back on, grasped me by the hand and out we marched through the doorway banging the large brass knocker on the solid oak front door shut as we went out. 'Now remember', she shouted as we sped down Park Walk, 'Whatever you do in life, never, but never, listen at keyholes! Won't do you any bloody good.'"

"I pieced it together a few years later, like a blushing jigsaw puzzle. Whilst she'd been fitting the covers on, the oh-so-grand lady and her boon companion had engaged 'Liz' in conversation. I must have been staring vaguely at the different pieces of objets d'art ornamenting the drawing room. Somehow or other 'Liz' let slip, forgetting herself and her place in the grand scheme of selection, that we, as a family unit, had travelled by car to Italy for a holiday that year. We'd had the temerity to get into our little old Hillman Minx and drive all the way. Of course, when 'Liz' had bent her incautious ear to the keyhole she must have half-suspected, otherwise why do it? She'd heard talk along the lines of 'What is the world coming to, my dear, when these little people, tradespeople for God's sake, start taking holidays abroad! I mean, what will they think of us on the Continent...' What indeed...! Good enough to kill and die for you. To protect your privileged position and pre-eminence in the higher order of things. But let's face it, Moonchild, only good enough to go to a holiday camp, maybe a week in a chalet at Clacton if you're lucky, or two weeks on a hop pick in Kent!'"

"You're getting really angry talking about it. Is it a lot better now?"

"You tell me. You're alive and can see for your self...Yes, even now I still get irate when I think of it. This was just one of very many instances, you understand. Not everybody, but a great proportion. Today is not quite so bad. The semi class revolution of the mid-sixties. Today it's more like the Americanised class system based on race, money and celebrity. Yet we still indulge it, Sweet Pea, still the shit of a two-tier educational system. Already a proportion of your peer group are elitist, courtesy of the advantages of a superior curriculum and private tuition. Privilege still operates...The really insidious part of it is that they get you. Make themselves seem superior so that if you're impressionable you end up wanting to be just like them. Especially living in an area like Chelsea the way it was back then. You aspire to their snobbery. Reject your own roots, develop sham affections and despise the very people who gave you life. It took me a long time, Sweet Pea, to get this fake shit out of my system. In fact, I'm still doing it right now, thanks to you. It's a cathartic process. Purging oneself of all the fake illusions and Venus Fly Traps of grand delusions that we stumble into...."

"Don't you have any pleasant memories of going on jobs as a child? Something to cheer me up on a grey day."

"Why should you need comforting, Sweet Pea? Everything is ahead of you... Well, alright, if I must. Our time is passing through our hands. Slipping effortlessly between our fingers. Spread your fingers wide and you can feel it. Jamming the present with the past. If I recounted everything that had happened to me up until this moment in graphic detail, we would both be dead before I'd got halfway through. Me of old age, and you out of suffocating boredom... Only one instance clearly stands out. Imprinted on the memory recorder. I only went on those jobs pre-school age you understand... There's a small dead-end street down the side of the Chelsea and Westminster Hospital. It used to be named St. Stephen's Way back then. The old Victorian building was extremely draughty and falling apart. It was re-built in the Eighties. Anyway, this particular day must have been quite close to Christmas. I'm not sure, but I think it was just a curtain job. Just a guy on his own. What he did I can't remember. Looking back I suppose that he must have been late twenties or early thirties. As usual, I sat quietly while 'Liz' got on with adjusting the poles and fixtures and hanging the curtains. He may have been attracted to her, but somehow I don't think so. It's hard with all the overt social changes to re-organise social behavioural patterns that far back. But I guess through the lens of time that he might have been gay... After a while he tried to engage me in conversation, asking me simple questions and the like. I just nodded and kept quiet the way I had been instructed to. This seemed to intrigue him. He was very warm and beautifully spoken. He went over to an old gramophone in the corner of the room and started sorting through some seventy-eight records. They were kept in plain oatmeal brown sleeves. The arm on the gramophone player had to be supported by an old penny coin and the music came out from a horn rather than a speaker... It was a grey day and starting to sleet outside... Jingle bells, jingle bells, jingle all the way... Sleigh bells in the snow... We're off to see the Wizard, the wonderful Wizard of Oz... I sat there in a tiny chair, enraptured. The new curtains were taking shape and the miserable winter's day vanished in that warm glow with the blazing wood and coal fire beaming in the grate. Nothing was said. He was very happy with the curtains and paid 'Liz'. But before we could leave he insisted on bringing out this magical-looking tin box with golden interwoven leaves decorating the sides. He then produced a large brown velvet pouch and started filling it up with loads and loads of coins from the box. 'Liz' started to get embarrassed and protested, but he wouldn't stop until the pretty pouch, probably the size of a football, was completely filled. He gave it to me, but it was too heavy for me to hold. 'Liz' took it and we said our thank-yous and good-byes, me shyly thanking him, and off we trotted past St. Stephen's Hospital in the slanting sleet to catch a number fourteen bus...When we got home I emptied the treasure pouch of coins onto the floor. Masses of pennies, ha'pennies, threepenny bits, sixpences, shillings and the odd half-crown, two shilling piece and farthing. I believe the lot came to over five pounds, which was a lot of money then. Nearly half a week's wages for the average person."

"That was wonderful. He must have really been taken by you. Was the old money more interesting?"

"It was original, Moonchild. The coins were far, far heavier than today's and had more character. Five or six coins jingling in your trouser pocket could soon make a hole. It would be futile today. Ten pounds a week then equals about three hundred and fifty now. Rather like the old German jokes and stories that helped Adolf into power. Workers taking their weekly wages home in wheelbarrows. We'd all be weighed down with small coins out of all proportion to their value."

"Tell me more about the wheelbarrows of German money?"

"Another time, Sweet Pea, I've got to somehow finish this film contract, design a website and push on with the story. Another time..."

The Dreamweaver first showed himself when I was very young. Nothing mind-boggling or sensational you understand. A collection of fleeting instances. A few peeps around the corner, a few hints along the way…caught in a dream and awakened by an early morning cup of tea and biscuit. Still slumbering, but able to sip some of the tea, leaving the remainder untouched with the custard cream. Slipping back down into that warm comfort zone. Able to slide straight back in … Getting dressed for playschool, peaking around the corner of the front door and Mr Skelton tiptoeing immaculately down the flights of stairs. Superbly attired in a pinstriped suit, gleaming black leather shoes, rolled umbrella and a black overcoat draped over his arm.

'Good morning, young man, lovely day for it…'

Well, I suppose it was. I just smile at him as he vanishes down another flight… Waking up already late. Being urged and pushed into my clothes. Mutterings. Still dreamy morning with dancing cotton-puff clouds of Morpheus smiling at me. Mouthfuls of porridge, busy hands checking my pale orange lunch box with the Dan Dare sticker. Going to the open front door and poking my head round it. Peeping out, waiting. Mr Skelton comes lightly tripping down the flights of stairs … 'Good morning, young man, lovely day for it.'… These sleepy vignettes were totally accepted. Nobody told me any different. Too many to remember, it seemed the way to be…Obvious incidences stand out…Being abruptly woken very early one morning. Older and a little less wiser. Sitting huddled in the back of the Hillman Minx with Sis. 'Liz' very matter-of-factly describing in the car what we are about to discover as we drive towards the World's End. How the door of the workroom in Rasay Street will be hanging off its hinges. When we enter the workroom we will find all five industrial Singer sewing machines smashed. Beaten to pulp with iron bars and claw hammers. The nicked indentations. How the cash box is tipped upside down on the floor with outstanding copies of invoices strewn all over the place. Two of the iron-grilled windows that look out onto a back alley will be smashed. Chairs overturned. All materials, outstanding jobs and work in progress stolen. The final insult of a pile of excrement dumped in the middle of the threadbare carpet…Nothing is said in reply in the car. Sis and I are aware that Dad hasn't renewed his insurance on the workroom after his huge losses the other month at the Cheltenham Festival. Always a sucker for the gee-gees…Sure enough the scene that we discover at the World's End is exactly as described. Recounted in finer, more accurate detail than I can remember. Nothing unusual in this, we took it for granted. A history of it stretching back generations, mostly through the female members of the family. The Dreamweaver was a friend who came to call and we fully expected him…After a while, as a very small child, daily events and the dreamworld became completely mixed up. Overlapping and merging into one another so that any sequences of reality became very blurred, surreal. Was it a dream or did it really happen?

Gran hardly slept a wink for years during her middle life. Every time she laid her head down to rest and closed her eyes she would dream a disaster. Her word gradually became gospel down Chelsea and Fulham way between the wars. People increasingly started making a bee-line for her front door…Had she seen anything about our Pat who'd gone missing in Toronto only last week? Is it safe for our Frank to travel on the Union Castle to Cape Town next month? Should our Daisy take that job in Felixstowe? Queries on all sorts of trivia. People wanting to know the future. Gran couldn't control these images until they took her over. Subjected her living to a walking misery. Plodding up and down, pacing to and fro, wearily wearing out the faded lemon-tinged lino just to keep from sleeping...Disasters and calamities. The Dreamweaver never gave her any respite. He took his toll of her sleeping unconscious, gave her a gift which extracted its reward by making her dread the nighttime.

My Great-Aunt Rose never had the same problems as Gran. She carried the air of a clairvoyant soothsayer around with her. Penetrating froggy eyes that unsettled you. A brusque manner with little truck for inconsequentials. Late in life, living in her little flat off Victoria Street, she allowed her talents to flourish. The nearby Church embraced her. She had become a local character. On Tuesdays and Thursdays in a hall adjoining the Church she was allowed to hold séances. Whether Rose was successful or not, I wasn't around to tell. Whenever I wrote to her and arranged a visit, the following always took place...

I had to arrive exactly on time. Clambering up seven flights of musty, stale-smelling, steep stairs. The all-purposeful knock on the door. Having overcome the 'Who is it? What do you want?' scenario, she would unbolt the four locks, unlatch the chain and peer at me through the doorway with her unsettling frogspawn glare..."Don't bring your troubles to my door!"..."Right. If that's how you feel..."...I would turn around and make to go down the stairs... "Alright then, you can come in..." Within five minutes I'm ensconced in a brass-studded, leather armchair drinking Earl Grey tea out of a Victorian china mug. Being told how much like her father I am, when in truth the only resemblance is our beards. Before long she's explaining to me how she talks every day to her late, departed Jim. They are in spiritual contact and able to converse. He advises her on all of her actions...Rose refuses to have gas or electricity in her flat. Lives by candlelight and cooks on an ancient, four-ringed primus stove complete with a biscuit tin oven. If there had been a pump-handle well for water in Victoria Street she would have used that as well. Any idea of a radio or television is strictly taboo. Only the local Victoria Gazette makes its way into this flat...I admire her. Rose is a hardy soul. Totally self-contained well into her eighties. Living daily with the dead. Communing twice a week with the loved and lost ones of sad and lonely people. Bringing some comfort and joy into dispirited peoples lives which the Church is unable to provide...She never questions me or asks after any other members of the family. And no, I'm not here because this querulous old lady has a lot of money in the bank...We usually end up after, say, four hours with her playing the piano and the pair of us singing a bloodcurdling rendition of 'I'm forever blowing bubbles'. This song brings tears to those thyroid eyes. It was Uncle Jim's and Rose's signature tune in the days when they used to razzle-dazzle all night at parties, entertaining and drinking an incredible amount...I never, never mention the Dreamweaver. I know through potted family history that she has committed a few deadly deeds in her youth. I suspect that he doesn't visit her anymore. Disgusted perhaps by her earlier life's performance... Rose tells me that she will visit me on a regular basis in the afterlife, instruct me for my own benefit.

But as yet, in the waning years, I've heard nothing from her. Not even a hint of contact. It doesn't matter for I forgave her for all the nasty family deeds, thank Kali for her deliverance and was truly appalled at her final demise...

"Hello, Sweet Pea, surprise visit!"

"Why do you always make it sound as if my visits are unexpected? Remember, you gave me a key to your front door and clearly said I could visit you whenever I pleased... Do you like this blue dress? I put it on specially for you."

"Now, now Moonchild. Yes, of course, I like it. Almost a shade of peacock blue... What do you expect me to say then?... No! Crap! Absolutely hideous! Makes you look old before your time. Blue is a cold colour fit only for gazebos and doesn't match your brown eyes. The length of the dress is disquieting and the overall effect doesn't project your presence sufficiently enough... Heigh ho!"

"Are we in a bad mood! All the work getting to you? Tell me more about the Dreamweaver. You've been very secretive about him. You're open about most other things. Something startling? A visit from him that really affected you... It's not something I've ever experienced. I hardly remember any of my dreams and I'm sure that most nights I don't dream at all."

"Everybody dreams, Sweet Pea. Usually three periods of REM a night. A way for the brain to gain a rest, recuperate from all the jangling images, sounds, information and responses it has to deal with every day. If we didn't dream we'd all go stark staring bonkers, crazy folk. Sleep deprivation, one of the oldest methods of torture. Denying us a chance to dream and release the turmoil we all gather daily just by opening our eyes. Most people never seriously consider what a wonderful machine we inhabit. The human body is a miracle of construction. Nothing is more fantastic on the planet Earth than a Human Being. It's easy as we trundle along from day to day to forget that. We all do it... I was writing about my Gran the other day, Sweet Pea. She was a great reader. Whenever she sat down for a while I always remember her with a book in her hands. The only photograph I have of her was taken with her sitting in a deckchair in a chalet garden overlooking the sand and sea at Jaywick. Book in hands, reading away. She used to love reading sea yarns. Her favourite brother, Herbert, spent a great deal of his life in the Merchant Navy. One time in the early nineteen-hundreds he was aboard a merchant trader that went down thirty miles off the coast of Africa. He was on the sea for over fifteen hours, but managed to swim ashore near the Cape of Good Hope. I think it was after that when he took a job in a diamond mine in South Africa and was killed a few months later in a mining disaster... Gran always talked about him. How Georgy reminded her of Herbert... Early death conferring glamour, sainthood. We never got to see them old. Imagine, Sweet

Pea, if Alexander the Great had lived to be eighty. His affair with Bagolas Old World knowledge. All the young boys and scandals to come. His weary veteran army all dead. Most of the special corps were aged over fifty when he inherited them from his father Philip. Perhaps he would have been deposed. Become old and grey with all the battle scars showing through. An old, limping, totally debauched Alexander. Senile, bald, grim at the last. Dominions usurped. Who knows? Would all the myths have survived? Would Iskendar still be revered today across large tracts of the Asian continent? I doubt it. All power corrupts in the end. The richest, most powerful man who ever lived. He never stood still from eighteen to thirty-three. It's better if our heroes die young. Surrender to their fate. That way their looks and deeds become immortalised, marbleised in our minds' eye. We can give free rein to our fantasies about them and they can never let us down…Herbert was like that for Gran. Hence she always read sea stories. Nothing complicated. Nothing Conradian or too deep. Simple, exciting sea yarns, which I now realise probably always contained Herbert. When she was a child and took a regular beating every day for daring to resemble her dead mother, Herbert was the one who tried to protect her. Supported her. Listened to her plight between sobs. Hard to live with cruelty each day, Sweet Pea. Must wear you down eventually. Crack and splinter any self-confidence and make you perpetually miserable and afraid…

I was stranded one time, living in an area of Leeds called Chapel Town. In the same street and only two doors away from the eventual Yorkshire Ripper, Peter Sutcliffe. It's too long a story to explain how I arrived there. Anyway, this particular night I went down to sleep. At the time I was carefully recording my dreams. I would try and force myself to wake up at the end of each REM period, grab the pen and notepad from beside the mattress on the floor and record it. Of course, once I started using these different methods, sleeping without any pillows, head facing north, no bed, forcing myself to sleep on my back because I'd noticed, so I thought, that when I slept on my side in the womb position I only dreamt in black and white. I'd been keeping this regime up fairly constantly for about two years by then. And, of course, during that time I hadn't had one meaningful dream. What had come naturally as a child, and had been rejected in the march towards macho-hood, had disappeared. By forcing the issue and attempting to re-awaken my dream world to reality, the Dreamweaver had taken offence and decided to teach me a lesson…

This particular night my dream life was completely vivid in glorious Technicolor. I awakened in the dream and realised that I was participating in someone else's dream. I was on a ship in a howling storm. Dressed in old-fashioned seaman's oilskins. Looking around me, the ship is very old. I'm at the tiller, foaming seawater cascading over the ship's decks in this raging storm. Awake without being able to see very far, blinding rain and salty spray whipping at my face. But I know there are hazardous rocks ahead which will run us aground. A torrential maelstrom mist vaporises everything as I'm hurled across the poop deck floor. Tiller spinning wildly out of control yet all the time aware that I'm traversing this dream through another's mind….Suddenly the scene changes and I'm walking along crowded back streets. I know it's Chelsea yet not the district I'm familiar with. Gas lamps giving off a strange eerie glow light the narrow cobbled streets. They cast amazingly grotesque shadows. People pawing at me as I pass. Drunken men, women and children. Toothless, dribbling adults beseeching me. Ribald joke and sneers. I'm apparently a stuck-up little madam. Quickening my steps. I'm manifestly used to these deprived, poverty-stricken sights. Part of me is appalled. Far more destitute and bleak than I ever imagined. Gutters overflowing with rotten refuse; putrid vegetables, pieces of maggoty meat, all swilling with the revolting stench of urine and water. Hurrying away with shouts and jeers echoing behind me. Strains of drunken laughter, obscene catcalls, thumping out-of-tune pianos and grinding barrel-organs piercing the foggy air. Frighteningly real and obscene. The squalor and the stench…

I awoke in a sweat, nightclothes soaked through. I wrote it all down. Unable to fully release the images. Gently stroking my wife and nudging her awake. Asking her to listen to me…I made her a cup of tea and read aloud the dream recall. Silence until I started to speculate that I was in someone else's dream… At first I mention 'his', but immediately reject the idea because of the period and timing. I realise it had to be Gran. The idea dawned, it seems so obvious now, that she had died. Hence me being inside her dream…It's important at such moments, Sweet Pea, to be clear and positive, otherwise afterwards people will always say you made it up. It's rather like the number of people who declare 'I know that' or 'I wish I'd spoken up', then again 'I knew the answer, but didn't say anything', if only…You have to be brave and do it or say it in the moment, be prepared to make a complete fool of your self. It doesn't matter and when the moment comes off it gives you the confidence for the next time…

I slipped my yoga clothes on and went down the ten flights of stairs to the payphone in the draughty hallway. It was around five o'clock in the morning by then…who to ring? I telephoned my sister, who was not best pleased…Later that same day I received a call from 'Liz', staring glumly at the glazed pane of glass in the hallway front door…Nosy neighbours making lame excuses for interrupting me on the telephone. Gran had been found dead that morning. Sis had gone round to her flat and let herself in with a spare key. Gran had died peacefully in her sleep…sailing away on Victorian cutters. Scanning the oriental horizon for her signs of her brother, Herbert. Leaving behind forever the dank, stinking, gas-lit confines of Edwardian Chelsea and the scar that stains you, the mark of poverty…"

"Were you very upset?"

"Well yes and no, Sweet Pea. How can you be upset when an old lady in her late eighties dies peacefully in her sleep. Given the choice we'd probably all select that final end. Nothing too traumatising. No farewells to comrades and into the gas ovens. No radiotherapy treatment, body hair completely shaven and taken before one's time in great pain. A surfing accident over at Newquay. He was such a strong swimmer, you know. Run down by a runaway truck. Wasted with Aids. Decapitated in a train accident when they said it couldn't happen here. Sitting on the toilet and having a heart attack. Too afraid to live anymore and seeking out phials of Hemlock and Belladonna to deaden the eyes. Yes, of course, I was bloody upset! Selfish. You don't find many people in this life who love you without reservation. Love you to the marrow without constraints. You never want them to go. It's selfish, Moonchild, but that's just the way we are. Her last earthly dream was her final gift to me..."

****

"What was it like living in amongst all those flats as a child?"

"Why are you so interested, Sweet Pea? You keep coming back with more and more questions!"

"People don't really talk anymore...Well, I suppose they don't...Anyway, the people I know don't...That old man who lives at the back of the church in Sancreed. Sometimes he talks to us when we play in the fields behind his house. But it's always about his dog, what it was like there fifty years ago. He's never even been to London. He doesn't seem to know very much..."

"Is he happy though, Moonchild? You don't need knowledge to be content. In fact, quite the reverse. He lives close to the land. Out in the countryside. Without even a Post Office or pub. Walks a lot with that collie dog of his. He strikes me as a pretty serene type of person. He's probably being cagey. He's not going to tell you about his poaching exploits, is he? Afraid even now that you might all shop him to the local Bobby. He's probably just pleased to find someone young to talk to. It must get very wearisome just passing the time of day with other old souls. All the opening weather gambits. The state of the water dam at Drift. The fluctuations in the price of fish. Think about it. Long nodding monologues on ailments and illness. The spectre of Death always looming large. General gossip about distant neighbours' grandchildren who he can't quite place in his mind. Why did that new youngblood farmer McKenzie at Grumbla bulldoze an ancient stone monument dating back some three thousand years?...He's hardly likely to say 'Did you see that Annabel Chong on the telly last night? What a gal! If I was even twenty years younger I'd fuck her till the cows came home. Give her a right good going over, Mrs Richards, that I would!' is he?"

"It must be really horrible to get old. What do you do with yourself?"

"We all get there if we're lucky, Sweet Pea. Anyway, different folks have different body clocks. I've met sixteen year olds who seem sixty in experience. Heroin runners and flesh peddlers before they'd even started shaving. I've met eighty year olds who to listen to them you would have thought that nothing of great significance or consequence had happened to them in the last seventy years. What about that lady at Mousehole, the early morning swimmer..."

"Margery."

"That's the one. Aged ninety-three at the last count. She rises every day at six and swims in the sea, all the year round, off the rocks at St. Clements

Island. Fit as a fiddle. Hardly a line or crease on her face. Still works part-time at the picture gallery on the harbour front, and still throws pots which she occasionally exhibits...You see, that could await you if Fate doesn't take a hand first... Different bodily metabolisms, different energy cycles...You're turning into my muse, Sweet Pea. When you left the other day, I sat down and wrote for ten hours straight until the typewriter ribbon gave out. I felt like I'd been drinking from the Hippocrene fountain on Mount Helicon...I shouldn't voice it though. One could get very superstitious about such things..."

"'Maybe that's a role for me in life. I can be your ...Muse?"

"Correct."

"That's great! I don't have to do or be anything...When the career's advisor comes round next term and asks me what I want to be, I'll simply say a Muse. What do you think the reply will be?"

"I hate to think. Probably recommend you for the Ed Psych...'I would say that this girl is in urgent need of a will to live. Silly little bitch thinks she can spend all her life being a muse. These responses and replies get sillier and sillier, Mrs Barnaby.' That sort of thing. Whatever you do, don't mention me, okay! You know what those teaching reformers are like! Leaving no grey Cornish stone unturned. A whiff of something slightly sinister and they jump on it with glee."

"Michelle said that you were a schoolteacher once."

"A long time ago, Sweet Pea, and best forgotten."

"The flats, please tell me what it was like. I can't imagine living among a lot of people every day."

"Alright...It was a thriving beehive of activity. Everybody, well, most of the men, seemed to work. Great droves of people setting off about their business every morning. Around seven thirty to eight o'clock. The second shift of office workers, store workers and school-children at eight-thirty-ish. Everybody knew one another. Over five hundred people shunted together in one hundred and forty-odd flats. They were all just pleased to be there and alive. I remember as a young schoolchild, complete with satchel, setting off every morning and walking along for a few yards with Mr Boothby. He was always friendly and had this tin leg. He never complained, yet sometimes in the thick of winter you could see the pain and discomfort etched on his face. After a short while, he'd be off and somehow manage to swing that tin leg over the crossbar of his bike...I remember laying in bed and hearing a lot of the men on the early shifts whistling as they set off. Some of them were really good. You've got to remember there were hardly any cars, Moonchild. My Dad was the first one to have a car in those buildings. Only a very few people had television sets. There was only one channel then. Seems laughable today. Also the radio programmes used to close down around eleven - eleven thirty at night. So you see everybody went to sleep. The sort of place where people didn't flush their toilets after midnight for fear of disturbing the neighbours...It wasn't all perfect. Nothing ever is. There were a couple of loud, disruptive Teddy boys, constant games of football and cricket in the evenings, weekends and holidays, which must have driven some of the occupants mad...Still, if you've fought in a war and killed people you don't worry about a couple of thugs with long sideburns, winkle-pickers and switch-blades. They were really spivs, Teddy boys came later. And the games were healthy. Just a noisy din and shouting a lot of the time...People looked out for one another. I suppose a carry-over of the Blitz spirit and the joy of V.E day...I can just remember the Queen's Coronation party. 'Liz' was one of the organisers. I was dressed in a suit covered in packs of playing cards. A type of Joker. Sis was dressed as a tiny pink fairy with a magic silver wand...In the central courtyard trestle tables were laid out all covered with food. Cheese sandwiches, ham sandwiches, cucumber and tomato sandwiches, fancy cakes, rock cakes, melting ice-cream, lemonade, orangeade. I suppose all the tenants must have chipped-in to a collection. All the children were given Coronation mugs, silver spoons with the Queen's head on the end of the handle, a commemorative gold-painted coach and horses, and a balloon...In the early evening, a band played and couples danced. Georgy was on the banjo. The music was a blend of popular, country and folk. Later on, people got drunk and sang old songs like "Knees up, Mother Brown" and did the Hokey-Cokey and then they Congaed around the seven blocks of flats a few times...Not like the seventy-seven Jubilee celebrations. Not a lot happened. In the streets and places I went to in Fulham, most of the younger ones, myself included, were totally spaced out of it on hash, grass, speed, acid, coke and heroin, whatever. The spirit was one of anarchy and let's have a last fling...God Save the Queen and her fucking fascist regime... Large banners proclaiming 'Let's put a real kween in the Palace'..."

"A few famous people came out of those buildings. Three to be exact. I never spoke to Alan Caddy when he was really successful. A founder member of 'Johnny Kidd and the Pirates' and 'The Tornadoes'. Later in the last part of the Sixties he was a record producer for Peter Frampton and 'The Herd'. I got to know him much later, Sweet Pea...If you're cold turn the fire up...I'd returned from a courier job in Morocco and was signing on. Staying a few weeks with 'Liz' at the self-same flat. Alan Caddy had returned from ten years living in America. Utterly broke like me and staying with his ninety-year old mother. She was an amazing old lady. Still getting up each weekday morning at five o'clock and going uptown to clean offices in The City. During the winter she still wore the fur coat that Alan had bought her with the success of 'Telstar'...Alan and I travelled together to the Labour Exchange on a number fourteen bus. Sitting at the front upstairs and sharing a crafty spliff. He looked very down at heel and drained. His American wife had divorced him by then and taken all of his money as well as keeping his daughter. He'd been forced to return with absolutely nothing, zilch. He was never a great talker, but we rubbed along on the four or five bus journeys we made together. Mainly discussing the old days. About his late father who had been a drummer in a local dance band in the Thirties. His mother died a few years later and that was the last I ever saw of him...In the late fifties Mrs Bell and her son, Ron, lived in a ground floor flat next door to some boyhood friends of mine. She was always great to me. Lemonade drinks on hot days and a boiled sweet at the ready. Ron seemed very shy. When I discovered that he was a professional cricketer I just had to go and watch him play...Sussex were playing Middlesex at Lords over the Whitsun Bank Holiday. Ron was the Sussex left-arm spinner. I sat all day Saturday in the lower tier of the grandstand and watched his every move. Eventually, when he came on to bowl his spinners, a left-hand batsman by the name of Peter Parfitt totally destroyed him. I was so embarrassed. Vicarious empathy. I could feel my sun-tanned face turning the colour of Tahitian rose-pink. Of course, I'd already declared I knew him as I scoffed my banana sandwiches. Fatal. His destruction prompted a lot of stick from the crowd, mainly other children around me...I never let on to Mrs Bell that I'd gone to see Ron play. Too embarrassed. I believe Sussex terminated his contract in the mid-Sixties and he disappeared into league cricket...Do you want anything to eat or drink, Moonchild? You know well enough to help yourself by now..."

"You said three people."

"Well, so I did... Alan Caddy and Ron Bell were a hell of a lot older than me, but always friendly to a little kid. If only a smile or a wink. George Barker wasn't. He was once described by a very famous television arts presenter and author as the only living Englishman to have the profession of poet written in his passport. Which I thought was a bit unkind to Ted Hughes amongst others. I would have written something else, Moonchild...Even as a very small child you sense people who believe they shouldn't be among you. Give off a disdainful manner and put on airs and graces, as my Gran would have put it. He dressed in what I suppose was an accepted poetic manner for the late Forties- early Fifties. Very large broad-brimmed hats. Blue dungarees before jeans hit Britain. An early form of brothel-creeper and sometimes a cape...Affected and sneering are the words I am searching for...He left before I reached school age. Many, many years later I recognised him in a pub in Norfolk. I'd been staying at Hunstanton and searching for the remains of an old country house that had burnt down and been destroyed between the two world wars. I saw George Barker when I popped into this country pub for some lunch. A total pisshead by then. Holding court in the bar in that surly, alcoholic fashion, and grinding the paraletically smashed young wife into the intellectual dust of the pub carpet. Very unsavoury..."

"Was he a good poet?"

"Yeah. But the trouble with knowing or meeting a performing artist in whatever field, is that if you really dislike them it completely colours your view of their work or performance. It shouldn't, I know. But if you find a person really obnoxious and then you see them, say an actor, perform you're inclined to find fault with the merest hint of a mistake. Just a whiff of a blemish. It's just human nature, Sweet Pea..."

"Why do you want to keep hearing this ancient stuff, Moonchild? It must be boring you silly!"

"No, it's not...Why do you still use a typewriter when you have an excellent computer...? If I was bored I wouldn't come around so much, would I? Who else is going to tell me about what things used to be like. The only relative I have that counts besides Michelle and Luke, who's only two and a half anyway, is my Grandmother in Nice who doesn't speak a word of English and doesn't know anything about England. She can hardly remember anything about France. The Second World War is a complete blank too her. She once said to Michelle that the Germans looked very smart and handsome in their uniforms. My Grandfather was supposed to have made a lot of money on the black market during the war, but I hardly remember him at all."

"You're unusual, Sweet Pea. Most girls of your age wouldn't give a fuck about what had happened two years ago let alone all the time I'm covering. Get a life! Go to the local disco. Get some computer games, go horse-riding, become a devoted fan of the latest pop band...I'm sorry, that was unkind. I should be grateful. You asking all these questions has re-opened a part of my life which had remained dormant until now. Closeted away for rainy days when I'm old, sat in front of the fire reminiscing. Of course, if I ever get there my memory will have gone and I'll be senile or worse...Habit and superstition. I foolishly believe that old IBM typewriter brings me luck. How wrong can you be! I know it's a pain where alterations are concerned. Just one click and I could change any mistake or name with the computer. But superstition is something we all concede to. People who say they don't believe in any form of superstition are just as bad. Usually very forcible about it. Pushing Fate away, deriding Lady Luck; lost in the cobwebs and undeclared daylight of ancient recesses of their brains. To deny superstition so vehemently is in itself an acceptance. Never trust anyone, Moonchild, who is fanatical about anything. Always suspicious. An abnegation of responsibility for themselves. Doesn't matter what it is. Religion, anti-smoking, Communism, Fascism, health, ecology, whatever...It's not to be confused with enthusiasm. Sorry I'm lecturing, Sweet Pea, hectoring, around and around...As a boy I used to sit and get my Gran to tell me stories. What it was like in Chelsea during the First World War. The friendly German butcher at the World's End whose shop was vandalised and burnt down in a mass arson attack just after the war began. How his family were pelted with stones and driven out, back to Germany. The newspapers of the day whipping up mass hysteria against the vicious Hun...What it was like cleaning five days a week for what was Chelsea's then surrogate Royal Family, the Bonham-Carters. Great Liberal politicians of the day when the Liberal Party was in power. My Gran was a great cook and when the Bonham-Carters threw special dinner parties she was always called in to prepare the meals. However, the only politician she ever liked or trusted was Lloyd-George. He brought in Insurance reforms for the poor and introduced the Old Age pension. I think the reason she liked him was that she cooked for him many times at those Bonham-Carter soirees and he always sent a shilling to the kitchen for her..."

On and on, masses of imagery. Flashed glimpses of chunks of other people's lives and times...How Pop as a young man used to travel on his days off to Crystal Palace to watch W.G.Grace play in his last years. Gran was so poor in 1915 that she used to borrow money to buy black-market horsemeat for her and the first two children. By 1917, she was reduced to stewing rats."

"Ergh...Rats!"

"Don't be precious, Sweet Pea. Better to eat stewed rat than nothing at all. Of course, she 'top and tailed' them first...I only know this through Gran. It's not something I've ever read about or come across. How the population of London in 1917 were really starving. You always hear about the Second World War rationing. All the jokes about Spam, spaghetti, dried egg, but never anything about the First."

"Rats though. That's really disgusting! I'd rather starve!"

"No, you wouldn't. Look, I'm a vegetarian, but I don't kid myself. If I was really hungry I'd go out and shoot a rabbit with a bow and arrow. We never experience hunger, Sweet Pea. What's the difference between a squirrel and a rat anyway. Rats have been getting a bad press for years. Squirrels are pretty with their fluffy tails. They look so cute don't they? But they are only tree rats after all. These darling little creatures being gamely fed nuts by hand all over Britain as we speak, have just carried out the virtual genocide of their smaller cousins the Red Squirrel. Yet you don't think any the worse of them do you, Moonchild? Sailors regularly ate rats. Soldiers in the trenches ate rats..."

"Stop it, please! I hate rats!"

"Okay, okay, but think, Sweet Pea. When you pop into the local supermarket do you ever walk slowly past the meat and fish counters and wonder how these polythene-wrapped pieces of flesh came to be there? Alright, unfair I know. You've been down on the quayside at Newlyn after a fresh trawler catch has been landed and watched the fish auctions. It's just, well, rabbits and pheasants aren't that much higher up the evolutionary scale than rats, are they? In a few years we will all be able to sit in front of our computers and trace our ancestry right the way back to the illusionary pea soup, the glories of DNA. I bet every one of us will discover an ancestor who was a cannibal. The world will probably be shocked and horrified to learn that the way the human race survived, came to be here right now, was through mass cannibalism before the last Great Flood. How we all ate a close ancestor of ours, ate them into extinction the way the grey squirrel has nearly taken care of the red cutie-pie. The past contained no protection of endangered species. Well over seventy percent of all known species are extinct. My Gran wasn't happy or proud about having to eat rat and I'm sure she only did it in a grave emergency. Like starvation. But better to eat something that revolts you than die from a misguided moral stance..."

"They eat horsemeat in France."

"So they do, Sweet Pea. You're half a horse-eating girl then...A restaurant in London specialises in horsemeat. Just a case of different countries, different customs and cuisine...Maybe my Gran had some Vietnamese blood in her. Rat is a delicacy in the Mekong Delta region. Rice. Farmers catch the rats as they try to snaffle the grain. Vietnamese restaurants serve rat fried, grilled or curried. Rice farmers make the main part of their living by selling rats. Tons and tons of them, particularly in the southern provinces...Rat is dish of the day."

"Please!"

"Okay. But the point is, Sweet Pea, what revolts you and me may make someone else salivate."

"Well, get away from rats, and tell me more about what it was like all those years ago when you were a child."

"You're very persistent, Moonchild. The spirit of Georgy drawing me back to a time and a place...It's all changed now but then there was a sense of community. Everybody spoke to one another. Followed different families' fortunes. Gossip prevailed as always and disasters struck just the same. But you weren't alone. Of course, one can take the sense of community too far. An elderly friend of mine, Bill Curzon, used to ride a motorbike. Must have been an old-style Norton. A loud, vexatious family named Martin complained about Bill riding his noisy motorbike into the courtyard after seven o'clock in the evening. Could you believe that today? Poor old Bill, through a council directive was forced to silently wheel the gorgeous gleaming machine from the front gate to his flat. Control gone crazy...The Martin's eldest son, Johnny, had a Diana air gun and used to shoot at people from his fourth floor bedroom window, but nothing was said. Can't upset his father, the local bus driver, he might run you down next time you're stood at a bus stop daydreaming...Today, old Bill would roar in at full throttle at two o'clock in the morning. When Mrs Martin pokes her head around her net curtains and shouts he'd give her a one-fingered salute. Even the fuck-off signs have changed. Next day Mr Martin would reach the bus depot and find his tyres slashed and the seats vandalised, and not-so-young Johnny would be charged with racism for shooting off his airgun over Mrs Fitzgerald's head...Nothing is ever perfect.

I was happy as a small child, existing serenely in my safe, secluded world. Quite content to play in the courtyard and the local Rec by St. Luke's Church. The problems arose when schooling loomed large on the horizon. The spirit of Georgy, love, cake and affection, had definitely not prepared me for what I was about to encounter. The grim, realistic outside world. Examples are plentiful, Sweet Pea, and I won't test your eternal patience with them...A defining moment came when I was eight. The school was a very modern, grand affair near Earls Court. Built in the early Fifties with a large, yellow-daubed water tower acting as a landmark. The rear of the school had an attractive pond containing lily-pads, fronds and very large Chinese goldfish. This pond looked out over a precious area known as Little Boltons...Of course, the goldfish regularly died each winter during a cold snap and had to be replaced...Every year contained two classes with about thirty children in each. I was always dumped in the second class. Each week we would have a maths test, spelling bee and an essay to write. Simple stuff. I nearly always won the lot and was usually chosen to read to the class. I can remember reading 'The Hobbit' out loud and used to smile much later when it became a cult book in the late Sixties. My fellow classmates contained Elizabeth Fontaine whose father became the manager/Governor of the Bank of England. We were all forced to view his signature on a fresh five-pound note...Dujan Indic, whose father was the Yugoslav Ambassador to London, Paul Vaughan, who was a child actor championed by Joan Littlewood, Alex Munroe, whose sister was a famous film actress of the day. Alex was always regaling me with stories of playing Pontoon with the comic actor, Sid James, on a film location set. Clive Usher whose father was a famous architect. And so on. Too many to mention. Gradually all these kids made their way into the first stream class. I never thought anything of it at the time. Yet even in my naïve, dumb state I was aware enough to see the class divide...If my Gran on a rare occasion came to meet me at the front gate after school, she was always left standing on her own by the other women. The same with the teachers. Idle glances and comments about your clothes. Masses of it really, but at that age you just let it go by. Most of it sliding over your head anyway. I suppose as a reaction to the school I was quite often ill. Broken arm, measles, whooping cough, German measles three times, smashed leg, another broken arm, nervous asthma. Long drawn-out visits to the Tite Street Hospital for special exercises on Mondays and Thursdays. Passing down past Oscar Wilde's old house and always staring at the blue plaque...This particular time I'd been ill in bed for a couple of weeks. Probably just a bug doing the rounds of the smog-infested city. That Sunday night I was pronounced well enough to return to school. I protested, but already the suspicion was growing that I hated the place and would say anything to get out of going...I can't remember what the day was like though I know it wasn't raining. School commenced at nine-fifteen and I arrived at ten to nine. Some children hanging around the playground and the eternal game of football in progress...I suddenly had to go to the toilet. Serious problem. Making my way, holding myself in. There was a toilet opposite the entrance to my classroom on the ground floor. Shock, horror! No toilet paper...Holding down a panic attack and gingerly walking back out into to the playground. The teacher on duty was a grizzly, grey-haired man called Mr Docherty. I stood before him with my head about level with his chest as he read his Guardian newspaper, ignoring his surroundings.

"Excuse me, Sir."

A catch in his throat signalling disapproval.

"Yes, what is it?!"

Probably disturbed his take on the Suez Crisis.

Nervous and ashamed. "I have to go to the toilet Sir, and there aren't any toilet rolls in the toilet, Sir."

"Aren't, aren't… well use your initiative boy. Go and look in the classroom and find some toilet paper."

"Thank you sir."

Head immediately back into his paper, which is held up ostentatiously in front of his face…Aboard a steamer coursing down the Suez Canal looking for stray French engineers misplaced around the time of the mad Mahdi…

Tenaciously holding myself in, I trudge slowly back to the classroom. Desperation seizing me. Searching frantically through the stacked piles of drawers at the rear of the classroom. All empty. Not a toilet roll in sight. The large, glass-panelled bookcase at the front of the class is locked. It contains all our reading material and individual exercise books which are put away for safe-keeping each day. If the mad Mahdi could have got his hands on these General Kitchener would have been done for…I'm frantically searching around the classroom caught between panic and the need for every action to be made slowly…Somehow I manage to walk back out onto the playground. Strange rumbling noises in my stomach. A horrible foul stench making its way up into my mouth. My mouth has become a cesspool of miasmic taste…Gradually the numbers in the playground have built up. The last ten minutes have seemed like a lifetime to me. It's still only nine o'clock as the church clock in the Little Boltons chimes…

"Excuse me, Sir."

"What again!"

Angry furrowed brow peering at me over the top of the printed pages.

"I can't find any toilet paper, Sir."

I'm anxiously viewing that newspaper. I want to grab it and take it to the toilet with me. If Mr Docherty were a kind, caring man, he would take out a couple of sheets of job advertisements and give them to me. My crisis would be averted and he could forget all about me and return to the day's news.

"You'll have to wait for Miss Parker to arrive."

I cannot hold back the idea. The whole of my insides are churning dramatically.

"Your newspaper, Sir."

I look at it lovingly. Two sheets of the Guardian in that moment would be worth pure gold dust to me.

"Go away and wait! You're not having my newspaper!"

Mr Docherty turns his back on me, grizzly head lost once more within the reaches of the Nile. Summarily dismissed. The insolent cheek of even contemplating using his precious sheets of relayed printed news. Somehow, and I'm not quite sure how, I manage to walk back to the toilet in front of the classroom. Toes turned inwards. Knees touching. The excruciating pain etched with the horror of the situation.

I get into the brightly painted yellow and green toilet. Sliding the silver-chrome bolt across the door.. Just making it to the toilet bowl, unable to pull the seat down in time...oh, the relief. The noise of my shitting and farting is thunderous. It feels as if my whole eight year old body is shitting out in that little bright thunderbolt. Panic has now set in. Shamed and red-faced at my own predicament. Then suddenly a glint hardens in my little blue eyes. For the first time I can truly remember I feel anger. Pure undiluted anger. The ridiculousness of my situation. I have a right to toilet paper just as the Egyptians have a right to control a trading canal that runs through the heart of their own lands. The only swear word I knew properly at the time kept running through my head. Bastards. Bastards. Bastards. The whole imperfect nature of this shit snobbery school wells up inside of me. I'll show the bastards. I slip off my short trousers and pants and slowly, but surely wipe my dripping arse all over the brightly coloured painted yellow and green walls smearing lines and lines of watery shit all over them. I turn to all four corners yet still my bottom won't clean. I flush the disgusting toilet bowl and climb up with my feet placed on the bowl and scrape my bottom firmly against the free wall below the cistern. Still incensed I jump down and besmirch my bottom all over the dark blue door... Outside I can hear the first signs of children entering the classroom. Putting back on my foul pants and short trousers and spitting on my hands. No wash basin provided, of course...I quickly slide back the silver-chrome lock and with great pleasure close the toilet door behind me. Leaving one great mess of shit streaked halfway up all four walls and door...Ignoring everybody I walked out into the playground. The beautiful freedom of being able to just walk without painful constriction...skirting left by the main entrance away from the late arriving herd and moving my way through the Little Boltons...I walked the mile and three-quarters back home. My pants and short trousers are in a disgusting state, but I don't care. I whistle to myself for courage and fight back tears of shame and genuine temper. Never before or since have I ever felt such real anger...

When I arrived back the only person at home was Gran...she came round during the weekdays to do the cleaning while 'Liz' ran the workroom down at the World's End...Thank God it's Gran. She doesn't make any fuss or pass comment. Simply smiles at me. Strips off all my shitty clothes and puts them in an old copper tub for boiling. Washes me down stroking my hair. Makes me a cup of Oxo in a blue-rimmed tin mug complete with a hunk of white bread. When I've finished this she puts me to bed...

"Sorry, I shouldn't have recounted that to you, Sweet Pea."

"It's okay. I felt really sorry for you having to go through that. Shit doesn't both me, I changed Luke's nappies many times when he was a baby...Did you ever go back to the school?...What happened?"

"Funnily enough, nothing was said at home. I suppose 'Liz' must have written a letter to the school saying I still wasn't well. No questions and nothing from the school...I managed to malinger on for another three weeks. Though, of course, I was better after two. That final week of freedom should have been an oasis of pleasure, but the whole smelly event kept building up in my mind the way things do. It seemed to penetrate my whole waking being with dread. Only the Dreamweaver provided any respite. I couldn't think of anything else. The sheer dread of having to return to school and face the inevitable inquisition...I thought of running away. Pretending to go to school and just drift around the parks all day. Induce such severe asthma attacks that I would be deemed unfit for any more schooling. But I couldn't put off my impending fate forever...

The dreaded day duly arrived and off I set like a convicted criminal awaiting the Hangman's noose...I arrived at about five past nine. Straight away groups of hop-scotching and skip-rope jumping girls sniggering and giggling in my direction. My face was scarlet all the way into the classroom and then into Assembly...Baldy Boon was our headmaster: a severe, taciturn man with arse-licking tendencies towards the right connections...About a year before he'd informed the whole school that from now on we would have Wagner's 'Ride of the Valkyries' played to us every morning before we began prayers. To elevate our appreciation of classical music and rid us of this rock and roll junk starting to infiltrate our senses...Peculiar and eerie looking back on it. Here was a man charged with looking after the clean scrubbed, molly-coddled, baby-boom generation only ten years after the end of the second World War, who decided to treat us to Hitler's chosen composer and favourite piece of music...I sat cross-legged at the back of the hall with the other three hundred and fifty children, feeling like a leper and beyond redemption...Sure enough at the end of prayers a delay in the classroom departures. My name was called out and I had to walk along the raised steps at the side of the Assembly Hall. All eyes following my every movement...I was quickly ushered upstairs to Baldy Boon's office above the Assembly Hall. I stood before him with at least four teachers including Mr Docherty and Miss Parker standing right behind me...Headmaster Boon was seated at his desk with a complete glass frontage behind him. Through this glass I could see all the children looking up at us and ignoring what was being said to them from the raised platform by the gym teacher, Miss Tomous.

"What do you have to say for yourself, boy?"

Baldy Boon's eyes glinting at me over steel-rimmed spectacles...I just look at him and say nothing. Some of the teachers are shuffling their feet uneasily behind me.. He doesn't give me long. Snorts...I can't really remember his speech. More like a diatribe. Mainly for the benefit of the teachers rather than me...About how he won't tolerate any rebels in his school. How one of the girls in my class, Susan May, had fainted on entering the toilet and discovering my artistic endeavour. How when she was revived she had developed a nosebleed and had to be taken home by Miss Parker in a taxi...I should learn to control my natural bodily processes like the other children. The rebellious nature of youth today. No respect, no regard. He won't tolerate it! The school won't tolerate it! The board of governors won't tolerate it!...But wait for it...He's going to expel me...No. That would be too easy. He's going to make an example of me in front of the whole school...No mention of contacting my parents. No reference to Mr Docherty. No concern at the lack of toilet paper or inadequate supervision... Still he's not satisfied. The natives behind him are getting restless. They want action. Some of the girls are practising with their recorders. A slow bee-like drone and hubbub...But Baldy won't stop. He's thumping his desk and making points...How we have all reached this crisis as a nation through a lack of respect and control. A lack of national spirit resulting in the crisis at Suez...I find myself wanting to laugh at him, but I know that would be stupid and only give him an excuse and opportunity he's been waiting for to extend the level of punishment... On and on he winds. Several times Miss Parker tries to interrupt him. I can partly see her reflection in the glass pointing to her wristwatch...He must have gone on like that for about ten minutes. It seemed an eternity to me...Eventually though, he catches up with himself. Re-composed his attitude. Glares at me for the hundredth time...The teachers troop out with me edging behind them. Baldy Boon bringing up the rear wielding his fabled cane of demon bamboo...Silence was called for in assembly. Headmaster Boon then re-addressed the expectant throng. Much along the lines already mentioned. The gist of it being he won't tolerate disgusting behaviour. No rebels in this school etc...Having exhausted his voice with the second tirade I'm called across and made to bend over in a ritualistic stance. Hushed silence from the attentive audience...Thwack...Thwack...I'm determined not to cry out loud and give Baldy Boon his pleasure...Thwack...I'm biting my lips hard as the tears start to career down my face...Thwack...I bite my tongue by mistake, but don't feel the pain... Thwack...I believe he gave me twelve of his best. Delivered with zeal and fortitude...Thwack...I was a dirty Egyptian wog who had to be beaten to order, commandeered and controlled...Thwack...Thwack...But I didn't cry out loud which must have angered him for I'm sure he slipped an extra one in...Thwack...Thwack...The gap between each stroke of the throbbing cane seemed timeless...Thwack...Thwack...Baldy playing to his audience. Glasses getting steamed up. I believe he stopped completely around seven and took them off. All the better to cane you with...Thwack...When he'd finished administering the thwacking pain I was made to stand facing the school and apologise. The final humiliation...At first nothing would come out. Baldy Boon nudging my shoulder, prodding me..."Speak up, boy...Speak up!"...

"I'm sorry."

"Say it again!"

"I'm sorry."

"Now, let that be a lesson to all of you. I won't stand for any rebellious behaviour at this school!"

Cliché rolled out after cliché...

Red-eyed and tearstained, I traipse off the raised platform to join the others moving towards the classrooms. Entertainment over for this Assembly time...resolved not to talk to anybody. From now on I shall operate in dumb, insolent silence. I won't read anymore to the class. I refuse to bother with any of the schoolwork. I will sit at the back of the classroom by the outside window and look at the cars and lorries passing up and down the Brompton Road. And they can take their school and shove it where the sun never shines!"

"That was really horrible. They're not allowed to touch us at all. I won't even let a teacher grab me by the arm!"

"Quite right too, Sweet Pea. The British always believed in beating their children into submission. You have to maintain some control, but I've always thought sarcasm, detention or lines ought to be able to do the trick...In those days a teacher could virtually get away with murder. All the sadistic elements revelling in their chosen occupation...Whack a child a day and keep the sex pain at bay. If it talks, gawks, walks, hit it hard..."

"Was that the end of it?"

"Not really. I never told the folks at home. Parents weren't allowed any input in those days. Unless of course you possessed the correct breeding, fame, glamour or oodles of money. Privilege dispensed and the rest could suck on bitter acid drops...I had to go to the school designated. Sis for example was sent to a school that was closer to home. No explanation. Just the way it was. You weren't consulted. Nothing's ever right, but today is more civilised...Events can shape and alter things happening rapidly. It was around that time that Georgy was diagnosed as having Hodgkin's disease...Like a malignant cancer, Moonchild. All the major glands gradually enlarge. In Georgy's case his liver, spleen and lymph glands. Deterioration is very rapid. A wasting away. No known cure and not much more known about it today for all the doctors say...Within a few weeks of the diagnosis, he was sent to a sanatorium at Buxton near Derby...Gran always said it was having those early morning swims during the War. Repeatedly diving naked into a pool of freezing icy water before the onslaught of the blinding desert heat...Who knows...People need to find explanations in such moments. A time of trial and hurt. If you can talk just a little about it, let some of the pain out. The old hoary cliché about the good always dying young. It seems like that. We never saw them old and depraved. Disillusioned and hard of heart,,,"

"God, you must have been upset!"

"I was, Sweet Pea, I surely was. It all happened so suddenly. Nobody ever told you very much in those days. They still don't really. All cosmetic window-dressing to create the illusion of healthcare in progress...What I was saying to you last week about the other side of Paradise. So often in our lives things are great and we don't know it. Always wanting more. Wanting to be better than the next person. For what? So we can feel superior. Acclaim ourselves as super beings. Pretend to greatness we can in no way justify...Georgy became ill not long after my shitty debacle at school. Nothing much was said, though I can remember listening to a heated conversation in our kitchen one day...How 'She' was not going to visit him on a regular basis. How 'She' had been seen out laughing and drinking with his best friend, Roy. How 'She' seemed unconcerned and was spied by a neighbour buying fresh summer frocks in a sale at Barkers...These angels of women who guarded me needed a natural villain and they'd found one without much trouble...A couple of months later, not long after my ninth birthday, the Family travelled by car to Buxton one Sunday. It was the only time we, the children, were taken to see him...Too upsetting for them probably the reason...The sanatorium seemed cold and grey from the outside. Set on the edge of town. High up and windy...Cold and austere in the way that old disused military barracks often seem...A place to hide one's face away from the world. As if sunshine never finds its way here. All the joy of life is going on somewhere else. The diseased have to be locked up. Shuttered out of sight in case of contamination...A weak wave and pallid smile greets us...A small nondescript room which two in-patients were sharing. I can remember sitting by his bedside and looking out of the window at the clouds circling the Peak District. The air was meant to be restorative and the adjacent mineral springs conducive to promoting health...Georgy had lost so much weight. From guarded conversations in the car, I'd gathered that most of his teeth had fallen out which had really dismayed him...Would upset anyone not yet thirty-five with an attractive young wife. When you're that ill inconsequential side effects can play on your mind as you're lying there with nothing to do. I mean, you might find this appalling, your vanity pricked, losing your hair and teeth seems devastating., But when you're dying, so what! If you could be cured then you wouldn't give a toss, right! Obtain implants on the National Health, apply for a scalp graft. Shave your head completely and flaunt it. Thirty more years active life is worth a few teeth and some hair...It's hard to accept. We are all so compulsively vain and secretly wish to live forever. Some magic elixir that will pickle our bodies in a time warp. Never do we think of the consequences, just the Human need to outlive our brethren...Old ladies well past ninety living in rooms on their own. One falls down on a rainy day. The fragile nature of bones and uncertain balance. The mind playing tricks. No one will help this old lady. What does she cry out with?...'Don't let me die...Please don't let me die.'...Born at the beginning of the Edwardian era. Having lived a life that would equal three of most others. Staring watery-eyed towards her ninety-seventh birthday. Fallen, trapped, unable to move...'Please don't let me die...Somebody help me.'...Voice rising to that of a pre-pubescent girl. Afraid...All old hat, but we don't deal with death very well in the western and WASP worlds do we. We deal with it by ignoring it where possible. Don't mention it and it won't happen. A complete downer, not something to be considered because it will never happen to us...'Don't let me die'...But they did, as her voice grew faint across time. Nobody cared and when the local authorities finally axed down the door it was all too late. All to no avail. The occupants nearby presumably thought it an afternoon soap with the sound control up to high...I was allowed to sit with Georgy on my own for five minutes...The last time...He asked me how I was. Putting on a show. Making an effort...I quickly ran through what had transpired at the school...The only person I told...Suddenly a flash of energy brightened his face. Took him out of himself for a few short seconds. Somebody else's problems...'Listen, don't worry, you were ill. You had a bad cold which gave you a severe case of the runs, that's all. Don't mind the school, could have happened to anyone'...He held my hand weakly and smiled with good-natured love and affection towards me...I felt better and relieved. His was the opinion I valued most highly. What did anybody else know anyway...We left as the diluted sun was departing. 'Liz' and young Sis crying quietly walking out towards the parked car. Gran's face set with hardened resolve...I never saw him again...Georgy died a few weeks later. A blessed release...A couple of days before he died I was playing on my own in the courtyard. The milkman was on a second delivery in the afternoon, which they had in those days. My tennis ball ran under the milkfloat and lodge by the single front wheel, trapped on the inside. I couldn't quite reach it and for some reason wouldn't crawl under the bulging milkfloat to retrieve it. Projecting from the front of the float was an arched black steering arm with a small brake on top in the handle...I pressed it and much to my surprise released the milkfloat... My tennis ball immediately spewed out towards the courtyard wall. I ran to get it. Picked up the ball and turned around to find the milkfloat chugging towards me. Surprise, surprise! Panic! Struck immobile with fear. An utterly stupid thing to do. Rooted to the spot. Indecision. By the time I chose to move it was too late. The milkfloat just rumbled and clinked on its shaky way and pinned my remaining right leg to the courtyard wall. Strove hard, shaking and jangling its bottles and assortment of orange and chocolate Micky delights, to drive that right leg of mine clean through the wall at five miles an hour...I started screaming and howling. Piercing cries of pain that brought the milkman mumbling out from a block of flats to regain control of his runaway, quaking mass of wobbly bottles. Milk bottles tottering and smashing on the concrete as he sets it in reverse...My right leg was shattered in three places. Placed in an old-fashioned plaster cast for nine months. All my remaining junior schooldays were to be over...Five months spent on a children's ward in St Stephen's hospital...Whispered fears that I would never walk properly again with that leg., Susurrated warnings behind face-high held hands that my future mobility was threatened forever...All the daily treatments and eventual repeated exercises when the cast was excruciatingly removed. Not a hair left on my leg as the nurse-inspired Doctor cut through the plaster like a lumberjack in black stockings and ripped the two halves away. I would be eleven before I could even limp successfully. Ancient methods that held your recovery back. Talk of metal pins to sustain the crushed leg. Some Swiss surgeon visiting the city who was pioneering plastic joint implants at the time...In a way I loved it. I must have. Not the pain, of course. It was such a stupid, self-induced accident. Freed from that junior school forever. Pain that somehow related to the early demise of Georgy. Turning the hurt and agony back in on myself...I spent the day of Georgy's funeral reading a western by Zane Grey in my hospital bed. Tears held down by 'The Riders of the Purple Sage'. Cacti, rivers, horses, guns and lassos to deaden the grief...It turned out that the accident wasn't purely my fault, Sweet Pea...You still awake?...That grass will destroy your mind. Home-grown Cornish weed will send us all to the funny farm...Roll me one, will you...Is a nod all I get? Go on then...Yes, it wasn't the normal milkman on duty that day, but the very obese, red-faced foreman. By law he was required to have had the main handbrake on to stop such an idiot as me. In fact, even a slight bump or push could have set that milkfloat off rumbling and rampaging through the streets of Chelsea. Dispensing crashing bottles for free to all the denizens and ripe fruits frequenting the borough in those days...Crinkle, crush, splay, as it disappears with tail-light winking round Manor Street into Cheyne Walk.

The runaway milkfloat came over the hill and smashed right into one of the decorative columns at the base of the Albert Bridge. When I hastily risked my eyes it had turned into the blessed Riders of the Purple Sage...Haven't you finished rolling that other joint yet, Sweet Pea?...You're really getting smashed, you know that!...A customer of 'Liz's' was a solicitor. Action was taken. Different lawyers came and visited me in hospital. Statements were taken. The police came...The Foreman had been the worse for wear through drink. Reportedly downed at least five pints of beer that particular lunch hour. Also, question: why was he so long in Mrs Quick's flat? A contradiction in name and terms...He was severely reprimanded, but kept his job, which I was naturally pleased about. Assuaged any lingering guilt...The dairy was forced to pay over four hundred pounds in compensation which pleased Dad and the local, illegal bookies immensely...I believe a new type of brake handle was introduced after that. Whereby it became impossible to just operate the handbrake without engaging the main brake..."

"How long have you been growing this giggle weed for?"

"Forever...Trudging out in the middle of the night to the secreted patch. Dispensing slug pellets all over the place. Lines and lines of string decorated with milk bottle tops to stave off the pecking birds. Spreading bio-organic compounds of fertiliser, even collecting horse dung to mix in the soil...I tell you what, Sweet Pea...Out of sixty plants only twelve survived. I hung them all upside down in brown paper bags in the attic. Dried them out for about eight weeks...Leo came round one night so I thought I'd try the home-grown out on him...nothing...I rolled pure, five-skin spliffs in honour of the Goddess and Sensimillia and waited...zilch...Leo and I got into our usual talking jag. Lecturing me on the joys of the Babylonian civilisation. We played a game of chess which never seemed to go anywhere. Leo was trying to convince me to be his driver and guide. He'd just purchased a huge Mercedes truck and was proposing a yearlong trip to Egypt...Studying the Pyramids, ancient scripts of law. We would attempt to cover our costs by finding some previously undetected archaeological dig around Luxor...Howard Carter is in hysterics from beyond the tomb...I suppose I must have rolled five of those stupendous spliffs. Nothing, so I thought...We looked up from the kitchen table together at the wall clock and realised we'd been sat in the self-same positions, talking for over twelve hours. The sun was due up and the time had flashed by in a wink of Horus' eye. The bird of unfettered conversation...The home-grown is great and has a way of creeping up on you..."

"Well, it's really marched all over me! I've got the munchies. Can I go raid your fridge and cake tin?"

"Whatever you want, Moonchild. I've told you before...Help yourself, okay!"

"Georgy's death was a great shock to you...Mmmm, I could eat all of this chocolate cake...You trapped the spirit of him in time in your boy's mind."

"I suppose so, Sweet Pea. Though he was too good for this world...I just continued to carry him around inside of me. In odd, traumatic moments in my life he's helped me out. I don't consciously think of him every day. In fact, until you started coming round, sitting there brazenly with chocolate crumbs coating your lips, asking all these questions; it was a part of my life that had lain uncovered, uninspected these thirty years past...'Liz' never really recovered from his death. She spent the next five years in mourning. Gran was a superstar though...within a month of Georgy's funeral, Jackie got married to Roy. They moved away to Colchester. I believe Eustace Watkins had administrative offices there...You can imagine all the chatter and gossip...'His body was hardly cold...', 'Couldn't wait to get him under the sod...', 'Little hussy didn't wait very long, did she?'...and so on. Everybody always agrees with you in times like these. Natural empathy of hate. People enjoy a good chew on somebody else's soul. Makes them feel better. For a few months Jackie became the scarlet woman of Chelsea. Soon forgotten though like everything else. Cast away into the pit of yesterday's tittle-tattle. New bones of rumour and scandal had already arrived to masticate on...Gran was made of sturdier fibre though. She didn't want to carry this hate and loathing around with her for the rest of her life. Nursing dark grievances...Jackie and Roy had only been living in their new house for a couple of weeks when Gran wrote to them. She arranged to travel over to Colchester for the day, have lunch and tea with them and then Roy would drive her back...Amazingly brave when I think back on it. Taught me a great lesson, Moonchild...Stop staring at the last chocolate wedge goggle-eyed and finish it...If you've got a major problem...Hurt, anger, grievance...Take it to the person or people you have it with. Clear it out from your system and then your life can happily roll on. It's pent-up pain and anger stored over years that causes people to get ill...I really admired Gran for that. She'd never like Jackie though she'd managed to keep it from Georgy. They say love is blind. Well, in Georgy's case it was two white sticks and a thick black hood...Gran travelled all that way to spend the day and wished them well. Hoped their life together would be happy and fruitful. From her conversation much later I guessed that Jackie must have been pregnant. Gran even continued to swap Christmas cards with them until the seasonal act petered out the way relationships often trail away..."

"Strange murky shapes become stunningly real. Time is in reality and all actions are explained. The presence of he Dreamweaver has lightly touched me, dusted my eyes and woken me up after so long. The dream reality takes over...The street market is one thunderous noise of hustle and bustle. Conflicting voices and sounds mix with flutes, pipes, gongs and drums. A rush of colour and smell. So vivid, so familiar. So real and exciting. Before the joy of recognition can envelop me, a sadness catches at me...People nod and smile, many with gap-toothed abandon and I am aware of her presence. A great sense of loss is overpowering me and I'm finding it hard to control my emotions within this multitude. I sense that she is gone from me again and it may take an eternity of time, thousands of years, to find her, if ever...The traders are selling their wares, crying out along the noisy streets, small boys laugh and run, tumbling and turning through the loose garmented folds of their Elders' legs. Above the noise and commotion a trader can barely be heard...'Frankincense, gum, best olive oil, perfume for the hair'...A water-seller beckons to me as I make to pass by. So as not to offend him I concentrate my eyes and lean my body towards a large niche in a wall by a small turning in the street. A silversmith is busy at work designing beautiful bowls from the finest silver. There is an outburst to my left as a rowdy group of clean-shaven youths are ejected from a tavern. It is early in the day for this behaviour for the sun has yet to reach its' zenith. One of the youths is shouting gamely, slurring his words and waving his arms. He's telling us he wishes to wallow in a debauched bordello...I accept the mode of dress all around for it is mine. Timeless across thousands of years. Each generation showing the small improvements in sandals, tunics, long flowing robes. The differing customs of each neighbouring country represented here. The Greek haircuts and the fine, ostentatious manners of the street have not altered...The black and perfumed hair of the strangers who smile at me in the heat of the day...Choking slightly from the stampede of street dust, thinking the Greek and Syrian presence here is so strong, so accepted as to be part of the hot, sultry flavour. Tasting salt on my lips. A Cappadocian merchant scuttles by. I realise he is on his way to the harbour to greet the latest great ship that has anchored...When a silk trader finally stopped me in my passage and told me of the catastrophe. That Eirene was dead. The heat of the day nearly overwhelmed me. The flies and the stench catching at my every breath. A buzzing in my head...

I decided to go to her house. I'm amazed how well I know my way through this warren of passages and alleyways...Coming upon a courtyard where women are washing the family clothes on smooth blocks of white stone. I'm thinking to myself as I smile at the women and pass by on the baked, rutted earth, that it's late in the day for them to be washing clothes and why aren't they properly attired. No modesty in their gestures towards me.

I realise that I don't like gong to this house. That I consciously avoid going to the houses of Christians. Their religious festivals at Christmas and Easter times are so depressing. These are famous festival occasions dating from olden times which they have usurped and preach to the rest of us how special they are...How left out the rest of us are made to feel. We cannot know and do not possess their faith. They laugh and sneer at our Gods and superstitious ways. But worst of all is when they are in mourning...

My path has entered a more respectable and prosperous part of the city. My sandalled feet are taking me towards the grand rich houses not far from the corniche...Nobody seems to notice me as I go up to the Grand House. A few blind beggars peer in my direction with their bleached, deadened eyes. Ears attuned to my footfalls, but they do not ask me for any money. A scabby donkey is chewing grass in an unconcerned way across from the entrance...I enter the Grand House unopposed and stand in the passageway. I feel awkward and out of place. I do not want to go further inside...People are starting to notice me, I can see that different relations of Eirene, all clad in black, are looking at me with a sense of confusion and displeasure...Finally, plucking up the courage for my love of her, I venture down the dark passageway and enter a large room. I stay standing just inside the doorway. The large room is coated in opulence. Riches that leave me feeling small and helpless. Valuable carpets cover the floor and adorn the walls. Plain rich patterns so intricately woven with fine threads of gold and silver. The room is laden with pots, vessels and bowls, all of silver and gold...

I cannot take the hard blank stares in my direction any more. I slip backwards out into the passage. Edging my way along the musty smelling walls...I find myself standing alone and weeping. Tears starting to trickle, now cascading, down my cheeks. My face is inflamed and running with water...I find myself dwelling on all the times we met. The social gatherings and the wonderful excursions. None of these will mean anything in the future without Eirene...I'm thinking to myself that I will not feel her presence or touch anymore at our lovely and disorderly parties. Those wonderful days and nights out. Watching with pleasure, Eirene enjoying herself. The shades and patterns of her laughter. Her wonderful voice reciting verses with her perfect sense of Greek rhythm...I'm thinking to myself that I have lost forever her beauty, her vivacious nature. That I have lost forever this woman who I have loved and adored so passionately across so many times.

Some old women near me are speaking in hushed tones and whispers about the last day she was alive... On her lips continually the name of Christ. In her finely chiselled hands she was holding a cross...I continue to stand in the passageway and wipe away the tears. After a while, trudging with drooping shoulders, four Christian priests go past me into the room and begin to say prayers. Fervent and severe supplications to Jesus or to Mary, I don't know their religion that well...

The group of us, of course, knew that Eirene was a Christian. From the first hour we knew it, when the year before last she joined our gang. But she lived exactly like us. More given to our pleasures than any of us. Her rich connections from this time had provided her with immense wealth. She gaily scattered her money, frittered away on harmless frolics, tossed unsparingly into the expense of our latest amusements. She paid no heed to the city's view of our pleasures, mocking their recriminations. Always next to me, but never afraid to join in. With reckless abandonment, she would gaily throw herself into our late night discussions and rows.

Her movement haunts me now in this musty passageway of lined mourners. I sense her being in a different form and body...We stand, unprotected, on a steep precipice underground. Rocks and waters all around. The soldiers are gradually making their way towards us, killing as they go. The cries of pain and death chillingly echo in our hearts. We hold hands and await our fate, helpless before the onslaught of tidal-blood genocide. We are being killed for the way we look and who we represent...Each time we never seem to reach too far into our allotted life spans together, before the barbaric traces of worldly power intrude on our oneness to separate us again. To leave us as floating corpses face down in the murky underground pools of brackish water...In this passageway I know of our past lives together, they are fully revealed to me...I am now alone and I hate it...This time around she happily joined with me in the gang. We thought we could survive longer by remaining shielded within the group...Whenever we met an opposing gang at a party or in the street at night, she never spoke about her religion. In fact I once told her, stroking her bare brown arms, that we would take her with us to the Serapion. But she seemed to dislike that...I knew of her beliefs which had never come between us before, it was only a joke, but I remember quite vividly now how much she disliked that. Withdrew her arm from my grasp and recoiled...

My eyes were lost on the black-clad, mourning women. Images spring forth to dance to and fro on their strapless clothes and I remember two other occasions of friction that come into my mind now...One night we were all very drunk. We had received a special shipment of wine from Antioch. In our heightened intoxication's we started making libations to Poseidon. Eirene smoothed the creases of her red-stained silk dress, withdrew from circle and turned her looks away. I felt guilt in my drunken joy and could not understand...Another party, another hot balmy night of unconfined revelrie. One of our gang leapt aggressively onto the table and cried out enthusiastically "Let our company be forever under the favour and protection of the great, the all-beautiful Apollo"...Eirene whispered in my ear, the others did not notice or hear amid the joyous mayhem..."Excepting me."...

The passage way is very crowded and I am a lost soul. Avoiding all eye contact... Gradually the passage way becomes silent and I can hear the Christian priests with their loud voices, they are chanting with a dirge-like, systematic methodicalness. They are praying for Eirene's young soul. The sounds and incantations leave me numb and cold. A shivering soulless dirge that brings no joy or love or hope into the hearts of those collected in this musty passage way...On and on the priests drone and I notice with how much diligence, with what strained attention to the formalities of their religion. They are preparing everything for the Christian funeral...Before she had no funeral. The last time her head floated just held to her body. Her corpse murmured to and fro in that underground graveyard. That killing ground of brackish water where we had waited together for our impending deaths...Suddenly I stand upright in the passage way, all grief skipped from me in an instant. An imprint and surge of a strange impression runs the length of my body. Indefinitely I feel as if Eirene is going away from my side. I feel that she has been made one, a Christian with her own people and that I was becoming a stranger, quite a stranger...I try to put these thoughts away and control my doom-laden feelings but I cannot help notice a doubt creeping over me. A joylessness. An urgency...I have been tricked by my own passion, by my memory of the past lives. By the brackish smear of water hitting my face as my body was hewn limb from limb. I feel I have always been a stranger to her this time...I wheel around and rush straight out from that dreadful house. I flee quickly before it should be sensed, before it should be changed. My love taken from me by their Christianity, my memory of Eirene...Running freely from the grand house past the pleading beggars and the startled donkey. My memory and love of Eirene could not be captured, could not be perverted by their Christianity...

"You don't look so well today. I bet you've been spending too much time on the 'phone and that computer."

"Good for you to ask, Moonchild...I probably have...Commitments and work have to be adhered to. It costs money to run this house, keep you supplied with chocolate cake...Only joking, Sweet Pea, don't go all serious and get huffy on me. I enjoy watching you eat. It might be a bigger turn-on to watch Annabel Chong munching away, but what the hell...If I relied on the income from my writing, Moonchild, I'd be a skeleton six feet under the sod. Laid to rest by the chapel up the hill with no bells a-ringing, no chimes of reward."

"Did the spirit of Georgy vanish from you when he died?...Was that the end of it?"

"I've got to give you maximum marks for persistency, Sweet Pea, you have a tenacious quality about you...People fade no matter how many pains you take to preserve their memory, embalm their natures and spirit...I told you before, until I started recounting these slight chunks of my childhood to you, his cherished memory had lain dormant in the day-to-day actions of my heart...That's not quite true...When I first came to this house I was not alone, if you remember. Beverley was already living here with her child, then a small baby. We weren't squatters, we paid rent through Sharon Vaughan who was by then living in Bristol...I wasn't really sure of the arrangements I just gave Beverley my share of the rent and expenses and she dealt with it...Attraction cannot be stifled when you're sharing a house with someone. Especially a house as cut-off as this. I kept to my room as much as possible. Stayed tight within the confines of our arrangement. But events happen, accidents occur and you both get drawn together through circumstance. Neither of us at the time as seeing anybody else. All is fair in sex and war...I realized the game was afoot after about four months. In my usual slow-witted way where sexual matters are concerned...I sat in the lounge late one night listening to music. Tom Petty and the Heartbreakers blasting it out. I glanced up and a totally naked Beverley was passing on her way through to the kitchen...Well, some hints are subtle, Moonchild, but that nuance was a ten ton truck driving straight through Tom Petty's voice and reaching out for my cock...We fucked that night, and morning and afternoon, ad nauseum and our stormy relationship kicked on from there. It stayed that way for about twenty months...Well, you know, Sweet Pea, you used to come around and stay a lot...Remember?"

"I never liked Beverley!"

"Well, that's as maybe. We just weren't compatible in any way, shape or form...Well, sexually, yes, that was the driving force...Even after that length of time I still didn't know who owned the house. I suppose we had gained paying squatters rights by then...I adored the child, but you can't base a relationship on the love of your partner's child. Blackmail intercedes that way until you find yourself detesting the thought of coming home...I stuck at it through the good times which by the end were down to about five days a month...I hate living with someone who doesn't speak to you for days on end. Acts like you're not there and bears a grudge for weeks. Takes a small, insignificant problem and blows it sky-high till it finally dominates the universe of your existence. Then just when you're about to pack your bags and leave, they leap on you sexually as if nothing had ever happened. All is sweetness and light till the next time which is usually about five fucks away...The poor child by then caught in this crossfire, unable to comprehend what the fuck is happening...But I'm stupid that way, Sweet Pea. I realized that Beverley was a very different type of lady from the previous wives and women I'd lived with before. All that Scorpionic angst. Therefore I tried to work at it in the mistaken belief that this continual feuding was helping me grow...Well, all relationships can develop you, I suppose. Trapped in lust with one of the Borgia women must have been fun...later, Sweet Pea...Lust can only get you so far. A little slice of kindness can go a long way. It also helps, Moonchild, if you actually like the person you're with...I know all this must sound infantile to you, but it's amazing how many couples I've met in my life where it's quite obvious to an outsider that they just don't like each other. Plain and simple as that spot that's growing on the end of your nose. Through too high a sugar intake if I'm not much mistaken...Don't blush, spots can be fun. That's when you find out who really likes you...Suck the pus from my spot. Extract the venom from my snake bite. Look after me when I'm old and grey and psychotic. No fucking then to delay the next argument. The seed has run dry and all our caustic loathing is way out in the open...

We murdered on this way as I say for about twenty months. I'd become so entrenched in the whole steamy relationship. Entranced in the way that nothing else really mattered...One night I laid there with Beverley and the Spirit of Georgy appeared to me...Up until then I'd mistakenly imagined false dreams and reincarnated remembrances, that I'd known Beverley in Rome. That we have been Albigensions who had been incarcerated then burnt for our beliefs in Languedoc. A seventeenth century civil war daydream of lying on straw in a barn and making love to her. Beverley's violent moaning and shrieking, succulent plump legs pumping up and down on that soft bucolic bed. We are in this ramshackle barn and I have to clamp my hands over her mouth for feat that the prowling Pikemen of the New Model Army will detect us...Across those lives and times I believed we'd known each other and I had become totally sucked in by her. In the way that I preferred her when she hadn't washed for days, when the blood was spilling from her wise wound and the moon was full...Suddenly, this night Georgy swims into my heart and mind as I'm nearing orgasm. The sweaty mass of flesh below me thrashing and moaning. A red warning light switched on in my brain. My soul was being destroyed and disappearing from my body. Georgy had sprung forward. My guardian angel had awoken me from my sex drunk state and was urgently instructing me to get out fast. Get away from this person. Save myself. His image kept flashing through my brain. Embedded in the semen drenching Beverley's anal passage...For days Georgy's presence stayed with me. I could feel his spirit permeating through all of my actions. His love trying desperately hard to protect me. Save me from a similar fate that had engulfed him with Jackie. Ignited his demise. Lost to that freedom of bursting into those semi-frozen waters as the Egyptian boys dance and cavort. Free from the constraints of war and reaching up above the surface of the icy water. The clear blue sky a ceiling you can burst through, beyond the limitations and restrictions placed upon you at birth. Everything is possible...Our arguments grew more vicious and demeaning after that. I was fighting back, fighting for my life...After a particularly nasty explosion between us, I left and stayed with your family, Moonchild. Your kindness helped save me. Simple things can mean so much in moments of great stress and anxiety...When I inevitably returned, Beverly announced that she was leaving, quitting this house to go and live back in town. To be near her friends...Within days it all fell neatly into place. I found out who owned this house. My Great-Aunt Rose had just died and left me some money. I made an offer and purchased this house outright. Too good a place to leave to somebody else, Moonchild..."

"Was that the only time Georgy ever helped you after his death?"...

"I think so, Sweet Pea though you can never be sure about these matters...Traces in the sky you don't notice. Movements that remain undetected...Since I've started recounting these parts of my childhood to you. Living under the spirit of Georgy. The feeling and good nature of that time in Chelsea. Whole wads of memory have resurfaced and I find myself having to fight them back hourly...What have you started, Moonchild?...It's no good you giggling away and looking all innocent. My days are plagued by great wedges of memory implants. Every movement seems to recall an impression. I find myself being haunted by my own childhood...Remembering how later 'Liz' told Sis and I that she really loved Georgy. How he'd wanted to marry her though they both knew this to be a fantasy...When she was pregnant with me, the three of them, Dad, Liz and Georgy, had gone to the races for the day on Epsom Downs. They sat with a picnic in bright summer sunshine on the slopes of the hillside. 'Liz' in the middle with the two men of her life on either side...Georgy so full of the impending birth. Talking non-stop about it. Drawing all conversations around to it. Worried continually about 'Liz's' awkward condition. Beaming happily at the thought of it...Later, Dad quietly mentioned that Georgy was acting more like the expectant father...Nothing else...Dad was always very spare and laconic with his statements. Just that little observation, nothing else. Nothing nasty or malicious. He and Georgy were always good friends...But I suppose you can't help, but notice these things. Sis was suitably scandalized when 'Liz' came out with this. She was that much younger you see, Moonchild. Georgy wasn't that special for her. His memory had faded and she could only look aghast at 'Liz's' statement of fact. How they could have been lovers...Sis never spoke to 'Liz' or contacted her for about three years after that particular evening. Assuming the moral high ground. Impregnated with disgust. Unaware of the Brother Sun, Sister Moon relationships throughout time. The Osiris-Isis legend...Sis's memory and take on events and happenings around us wasn't very good. She had forgotten, perhaps she never knew. You imagine when you're growing up that everyone around you has access to the same knowledge, gossip, common ground. But now Sis's recall was a complete blank on the matter...One of my best friends in those flats in Chelsea was Nick Douglas...I can still remember when I first met him...we must have been about four years old. I was with Fran walking up Manor Street from Cheyne Walk. I suppose, on reflection, we must have been to Battersea Park for the morning. As we drew past the Beehive pub and level with the first block of Fran's flats, this small fellow playing in the dirt, frying ants to death under a magnifying glass in the noonday sunshine, looked up and called out to me. His family were about to move into our flats and he was announcing his presence to me...Through the years, a relationship sprang up. Hanging out with Nick in the courtyard after school. All the usual scrapes of the day. Nick was the first person I ever knew who grew his hair really long. His idol was Brian Jones of the Rolling Stones and his hair was longer...Old ladies tutted when Nick walked past and mentioned words like unclean, lice, girlie, get a hair-cut, they should never have done away with conscription you know, Doris...Nick had a sister about eighteen months younger called Cathy...I used to moon over this girl, Sweet Pea. Forever identifying with an Everly Brothers record, 'Cathy's Clown'...'Here he comes'...Yeah, that was me, but she never showed any interest. Never even asked after me when I limped by on crutches...I can't even remember Sis and Cathy being very close either...Nick and Cathy's dad was a clerk in some offices near Putney Bridge. Well, he was until I was about eight. No-one ever said if he'd been sacked or simply just upped and left his pen-pushing for ever. He quickly became the courtyard drunk. Every estate of flats has to have one. He wasn't a particularly nasty man. In fact he was very intelligent, kind and generous when sober, but aren't they all!...No, they bloody well aren't, Moonchild!...Whether he got drunk easily I don't know. Perhaps five points of strong beer just took him out...Into the courtyard he would wander, surveying in his rollocking gait, sometimes singing, usually around eleven thirty at night. Quite harmless. Later on, he got into the habit of sitting on the grass, carrying on conversations with invisible friends. Nick and I would go and get him and help him up flights of stairs into his flat. Completely pissed to the four winds. He carried on like that for the next thirty years. Where he got the money to drink with I have no idea...Much later he became a stalwart regular at the now defunct Queen's Elm pub just past the Brompton Hospital. Laurie Lee will be turning in his grave...Mr Douglas gradually assumed the role of Potman in the Queen's Elm and Laurie Lee encouraged him to sit in on their esoteric, befuddled deliberations and discussions. In fact, they probably got regularly pissed together for about twenty years. Cider with just about everything I would imagine...Sexual urgings were springing up in Nick and myself. All about your attractive female bodies, unable to touch or comprehend. The smutty books and all the in-jokes. You feel like the last boy left on the planet who is still a virgin. Of course, later you realize that all your male peer group, with a few exceptions, were lying through their back teeth. But you don't know that at the time. Aren't quite sure what to believe...Nick kept telling me how he used to wait till Cathy was having a bath. Refusing to go to the toilet. Knowing full well that his dad was down the pub and his mother out doing a cleaning job on the side to supplement what was then aptly-named National Assistance. Nick would burst into the bathroom. Funny how I never thought to ask him about the lock on the door. Anyway, he kept telling me these same stories. How Cathy's breasts were growing apace...He was telling me! I knew every minute inch of that body from a distance of five hundred yards and never even had the courage to speak to her across ten years...Cathy didn't seem to mind Nick's interruptions, in fact, after a while she actually encouraged them...Next he whispered to me, swearing me to secrecy as always, how she let him fondle her expanding breasts, how she liked it when he played with her brown ripe nipples...I was all agog with this. Revolted and fascinated at once. I looked at my own sister and just couldn't understand it. Then the strains of 'Cathy's Clown' would burst from the radio and immediately imagining that if she was my sister they would probably have to lock me up. Bring back the dreaded conscription just for one. Put me in the sticks and stone me to death for breaking a taboo and I wouldn't mind. Just to fondle and caress those sweet nippled breasts of expanding persuasion...Many weeks after the continuous bathroom interruptions and stroking of Cathy's breasts, Nick's demeanour definitely took on a superior swagger. I was still a spotty youth and he was an experienced man...They had started waiting till the coast was clear. Mum and Dad out of the flat. No doubt about it. They were doing it. Nick had to tell someone. If I ever even hinted at a word of it he would kill me...I mean, who as I going to tell, Moonchild! Like, hey, Sis, do you know that Nick Douglas is fucking his sister Cathy and she actively encourages it...What if she got pregnant? Would it be a mongoloid child? How come she would fuck her own brother and not give me the time of day! Me, who was infatuated with her! Me, whose entire wet night-time fantasies were built solely around her very existence...I reckon Nick and Cathy must have carried on that way for about a year with their furtive couplings. By now Cathy was very beautiful and sexy with it. Still not quite fifteen but I noticed how all the older men had taken to watching her. Chatting her up. Wolf-whistling whenever she happened by. She became the sex siren of the courtyard for a while. All the wives noses put out of joint...'You young hussy. Look at her showing it all. Thinks she's a sex symbol like Diana Dors, she does. Just you wait till she's got a couple of kids with another on the way and a layabout husband like mine. See who gives her the glad eye then!'...Nothing like a little sexual jealousy to liven things up...Me, I was mortified. Disgusted and enthralled to the merest whiff of her presence, a heady fragrance of unperceived love lost on this developing sex siren...I managed to piece it together later. Nick would never tell me fully. Too embarrassed, hurt, ashamed, whatever...One night old man Douglas came home well drunk as usual. Cathy was having a late evening bath. She always seemed to be in the bathroom when Nick spoke of her. The old man must have burst through the bathroom door. Maybe Cathy had Radio Luxembourg on full blast or thought it was Nick coming in for a late surge. Unlikely because Ma Douglas was sat in the lounge reflecting back the black and white television pictures...The old man made a grab for Cathy in his drunken, lecherous state. She tried to fight him off. By now their whole block could hear what was going on. Cathy screaming, old man Douglas yelling, calling her a whore and trying to get his hands and prick all over her...Nick was out, but Mrs Douglas, with help from some concerned and inquisitive neighbours, managed to rescue Cathy from his thrusting intentions...Old man

Douglas relapsed and cried. Apologised in his maudlin, drunken condition. Pleading with them not to call the Police...And do you know what, Sweet Pea? Mrs Douglas agreed. Hush it up. After all he didn't actually penetrate her, did he. Just drunk that's all. Probably mistook her for his wife...Oh yeah...Five stone difference...What the hell...Got to keep it quiet. Just an unfortunate occurrence...Cathy packed her suitcase and left home next day. School-leaving age was fifteen in those days, Sweet Pea. I don't suppose the local educations authorities were going to hassle her over a couple of months...Cathy went and stayed with a girlfriend and ended up taking a job in a shoe boutique uptown in Carnaby Street. Queen Bee among the stilettos and brogues...I never ever saw her again. She never, as far as I know, ever returned to see her family again until old man Douglas was dead..."

"I don't blame that Cathy. That was horrible! If my father, Chris, had ever touched me like that I would have gone straight to the police!"

"Sure you would, Sweet Pea, and you would have been right. But it can sometimes be difficult to prove...Times have changed. A lot of sly abuse used to go on then and nothing was hardly ever said. I suppose in a lot of cases the victims were too scared to speak out. Too ashamed. In many instances the mother or elder woman is compliant. Petrified, I imagine, that they will receive a torrid backlash. That the delicate balance of the family structure will be shattered. Just plain selfish, uncaring, guilty; often it may be a repeated cycle of family abuse. Probably happened to them and they just accept it...We can conject all we like, Moonchild, but it goes on...I mean, Christ, I find myself thinking twice about smiling at young children in the park. Giving off any sort of response these days...'Yes, Officer, he definitely leered at my young Gary. I could tell straight away his intentions were of the perverted kind. He should be locked up and castrated, he should, Officer. What you going to do about it then!'...It definitely went on, Sweet Pea. I heard all the stories in my spotty years. I saw some of the traced edges of it...Scout troops, choir practice, girl guides, foster homes; the friendly English master who invited you on your own for tea at his house after school and 'Don't tell anybody.'...Furtive tumblings in the park after dark. Everybody mocked the local pervert when he ogled us playing at the Rec...Society didn't exactly turn a blind eye, just ignored it. It had always gone on and maybe it would just go away...When was the last time you saw your father, Chris?'

"Well, you know...he left over two years ago. Took off with Michelle's best friend, Gloria. They went to live in Prague and we haven't heard a word from them since."

'What about maintenance, Sweet Pea?"

"What?"

"Money, dosh, lolly for Michelle. You are entitled to money from Chris...Well, he's responsible for you and Luke that's for certain."

"I think Michelle is just pleased to be rid of him. She doesn't want any money from him. She said so. He would only demand something in return. Anyway, he's never got any money you know that!...I bet he still owes you, right!...I don't care if I never see him again. It's just great not to have to live in a house with continual squabbling, arguments and fighting. Every day was like the conflict in Kosovo when he was around...Michelle's a whole lot happier without him."

"Don't feel too upset about him, Sweet Pea. One can never offer consolation. I have no idea how it must feel. If you've never experienced a particular emotion it's hard to empathize. You can surmise, identify, shed tracts of tears, but never fully understand. I've lived with three women in my life who were all adopted and never knew who their real father's were. In all cases, they wouldn't pursue it. All three of them were haunted by it. When you'd finally delved below the outburst of the latest argument, the missing father scenario would invariably resurface. I felt for all of them. It was easy for me to say that at sixteen I would have set out to discover my originators, would have wanted desperately to have known. To have cleared it out so as to be able to move on. Discovered the original birth certificate. Hospital records, adoption agency papers. It's easy to sit and say these things because they don't involve enormous pain. Nobody gave me away. I was secure in the love of being wanted. No great bottomless pit of unknown ancestry or aching chasms of early life to contemplate. No guilt. That was the interesting part. The child, those three lovely ladies, all felt a deadening thud of guilt in the pit of their stomachs, their soft round bellies. As if they weren't good enough to have been wanted. As if somehow it as their fault for being born...You cannot ride easily past that, Moonchild. All the soothing words and therapy sessions in the world won't help that much. You can delve deep into yourself, project yourself down to minus six months and induce the pain and anger with primal scream therapy, but the fact still remains...'I was given away into the hands of strangers'...Now, all three of these lovely English roses loved their adopted parents with a passion and were grateful. Given the best that money and genuine love and affection could buy. They were all three carefully told that they were adopted. Tactfully broached, usually between the ages of eight to ten. Just old enough to accept to a degree what was being said to them and importantly before they heard it from another source...Anger was the over-riding emotion. Anger at the injustice. Anger at being conceived witlessly. If they were conceived knowingly then why were they given away. Passed on heedlessly to desperate loving couples of a barren disposition...In all three cases, I tried hard to convince them that they should track down their roots. Discover their real source of birth. Each one would go through a period of pretending to adjust to the idea. The super-human effort, pain and anger involved. Then the negative rejection through a fear of finding out you're not a princess with an unharmed green pea residing under your mattress. More likely a factory girl squashing the tough mind of a melon to death. Crushing a screaming potato...Each one wished to cling to their middle-class fostered roots of respectability, love, money, large houses, adopted fathers' jobs like bank clerks, electrical engineers, schoolteachers...The fear and uncertainty of what you will discover...A young Canadian flyer on a good-time mission down Bristol way during the second World War...A Danish diplomat having a boozy thing one crazy weekend in London in the early fifties...An Irish race horse trainer who became over-enthusiastic and exuberant with a winner at the Cheltenham Festival and took his victory to its logical conclusion one beery night of heavy, non-stop party time...The horror of what these ladies would find. Complete history re-organised. No android existence smoothed away, relegated to a fuse love. Nothing the adopted parents can do. They live with these secret urgings and announce the truth...Common denominators, Sweet Pea. All of these three ladies were completely different in style, manner, personality, yet when the social veneer was scraped away the same dread, pain, guilt and stress matched. Unresolved. Whether they implanted the seeds of that unresolved tension into their own children I'm not sure. It must be there. Must exist in the way of strange, unaccountable gaps...I'm positive many such other ladies have dealt with it better. I just happened to draw a similar type, choked up with unrequited love. A need, a dread...The former Canadian flyer is already dead. He never even knew he'd fathered a child during those best years of his life in the war...Even more remorse. Unresolved futility. I lived and he never even knew. Nobody ever thought to tell him...Perpetual raging hate transfixed towards the real mother who, of course, has subsequently reared a family of her own. When approached she doesn't wish to countenance it. Doesn't wish to acknowledge or contemplate it. Dredging up the past. Better to put I back in the time-box when she was just a young slip of a girl. Just a young lass, so dazzled by the uniform and the soft drawling burr of that accent. The sheer delight and excitement of nylons, chocolates, cigarettes and food parcels. They all deserved a just reward. A thrillingly wet country kiss leading to a few hasty couplings and sweaty leg-overs...His name had been John in his diplomatic days, but now he is a Julie. She runs a very exclusive dressmaking business in Copenhagen. You set out to discover who your father was and end up with two mothers. Julie's most pleased to see you, gushingly sincere. But it doesn't sit right. You've met your father and he's a woman. She can't clearly remember your mother, since the operation her memory of the past Him has become very fuzzy. Julie thinks maybe she was a typist or record clerk. One of those diplomatically arranged one-night stands, you try and trace her, but with the switch-over to computerized records a lot of information has been lost or scrapped. No family connections are revealed and the only faint hint of a linking thread suggests she may have emigrated to Australia on the package deal of the early fifties. So there you are. A mermaid cut-off at the waist awkwardly going for coffee in Copenhagen with your father, Julie...You can check against the adoption agency papers and sure enough your father was an Irishman from Cork. As luck would have it he's still alive after all these years. Why not! All your dreams of him being dead are vanquished. Plucking up the nerve and courage, you travel to Ireland and, without too much trouble, discover where he is living. When you arrange a meeting and finally come face to face, he denies everything. A mistake. An error. You present him with all the relevant documents and he flatly refuses to accept their statement of fact. He just knows he isn't your father. After all he would know a thing like that, wouldn't he! He's fathered ten children himself and has over thirty grandchildren to prove it. No matter what you say he refuses to accept you. What recourse? The poor girl caught up in the social whirl of a Cheltenham Festival weekend so long ago is dead. You cannot question her and her remaining family have a complete blank where your birth is concerned. You travel back from Ireland with an empty, desolate feeling that you will never be resolved. If only you'd left well alone and left your real parents in the fantasy land of your fertile imagination, residing along with kings and princesses, warriors of great valour and ladies of stunning beauty…"

"Did that all really happen?"

"What do you think, Sweet Pea…No, of course not…Some of the imagined stands might be true…But as I said, none of the ladies I alluded to would ever trace their real parents and unless their attitudes have changed in the subsequent years that still remains so."

"Well that doesn't make me feel any different about Chris…I can't imagine him ever becoming a woman. I don't care if I never ever see him again."

"There, there, Moonchild…I was very lucky and fortunate to be raised in the Spirit of Georgy. My family lines and history were clearly drawn. I had access to all the family stories as a child. The different characters and personalities that go to make up who I am. Sis and myself were never left in any doubt with regard to our roots. For that I am thankful, Moonchild, and accept that growing up under the loving canopy of the Spirit of Georgy was very special and precious…"

*

The Victorian styled school building lays at the bottom of two converging side-streets on the outskirts of Penzance. To pass by the school to reach the sea front you have to negotiate a series of narrow alleyways and blind detours to the uninitiated. Just room enough in these narrow confines for two moderately slim bodies to pass each other without brushing shoulders. A labyrinth of mazy shortcuts that at last bring you out into the reflected, dazzling sunshine bouncing off the Italianate houses. The sea breezes nearly knocking you over with their salt tasting, tangy freshness…St. Michael's Mount dominating the skyline and peninsula, a reminder of past glories and the affluence of Tin in the Bronze Age…The late nineteenth century school building has long since ceased drumming in times-tables, imposing corrective grammar and imparting a smattering of the sciences. All the awkward gangling school children; pig-tailed, pudding basin haircuts, dreamy futured waifs, have been confined to the educational dustbin of futuristic learning. They are now trawler fisherman, farmers, redundant tin miners, bakers, florist, dressmakers, grocers, tourist guides, council workers, stonemasons, supermarket jetsam and school-teachers….

No sign indicates that this school has long been a photographic laboratory. A suppository for yes, other schools annual photographs. Chief suppliers for estate agents and tourist offices…Feeling like a first day pupil and finally entering through the right door still marked Junior Infants. The cloakroom to my right is no longer a heaving mass of clammy articles, muddy Wellingtons, school scarves hanging from overcoat pegs or draped in the late assembly rush across the stone floors. Two bright silent copier machines look on at my progress. Promotional pictures of St. Michael's Mount and Lands End sheen from the off-white walls...

"You're punctual. Good! I like that. You can tell a lot about a person by their sense of time keeping...Take a seat...Are you in a hurry? No other appointments?...Splendid. Because this will take some time if you don't mind...Excuse me one second...Megan!...Megan!...Good. I don't wish to be disturbed at all, you understand. Any telephone calls for me tell them to call back this afternoon. No-one, I repeat no-one is to come into my office. Is that fully understood, Megan?...Right, thank you...I asked my assistant, Teresa, to track you down, discover your telephone number. You're a very elusive person. Nobody from the Economic Development Office or the Film Commission would supply me with any information about you..."

"I like it that way."

"You impressed me when you rang me about that Economic Development book. Remember? I've got a copy here somewhere... Very impressive. Defines an economic need...Do you remember our conversation on the telephone? Do you always hold conversations like that?..."

"I do...And no, I don't...Well, at least not with just any old body, Mr Dangerfield..."

"Good! I was hoping you would say that...If I remember your drift correctly you were talking to me about Truth. How there is no such thing as exact truth. How as a people, society, we just agree upon a number of facts to save us time because they are probably true. Example...The world is round and you haven't got the time or the money to dispute it. And anyway, the Flat-Earth Society seems an apt home for nutters. You believe that the American astronauts landed on the moon in 1969. If it was a grand hoax then, so be it. You haven't the necessary energy or inclination to disprove it so you accept it as fact. You believe that six and a half million Jews were gassed by the nazis before and during the Second World War. Later generations may try to prove otherwise, but you accept on trust the relative data on the Holocaust...These different examples represent differing levels of truth that we take for granted and live with everyday. Otherwise we would be forever attempting to prove as true everything around us when pure truth doesn't fully exist in the first place as an essential fact...Am I right?..."

"Yes."

"I'll leave the rest of your examples to one side...There is no such thing as truth...There is my truth, your truth, our accepted agreements upon facts which can be shown to operate in a linear timezone...Now, you told me that you yourself inhabited for many years a make-believe, Walter Mitty-world full of fabulous lies and self-made prophesies. That one day your Billy Liar world caught up with you and all the lying, make believe and cheating just fell away from you like scales dropping from your eyes...You became the Truth Dentist!...Am I on the right lines?"

"Near enough, Mr Dangerfield."

"Splendid, splendid...You'll have to excuse me approaching you like this. It's not often, in fact, rarely ever, that a salesman holds my attention for over half an hour on the telephone and manages to sell me an advert for five thousand pounds in a book I have no interest in, by selling me the Truth...How old do you think I am?"

"I'm not very good on age...sixty?"

"I shall be seventy-nine next birthday..."

"I would never have guessed."

"Flattery will get you everywhere, dear boy...This will take some time, but don't worry, I'm going to make it worth your while financially. That is if you accept my two propositions...Many years ago I used to be a travelling salesman for a cosmetic company. One of our best selling lines was shampoo. Cutting a long story short, I became infatuated with a young hairdresser named Adele. She was twenty-two years younger than me, but that didn't seem to make any difference to her...Do you believe in love?"

"Yes."

"Well, that helps...Adele was working as a stylist for a salon at Wood Green in North London. We carried on a courtship for over a year and then we got married. Both of us had always had a fascination for Cornwall. My personal hobby has always been photography. Just after the war, I owned one of the latest Graflex cameras in the country. Well, we decided to use my savings and buy a house down here. Things were very different then. Still open season in a business sense...Do you know how I started this business?"

"Schools?"

"No. The schools and estate agents are the cream. The core business is Lands End...Every day through the holiday season I would go to Lands End and take pictures of the visitors and tourists. Take their names and addresses, secure a returnable deposit and mail the resultant photographs on to them. Simple cash transaction. After a while we began developing the negatives ourselves. Made sound commercial sense to keep the whole operation in-house. Then I started employing people to develop and snap for me. The rest is history as they say. Of course, Lands End is now a highly prized concession. But first on the scene brings its rewards. The business just took off. I found this disused school some twenty-five years ago. Nobody else wanted it. Very cheap then...Later I'll show you around. The whole development process is housed underground at the rear...Did you notice that?...I'll wager you didn't! For all the school, estate agent and tourist office contracts the real moneymaker is still Lands End. As we are talking, I have ten photographers out working there now. Just a licence to print money. But with Adele's help, I started from nothing. From scratch. Adele is a very hard-headed business woman. We invested wisely and now we are the largest in our field between here and Bristol...Not bad, eh!"

"Very impressive, Mr Dangerfield. Very impressive!"

"Call me Mike, there's a good chap. Everybody else does. I prefer it that way...Love, that's what drove me on. Love for Adele and the two children. My life has been perfect. Well, I thought it was until three months ago...We are always employing casual staff. Part of the seasonal nature of the business. Though I must say Lands End has developed over the years. Very busy now from March to October. Since the new owners invested in the underwater grotto, new hotel and the other theme park features...About four months ago, I employed an Australian called Daryl. Son of a bitch!...Would you like a drink?"

"No thanks.'"

"Well, excuse me while I pour myself a large whisky. Just makes me angry mentioning his name...He did bits and pieces for me. I was hoping he might turn out to be another Sven...You must know Sven?"

"I've heard of him. The computer whizz-kid who developed a cheap system with an easy-to-use program."

"That's the one. He started out working here for me you know. Brilliant mind. Plenty of energy. Fix anything. Totally re-organised the business. Computerised the whole company. Brought in all new equipment. Very cost effective. I made him a partner. When I hired him he was just a Norwegian student on a two-week holiday in Penzance who had run out of money. Can you credit that! Now look at him! Floated his company for over thirty million pounds last year. New York office turning over record profits. A real gem our Sven...I had hoped that Daryl might be made of the same material...little shit! There's something I have to tell you. But only if you promise me not to repeat it."

"You have my word."

"Splendid!...Six months ago I was diagnosed with maculd in my left eye. I can hardly see out of it at all. It's like trying to look through a distorted fishlens camera. Nothing they can do... A few weeks ago I travelled up to Moorfield's Eye Hospital in London. Saw a young Australian eye specialist called Doctor Ng...Can you imagine that. Strange name, just Ng. Chinese parents out of Shanghai or whatever they call it today. To me it will always be Shanghai..."

"Shanghai Lil."

"Pardon."

"Well, Shanghai Lil...Never mind. Carry on."

"Thank you...My right eye is going as well. They can't tell me how long. Fibres spreading like tentacles which will totally envelope the eye-ball. They could operate. Laser surgery. But then this Doctor Ng, well, he was keen to try. I'm a fascinating case study apparently. But when Adele questioned him closely he estimated there was only a ten percent chance of success. The creeping fibres are too near to the retina. The laser could burn straight into my retina and leave me completely blind. Well, I'll take my chances. Better to see something through a fuzzy, distorted image than have no vision at all!"

"Is there nothing that can be done? No other specialists to see, excuse the pun. No other ops?"

"Doctor Ng is the best in his field. Very young, but the best. Don't you think I haven't explored all the alternatives, avenues, quacks and cranks! It's just a fact of life. In the foreseeable future I shall be reduced to making my way with a white stick. Completely helpless. Totally reliant on a paid nurse to help me every day."

"I'm sorry."

"Don't be, dear boy. It's just what life gives out. Who knows what fate awaits us all...I've had a good run. It's better by far if you don't know what's around the corner. If we all possessed second sight I'm sure at least half the world's population would instantly commit suicide!...My whole life has been turned upside-down. This Daryl shit and Adele are sleeping together, I just know it! I won't deign to call it having an affair, that would raise it to a status it doesn't deserve. As you must realize he's at least half her age, silly cow, probably thinks he can sleep his way into some money...I'm totally distraught over it. In our thirty-five years of married life I've never suspected her of ever having an affair until now. It's ruining my life...But I'm being clever about it, dear boy. I haven't sacked him, he's still out there snapping away today, as far as I know. I won't confront Adele with it until I have some hard tangible evidence...Now, that's where you come in. I believe in Truth and the idea just popped into my head. Who better to find out for me that the Truth Dentist!"

"What exactly would you like me to do, Mike?"

"Do you have a camera?"...No...Well, I'll lend you one of mine. All set up for you. Neither of them know who you are, have any idea about you. Look, I've made a list of Adele's weekly appointments. Times and dates. Friends she usually meets, that sort of thing. I want you to follow her carefully. When you find out exactly how and where they are meeting note it all down. The Leica that I'm going to give you possesses a long range lens. Just take some shots of them together. I don't want you taking pictures of them doing it. Just shots together. Arm in arm, kissing, that sort of thing. Alright?"

"When do you want me to start?"

"Straight away, if you can. Now, as regards money. I'll pay you five thousand pounds cash. Half now and half when you get the pictures and the times and places of their meetings."

"You said two proposals."

"So I did, excuse me while I pour myself another drink. Might as well while I can still bloody well see to do it!...Thank you. That's better. I seem to be oscillating between rage and despair...I said to you that I believe in love, right! Well, I wish to help people. I've studied a lot of the magazines on the market for single people to meet. I think they're all useless. So when you have the evidence on my wife and that Aussie shit, Daryl, I'd like you to study the market place, all the date-time agencies, that sort of thing. With a view to us producing a monthly magazine for genuine people looking for the love of their lives. Nothing smutty or over ambitious, just a plain honest contact magazine I'll pay you another five thousand pounds for researching it. If you think we have a chance then I will make you the Editor of the magazine, set up a separate company and you will get a partnership. Now, here's five thousand pounds cash, half for the investigation and half for the magazine research... Now are you prepared to accept both jobs?"

"Yes."

"No questions, dear boy? Nothing you wish to interrogate me about?"

"Look, Mike, I understand fully whether the magazine will be a winner is open to question. I shan't know that until I've attempted some research. Produced a few figures, see how much advertising revenue we can come up with. As for the other painful matter. Well, it shall be done."

"Splendid, splendid. I had a feeling you would be my man. Now, of course, it goes without saying everything I've said here today mustn't leave this room, you understand. No blabbing to friends. You're not a toper are you?...Good, I didn't think you were. Drink loosens tongues...Look at me drinking this whisky. Do you know this is the first time in my life I've ever taken to drinking in the daytime. I just can't bear the thought of that shit Daryl with his hands all over my Adele."

"Don't worry, Mike, I'll sort it out for you. What are you going to do when you have the necessary proof?"

"Why, sack the little shit and send him packing back to convict land. Confront Adele with the accusation and see what she has to say for herself. Silly cow is nearly old enough to be his grandmother. Let that be a warning to you, dear boy. Never fall in love with a woman who's over twenty years younger than yourself. This is what happens! After years of love, peace and success you find it all blown away. Regret seeping through your every action. And you end up like me, unable to see properly to be able to do anything about it.

Look, here's the money plus my mobile telephone number. Keep in touch, say, every two days. On your way out the receptionist, Megan, has a package of magazines and contract dated for you to search through regarding the magazine. I shall tell Adele that I'm hiring you for magazine research just in case something goes horribly wrong, or Megan or Teresa blab their pretty mouths off. Adele still won't know who you are. Good luck, dear boy, put me out of my misery and keep in touch...Arrgh, I almost forgot. The camera... It's easy to use. Goodbye, dear boy, let's have some truth!"

*

"God, the path to this house is getting more overgrown by the day! Look at my legs they're all scratched and bleeding."

"Sit down, Sweet Pea. I'll make you a cup of tea or if you prefer it you can have a coke from the fridge...Is that a nod I interpret with regards to the tea? Good...I can use some of the boiled water when it's cooled off to wash your legs with...no nettle bites? Better still. Saves all that furtive hunting for dock leaves. When your legs have dried off we'll put some comfrey ointment on them...Don't pull a face it doesn't sting...I'm not going to cut back the pathway. I deliberately leave it overgrown like that. Keeps out unwanted guests and intruders. Very few people make their way up above the road and along what passes for a car-track to the front door. Seclusion is just the way I like it!"

"You're becoming a hermit, do you know that...That's what's going to happen. Half the country will end up never going out. Never walking in the spring sunshine and getting their legs scratched...Look at your face. What's the word?"

"Pallid. Pasty. Wan as the disfavoured knight...You're right, Moonchild. We will all end up living in our computers. The world is safe in here. I have some idea of what is going to happen. Everything is squared-off. Follows a logic... Alright, if you're into porno pics or if your internet credit account is being raided by fraudsters and computer pirates it can be a drag...But hey, that's a small price to pay for an explainable world. We can all live with the odd glitch...The real world, Moonchild. Now there's a nasty place where things can happen without warning. Highly dangerous! Just going out your front door requires an act of faith...Better? There you see. Tea and comfrey, sympathy and a joint. Worth the hassle, right?!"

"I didn't realize you were into photography. That's a very flash camera!"

"Better still. Rolling a joint and cracking a joke. Next you'll be telling me the ballet mistress has selected you to dance the lead in the latest school masterpiece...?"

"I wish. All the stretching exercises kill me. I'm still a growing girl...Don't look like that, you could get locked up for it...I'm sure it's not healthy to stretch so much while you're still developing bodywise. After the last couple of workouts

52

I've been really shattered…I'm giving up anyway. They say I'm short in something called aptitude…"

"Your talents lie in other directions, Sweet Pea. Look at those water colours you did last year. They were marvellous! Made the school exhibition night!"

"I know, but I'm bored with painting now. School bores me. Sat in a stuffy room all day. About once a week, if I'm lucky, something interesting or exciting happens. Boys always disrupting the class. They think they're clever and funny. Well, perhaps a couple are occasionally. I don't want to be the school swot. I wish I could leave now. If you were my teacher that would be different. You're interesting. I don't find myself dropping off to sleep when I come round here. Well, not too often. Maybe when I've had an extra joint. Sometimes you'll be talking for over half an hour and I've been off somewhere else. You haven't noticed and I look up at you and smile and on you go… You get carried away, excited about all sorts of things…Most of my teachers just look bored out of the skulls, if you ask me. We never seem to have a really wicked time anymore like we used to…They're always complaining about being over-worked. Seems a cushy job to me…Why do the Government keep changing all the syllabuses? All the marking they have to do and we are such as ungrateful bunch. Not interested in learning…Did you know they are going to introduce drug testing at the school? Michelle was scandalized. She started raving on and on about it. I couldn't stop giggling. She got madder and madder. What the hell was I laughing at. What did I find so funny. She'd already done two lines of coke. She didn't get it. It was hilarious."

"She should smoke it. Eat hash, freebase coke. Much better."

"But you don't! You always smoke and I've never seen you take coke."

"Reserved for special occasions, Moonchild…I don't really like it that much. When I lie in bed a metallic smell seems to ooze out from my pores. Instant speed-like rush. Makes you think you're cleverer than you really are. I lived with a coke dealer for years, one of my oldest friends. I could have as much as I liked within reason. Never really turned me on though. Now, crack is a killer. Instant rush, lasts about five minutes if you're lucky, then you crave more. Rock after rock disappearing up in smoke. Love the smell and taste though. Very dangerous drug. You know why, Sweet Pea? Because it's so nice, so delicious. Easy to become a crack addict. No problems. Myself, I avoid it now where possible. Still, when we've got something special to celebrate one day we'll try some…Now, your legs feeling any better? Fine… I'm not into photography, jut a little number I have to do for someone."

"I bet you didn't have all those problems when you were at school. No drug to worry about when you were living under the Spirit of Georgy."

"It makes me laugh, Moonchild. Firstly, the way the great minds of the media and fourth estate always refer to drugs…Still, I mustn't get into that we could be here forever. Secondly, I haven't got the time right now to go through the history of drug taking over the last ten thousand years. Suffice to say that drugs have always been with us, Sweet Pea. As old as the hills, the winking mountains have seen it all...The Spirit of Georgy never left me, but it certainly diminished when the Sixties were ushered in. Senior school was much more fun. I attended a school in Fulham, off the Fulham Palace Road by Bishop's Park and Fulham football club. On thick smog-driven wintry days the fog used to roll up from the Thames in coughing waves and engulf us. Funny how you think you'll never get lost in a pea souper. All sense of direction completely disappears. You become convinced you're heading in the right direction then find out later you've walked three miles out of your way and end up feeling helpless and lost...Drugs! The lovely thing about drugs in the Sixties, early Sixties, was that you could be totally out of it, zonked to high heaven and most of the population wouldn't know...My senior school was very large. Over twelve hundred boys at any one given time. So massive, a street separated the school buildings in half. We were too large a group to ever be able to assemble all together at once. On the corner of the street was a private sweetshop-cum-newsagent. Our very own tuck-shop. From the early Sixties it was quite easy to score any day you liked. Some boys always lounging against the shop wall willing to sell. Remember, we were in the heartland of the metropolis. The only drugs you could readily get were speed. French blues and purple hearts. A shilling a tab. We were all popping pills. That's an exaggeration, Sweet Pea. About a third of us were pill popping from aged about thirteen upwards. Nobody knew what the fuck was going down... The other day an old school friend of mine contacted me. A letter forwarded on from 'Liz'...We'd last met about twelve years ago and had an argument. More a falling out. People can change across the years and I'd taken exception to his driving a Range Rover at eighty miles an hour down country lanes, totally blind. Why rush to kill yourself and your passengers for the sake of ten minutes...Machismo shit and I'd taught him to drive, for god sake! Sorry, Moonchild. Tangents appearing all over the place. Anyway, we re-communicated after all that time and he decided he wanted to make up a special CD for me. Downloading for free from the Internet. They had a court case in America about it last week. I believe you have to subscribe ten dollars a year to Napster now unless you go to Duet and they aren't so good. Anyway, he sent me this CD which contained all of our favourite music from when we were fourteen and fifteen. Really took me back down memory land I can tell you. Prince Buster, a very young Julie Driscoll, Booker T, Bob and Earl, Sam and Dave, I'd forgotten how much I used to like Smokey Robinson. All the old Soul Classics. We used to go to all-night sessions up west when we were fifteen. A place called the Scene Club off Shaftesbury Avenue at the back of Piccadilly Circus. Usually a live band called the 'Ricket Beckers'. Mainly Ska music. What I remember most is the sweaty, cigarette filled atmosphere. The dark corners and faded lights. Girls with bangs or beehive hairdos going to the dance floor and putting their shiny handbags down. Somehow this always seemed significant to me. Dancing round and around these glimmering handbags on their own. Everybody out of it on pills. Total space city. Very little violence. The occasional guy sat at the back of the club with an axe hidden inside a leather jacket. Aggression was in the way we moved, in the incommunicado signs and secret formula that relayed cult messages. We weren't primarily in the Scene Club to get laid. We were there to feel the music and dance to set the world on fire in a supercool mode. God, I wish I could have danced then as well as I do now. All stiff and awkward. Self-conscious and over-prone to preening..."

"We could dance, if you like. Put the CD on and play some of those old soul classics. I'll dance with you. I've never really listed to any soul music. There's none in your vinyl collection. You seem to have lots of Jazz, Classical and Acid Rock Music."

"Another time maybe, Sweet Pea. You've got to be in the mood. Hard to recreate that specific culture. It didn't last very long. Cool age mods and then Acid Freaks took it over. Subverted it. It was chiefly a London working-class culture that peaked for about eighteen months in the early Sixties. Then puff, gone in the blink of an eye, in the time it takes to pop a purple heart."

"Didn't you take any other drugs?"

"Only one child from my hideously snobby infant school made it through to the senior level with me. A dude called Rick Maghoo. A really beautiful looking guy born in Mauritius. He was of French extraction and he was a wary kid of friendship. His father was a Chef at the Savoy Hotel and ploughed all the spare money he had into buying up dilapidated houses in the Fulham area, renting out rooms and renovating the houses to sell them on. Quite entrepreneurial for the time. I would sometimes go round to Rick's house off the Fulham Road. For a while they had a Nigerian student lodging with them. We must have been about fourteen, I guess. One evening this friendly student invites Rick and myself up to his room. Rick seemed to know what was going to happen. The student was a very affable guy and rolled a couple of pure grass spiffs. Zonk! Straight out of it. A different world was instantly revealed. Some things you like immediately, Moonchild. I have always loved grass and hash from the first turn on. Never incapacitated on it. Fully conscious and able to think. Never ever made me sick, never made me aggressive, never ever gave me a hangover. Alcohol was always a drag for me. Brought up in a dependant alcohol culture. You go on a pub-crawl aged sixteen with your friends down North End Road market. Probably imbibe five or six pints of strong beer. Quite legless. Pissing endlessly. Willing to punch complete strangers heads in for the merest of slights. Quite out of character. You eventually stagger home having steamily groped some pissed like you girl up against black-spiked railings in the street. Oblivious to passers-by. You lay down on your bed and the room starts swimming. You fight hard to hold down the urge to be sick. If you're lucky you make it and queasily fall asleep in your beer-stained clothes. Otherwise the toilet bowl and seat are awash with vomit if you get that far. Next morning you feel like hell has frozen over and your mouth tastes like shit...Nothing. No great thoughts. No pearls of wisdom dispensed by an alcoholic. No catching of traces of movements. Seeing beyond the plastic furniture of everyday existence. For me there was no choice. I suppose a lot of people must enjoy drinking, it just never appealed to me. I appreciate a decent glass of wine with a meal and that's about it, Sweet Pea. If I'm really ill, I'll have a teaspoon of French brandy in my coffee. Otherwise you can forget it. The trouble is it can alienate you living in a country based around a pub culture. After a while, drinking endless glasses of lemonade or coke as all around you are getting pissed pales. Even now, in these so called enlightened times, try walking into what passes for a normal pub at nine o'clock of an evening and asking for a fresh cup of real coffee. Nothing really has changed that much. Still the same peculiar, hard-assed stares, blank incomprehensible louts. We've got a right one here. Cheers, pal, any more street smarts up your sleeve?"

"I like that about you. I think it's great you don't drink. Chris was always down the pub spending our money. That's how he and Gloria really came together. Always out on the piss. I feel really threatened by people, especially men when they drink. All that leering and shouting."

"Well, Sweet Pea, there you have it. School probably wasn't as awkward for me. Everything stayed much the same education-wise for about twenty-five years after the Second World War. But drugs certainly existed in a big way in the city. Of course, speak to that generation now and they will deny it. Convenient amnesia. A lot of the kids left school at fifteen and went straight into work. Times were very different. Optimism paraded in the air, percolated through society. Fears regarding an atomic war were held down. We were the Baby Boomer generation and ours was the world to inherit. Just don't mention a nuclear holocaust and it might go away. People had laid down their lives so we might have a chance. The class-ridden divide was supposed to dissolve. We were going to be an educated, new order, affluent society working a constructive twenty-five hours a week. Going for country walks on our off days and feeding homogenised glue to the concrete and plastic cows of Milton Keynes. Just how wrong can you be, Moonchild! It's like steering a ship, charting a course for America and ending up beached on sandbanks off the Essex coast. No they don't throw you a hope. They act like Cornish smugglers. Chop you up before you even reach the shore and sell your flesh for cooking meat. Steal all your possessions, strip the sinking ship clean and set fire to it. Left as dead meat on a spit with your suitcase of precious items on sale at a cheapo price in Brixton market. Rootin', tootin' strangers walk on by in your cannibalised underwear. On the rocks and your dead glassy eyes stare up from an alfresco salad."

Mike Dangerfield asked me if I had any questions and I never thought to enquire about photographs. Not blessed with the brains you started out with! God, he must think I'm a two-bit idiot...No matter. He's taken care of everything. Carefully placed between the folded sheets of Adele Dangerfield's weekly assignations and appointments are two small colour snaps...What would you expect from a photographic company right...Adele Dangerfield is a brassy-looking blonde with hard grey eyes flecked with blue. From my calculations, she must be at least fifty-seven. Our antipodean gigolo, Daryl, appears about twenty-two, twenty-threeish. Long matted blown hair streaked blonde and modelled upon seventies rock bands. Harmless enough looking shots...Hey, what do I expect. The trouble with a job like this is you start imagining you're some kind of special Private Eye operating out of Los Angeles or San Francisco in the late Forties. The hard-bitten worlds of Dashiell Hammett keep reverberating around your brain. How, on instruction from the continental Op, he once followed a guy for two weeks across the Midwest of America. Trains, cars and buses. How to remain invisible. Dress in the style of your time. Nothing too ostentatious or flashy. Learn to merge with the crowd. Keep a regular supply of props with you. Daily newspaper, book, nondescript raincoat. Always try and keep at least two people between you and your quarry. For two working weeks, Dashiell trailed this mark and never once was spotted. The glamour we impose on a down-at-heel humdrum job. All the Forties and Fifties B-movie film noirs. The directors didn't know they were making film noirs at the time. The phrase hadn't yet been coined by the French film press. Just producing cheapo second reelers from any half-decent pot-boiler they could get their hands on for as little as five thousand dollars for the option and rights with no percentages. Raised to an art form and we all imagine it's so easy. Got to avoid that pitfall. Keep it simple and be crafty in a small inquisitive town like this, where strangers can meld with the brickwork like painted circus ponies galloping down the main street.

It's funny how the floods of tourists seem to be existing on a different plane to the rest of us, and except for choking up the traffic have no real input. We just want your money, if it rains, all the better to fleece you with and bye-bye, come again next year. Dressing simple and taking a black bag with me to disguise the Leica camera. I've practised with it a few times to make sure I don't fuck up. Keeping the clothes to plain colours, leaving the car dirty and remembering to fill it up with petrol. Smearing clods of dried mud over the license plates. Can't seem to get Humphrey Bogart and Jack Nicholson out of my mind. I must stop this! Fantasy taking over. Just remember to keep cautioning yourself against over elaboration. Pay attention to detail. I like Mike Dangerfield, I feel for him and he deserves the best of straightforward action.

Waiting across the street from the hair-dressing salon 'New Waves'. Adele Dangerfield has an eleven o'clock Tuesday appointment. A muddled group of tourists shuffle by confused at the sunshine and nearly obscure my view. But there she is, sliding by them and in through the salon glass doorway. A quick glance of a petite, trim figure, expensive clothes. Nearly missed her for the scarf draped over her head. Waiting, waiting, becoming one with the brickwork. A policeman has walked past at least three times. The ice-cream seller across the way keeps glancing in my direction. Fuck 'em. Just ignore them. Christ, how long does it take to get your hair done. Now I'm wet from a May shower. I'm starting to believe that everybody is watching me. I've read this same newspaper at least five times. Bloody print stains all over my hands. Why can't these broadsheets use sealed print like the tabloids. She's been in over two goddamn hours. I could have sworn I saw that suspicious policeman bruise by in a Panda car. The ice-cream seller probably thinks I'm a rival eyeing up his pitch fresh off the plane from Palermo. Now all the lunch-timers are out and about. She could whisk out from the 'New Waves' salon and evaporate in a mass of bodies. Still no goddamn sign of her. I've parked my car in the nearest car park to the salon, let's hope she's had the sense to do the same. But I've only paid for a two hour ticket. Mike didn't mention anything about expenses, but I can't complain with the amount he's paying me. There she is! Scarf discarded. Hair tightly permed to her head and looking every inch the Penzance chic lady. Just thirty years out of date that's all. Who gives a fuck. C'mon, get across the street. God the ice-cream seller's got so used to me he's about to say hello. Ignore him, look straight ahead and mind that bloody car! Hell he's honking at me, almost caught my leg. But hey, she's not interested, not looking around. She's a fast walker I give her that. What now? She's going into a shop, goddammit! Still that ice-cream seller can spot me. All these bloody obese tourists staring idly off into space. Get on the beach, the wind and the rain are good for you. No, it's not pollution, the sea always looks like that. The fact that the town's sewage pipers only reach out half a mile and the tides bring all the effluent waste back in is just a hazard of an English seaside resort. You never complained about swimming in shit thirty years ago, why worry now! Concentrate. Now what! Christ, she's gone into another shop. I feel like a real dickhead having to keep stopping like this. I can't just keep staring in at the shop windows. Hardly a window display at all. Now the women inside have noticed and are pointing at me. If I walk on by I'll be past her when she comes out of that leather goods shop. Cross the street. No, avoid that cyclist. Goddamn idiot! Don't they ever look or ring a bell any more. Aargh...at last! Come on, just head towards your car there's a good woman. I do believe she is. Nothing too flashy. A four-door white BMW. I nearly lost her at that last set of traffic lights. Lucky there was nothing cutting across from the side road. God, she puts her foot down hard. I mustn't get too close. I haven't seen her look in her mirror once yet. She's turning into that 'Vineyard Bistro' up above the heliport. Great! Only two other cards in the car park and me standing out like a flightless grebe on sentry watch. Duped again. I can't really park unnoticed on the side of the road in front of the entrance to the 'Vineyard Bistro'. Approaching on foot. This must be a rendezvous point. How will Daryl arrive? No need to ask that question anymore he's just walked past me and nodded in my direction. Dashiell Hammeett would have fired me on the spot and the continental Op would have cancelled my contract. I'm not cut out for this sort of work. Too conspicuous and hesitant. Scared of losing them when I have the white BMW in my sights. I must admit they are quite blatant in their actions. Openly meeting for lunch in a well-known expensive restaurant on the edge of town. Tongues must be a-wagging. Poor Mike Dangerfield cuckolded for all the world and his one-eyed blind dog to see. Now, c'mon, kid, use what little brains are left to you. There is only one way out from the restaurant. Walk casually back to the car, make as if you've taken a wrong turning. That's it! Stop pretending you're in a gumshoe film and blue meanies are about to mug you, make a meal out of you and feed you to the gulls. That's better! Control breathing. Now drive back down to the coast road and park across the way. Look out to sea and concentrate on the passage of the 'Scillonian' making its way out from the harbour and heading for St. Mary's. Keep your eyes on the raised wing mirror and pretend to watch the birds flying in the "Scillonian's' wake ready to feed off the crumbs of refuse. That's me, feeding off the crumbs of Mike Dangerfield's life and disillusion. How long is this tryst going to take? Maybe there are rooms above the 'Vineyard Bistro' and Adele and Daryl have hired them for an afternoon fuck. Stop it! Now what! "Sorry, I'm a complete stranger to these parts. Why don't you go and ask at the reception desk at the heliport. They're bound to know.

Christ, so I look like an information bank sat here! Do something. Roll a spliff. Play with the camera. Over an hour. I'm starving at the thought of their meal. At last! They're walking towards the car arm in arm. Oblivious to the suspicious eyes of strangers. Adele's completely in control, you can spot that from their body language. Here we go again. Stop being so bloody nervous. Relax and enjoy it. We're on the road to Hayle. Past the languishing harbour and across the swaying iron bridge that leads to the Towans. Bumpy road. Crucifying my exhaust box. Lurching up and down like a throat sore guillemot. I know where you're going. Heading for those cottages and chalets out near the beach. Just along from where Virginia Woolfe used to stay and wrote 'To the Lighthouse'. Beverley nearly purchased one of these cottages a few years ago, but the surveyors report forecast that they would all be in the sea in twenty years time. Continual erosion eating up to the foundations. Can't sell these properties for love nor money. Either Mike Dangerfield owns that one with the shrub garden at the front or Adele must be renting it. None of my business. Hideous lime paint. A lovers' retreat on a cloudy wet, Cornish spring day. Sun just starting to peep through. What to do? Leave the car, dumbo, and make your way on foot. That's right, now find a good spot and nestle down in a sand dune. Just a few strands of greenery sprouting up to provide cover. Keep the camera wrapped around with a few sheets of newspaper. Fine grit blowing this way will scratch at the lens. Just hope they kiss and cuddle in an open show of post-coital pleasure. I'm freezing, laid out here. Wind off the dunes blowing right across me. The beautiful view is spoilt by the rotting smell of seaweed permeating everything. Fine white sand blowing in my face, ruffling my jittery feathers and penetrating St. Ives shrouded in a grey filmy mist, but it doesn't bring me any pleasure today. So typically Cornish, hanging in a mist on a wet spring day. Even the birds are too pissed-off to whistle. They have now been in that lime-green cottage for over an hour. I can't see any smoke coming off the roof and it's well past four o'clock. At last. No communication between them. Just business-like, casual and unconcerned. Stop being so nervous and just click them, they can't see you! Blissfully unaware. That's it. Keep smiling. Camembert, camembert, camembert, click, click, click, gotcha! No wreathed smiles. No clutching embraces, no sweet nothings, but I've got you on film, dears. Stay awhile, pointless following them anymore. Right, get down the address, what is the number? Sixteen. Breaks down to seven. Can't see any great significance or relevance in that. It's one of my lucky numbers, the old power number before Uranus was discovered but hey. I don't think Adele and Daryl are particularly worried about that. That's it, you've given them enough time to get away. God, it's nearly five o'clock. Dashiell Hammett earned every dime of his money. I feel exhausted. My knees are very damp from laying face-down in the dunes and my body's frozen, yet beads of sweat have caked my hair, plastering it to my forehead…

"You're very edgy and nervous today. Don't you want to see me? Would you rather I left?"

"It's not you, Sweet Pea. You're the only human being I know that I can be completely open with, just myself, blistering warts and all."

"What is it then? Would you like me to make you some lunch, tea, roll a joint?"

"No, I'm okay. I had a visit from the Dreamweaver which really depressed me. Made me realise yet again how we are all just plastacine figurines dancing round and around in endless cycles, totally at the whim and behest of Fortuna."

"Cheer up, you're usually so positive. Tell me the dream if you like. You're lucky you have a Dreamweaver. My dreamworld is a big fat zero. Though, funny since you started telling me about the Dreamweaver, I've remembered tiny snatches of a couple of dreams. You were in both bits."

"Like Carl Jung said regarding synchronicity, the more you start to notice them the more they occur. Sometimes I dream events that have already happened to me. I suppose it's a form of verticality in reverse. Later, Sweet Pea. During the Fifties when television was gaining a stranglehold, Hollywood studios employed some terrific artistic designers to produce promotional posters for their films. Really epic pop art displays to lure in the punter. Now, of course, they hold exhibitions of them in major galleries. I remember clearly being fascinated, excited and thrilled all at once when I first saw a poster for 'The Searchers'. I think the family had been on holiday to Devon and when we arrived back 'The Searchers' had just been released. Staring with awe at this poster on Paddington underground station. I couldn't wait to see the movie and it didn't disappoint me, unlike so many other things. Years later, when 'The Searchers' was shown on television, I always contrived somehow to miss it. Something would always happen. One night, when I was about twenty-six, I laid down to sleep and dreamt the entire film in glorious Technicolor. Complete from first reel to last. The only difference was I followed the action from inside the film and I'm sure some sequences, which John Ford must have cut for the final edit, were included in my dream. This re-dreaming of past events, real or filmed, doesn't happen a lot, but it occurred last night. The Dreamweaver was reminding me, throwing me a line and instilling some sense of purpose, least I forget. In the dream, Caroline comes to see me in my bedsit in Bristol. I'm working as a door-to-door encyclopaedia salesman for Robert Maxwell's Pergaman Press. We are all broke students, idlers, wasters and drug addicts on the loose. Caroline is a plain twenty-two year old blonde who has taken a shine to me. It's the early Seventies and Jimi Hendrix and Ritchie Havens are blasting out from our coffee shop jukebox everyday. Caroline is a law student at Exeter University who has, so she says, taken a year's sabbatical. She explains in depth to me how her jaw has not developed properly, I forget the clinical term, how she had a wire placed in it when she was fifteen and will have to wait another three years before it can be removed. Something about the bones setting. On our wet sojourns west, on behalf of Pergamon Press, to sell these eighteen volumes of cannon fodder knowledge with free gifts of a Bible, four children's classics, an atlas and a moneybox to encourage you to save, we communicate constantly. Caroline never stops trying to educate me to the ways of life. She believes I'm passing by, missing out on. We travel quite far afield from our Bristol office base. On any given day we might hit an Army camp at Watchet, new estates of pretty boxes in towns like Cheltenham, Swindon, Warminster, Trowbridge, Bath, Newport, Newbury, Taunton. All that travelling time spent in the car together. Laughing, bitching, animated discussions, listening to music. Rolling spliffs, what we all hope to become, to be, our lives are ahead of us and this is just a downturn to gain us some much needed cash we all lack...Caroline constantly regales me with stories of this wonderful summer job she had last year working for the promotional arm of John Players cigarettes. How they supplied sleek Ford Escort cars, white suits with skirts for the girls. The job was well paid and simply entailed travelling around to different retail outlets with new promotional literature. All helping to promote the sale of the evil weed: two hundred and fifty pounds a week and a company car. Compared to the maniacal, desperate struggle to sell these encyclopaedias, it sounds like paradise on Earth. Caroline always snuggles up close to me in the car and tells me wonderful stories. We are just part of a five or six party crew and hunch up in the back. She whispers in my ear, tongue touching the lobe, darkly hinting at unspecified drugs which obviously don't match the weed we are smoking. Forever promising she will get me this wonderful summer job. Day after day encouraging me. How my friend Rick Maghoo can come too - Caroline doesn't really like him, but as he's a friend of mine that's good enough. I've made it quite plain that I like her as a friend, as a person, but not as a girlfriend. We never sleep together, ever share a bed or even a sexually orientated kiss. Finally, one day an official letter arrives from John Players Head Office offering the three of us an interview. Caroline has connections from last summer, an 'in' with the general sales manager. Yes, they are looking and would be pleased to see us with a view to employment starting in the Spring. Caroline is so excited and happy. This particular morning she comes bouncing into the bedsit with the letter, full of the joys of youth, the energy of being alive. Her shortish blonde hair continually flicking from her ears as she talks in excited speech patterns. Our ship is coming in and won't it be fine. Rick is very non-committal as usual. He and Caroline don't really connect. We work in separate crews in different areas. At the time, we are all boracic lint. I manage to sell a few nerve breaking sets which provides just enough for food and some back rent on our cheapo bedsit off Whiteladies road in East Shrubbery. The shrubbery is a crescent road running through the name change of West to East and, at the heart of the arc, resides one of Bristol's police stations. Somehow between us we manage to scrape together enough money for the train fares. We can only afford one-way tickets and just hope we get the jobs and have the nerve to ask for a small advance to get us back home. The evening before we are due for our appointment Caroline comes round unexpectedly. We have all taken the day and evening off from selling encyclopaedias and Rick is over at his girlfriends. Caroline shares a flat two streets away with a couple of nurses from the Royal Infirmary. Caroline is behaving very oddly. She's brought some of her most precious possessions with her and gives them to me for safe-keeping. An ugly looking rubber troll. A five-by-five near life-size colour portrait of Bob Dylan. About ten LP's of bands like 'The Fugs' and 'Moby Grape'. A real woollen cape with golden spangles embroidered around the neck and hem. This cape was a present from her jet-setting mother who she hadn't seen in four years and was last heard of staying with Robert Graves in

Majorca. A pair of lemon and gold espadrilles. About fifty paperback books and a magical silver tin box of ornaments, stones, trinkets, bracelets, bangles and the like.

"Will you keep these safe for me?' Is there something wrong?"

"No, nothing. I just want you to look after them for safe-keeping".

"Hang on, Val and Sue don't strike me as tea-leaves working a nursing shift."

"No, no, nothing like that! Keep them please they'll bring us good luck for tomorrow, I'm sure."

With that she gave me a peck on the cheek, slipped a single skin pure grass spliff into my jacket pocket and left. I imagined it as just the effect of heavy drugs giving her delusions. I was quite naïve regarding heroin and cocaine in those days. Caroline was always on at me to stay the night in her room and share a needle with her. I just laughed it off, recoiled away in mock horror and said I was quite happy with nicotine and hash, thank you very much. I put her strange behaviour down to this. I mean, why else give me all of her gear. The amount of her precious belongings was about as pathetic as mine at the time. We had little use for possessions. Still, it was a responsibility to be entrusted with her favourite things and I respected that.

"The day of the appointment and the sun is shining, glinting off the windows of the parked cars in Whiteladies road. Gleaming in our reflected looks. Success beckons and the world is a wonderful place. Cramming aboard an early morning bus, the warmth and good nature between us wreathed in smiles. We pull faces and giggle as the bus lurches on its way to Temple Meads' mainline station. Even Rick has relented and is relaxed. And why shouldn't he be! Caroline keeps telling us, reiterating a tale of success. The coming interview is assured so we can travel on our way with insouciant ease. The rest of the journey is a fatalistic blur. Changing at Paddington then Victoria Station and catching a mainline train to Watford. Only snatched glimpses of the redbrick buildings around Victoria. The final part of the journey is a smooth ride to our destination. We reach Watford with plenty of time to spare. Pooling our slender resources, we decide to arrive with a little slice of style. We hail a cab outside the station, give the address of the John Player office and off we set. It turns out that the Asian cab driver has only been working in Watford for two weeks. He drives us up and down the main business thoroughfare, but he can't find the building. We are starting to get annoyed. I'm brandishing the appointment letter and Rick's getting very heated. After an angry exchange with the cabbie, we leave the taxi without paying. The driver is so apologetic. Our time is suddenly short. We were early and now we will only just make it. Rick hails another cab and shows the address. This grey-haired gnarled old cabbie has been driving this beat for years. No, he's never heard of it. We eventually find the street, but the number and building don't appear to exist. Up and down we drive, jumping out from the taxi and accosting startled strangers. Everybody is agreed upon the fact that the building we are desperately searching for has never existed.

Caroline says nothing. Totally cool, completely unresponsive. Rick becoming very animated. Temper boiling over. Grabbing at Caroline as we leave the taxi, shaking her roughly like a marionette being jerked up and down. She says nothing. The more Rick explodes, the calmer she remains. Just looks blandly into space. We walk back to Watford station with our heads bowed. Rick cursing all the way and walking ahead of us. Rick has just enough money on him to get the two of us to Barnet where his parents now live. We will try and borrow some money. Walking languidly up and down the platform, still in a daze. Rick refuses to share the same part of the platform as Caroline. She has no money left on her. I'm caught between the ominous dark cloud of Rick's fuming temper and Caroline's helpless bland stare. I walk along the platform with her. Taking out my red packet of tipped Chesterfield cigarettes. Six left and gazing at them with her. It's pointless asking any questions. She just won't respond. She will hitchhike back to Bristol on her own. I don't know why, but I feel sorry for her rather than angry. I share the remaining Chesterfields out with her equally, kiss her on the side of her right cheek and watch as she climbs up the flights of station steps, disappearing like a sleep-walker out of sight to hitchhike her way back home.

"Why have you stopped? Was that it? What happened to Caroline?"

"Hang on, Sweet Pea, I'm thirsty. I'm going to make a pot of Earl Grey tea, if you don't mind. There's more, just be patient."

"She made the whole thing up. Cooked-up the appointment letter herself and went with you and that Rick Maghoo on a wild goose chase. Why? She must have realised what was going to happen. It could only end like that. It was crazy! If she was that mad about you she knew it could only end in disaster."

"That's better. I was very dry, Sweet Pea. Part of the process of dredging it all back up, I suppose. First I re-dreamt it last night, now I'm re-telling it. All the conflicting emotions of the day come flooding back."

"Go on then. What happened?"

"God. You're impatient today, Moonchild. Well, Rick managed to borrow some money. Final memory of his father shouting at us, how we would never amount to anything. Cursing us. Rick's mother running after us down the garden path crying, thrusting twenty pound notes into Rick's hands which he kept throwing onto the gravel path. I picked them up. It hadn't been a good day. We hitchhiked our way around the metropolis and arrived at Heathrow airport by about four o'clock in the morning. The whole day had been a strain as you can imagine. Our fictitious appointment had been for two o'clock the previous afternoon. As luck would have it, we met up with a long distance lorry driver playing in the ten-pin bowling alley and he drove us all the way to Bristol. He was heading for Cardiff so that was just ideal. Rick wouldn't even allow me to refer to what had happened. The subject was strictly verboten. The following day one of the nurses, Val, came around to our bedsit. Had I seen Caroline? She'd never returned to her flat, Sweet Pea. We left it a couple of days, she may have decided to carry on to Exeter for a while. Who knows what was passing through that mind. After a couple of more days and no news of Caroline I went to the police station dissecting the arc of the shrubberies. Really surprised at the number of pictures on the station walls of missing girls. Until you're caught in something like that you never realise. A few hours later a police sergeant came around to the bedsit and interviewed me. Everything came out. All about the abortive job and Caroline's possessions in my bedsit. Must have seemed quite suspicious to him. I, of course, avoided any reference to drugs. The police sergeant kept picking at my brain and I remembered visiting a woman who Caroline said was her Grandmother. We must have been trying to sell encyclopaedias in the Bath region. The house was empty when we'd called there and I'd thought nothing more about it. The police sergeant drove me around the outskirts of Bath for half a day till I finally remembered the house. The elderly blue-rinsed lady turned out not to be Caroline's Grandmother at all, but an old family friend. She had Caroline's mother's latest address c/o a post restante in Kandy. The police rang through to Exeter University but drew a blank. They mailed through some photocopies of her photograph, which were pinned up on the University noticeboard, but no response. Months later, she still hadn't turned up. No one that I was in contact with had ever seen her since. Every morning when I sat up in bed the surly looking grin of Caroline's rubber troll acted as a reminder."

"Was that it? The end of your dream?"

"That covered last night's dream, Moonchild. The Dreamweaver had prompted yet another reminder. But Caroline's disappearance didn't end there. I left Bristol about six months later to go and work in Alsace-Lorraine. Periodically, over the next two years, I would turn up in Bristol to see different friends, renew old acquaintances. Never for longer than six weeks at any one given time. Always at some stage the memory of Caroline would re-surface and I'd find my way to the police station on the east/west Shrubbery divide. Caroline's picture would still be adorning the missing person's notice board. The number of photographs of missing women was growing a piece. I would always go through the same routine. Questioning the always-new desk sergeant who would dig out the records of Caroline's file case. The police were forever patient and helpful, but nothing. One big blank zero. One time the Dreamweaver really haunted me when I was staying at a house in Clifton and I was forced to travel out and visit the surrogate Grandmother near Bath. Seven years had elapsed by then since that ill-fated fictitious appointment in Watford. Still nothing. No sign of her in all of those intervening years. Not a word. Caroline's mother was living in Taos in the States by then. I wrote to her, but never received a reply. Memories start to fade, Sweet Pea, and the glutinous guilt is layered down into the subconscious. Nothing outside of the mischievous ways of the Dreamweaver to dredge it up. We grin, pray for good health and carry on. Disasters, forgotten, hopes resurrected until…"

"Until what? I hate it when people do that! They go to tell you something then break off. It's like the last few bars of a song missing or if you're reading a detective story and a previous reader has taken out the last few vital pages. What?!"

"Well I've got this far, Sweet Pea, and suddenly started deliberating whether to tell you. The Fred and Rosemary West case. Do you remember that?"

"Vaguely. I was quite young."

"You were about nine at the time. They were the lovely caring couple who killed around the Bath and Bristol area. Scouring the A roads late of an evening picking up stray hitchhiking women...Caroline's photograph wasn't amongst the first group of corpses. The West's had a second house. One night, I switched on the television news and there were six pictures of murdered women on the screen. They all looked so young and innocent. I jumped straight out of my chair. Caroline's picture was staring out at me."

"Hell, that's awful!"

"Hell's quite good, Moonchild. I couldn't let Caroline go. I kept replaying that last scene between us on Watford station. She's left at about two-thirty. A series of good lifts would have put her on that Bath, Bristol road around nine, ten o'clock at night. I dreamt she'd reached Trowbridge on the A4. Her lift would have driven her through the town and dropped her at the Bath, Bristol crossroads. The perfect spot to hitch. The wide-open spaces and the smell of dewy grass. The stars starting to twinkle and the cold coming on. Not caught up with the cars heading for Bath...A seemingly friendly couple with a young girl stop. Straight away Caroline's fears subside at the sight of Rosemary West and the daughter. Caroline was very intuitive, but being so close to Bristol, such a strange day behind her, she probably put any qualms and misgivings behind her. Agreeable conversation in the van, the young girl so friendly. Unable to see Fred West's face clearly in the driving mirror. They have just got to stop off for a few minutes and then will drive her on to Bristol. Does she mind? Well, of course not. Safety in female numbers...now there's a catch. Would she like a cup of tea, coffee, coke or maybe a beer? Bedraggled Caroline who's probably not had a drink since eleven that morning as our London bound train sped out from Reading station. Maybe one of her lifts brought her a cup of coffee, but she couldn't enjoy it for the leering looks and smutty banter cascading her way. Caroline accepts and enters the house of her death. How long before she picked up on it? Did they doctor her drink? The sanctity of womanhood betrayed by that killing bitch West. Poor Caroline sexually assaulted, killed, chopped up and buried under concrete in the garden with only her dental records left to reveal her identity. They nightmare of her screams and struggles. Keep seeing her smiling face, her awkward embarrassed manner as I gave her the three Chesterfield cigarettes. She's just happy I'm not cursing at her. She knows I don't understand. I should have put an arm around her. Left the fuming Rick Maghoo and hitchhiked off with her. Years later, when I told Rick that Caroline had been murdered, he feigned disinterest and said 'Who?' Did she struggle hard? Was it quick? How much pain did she feel? How much fear? How often did they fuck her tied up like that?"

"It wasn't your fault! She partly brought it on herself by lying and making up the job appointment at John Players."

"No, Sweet Pea. Very charitable of you but no, all the same. Caroline had no right to die like that in naked fear. She was only a young girl. Really just searching for a little love. Left to scavenge for herself. Dabbling in heroin. It turned out she'd actually been sent down from Exeter University for repeated stealing. I don't care what she'd done she didn't deserve that fate. We are all guilty, Sweet Pea. Her mother, the university Dean, her surrogate Grandmother, the nurses Val and Sue, me especially and Rick. We all contributed to her being on that road, reaching that moment when evil pounced on her disguised in Samaritan clothing and brutally butchered her. What disturbs and unnerves me, Moonchild, is my dubious connections to three mass murderers of the last forty years. I lived in Chapeltown, Leeds in the same street as the Yorkshire Ripper, Peter Sutcliffe. Only two doors along. He was such an ordinary man, they all said afterwards. Average my arse! He used to fire his air rifle across the lengthy back gardens at fellow neighbours using the alternative pathway. Twice shot at me, narrowly missing on both occasions. My wife wanted to go and confront him. After a ferocious argument, I persuaded her otherwise. Sometimes it pays to turn the other cheek. Much later on I was living with a lady who was studying for a degree as a mature student. The subjects of her thesis were the Moors Murderers, Ian Brady and Myra Hindley. These characters made Annabel Chong appear like the Virgin Mary. I agreed to let this lady read her completed thesis to me. I don't often get depressed about human nature, Sweet Pea, but the darkness and evil of that couple seemed to overshadow the Sun. Permeated our house and left me forlorn for days."

"Look on the bright side. You avoided them. You weren't a victim."

"True, Sweet Pea, but the darkness lingers on. I lived in Morocco for a year in the mid-Seventies. I had an old Swiss ambulance complete with siren. It was a split-screen Volkswagen van still painted in its original red and white colours. I journeyed to Morocco with my first wife and we free-camped most of the time in and around Agadir and Goulimime. One particularly good spot was just outside Agadir, overlooking the sea. The stretch of firm sand lasted for about a mile and was solid enough to park the van, Jungan Magdalla, on. We would free camp in the same place for three weeks then drive into Agadir and stay on the official world club camping site for a couple of days. This gave us a chance to use the washing facilities and generally relax. A twelve-foot high metal wire fence enclosed the camp compound. You could ease off during these stays. Stock up on provisions, service Jungan Magdalla, fill up our twenty-five gallon plastic drum with fresh water and launder our clothes in the camp washing machine. I suppose we'd been living in Morocco for about six months this particular night. I was attempting to write a novel during the day, sat at a plastic table on the beach under a canvas awning, but I could never get started. Each night, before we went down to sleep, I would meditate then prepare myself for a dream recall. Writing pads and pens at the ready. Forcing myself to sleep on my back. We would lay in this glorious solitude. Just the swishing sound of Atlantic Rollers hitting the rocks further

along the coast at Tarazout Plage. A very peaceful place. My dreams were
hotpotch and disjointed. The Dreamweaver had decided not to grace me with
a visit and a touch of dream reality. A form of hubris which I was straining
hard to fight against. The cab of Jungan Magdalla was separated from the
rest of the van, unlike the later models. We used a blind to compartmentalise
our very limited space. The plastic water drum and two large metal trunks
were locked on the roof rack. Before we went down to sleep I always
checked the front cab to make sure nothing was left exposed. This night I
made a mistake and left my wife's rucksack on the passenger seat. The
contents included a special antique Chinese dress, favourite knickers, jumper
and blouse, books, jewellery and a cape. I was on my third rem of the night.
Dreaming away in a bar in London in the late Sixties. Refused entry back to a
place and time I had long ago rejected. An old friend, Crocket, was explaining
this to me when a hand seemed to reach deep down inside my self and pinch
at me in my most secret recess. An explosion of noise rented the air. A bang
so loud it obliterated all life. My wife and I sat bolt upright in unison and
screamed in a bloodcurdling fashion that would have done the hordes of
Genghis Khan proud. A gang of Arab vandals must have circled the van just
after dawn, spied the rucksack on the passenger seat and realised it was
impossible to pull the rucksack through the split screen side windows. They
foraged around in the sparse undergrowth by the side of the beach and found
a mini boulder. They must have jiggled this thieving stone between them and
charged at Jungan Magdalla hurling the mini boulder straight through the split
screen windows. Sending the metal bar backwards and shattering the two
panes of glass. Grabbing at the rucksack and hot-footing it down the beach
with synchronised howling screams straight out of hell echoing behind them in
the early morning light. Little physical damage was really done. I replaced
the two windows and metal bar that same day in a scrapyard on the outskirts
of Agadir for a paltry twelve dirhams. The antique Chinese dress was
irreplaceable and I was never allowed to forget it. My manhood was called
into question till I was prodded into a machismo stance. I trailed the three
tracks of footprints of this boulder-throwing gang for about three miles along
the beach. Suddenly a converging and mishmash of footprints as if a lost
caravan of Touareg nomads had lingered here less than half an hour ago. A
berber village nearby this spot stood brightly illuminated in ramshackle style.
Naked children playing in the dirt and sand. The inquisitive eyes of these
friendly people viewing the agitated Western strangers. We wandered down
into this berber village and asked questions in French and stilted, broken
Arabic which were innocently ignored. The rucksack stealing gang were
obviously hiding out there, but I wasn't about to conduct a search hut by
ramshackle huts and they had to live and survive alongside Arab gangs and
we were just rich strangers who would soon be gone, out of their lives for
ever. We could see that they wanted to help us, but were afraid. That
intrusion in my dreams, that naked pinch touching right to my core, deep
down inside my subconscious, would not leave me. Over the years,
Moonchild, I would tell the story, garnishing and expanding it with each
different telling. But I couldn't get the correct sense of what had happened.
That evening when I switched on the television news and saw the picture of
Caroline I knew straightaway. Knew without fail what had occurred at the free

camp outside of Agadir. My dreaming consciousness had been touched by pure evil."

The sky over Penzance is dark and foreboding. Thunder and lightening striking through the folds of clouds over the grim harbour walls. It's only midday, but it feels like the end of the earth. The side street of terraced houses leading down to Dangerfield Photography is awash. Streams of dirty rainwater gushing over the sepia brown paving stones and forming mini ponds that engulf the hubcaps of illegally parked cars.

"Come on in, dear boy, you resemble a drowned rat. Put your umbrella over in the corner and hang up your raincoat. No, don't open your umbrella I have enough bad luck already. I must say, dear boy, you are quite probably the worst photographer I've ever employed. To maintain complete secrecy I developed your roll of film myself. Were you pointing the Leica in the right direction! Were you looking up at the sky and hoping! Don't you know anything about shutter speeds?"

"But I got you a clear enough shot of them to be conclusive. Yes?"

"That you did. I'm in total torment over it. I've sacked the little Australian shit, Daryl, and sent him packing. I have many friends in this town, you know. Adele cried and begged forgiveness when I confronted her with your smudgy photos. Harping on about our children and how they mustn't find out. Silly cow! They've known for months! How can we keep it quiet from our friends. Well, she should have thought of that when they displayed themselves all over town for the gossipmongers to latch on to with glee."

Mike Dangerfield gabbles on this way for another twenty minutes or so. Rarely looking me full in the eyes. At one stage sniffily pushing a brown envelope containing the second part of my fee for the trailing job towards me across his expansive wooden desk. It's dirty money like the mackerel splattered sky peeping through Mike Dangerfield's office window. Adele Dangerfield is a very lucky woman. Mike's advanced years saving her. One time on a space-selling gig in Manchester, Simon the Punk arranged for Tommy the Axe to guard me safely to Piccadilly Station. I was carrying twenty thousand pounds in cash on me after a particularly successful selling operation. The man who had hired me for this gig had taken to employing a minder in imitation of a successful television programme of the time. This minder was AWOL from Her Majesty's Forces and was supplementing his income by turning over Post Offices in the Bolton and Preston districts. I was an obvious mark. If this psycho soldier on the run would shoot a sub-post office manager in the leg with a sawn-off shotgun for two thousand pounds what would he do to me for ten times as much. I knew the word was out and appealed to Simon the Punk for help. Tommy the Axe was a heavyset fella in his mid-forties. Very genial and unprepossessing. His reputation went before him. When he took care of me that day he'd only been out of prison a year having served twenty for murder. As a young married man, Tommy had arrived home early one morning off the night shift to find his young wife in bed with his best friend. Tommy said nothing upon the discovery. Calmly turned around and walked out of the bedroom and went downstairs and got an axe out from the woodshed in the backyard. Neatly re-climbed the carpeted stairway on tiptoe. Burst back into his bedroom where his wife and best friend were getting dressed. Without a word he proceeded to hack them both to death. Ended up lopping off both their heads. Now maybe Tommy the Axe might, just might, have got off in a French court of Law on a crime of passion plea. Especially as he'd made no attempt to hide what he'd done and had calmly rung the police and informed them. Sat down with a cigarette and a cup of tea, all besmirched in blood, and awaited their arrival. But, in Blighty, that counts for nowt. His reputation was made and the best years of his life were spent in prison, contemplating his gory decapitation deeds. Tommy the Axe saw me safely to Piccadilly Station and insisted on putting me on the London-bound train like I was an invalid of a nervous disposition. He flatly refused to accept any money from me and just grinned saying it was a pleasure to be of assistance to me. The psycho soldier was never spied. Simon the Punk must have put the word around and he wasn't taking a chance. Tommy the Axe didn't expect the Post Office penpusher to be so easily frightened and panicked into submission. If I was a menopausal Adele Dangerfield right now, I'd thank my lucky stars for the rain shooting down my bedroom window pane, feel the precious fine hairs on the nape of my neck and offer up a prayer of forgiveness. I'm concentrating back on Mike Dangerfield now that he's vented his spleen.

"I didn't know what to do with myself last weekend, Truth Dentist, so I came into work on the Sunday. I was the only person here. I sat right here at my desk and cried like a baby. I was startled out of my despair by this continual thudding sound. I went outside and saw this small boy kicking and kicking at the driver's door on my car. I stormed straight up to him and he didn't budge. Kept right on aiming his kicks. Stop that, you little shit, I yelled at him. What do you think you're doing. He just looked straight at me Truth Dentist and sneered. How old are you I asked. He just glared at me and said what's it to you. Well, come on, how old are you boy? Eight, he replied, and it's none of your fucking business. I was angry at this little turd, as you can imagine. I towered over him and said, what would your father think if he saw you behaving like this? He stopped assaulting my car, turned around fully towards me and said, I ain't got no fucking father, then calmly as you liked walked off. I was stunned by that, Truth Dentist.

"I came back in here, sat down and poured myself a large Scotch and all the ills of the world seemed to descend on my shoulders. All these poor little buggers running around without proper parental control. No proper care or attention. Denied a loving family structure. My life seemed an utter mess, a waste of space, I was absolutely distraught and this poor little bugger seemed to epitomise my very hopelessness. Now you can see why I'm so keen to start up this contact magazine for genuine couples looking for love. What have you done so far? Do you think we have a chance of success, dear boy?"

"Well, Mike, I've searched through the marketplace. Examined the obvious top-liners like Dateline, Singles, Lonely Hearts etc., one of the more

to both of us, wouldn't it...Every morning I get up and try and remember that I'm not bound for the gas ovens today. I have all my limbs and facilities intact. I was born in a privileged country and don't have to beg on the streets of Calcutta or Chittagong for my daily bread..."

"Thank you, dear boy. I asked you an impossible question and you're quite right, I'm just a tired old man feeling sorry for himself. I'm lucky and I don't realise it. I have simply to accept what happened to me emotionally and get on with it. Throw myself into work. After all, why should I be different to everybody else. What gives me the right to expect superior behaviour from the people around me!...Yes, carry on with the magazine investigation. Of course, I will pay you the second instalment on the research, as agreed. Keep in touch and we will analyse our prospects, dear boy."

"Thank you, Mike, that's good of you...What I have to try hard and remember is that just because I took a vow to tell the truth doesn't mean to say that anybody else does. The rest of the world might well be lying..."

*

"What are all these singles and contact magazines doing here? You're surely not looking for a lover or a wife are you? I mean I can't believe you'd resort to these! Are you that desperate...?"

'Yeah, Moonchild. I'm hunting a fifteen stone, thirty-something Manchurian blonde with pots of money who's looking to uproot and move to sunny Cornwall! Discover the man of her dreams and live in perpetual sin and degraded filth till the end of her days. Fuck till the stars fall out from the sky and the oceans pound over the earth storming right through these doors...what the fuck do you think!..."

"Well, I couldn't believe that! You always seem so content and happy living on your own. After all, you've already been married three times, haven't you? You've always said they were all hopeless disasters. And there was those two years here with Beverley as well! You don't seem cut out for relationships."

"Well, thank you for that voice of confidence, Sweet Pea! I mean, is there anything I can do for you today?...Tell your fortune perhaps? Read your tea bags, recast your horoscope, do a fresh reading with the cards? I'm sure horror and sybaritic indulgence await you."

"I'm sorry...what's the explanation for these then?...I see you've even got a list of the contact sites on the net. What are they?...Conversation and discussion groups for the lonely at heart...have a chat and e-mail the lover of your choice...go wicked on-line and meet your predestined cyber partner!..."

"I do believe you're jealous, Moonchild. Been at the acid drops, have we?...But if you must know I'm researching the possibilities of setting up a contact magazine for genuine couples to meet. No advanced fees, no strings...look, we are not puppets...See, can't cut the wires. No weirdos or young psychos like you need apply kid...just a job for Mike Dangerfield I told you about. He's currently in agony and torment over his wife's infidelities and wants to produce a genuine contact magazine based on altruistic principles...now is that okay with you, Sweet Pea?"

"Sure. And I'll thank you to remember I'm not a goat! I'm no longer a kid or haven't you noticed!...Mike Dangerfield is a sweet old man. I saw him at our school last year. He was giving out the end of year prizes. Dangerfield Photography produce all our school photographs and they also sponsor the kit for our school football team...Isn't it horrible the way folks act towards their loved ones! It really distresses me...It's like Michelle and Chris all over again. Tearing each other apart and destroying everybody else around them!"

"Don't get upset, Moonchild. Worse things happen at sea. In fact, worse things happen right on your doorstep, in sleepy old Scancreed..."

"Not in Sancreed...I don't know of any diabolical happenings where I live!"

"How are you fixed for time, Sweet Pea? This could take a while...are you up for a horror story today?...Very close to home on the bone, it might upset you..."

"I've got all day. Nothing better to do...do I seem that fragile? A delicate, spring flower that's going to be blown away with the first gust of wind...You see what an influence you're having upon me. Michelle was going on about it last evening. How I'm sounding more and more like you. Using some of your words and phrases."

"Well, thank you for yet another vote of confidence, Moonchild...some of us are susceptible to assuming the speech patterns and blocks of phrases of the people we spend a lot of time with. Mimetic flattery. It's natural...let's hope I can stave off your ennui and capture your desultory attention!"

"I didn't mean it that way and you know it!"

"Sorry. Being too precious. Too little contact with people...do you remember American Joe?...Good, you should...Sancreed is always a hamlet that fascinates me...Many years ago, on a lovely warm sunny summer's day, Beverley persuaded me to drive out there...Turning off the A30 and going past Drift Dam. Then the lazy tree-lined lane, bending its way. Gossamer strands seemed to interlace the tree-topped winding lane...Beverley had spent time out there when she was a teenager...showing me the ancient church and graveyard. Explaining to me how there used to be a leper colony in Sancreed. During the forties, a Gurdjeff Centre existed there for a while...Coming upon the single red telephone box sheltering by a three hundred year-old oak tree...Parking the car and going past the oak tree through the backyard of a farm that leads to the three thousand year-old Holy Well...Climbing down carefully on the slippery granite slabs. Bending my head very low to drink from the trickling waters...No more than a mile, as the

Cornish crow flies, from the excavated hill fort settlement of about the same age...No shops, no post office, no pub. Just a row of ten council houses facing open fields. A wooden church hall for fetes, the occasional dance, a snooker table to entice the youth...Four chalets at the back of the church, a leftover from the Gurdjeff days. Three or four scattered farms and that's it...The back road to St Just via Grumbla. A higgledy-piggledy collection of workshops a mile past the council houses that proclaim themselves to be the Sancreed Business Centre, but are usually deserted and shut up. A bee-keeper at the rear of the wooden church hall and a pig farm cresting the hill on the road to Grumbla..."

"Why are you telling me all this? I mean, I live there, though I didn't know about the leper colony or the Gerd...what is it again?"

"Gurdjeff...Georgei Ivanovitch Gurdjeff...Well, I was remembering that first time with Beverley and got carried away...how taken with the place I was. Also, I thought I might incorporate it into a story so I suppose I was practising a description on you. After all, you are a Sancreedian The best years of your life have been spent there...How often do you lie in bed at night and think of the Beacon a quarter of a mile behind your head. What it was like when the locals lit it to announce the Spanish Armada. How they went back and refuelled and lit it a few days later when stray Spanish privateers ransacked and burnt Mousehole and Paul...The victory fires for the Battle of Waterloo. Criss-crossed fiery lines of blazing beacons linking up across the land with the sounds of church bells, to proclaim the famous victory..."

"No, I don't lie in bed late at night and imagine that...the best years of my life, thank you, are ahead of me...if I can't sleep I've usually got my headphones on listening to music or I get up and play a game on the computer..."

"Well, the previous occupants of your house were Angela and American Joe. They purchased the house under a new government scheme at the time and sold it on to Chris and Michelle at a healthy profit...I don't agree with private ownership and selling council property, it defeats the object of why they were built in the first place. But if you were going to buy a council house anywhere in Britain then Sancreed would be the perfect choice..."

"I only vaguely remember Angela and Joe. They had two children and a small baby. Kipper refused to leave the house and stayed with us."

"American Joe had grown up in Frinton-on-Sea. When he was ten, his parents moved to the States. He came back to Britain in his mid-twenties sporting a mid-Atlantic accent, which was how he got his nickname...Like many alternative types he drifted down to West Penwith in the mid-seventies. Found an old disused touring caravan and promptly moved it onto the free squatting sands and dunes of Rosesudgeon Common...I know, the site has been bulldozed now, by order of the council and turned into a rubbish tip. But I'm talking before you were born, Moonchild...One day, shopping in the market up the top of Causeway Head, American Joe was fingering a zucchini and looked up to see Angela. They were both stunned by this reunion. As children, they had only lived two doors apart in Frinton-on-Sea and played together a lot. They'd lost all contact these past sixteen years and here they were in an out-of-the-way place like Penzance, staring and smiling at one another over a display of organically grown carrots...Over a cup of what passed for coffee in this seaside resort, Angela offered American Joe food and shelter out at her house in Sancreed...The local inhabitants were becoming militant over at Rosesudgeon, and what with American Joe's dealing ways a move seemed opportune...Your house, Sweet Pea...Angela was married to Mylo. He'd been an electrical engineer working on contract out at Goonhilly Downs, when he was struck down with a degenerative motor-neurone disease a couple of years before American Joe came on the scene...Joe's arrival was great for Angela and the kids. Mylo was confined to a wheelchair and Joe immediately started helping with him and building up a relationship. They became buddies during long nights of joints and beer, stories of Joe's time spent with the Hog Farmers. Shooting the breeze. How Joe had lived for a while in Haight-Ashbury in the summer of sixty-seven when it was psychedelic city, the new Space Age. Joe was getting his shit together, developing fresh connections up country and starting to deal dope seriously for a living...Now, you can imagine what happened in time, Sweet Pea. You know the layout of the house...Mylo was sexually incapacitated. Angela was still a young, attractive woman even though they had two children...Quite naturally enough, Angela and American Joe started sleeping together. Mylo knew and gave them his blessing. It was the perfect answer to their problems. The extra income from Joe supplementing Mylo's meagre disability pension...Sancreed, an out of the way place without even any street lamps. Ideal to deal dope from. Who could prove otherwise? The perfect ménage a trios...This happy family persisted for about a year. What could be better? Mylo with sustained buddy-buddy company. The children with an active surrogate father. Angela with sexual contact to relieve the tension. Differing folks dropping in for a chat and a cup of tea by the wood-burning arga stove, joints all round, as they score. American Joe even developing coke specials for the highly-prized rich customer, usually a famous rock guitarist slumming it in retreat on a picture-book chocolate-coated farm. Heaven...The devil whispered in Angela's ready ear. A hostile pagan troll subsisting beneath the Holy Well beat on Angela's eardrums. The ghost of a rancorous leper who despised life supplied her with a dark vision. The evil sprites of long ago who lead the hill fort dog soldiers to their doom on a misty Cornish night of slaughter and iniquity, raised a crooked smile in her direction. Maybe Angela had offered up the blood-red juices of her moonstorm, mixed with American Joe's semen, stirred them in an old bronze goblet with the snake design. Slavishly made her way up to the tip of the Beacon. Offered herself to the raging hag of the night, rendered a sacrifice, begged. If only she could have just one wish granted...Angela started to connive. Whispering, late at night, while dead sperm heads grazed her inner thigh, slick words melting into easily seduced American Joe's ear...It was fate that had brought them together. They had always been meant for each other and their disparate parents' wanderings had failed to keep them apart. Kismet had played a hand and thrown them a life-line of love. Everything would be perfect if...Angela started paying extra attention to Mylo. Their language echoed around the lounge and kitchen windows. Life was so sweet. Joe had become moody and withdrawn. His chess games with Mylo often leading to arguments. Tetchy with the two children for no apparent reason. Everything was fine as it was. Why change a situation that works. American Joe gently caved in to Angela's persuasive charm. She turned his mind till he envisaged her dream. Saw the possibilities, the vision. When he fought hard against her overpowering will, she withheld her sexual favours. When he proclaimed his innocence she scoffed at his immaturity. When he pronounced his satisfaction with their present arrangement, she chided him for his selfishness. She never left him alone. Never gave him any peace. Openly stroking Mylo's hair and always siding with him in any fractious dispute with Joe. When American Joe finally submitted to her greatest wish she rewarded him with savage sex that shook the windowpanes loose and left a dark dank spell lingering in the corners of the house. Furious sex that knew no release, only continual pain of pleasure till Angela gushed white-hot from every orifice. Her arsehole bewitched by the raging hag's demands.

"American Joe unable to hold firm before this carnal flood and totally submerged personality and faith disordered. Disorientated by the constant hardness of his prick. No longer a godhead, but a devil-driving, mechanical machine that must have revenge. Death in the sexual act. Death and revenge the devil's prayer of the hour, the incantation that Angela willed on them both."

"It's making me shiver just thinking of all that going on in my house. You've made it all up, of course. This is just a tiny schlock horror, story to frighten me...Right?"

"Wrong, Sweet Pea."

"I shall never view our house the same way again. Which room did they do it in? No, better not tell me. I've got to know the rest of it now. C'mon, you've already shattered my illusions about Sancreed. You might as well finish me off!"

"Mylo was, of course, on heavy medication, Moonchild. A whole mass of tablets, infusions, thrice weekly injections, as part of the treatment. Angela took to personally supervising his medical care... She took to educating herself and started getting off to Penzance library and spending time in the reference section. Looking up and digesting tales of Livia and her ancient remedies for revenge. One of Mylo's daily dosages was in liquid form so it was quite easy for Angela to add a small tincture of strychnine. Nothing too severe, you understand. Her sister worked in the pharmacy of a Plymouth hospital. Probably Angela came up with quite a plausible explanation for requiring quantities of a deadly poison. Angela took precautions. American Joe must have known the plan, it was important for her to involve him fully in the deed. A death pact of carnal desire. Young Doctor Gray visited the house three times a week to give Mylo his injections. A very susceptible young man, Doctor Gray. Quite taken in by Angela's concerns over Mylo, his deteriorating condition. Heartfelt conversations with Doctor Gray as she walked him to his car after each visitation. She must have planned that the strychnine would take about twelve weeks to work properly. You have to remember, Sweet Pea, like most poisons, strychnine if administered in very small quantities, minute amounts, can be beneficial to health. So it was important for Angela to be quite sure that the daily amount was just deadly enough to build up over time. She took up an invitation from Doctor Gray to attend a play at the Minack Theatre. Nothing too obvious, you understand, Moonchild. Doctor Gray was an eligible bachelor on the loose. Maybe they had a sticky session of heavy petting in his car one night returning from an opera in St. Ives. Just enough to encourage him. Oh, Doctor Gray, I can't! I'm sorry, I didn't mean to lead you on. You'll have to excuse me. I can't suppress my feelings for you. But no, I definitely can't hurt Mylo like that. It's not fair. Doctor Gray suitably chastised, shamed into greater attraction. Aware of an attractive young lady with a healthy sex instinct denied her conjugal rights through illness. The subtle offer of a future liaison. Angela probably passed American Joe off to him as homosexual. Doctor Gray was so secretly besotted by that time that he would have believed anything. Surprise, surprise, Mylo died from strychnine poisoning after about twelve weeks. Of course, we know it was poison, Sweet Pea, that's easy to see now. But what could be more natural then. Local inhabitants and friends would call it a blessing in disguise. Poor Mylo, such a young man to be struck down like that. But hey babe, better than spending the rest of your days in a wheelchair, then bed-bound. Withering away, a bleak shadow of your former self. He was going to die young anyway, just happened a few years earlier than forecast, that's all. Doctor Gray duly signed the death certificate. Just an early onslaught of a fatal motor neurone disease and well, what do you do. No autopsy required. No suspicions. No questions. Poor Angela the bereaved young widow in mourning and being comforted by American Joe. They had accomplished their deadly deed quite easily without any qualms or misgivings and now they had each other, but they still had to be careful. Tongues can wag in rural retreats like Sancreed. The children under their charge might grow suspicious. But hey, what could be more natural than a young widow with her poor late dear husband's best friend. Due respect for time and niceties. Doctor Gray no longer required. His odd visit carried out in front of the children, solicitations and condolences gratefully received but hey, I don't think I'll go anywhere with you tonight. Just enough to ward him off till another attraction springs forth on his eligible round to take Angela's place. As, of course, it did. A young farming widow over Zennor Way was to become Mrs Gray, the Doctor's wife, within the year. Even guilt tied in to Doctor Gray's decision. How easy to allay any faint trace of suspicion. American Joe now the man of the house. They could wait to get married. Which they did, for a year. Easier to buy the council house that way. They secured a mortgage with the proceeds from Mylo's death policy, the insurance company happily paying out. A fifty-percent discount on the value of the house from the West Penwith Council and they immediately sold it on. Chris and Michelle, the lucky purchasers, while Angela and Joe moved into another privately-owned council house on an estate in Penzance. Just to keep the children happy, was the put-about reason. Now that they were growing up they were becoming restless stuck out at Sancreed. Better for Joe's business dealings being in town. Away from the memory of Mylo."

"Is it that simple to kill someone? Just poison them and nobody suspects!"

"Don't get any ideas, Sweet Pea. Of course it's not. Remember, Mylo was very ill. They were quite cut off, you should realise that Angela was very clever and devious. She administered the strychnine over a three-month period, like I said. I mentioned Livia. A famous Roman poisoner. Notorious for killing over long periods of time. Just a little a day is all it takes. You just have to possess a lot of patience to kill someone that way. Doctor Gray was putty in Angela's hands. Just asking to be duped. Also working in their favour was the nature of Mylo's illness. With a disease like that you can never tell how long a patient's going to live. Could be one year, could be ten. Who knows. Cornwall is a bit of a medical outpost. Nobody's really got time. Every practitioner and hospital is under enormous pressure. All this worked in their favour. The children were just young enough not to be a danger. Still only six and eight at the time. The rest all just fell neatly into place. Angela and American Joe accomplished it. Sure there were whispers but hey, you can live with those as long as the suspicions of the police or medical authorities aren't aroused. Plus the really prize benefit of Mylo not having any living relatives left outside of the children. No inquisitive brothers or sisters turning up later to ask awkward questions. Observe the obvious sexual chemistry on show between Angela and American Joe, flagrantly apparent at close quarters."

"So, that was it. Next. They got away with murder and nobody found out. But how do you know then? Did one of them confess to you? Perhaps your Dreamweaver led you to Mylo and he revealed all."

"Good! You're thinking better, Moonchild. Remember, somebody always knows, Sweet Pea. My knowledge source will have to remain a secret for now. It's amazing how many murders go unsolved, undetected. The police departments in Los Angeles are awash with unsolved killings, and those are just the ones they know about. The numbers have risen incredibly. Fifty years ago you might get forty-to-fifty murders a year in the district of Los Angeles. Now more like four to five thousand. They should rename it the city of Deadly Angels. But murder is definitely on the increase in a big way. Murders in Britain are up over a thousand percent over the last fifty years. Los Angeles is not alone, it seems to apply right across the western and wasp worlds. I was talking the other day about my having tenuous links to serial killers yet this Doctor Shipman in Greater Manchester and Todmorden puts them all in the shade. The chances are he murdered over four hundred elderly patients. That's a lot of karma to work out in his future existence if he ever gets another chance, Sweet Pea. Don't look so worried. Demons aren't about to swoop in on us and machine gun us down as we sit here and talk. You have to be brave and live for the day. Karma is an out-of-date concept at present in the west. The odour of the late Sixties lingers on the word. But I believe in it. About six years ago I started using American Joe as my connection. Easy to reach and always holding. Never a problem and a reasonable price and quality. Angela was always very pleasant to me and I somehow managed to reciprocate for my own selfish ends. The moves we make that lead us down pathways we should never tread. That's how people get murdered, Sweet Pea. My old friend, Freddie, cautioned me when he found out who I was using. How come American Joe had never been busted in all these years? It's virtually impossible to stay undetected in an area as tight as West Penwith. The drug squad knew all about Joe. They had been following his operation for years. Every so often Joe would offer up a victim. Some small-time client he could afford to lose. By this time, Joe and Angela had moved away from Penzance to a beautiful cottage not far from Zonnor. Up a track with a sensational view of the sea. Down by Rose Valley. Freddie's words of warning always rang in my ears whenever I journeyed out there to score. Was Joe going to offer me up this time? Paranoia sweeping over me. Always phoning him at the last possible moment. Forever on edge after I'd collected and left the cottage. Sometimes helicopters would be buzzing and patrolling overhead which made me extremely nervous. You never really know, can't be sure about these wheelings and dealings. If they could kill Mylo so easily then they sure as hell wouldn't have any compunction about setting me up for a police bust. The oldest child, Patrick, must have been about sixteen by then. Do you remember him, Moonchild? A very attractive-looking guy with a slight speech impediment. He was apparently a living double for Mylo. Looks, actions, movements, temperament. People who'd known Mylo said the resemblance was uncanny. American Joe and Angela threw him out from the cottage in Rose Valley when they first moved there. Left poor Patrick to scavenge and scrounge till he was finally arrested for repeated breaking and entering. Poor Patrick never stood a chance. Disowned on the basis of what he looked like. Can you imagine that, Moonchild? Every day as Patrick grew, American Joe and Angela were being confronted with the living ghost of Mylo right under their very own roof. It must surely have got to them. The daily reminders, the furtive counsels and false whispers in bed at night, waiting to pounce on any mistake by Patrick. Poor boy, he wasn't the brightest and never stood an earthly chance. The girl, Corrina, was dark like Angela and stayed within the fold. Corrina had bluish patches under her dark eyes and soon developed a heroin habit before her fifteenth birthday had been celebrated. She also was eventually moved on though her fate was luckier than that of her brother's. She was attractive to men which helped her sustain her habit and would always find a bed for the night. While her looks lasted. You mustn't start going around repeating any of this, Sweet Pea. That's what comes of living on your own. Here I am shooting off at the mouth when it pays to keep schtoom. But it's a human habit. Disease. We are naturally gregarious animals by instinct. A shared secret is so much more fun. Almost impossible to remain silent. We are like verbal magpies, forever running-off at the mouth. Always endangering our lives through wanton gossip. Stories to pass the time with juicy insights on fellow human beings. Angela contacted a virulent form of cancer about three years ago and died before her forty-fifth birthday. American Joe nursed her right to the end. Faded and cracked sepia snaps of them as tiny children playing together in Frinton-on-Sea, paraded the wall above her sick bed. Joe was utterly distraught and suicidal at her death. Their boy together, Warren, upped and roamed away and has never been heard of since. Probably sold into slavery in a back street in Marseilles. Maybe begging on the streets of London with the other thousands of young teenage homeless. Perhaps he's sleeping rough in the graveyard in Sancreed and you are secretly nourishing him, Sweet Pea. The Drug Squad chose the timing of Angela's death and the disappearance of young Warren to finally bust American Joe. Before the dust had settled on Angela's grave in Rose Valley, he was convicted and served two years with remission in jail in Exeter. Since his release the other month, he's a broken man. American Joe of yore a fading memory. His health is very poor and he's very sick with only a few weeks to live. Now, Moonchild, you could say that all came about through chance, but I don't believe that. What was a comfortable existence for Angela and American Joe for many years had been rent asunder and they will both have died before the age of fifty. Guilt on their conscience, blood on their souls, if misgivings like that ever held a place in their lives and I seriously doubt it. Nothing penetrated their belief in one another, Angela's willpower and resolve to have what she wanted at any cost. American Joe was her sweetheart's desire and that's all that mattered to her. I believe that karma sought them out and dealt them both a fatal blow in memory of Mylo.

"I'm faltering, Sweet Pea. Adrift without rudder and motionless. Becalmed in the doldrums contemplating anal dog days and all washed up. I awoke today as the sun paraded in reflection through the lining of my red velvet curtains and realised that Darwin's theory of evolution is suspect. Einstein's theory of relativity is quaint. The equation that has dominated this century past is just that. An equation that no longer satisfies. Landmarks of the human race that have helped us get this far are about to be jettisoned without a backward glance. The missing link is alien contact. Somewhere along the line, we were sifted apart from our primeval peer group and sprayed with minute particles of cosmic dust. My life lived in the Spirit of Georgy has gone. Transfixed in a love-zone that can never be recaptured. Drifted away into the phantasmagoric past. Contemplating it here with you, Sweet Pea, I might as well be a time-traveller purchasing two prize ringside seats for the fall of Troy. Able to watch the greatest wooden horse in history from a privileged vantage point. Spy Cassandra on the sturdy ramparts tearing her hair out in anguish, shrieking with blood-curdling prophecy and proclaiming doom. My dream veil won't lift. Glimpsed images keep misting my eyes. The oatmeal lining of the velvet curtains seems to be reddening with the day. My dream bedevils me. I'm attacked by a dog, a half-breed Doberman Collie, who keeps biting my arm savagely. The dog likes me, but continues to attack. Then the dog changes, transforms into a woman. Pleading with me before the green-tinged brickwork of a harbour wall. The nature of my sexuality, oscillating between carnality and the childhood dream of the perfect union of love. I cling to the union of love in the dream, but the changeling Princess, by the harbour wall, springs back into the ferocious dog that won't give me any respite, any peace. Now I'm in a swimming pool, my eyes are looking up, running along the level of the breaking water line, now bobbing up my head, puncturing the filmy surface. The harbour wall Princess has become Andromeda, the daughter of a friend, Lawrence Rogers. With the flattened heel of her hand, she pushes my bobbing head down. Keeping her hand level with the surface water, making sure that I sink. I am drowning. Trying desperately to resurface for air. Andromeda's water-contorted face smiling evilly with concerted concentration. Laughing gleefully and driving my head under the water again. Damming me to a watery grave. I suddenly cease struggling. I am going to die in this pool and I really don't mind. All panic has gone from me and I surrender to the drowning sensation. I love the water and I'm happy to expire in it. Content to drown in the water from whence I came. One more time, the buoyancy of my body levers me upwards and, to my surprise, gasping for air. A solemn faced Andromeda lets me live. She even helps me clamber from the pool as I'm convulsed with coughing and spluttering. All that will pass through my mind is the line about waving, not drowning. For now I am a survivor. The muscle-bound arms of life that pin you down, entangle you up in the reeds so as you no longer recognise who you thought you were."

"Mike Dangerfield cancelled the contract for the Lonely Hearts magazine and I am sick as a gorilla. Too dangerous now, dear boy, was his brief explanation. Too much of a heavy investment when a war in the Middle East seems imminent. A cautionary tale. The escalating violence and tension on the Israeli/Palestinian divide. All hell about to break loose on the Gaza Strip. I believe, dear boy, we are about to enter a major conflict. If Israel is entrapped in a full-blown war then business will suffer. Already the stock market is jittery. They have to hedge their bets, dear boy. Not a good time to start a magazine. Any old lame excuse, Sweet Pea. The give-away was no Truth Dentists, just Dear Boys! Emasculated from the waist down. He didn't even pay me off properly after I'd done all his dirty work for him. Gratitude and moneyed words belie the true nature of the beast. Still what the hell did I expect, Moonchild! Mike Dangerfield was plainly back under the thumb. I could tell it from the distant tone in his voice. Adele Dangerfield, exacting her power. Bellatrixing her way back into her rigid calved shaven legs and brushing back her coarse blonde hair. Sliding with her semen licking tongue the ice-cream cornet of knickerbockers, compromise and forgiveness. And can you just ease the zip a little, it's catching at my pubics, there's a dear. Just a few juicy licks and she's cruising once again with her certainty of power. Money control regained and she has her sticky fingers back on the purse strings. Smirking and consigning the Truth Dentist to the waste bin as an act of revenge. Kicked into instant oblivion by the black pointed tip of her expensive high-heeled shoe."

"I'm sorry about the contract for the magazine. Still better now than when you're further down the line. From what little you've told me, he's an old man grasping at straws. He wants desperately to believe the best of his wife and will probably pretend her affair with that Australian guy never happened. Just a bad dream."

"God, you're so sensible, Sweet Pea! I could eat you up for your cleanliness, freshness, clear-sightedness and youth. Any more pearls of wisdom to drop before this old swine?"

"Yes, if you must know. I've been meaning to say this for a long time now. I've been waiting for the right moment, but that never seems to come so I'm just going to blurt it out...Okay!"

"Sure, Moonchild. Say whatever you want. No secrets that can't be revealed. No hidden anxieties that can't be laid bare here!"

"Okay then. Will you PLEASE stop calling me Sweet Pea. It was great when I was ten. I know you mean it as a form of affection and I realise you don't mean to belittle me, but it's been driving me crazy for months! Every time you come out with it, which is usually once every five minutes, I blush with embarrassment and anger inside. It's got so its' really making me mad. I keep having to choke back a bad mouthed response. I know you don't mean to be intentionally condescending. It undermines me and makes me feel like a little girl again. Am I sweet like sugar? Sickly sweet like saccharine? When I go to the toilet and I'm peeing I always think of it. Will you please stop calling me it before I decide to call you some name you really won't like!"

"Hell, Sweet Pea. Shit! Habit, I guess. I had no idea, I never realised. How the fuck could I? You should have said before. I didn't mean to be offensive, Moonchild."

"And that's the other one. I'm no longer a child though you seem never to notice that! I could sit here naked and masturbate using one of your homegrown cucumbers and you'd still carry on telling me some story. Totally oblivious. What am I, the Invisible Woman or something! I know. I know. You've told me a thousand-zillion times. How you were present at my birth. How you drove through the snow from St. Just and the car broke down. How you continued on foot for the final mile in a snow blizzard because you'd promised Michelle and you'd never seen a child born so you thought it your duty to be present. Gulp. You arrived. God, this is so embarrassing for me. You finally arrived as Michelle went into labour after her water had broken. I was a home delivery under fifty-power candlelight which made it very special for the people present. Though of course, I can't remember a fuck about it! How the snow-moon was full that night and seemed to dominate the whole sky above. Just as you arrived, it miraculously ceased snowing. How the rays of the full moon were incandescent...Is that the word? Good! Incandescent and completely illuminating the bedroom with light. What with the candles and the full moon, it's a fucking wonder I wasn't born snow-blind or something! I was your special Moonchild, born on an auspicious full moon and you've hardly failed to mention it every day that we've met for the past fourteen and a half years right!!?"

"Jesus, Moonchild... Sorr..."

"There you fucking well go again. Can't you get the idea through your cottonwoolled head. I'm not your Sweet Pea or your Moonchild any longer. I'm a growing woman with breasts and a bum or haven't you noticed! I never want you to call me by either of those names again. Every time you do I'm going to kick you hard in the balls. Got it! Every time you make a bollocks of it I'm going to kick you right where it hurts most till it goes in...Right!"

"Jesus, Moon...Right! It's so hard. It's become automatic after all these years. If I'd realised it was annoying you so much. What can I say, Sweet...Ouch! Hey, that hurt! It's a good job you only caught me in the thigh and are wearing trainers. Jesus, you really mean it don't you!"

"Good! I seem to be getting through to you at last!"

"Well, what do you want me to call you then?"

"Well, you apparently came up with the name Yolande, according to Michelle. Sometimes I hate it. That's when I seriously dislike you. Being teased at school when I was younger. Yo-yo, yo-yo, got you. And such shit! Most of my friends call me Yo. I don't mind, it could be worse. So from now on if you don't fucking well mind you can call me Yo. Okay!"

"Yo it shall be. If I can remember, it was a three way split between Hannah, Almeira and Yolande. I can't recall now why Yolande got Michelle and Chris's final vote. By the way, Yo, you don't have to continually swear to make your point. I may well forget sometimes in haste and you will just have to put up with it or stop coming to see me altogether if it irritates and upsets you that much!"

"Don't be silly. Don't get on you high horse with me! I'm going to keep coming around and you know it. Please, just don't call me those names anymore and we can continue on just like nothing had ever happened. Okay?"

"Whatever you want, Yo."

"Tell me more about what it was like living under the Spirit of Georgy. About those times, how life was different then."

"I'm trying hard to conjure up his image, Yo. The magic of his presence. But it just won't come, the spell is broken. Georgy is fading away from me. All the flashed memories of him have been revealed. His essence captured and portrayed. Now he is returning to the pack. Inhabiting the barren lands the other side of Paradise. The place of dashed hopes and dreams. The modern day, lumpen proletariat clustered together haphazardly for what passes as a social veneer. Georgy has regained his invisible face. Always a sense that this life is like a minor play with greater figures watching over us. Lording the skies and blazing across our insignificant lives like major comets. Rather like the ancient Gods of Greece viewing the Trojan War. We are the living small-fry, the foot soldiers sacrificed to win the battle. We make no account on the grand stage of events. Contribute nothing to the pages of history. Our actions don't even warrant a footnote in the grand design. We are the accountants, apothecaries, advertising dogs-bodies, butchers, bakers, brewers, bus drivers, cashiers, canvassers, clerks, computer salesmen, driving instructors, dockers, dress-makers, dodgers, electricians, estate agents, erstwhile fakirs, florists, farmers, factory workers, fisherman, grave diggers, glaziers, greengrocers, gardeners, hawkers, horticulturists, hairdressers, ice-cream sellers, impostors, itinerants, jam makers, jacks and jills of all trades, jobsworths, knife grinders, kebab sellers, key cutters, laundry-women, lackeys, locksmiths, mechanics, machinists, meter maids, newsagents, nurses, no-hopers, nutritionists, opticians, odd-jobbers, orderlies, publicans, printers, painters and decorators, quarrymen, quartermasters, quasi-optimists, receptionists, rat-catchers, railway car attendants, road-sweepers, switch-board operators, seamstresses, swimming instructors, space salesmen, tin miners, travel agents, taxi-drivers, taxidermists, usherettes, umbrella sellers, underground workers, vivisectionists, veterinary surgeons, vicars, welders, woodchoppers, wine growers, Xerox repairers, x-ray therapists, xylographers, yoga-teachers, yoghurt producers, youth club workers, zoo keepers, zoologists, zymologists.'

"Phew! You deserve a cup of tea after that!"

"It's an old trick, I've done it before. I just had to get the under-current of anger out of my system, my grief over Georgy still lingers and hurts. We are the faceless ones, Yo, occupying the other side of Paradise. Just like Georgy. We are always seeking a lottery ticket that is so wild and high we will never have to buy another. That promise of success, luxury and wealth that most of us will never realise. Disadvantage is the order of the hour. Life is based on the principal of what you cannot afford. If you have to ask the price, you can't afford it, right! The continuing poverty of the Third World is a constant reminder of how lucky we are, but it doesn't pay the rent! Every time you switch on the television, go to the cinema, log on the Internet, glance at a billboard, look in a shop window, marvel at some skywriting, receive your daily does of junk mail, spammed trash; you are constantly prodded into believing this could be you. This is what you are missing out on. This is what you don't have. The messages aren't subliminal anymore. They don't have to be. The medium isn't the message, the medium is all there is. Subtlety went out with the ark. This is unobtainable, but please try all the same. For the majority of us it only deepens the daily depression which is a part of the plan. The jobs that we do that make the wheels of society revolve are not considered glitzy enough. Not fashionable enough. Not adventurous enough. Poor us! All this only goes to deepen the revulsion with ourselves. Disenchantment. Why aren't I brainier, handsomer, younger, more naturally talented, supplied with a splendiferous gift at birth. The modern day, lumpen proletariat shall inherit nothing but a painful longing. Thank you, stick the tea down on the table."

*

Walking my way back home across the fields to Sancreed. Already my trainers are wet-through from the shower of rain. I'm pleased I told Paul to stop calling me those childish names. It went pretty well. He only got slightly upset. So what! Really neat. Back on the road. The water level is really high at Drift Dam. What was it Paul said about the flooded village? How when the water level is really low you can see the top of the old church steeple peeping through the water, reaching up like the outstretched hand of the Lady of the Lake to receive Excalibur. I like that. What disasters will I find when I get back. Always something wrong. Always a calamity. Those pink-terraced houses across from the Dam have all got scaffolding up. For Sale notices plastered all over them with those pictures of man-eating dogs. What was it Paul said? The lowest common denominator is a drill. I don't mind drills, well, I'm not crazy about them. But noise doesn't bother me that much. It drives

Paul crazy. He's living all alone in that big house without any sounds and the slightest noise, could be a helicopter passing overhead from St. Just aerodrome, sets him off ranting and raving. I hope I never get like that. It's so quiet and peaceful out here. Boring as fuck, if you ask me. I suppose I'll have to baby-sit Luke again. I promised Julie I'd drop in and see her. She seemed so excited this morning. Can't be the job. Must be as boring as fuck to sit at a supermarket checkout all day. Ringing up food prices, listening to all the customers' grumbles and complaints, the weirdoes and their smelly clothes and the sunshine outside. I couldn't stand that. Shit! Merde! Why do the cars have to pass so close! I'm walking on the right side of the road yet still that Range Rover nearly brushed against my jacket. That guy's always eyeing me up. Real weirdo if you ask me. These farmers' sons think they can have anybody they want. Gold chains jangling around their rubbery necks, Barbour jackets, green wellies. I hate them. Everything seems so real today. The smells, I can taste the trees, the grass. I can lie on my back in the damp grass and be in the sky. A clear blue oasis flooding into me. I'm awash with the sky, with the pure light, the angles of reflection. I don't care if my clothes are all damp and grass-stained. Little old Sancreed. Paul loves it. He should try living here! All that talk of ancient settlements, a leper colony by the church. Jesus, gives you the creeps just thinking about it. Were the lepers allowed to go for walks on their own? Did they have minders with bells? It's making me shudder. I shouldn't be so unkind. Uncaring. God if I ever get leprosy I hope I die soon. I couldn't take that. Aids as well. HIV must be like a modern day leprosy. Who was that guy they told us about last term? Albert Schweitzer. Spent all his life as a missionary treating lepers in the Gabon. Even formed his own colony. How come he didn't contract it? Paul started telling me some awful stories about him, but I kept my hands clamped over my ears till his lips stopped moving. He always knows something about any given subject and starts telling you awful tales. I wish he wouldn't do that. Makes my skin crawl. You could take the kindest most caring person in the world and Paul would have some dirt on them. How they ate little children for lunch, or killed their father before they became famous. Oh you know so and so, he was one of the Sicilian Mafia from Palermo. Responsible for thousands of deaths till he reformed and eventually became Head of the World Health Organisation. Changed his name and nobody took the trouble to find out till after he'd died. Nobel Peace Prize and all that Shit. I don't want to know stuff like that. It's so fucking depressing. I like to think the best of people. It's so easy to always imagine the worst. Another weirdo. Must be this jacket. Now he's honking his horn. Okay, okay, I can see you. Wave, make him happy. There's a good girl. I don't like him either. He's got a pregnant wife, but whenever I see him alone, he's always eyeing me. Dirty bastard! What was that other group? The Gerd-something. Sounded really weird to me. I can't believe all these different groups and organisations used to live here. Not in sleepy old Sancreed where nothing ever happens.

"Where have you been? I'm waiting to go out!"

"I've been over at Paul's if you must know. I didn't realise there was some kind of emergency on."

"Don't get sarcastic with me! You're turning into a right little madam. I suppose Paul has been filling your head with loads of daft ideas again. You spend far too much time over there with him. Listen, I want you to baby-sit Luke."

"Surprise, surprise."

"Now that's enough, Yo. I need your help for once. I've left some burgers and a bowl of salad in the fridge. Something really wonderful has happened."

"Oh yeah?"

"Now, don't get too excited, it wouldn't fit your cool demeanour. I was in Penzance this morning and met this wonderful fella called Gerry."

"Here we go."

"Just listen for once. You're so sharp these days you'll cut yourself! I can hear Paul's cutting tone in your voice. I've fallen crazily in love, Yo. A real thunderbolt from out of the clear blue sky. Gerry is an American lecturer in English Literature. He's over here for a Thomas Hardy appreciation week, which is held each year in Bridport in Dorset. Apparently..."

"You're not interested in English books, you're always saying so. How English writers are junk. Just hung-up pale limitations of French authors."

"I now, I know, please, Yo, don't do this to me. Just listen honey, please. Hardy wrote a short story about love and missed chances based around a girl who lived on the Isle of St. Mary's. Well, I can't remember the name of it right now, but Gerry has travelled down here to get the flavour of the place and tale. He's giving a talk on it next Tuesday at St. John's Hall in P.Z. I was just casually drifting round the shops in Causeway Head and we accidentally bumped into each other. Straight away we hit it off. It was instant magic. I went all weak at the knees and you know I'm not usually like that, Yo. He's taking me out for a meal this evening at Rosie's Restaurant in Chapel Street. Now don't pull a face, honey. He's divorced and on the look-out. You'll really like him, I'm sure. I sense this is the one, Yo, so don't spoil it for me. When he arrives, please try and be pleasant for once. It won't cost you anything, will it. Now, honey, do me a favour. Can I borrow your Louis Vuitton cotton jacket? I promise to take special care of it."

"Sure. Anything else? Perhaps my Hi-Top trainers or maybe my silk chiffon dress!"

"God, you sound just like your father, Chris, when you bitch like that. Please don't spoil it for me! All I'm asking is that you make an effort to be especially nice to Gerry when he comes. A little charm goes a long way, honey, and you've got loads of it when you try. And since you've asked, I wouldn't mind borrowing your Bakelite bangles. You don't think they'll make me look too tarty, do you?"

"No. The bangles go with the jacket. You'll look great in them. This must be really serious then."

"Yes. Now look, don't keep Luke up too late. He's already had his meal and he can have one, only one, chocolate bar. Got that!"

"I promised to go next door and see Julie."

"No! You know I don't like Luke going in that house. The Cornish can be very dark. If Julie wants to see you so much she can come over here. Did you hear a car? Christ, that must be Gerry and I'm not even ready. Here, you let him in. Offer him a beer. Now I'm warning you, no shitty Miss Smart-arse stuff, okay! Gerry's a very special, gentle guy. I'm going upstairs to get ready..."

"How much longer do you think she'll be, Yolande? I've made a reservation for eight o'clock."

"I shouldn't think Rosie's Restaurant will be heaving with customers Gerry. Do you want another beer?"

"No, no, I'm driving. I know just how particular your English police are regards drink driving. Hey, little fella, that's a big gun."

"He's going through the stage of shooting everybody who comes into the house. He's already killed me over twenty times this evening. Do you want some music on?"

"Nah, nah. Will Michelle be much longer?"

"Here she comes now."

"Jesus, you look sensational, Michelle! Love that jacket."

So you love my Louis Vuitton cotton jacket, do you, American man? God, he's so boring. Can't take his eyes off Michelle's body. Two bottles of wine and she's anybody's. I suppose they'll come back here and be humping all night. A moaning and a groaning across the hallway from me. Loads of loud shushes and stupid laughter. God, I hate living here. I love Luke, but I'm nothing but an unpaid babysitter and wet nurse.

I couldn't believe Julie getting married to that jerk, Adam. She didn't say it, but I bet she's pregnant. Two years at college. She was going to be a teacher or work in a travel agents. Now look at her. Not yet twenty-one and she's fallen for a child. Getting married to the village idiot, Adam. She'll soon have another kid. Stuck working part-time over at the supermarket in St. Just. Her mum looking after the screaming kids and always complaining. There'll never be enough money. Just thankful and having to fight to get a grotty council house. Adam off on the piss with his dumbed-down mates all the time. He'll soon take to hitting her and raping her when he's drunk. Julie completely stranded at home with two yelling brats. No money, no prospects. Fat and finished. Her life in tatters. All those hopes she had only a couple of years ago. She used to seem so bright. Has she never heard of the pill or contraception. Shit, I don't want to end up like that. All washed up before you're twenty-one. Some beery guy fumbling all over you every night, just wanting to get his prick into you. Probably thinks he's really neat. Thinks his shrunken penis is really wicked in the sexual stages. All of five minutes of sweaty real-time action. Then wham bam. All over. Laid on his back, hogging the bedclothes, his stinking feet smelling the place out. Great, can't wait. I can just see all the old bloated dears nodding their heads wisely in my direction. Like I should be so pleased! Like I should be so happy that some thick Cornish farm labourers gonna make a decent woman out of me! I should be so lucky! Well, up your's, grannies. I can really do without that, thank you very much! I've already spent the last three years bringing up a baby, thank you! What does that mean, that I only get four years of freedom till I'm eighteen then hey presto, that's it! That's my life over. I simply become a reproductive machine. A form of glorified cow to keep the race growing...Paul always says that the world is over-populated. How the planet could do with twenty years of no children being born at all. I agree with him. Come to think of it, it's the only fucking thing you can do without having to get a license or some qualification. I already know of three girls of my own age from school who've had babies. Shit, that Demelza Cooke girl was only eleven. Well, that's not going to happen to me. I can't stand the thought of spending the rest of my life living in sleepy old Sancreed. Drives me nuts. Every time I wake up in this room now, I can't get that horrible story about American Joe and Angela out of my head. Makes me feel creepy all the time. I wish Paul hadn't told me that. I sort of sense that Mylo used to sleep in this room. I could move into the spare but it's so small.

"Can I come in?"

"You are in!"

"Well, it is my house, honey. You don't have to hide away in your room just because Gerry's here. Luke's been asking for you all morning. Why don't you come downstairs and have some breakfast?"

"I'm not that hungry. Anyway, Luke knows where I am. I'm entitled to privacy just like anybody else!"

"No-one's trying to eat into your privacy, Yo. It's just, well, not that friendly. You'll scare Gerry off if you carry on behaving like this! C'mon, honey, make an effort for me, please. This is my chance. Jesus! All these clothes and cosmetics! I didn't give you the money for you to waste it on all this! I thought we agreed you were going to get a new computer to help your schoolwork. You also said you were going to update and get the latest Windows. What's this? Kiss My Ass products. Bottoms Up freshly squeezed body lotion. When my mother finds out how you've been spending your money she'll think twice about the legacy when you're eighteen!"

"It's my money. Anyway, what gives you the right to come into my room and start going through all my things. Where's the Louis Vuitton jacket and the bangles then?"

"Oh, Yo, I'm so sorry. Look, I promise to have it dry-cleaned, I couldn't help it! A glass of red wine just slipped like it had a mind of it's own. I'll make it up to you."

"Shit!"

"Don't talk to me like that! Christ, what's this book you're reading!"

"Hey, give that back!"

"The Wise Wound. My god, you shouldn't be reading this! Bloody Paul again. Why have you moved your bed under the window?"

"If you must know I'm going to sync my periods into the phases of the moon. It says in the book that by sleeping with the curtains open and letting the moonlight shine on you, your periods gradually adjust to a correct rhythm. So that after a while you menstruate on a full moon and ovulate on a new moon. It also says that, after a while, if two women live under the same roof their menstrual cycles become synced. As we are mother and daughter, that should happen quite easily."

"It's not enough that you hide away in your room like this, surrounded by all these bloody clothes, perfumes, jewellery and body lotions. I kept wondering what those mail order parcels were that kept arriving, I thought they were hardware parts. Now you're upsetting Luke, making Gerry feel unwelcome and, just to cap it all, you are trying to gain control over my menstrual cycle!"

"That's not true! I just said..."

"You're too Little Miss Smart-arse, that's for sure. Now, c'mon, Yo, get your shit together. Dress yourself and come on downstairs. Don't put on any of those provocative clothes and no wisecracks. Make yourself agreeable and I won't tell Gran how you've been wasting your money on clothes and make-up."

"Blackmailer!"

"Yes, that's right and, for Godsakes, don't start talking to Gerry about this Wise Wound book. You know how easily men are revolted by any talk of periods or ovulation cycles."

Suddenly, it's happy families all round and I'm supposed to join in this shit. God, Gerry's such a middle-aged nerd. I can't believe that Michelle is so crazily in love with him. She's getting desperate, that's all it is. Looking hard into the mirror each morning at all the lines and creases appearing all over her face. She wants out. A new life in America. Gerry is besotted with her. Fallen head over heels in lust. She's a lust bus on wheels. Suddenly, it's Luke this, Luke that. How the little fella would stand a much better chance educational wise in the States. A healthier, more go-ahead country in which to raise children...Oh yeah?! Who you kidding, mister! Let me see, I've got my school satchel with the stars and stripes, my lunch box with the vampire sticker, exercise books and, oh yeah, nearly forgot, my .22 calibre pistol just in case I bump into a rattlesnake as I run for the school bus. I'm sure Gerry must be aware by now that Michelle has a lot of money and is guaranteed to receive more as Gran gradually loosens the purse strings. Michelle can't have failed to have told him. The only bugbear around here is me. Would I fit in? I simply couldn't go through all those High School charades. Gamesville New Mexico and we'd better cap your teeth dear. Hey, honey, you've gotta adjust. Be a part of the new life. Get all that old European shit out of your system. Embrace the New World and forget all about your French and English ancestry. You can still go and visit your grandmother once in a while in Nice if you like, honey, but I wouldn't recommend it. No, sirree. Gotta adapt, fit in. Well, I ain't going and that' for sure. What about my friends? Suddenly sleep old Sancreed doesn't seem so bad. Anyway, what does Michelle really know about this guy? He could be a serial killer con artist on the make. Two days and a few quick sweaty fucks and they're all ready to set up house together. Never mind me, my feelings. Michelle prancing around the house, barely wearing any clothes. I find that really embarrassing. Cringing at the way she's behaving. That silly little girl laugh that she's discovered overnight. She keeps talking about snakes. Have they got a snake temple in Santa Fe? Has Gerry ever seen a real snake dance? How snakes are the most beautiful creatures on God's earth. Did you know, Gerry, that snake venom, used in very small quantities, is a cure-all panacea, very beneficial to promoting health and sexual rejuvenation. Snake oil lubricants, wink wink. Silly laugh glides once more across the lounge carpet, shaking her arse like she's a snake charmer on heat...

Suddenly, we are all sitting down to eat together at the dusty dining room table. Michelle is cooking these really big, blow-out meals. Neat, Ma. The message being, the way to a man's heart is through his prick and his stomach...Suddenly, I'm a little girl again. Show Gerry your school uniform, Yo. What am I, a performing pit pony? My last term school report appears which was deadlier than the largest New Mexican rattler alive. Then the strange remarks. Hooded eyes of obvious meaning. Weren't you supposed to be going out with Julie tonight, Yo? Hasn't Rainbow invited you over to a party at St. Just tomorrow afternoon, honey! She knows very well that I haven't spoken to Rainbow in over three months since she stole a pair of my quart socks. Little bitch! She's full of the colours of lies and I hope she's happy with that donk, Billy Richards. They deserve each other! Anything to get me out of the house. I've noticed Gerry casting sly looks in my direction, eyeing my legs when he thinks no-one's watching him. He's like those guys who wear large wrap around shades and think that makes them invisible. Creepy Yank shit, if you ask me.

I feel cut off today. Very alienated. I can't stand it in this house at present. Michelle waiting on that Gerry hand and foot. Hanging on his every word like he's some great American overload slumming it down here in grotty old Cornwall. Michelle pretending all that fake interest in Thomas Hardy. She's never read a bloody English novel in her life. Always going on about what a great writer Francoise Sagan is. Oh hell, I feel so fucking miserable! What have I got to look forward to? Bloody school, babysitting Luke and end of term exams. I won't be seeing much of Julie now that she's hooked up with that Adam. She made it plain last night that two's company and three is definitely awkward and a drag. Michelle keeps putting me down. Taking the piss this morning out of my French Connection ra-ra skirt. And oh, Yo, your eyelashes are really growing fast. You must have had a visit from the sandman of lashes overnight. Oh yeah, Ma…Gerry laughing so hard it's like he's a distant cousin of the Mule Brigade. If you must know, these are called Lashes of Fun by Shu Uemura. They are neatly-looped false lashes, okay. Shit, they nearly collapsed in hysterics. Lashes of fun! Ha-ha. The only relief was when Luke shot me again. Fashion! If really neat fashion came up and hammered them over the head they wouldn't know what it was. I've noticed that Michelle takes the piss out of me to entertain Gerry, but she's quick enough to raid my wardrobe to keep him interested. When she came flouncing out of the bathroom this morning she was wearing my red silk bra and panties by Prada. God, how I hate bank holidays. Nothing ever to do here. I climbed up to the Beacon early this afternoon and looked out over Sancreed. Rolled a joint in the wind and stared hard at the land. All the houses and farms looked so insignificant. Everybody going about their little lives. The arguments and jealousies behind closed doors. I don't want any of that. I'm not super-special, but that's not for me. When we were all watching the news last night I started crying. Gushing with tears. All the terrible things that happen every day. People being killed in Jerusalem, the Gaza Strip and Belfast. It's horrible. Michelle started going on at me about how that's life. How hard Gran had it during the German occupation. How she coped. Jesus, even Paul wasn't born then. Gerry nodding in total agreement with her like a ventriloquist's dummy. He'd agree with anything she says right now. I bet things would soon change if Michelle moved to Sante Fe like she's threatened. People are so hard, so uncaring. They watch the news like it's a game show or a Big Brother lock in. I hate them! They are all so unfeeling, so heartless…"

*

"God, you look so bedraggled, Yo. Have you been crying? What's wrong?"

"Can I simply sit here and roll a spliff, make myself a cup of tea and just gaze out of the window?"

"Of course you can! Listen, as you're playing hooky from school you can do whatever you want. Okay! And you're dead right! Even though I say it myself, cliché rolling in upon tidal cliché, this is one of the best views you are ever likely to get. On a clear day like today, you can see the outline of the Lizard. St. Michael's Mount glinting like an ancient fortress in the sun. The red and blue sails of the yachts scudding across the bay of Penzance. All is right with the world and even the tourists are happy. Sand between their toes, well, almost. Sticky fingers from melting ice-cream cones. Crimson torsos and bare-breasted ladies who should know better. What are you laughing at! I'm giving you an instant impression of heaven, a tiny slice of paradise as seen through my lounge window. Advertising agencies would pay millions for this. Hack and cleave their nearest competitors to get a chance at this view."

"Why don't they then?"

"Because I'm not going to tell them, that's why! Some things have to remain sacrosanct. Do you really want me to prostitute the view from this house? Have agency photographers crawling all over this place. Smoking all our dope, drinking all our tea and coffee. Jabbering on and asking inane questions, telling us repeatedly how superior the view is from a beach hut in Tierra del Fuego Queuing for the upstairs loo and pissing all over the floor. Making passes at you and can we just have a couple of shots of Yo on the roof of kitchen extension with her clothes removed. Furtive empty promises of modelling contracts for you. Instant glamour on the roof and who gives a fuck till the next assignment."

"Well, I wouldn't mind a modelling job. Do you really think I'd stand a chance? Here, is my nose too long in profile?"

"Yeah, far too big a hooter. Definitely a plastic surgery job for you, my girl. You'll have to have silicon implants for your boobs as well and, as for those bags under your eyes, well, they'll have to be got rid of with some type of suction device, make-up will never hide them."

"Do you mean it?"

"God, you're so sensitive today Yo. Did someone piss on your chips last night? Your random attempt at firebombing the school failed lamentably? The church in Sancreed has put up a poster of you on its' closed doors declaring you to be a danger to society?!"

"Can I roll another spliff?"

"Look, I've told you before, help yourself. What's mine, is yours. Just imagine, before the last great flood, three and a half thousand years ago, that lovely blue lagoon of a Penzance Bay was all forest. St. Michael's Mount was situated some five miles in land. Phoenician Traders used to journey by sea here to trade for tin. Our Celtic forbears used to track across land from Galicia in northern Spain to barter for precious tin. This sleepy outpost was a prime mover and shaker in the tine stakes. Hard to believe now that this was an affluent land while the rest of Britain struggled. Open cast mining the order of the day. No need for tunnelling underground and working in temperatures exceeding a hundred degrees Fahrenheit. No need to be paid purely upon production, only a good wage if you're lucky enough to hit a rich seam. No tunnelling out under the ocean, like those mines along the north coast between Zennor and St. Just. Tin abundant and all around. Masses of the gleaming stuff and all the powerful kingdoms of the ancient world were desperate for it. Tin goblets and amulets found at Knossos, the ninth ancient site of Troy, UT, digs in Egypt like Tal al Amarna, Thebes, Bani Hasan, all along the thousand-mile stretch of the Nile delta. This backward, forgotten land was the King of Tin. In those days, the Isles of Scilly were connected up to the mainland. You can still follow their course from the head of the dragon that starts above the hills at the back of Carnyorth. The lost lands of Lyonnesse. The magic land that time forgot. That's why all those ancient settlements like the one near Sancreed are here. That's why all the lunar/solar nineteen stone circles. When societies are rich they turn to religion, mysticism. When food is abundant people wish to feed their spiritual selves, seek a fuller explanation of their human condition and offer up sacrifices. Now look at it! Reluctantly accepted as a part of Britain. At least the old Cornish Brythonic language is being revived. Production companies like Wild West films making fifty minute shorts in Cornish and not before time. We should become an independent kingdom, as before. Kick out this clown Prince of a fool and reclaim ourselves, rediscover our true heritage as of yore before the last great flood. Our history of tin-mining has been discarded. Our trawler fishermen have to rely on cocaine and hash smuggling for a living. We have to greet and embrace all the Emmetts and fleece them of their money and smile indulgently, be pleasant to them through all the uptight urban complaints about our backward nature and ways. How come you have all these expensive clothes and accessories, Yo? I shouldn't think your average young lady of similar acquaintance would even dream of such items. A millionaire's daughter perhaps, cosseted by her surroundings and opulent life-style. What are these? Gucci sunglasses and what's that smell? What perfume are you wearing? "

"It's an eau de toilette by Fiorucci. Do you want to hear the blurb?"

"Sure, why not. The defining fragrance that leaves us all noseless."

"This one is called the Lolita of teen fragrances, an Italian chocolate and parma violet scented perfume."

"I'm stunned. I've been wasting my precious time all of these years. I should have been composing trendy phrases and descriptive lines for all the fashion houses and perfume manufacturers. God, what's this! Glitter Babes nail polish!"

"Please, don't go through my bag. I hate it! Michelle is always doing that. I don't come here and start looking in all your cupboards and drawers, do I! Just because you're young, people think they can take advantage. It's not fair. If you continue to treat me like a child, I'll behave like one. Treat me properly and I might surprise you."

"Steady on, Yo."

"Hasn't Michelle ever told you our family history?"

"I don't think so."

"I'm surprised at that. You being so inquisitive and all. Well, you probably already know that my French grandfather, Michelle's dad, was over sixty when she was born. Really, really old. He's married a second time after the Second World War. Gran was at least thirty years younger than him, though I'm not sure of her exact age. Anyway, cutting a long story short, my grandfather lived in Nice before the First World War and apparently made a large amount of money in investments. His own father died when he was seventeen and left him a lump sum, he was given some inside information on the bourse and made a killing. He always told this story to show how clever he was, but as a very small child I never quite understood him. He said that he knew there was a war coming so he invested all of his money into buying a block of one bedroom flats which had just been built in 1913. In those days, the block of apartments was on the outskirts of Nice. Most of the tenants weren't much older than my grandfather when they first moved in. Am I boring you?"

"No, no. I was just checking on the email. Sorry, carry on."

"Well, under French Law unless a tenant fails altogether to pay their rent or commits murder you can't evict them. Also, in France, unlike here, you can't just raise the rent every six months as you were telling me the other week. People, tenants, have rights. What really angered my grandfather was that most of the tenants were still paying the same rent he'd set in 1913. Can you believe that! When he would start talking about it when I was a little girl staying with him in Nice, he would work himself up into a frenzy at the dinner table, grow very red in the face and seem like he was about to choke to death. There were twelve flats in all and something like ten of the original tenants lived on into their late eighties and nineties. Of course, after all that time the block of flats had gradually become a part of fashionable area of Nice as the city grew. Are you still listening?"

"Sure, sure. You sent me off then, Yo. I was having visions of Nice, pre the Great War. Your grandfather, the smart Edwardian, or whatever it was called in France, entrepreneur. This little block of apartments on the outskirts of the city...well."

"I've never realised till today how rude you are sometimes. I always concentrate completely when you're talking to me."

"Bitchy."

"Anyway, the rents had virtually all stayed the same since 1913. That's why my grandfather used to get so upset. Then when I was about ten, the last remaining six tenants all died within a year of one another. That was neat, wasn't it! My grandfather was then free to sell the entire block to a large property developer who promptly knocked them all down and built a luxury hotel on the site. I don't know exactly how much he got. Michelle thinks

Granddad was conned by an old business confidant who was in league with the property developer. She estimates he received at least fifty million francs."

"Jesus, that's..."

"I know exactly how much it is, thank you. I have to do maths every day at school."

"But not today."

"I'm starting to with...Well, Granddad died last year. Gran naturally inherited all of his money. That only left Michelle and my Uncle Alain. Granddad had stated in his will that Uncle Alain was not to receive a single franc, even though he was the eldest. If Grandma had ever given him any she would be disinherited. Uncle Alain is gay and Granddad really hated that. He was very old and you know what men of his generation were like. Well, as you have probably worked out by now that only leaves Grandma, Michelle, myself and little Luke. Grandma know what a spendthrift Michelle is and how she can get these crazy ideas so she's taken to doling it out in fifty thousand lumps every six months."

"Pounds or francs?"

"Pounds, dumbo. Grandma also gives me at least two thousand each time. Last time I got five on the condition that I allowed three thousand of it to be invested in stocks and shares for me."

"I saw you being born and didn't realise I was watching a little rich girl in the making."

"I really don't like your attitude today, it really sucks. I don't want to talk any more. I'm going to leave now unless you promise to fuck me later."

"Pardon?"

"You must be going deaf in your old age. I want you to fuck me okay. I've been wanting you to for ages and now I feel ready. I keep dreaming about you. I know that you're very old and have wrinkles around your eyes. That you talk too much and can sometimes, a lot of the time, be boring and tedious, but I don't care. You're also neat. I just think you're uptight because you haven't had any sex in a long while. All that celibacy stuff, all the yogic exercises and trying to channel and control your sexual energy will drive you crazy. I want to do it. I'm sure it will do you good. I promise I won't get pregnant. I've got over three month's supply of Michelle's pills. Since she's started sleeping with Gerry she's stopped taking them. Hoping Gerry won't ask her, I guess, and that she gets pregnant again."

"I'm speechless!"

"Well, that'll be a first!"

"But Michelle has only known Gerry what...five days...?"

"Don't change the subject like that and try to slide off the point. Am I so unattractive to you? Don't you desire my body? Don't you secretly have fantasies about me which you won't even admit to yourself?"

"Hang-on, hang-on, who's in charge here. This is my house, my life, my thoughts, okay! I love you because I've know you since you were minus nine months. Since I've become a little cut-off in the last couple of years, your friendship and our conversations and time together have become very important to me. But I've never thought of you like that. You're just a young girl!"

"Liar. You're a fucking liar and you know it! I don't want to hear anymore of that little girl crap either!"

"Where are you going? Don't go off in a sulk like that. Please."

"Will you agree to my greatest desire then? WILL YOU FUCK ME! PLEASE!"

"Do I have any choice in the matter if I wish to keep seeing you?"

"No, you bloody well don't! I can't believe this! Here I am, a fourteen year old virgin, having to fight off lecherous farmers, run the gauntlet of the boys' dirty remarks and grubby hands at school. Half the male population of Sancreed is trying hard to get inside my knickers and I'm having to beg you to do it! Are you scared of me or something? Am I so unattractive to you? Don't worry about Chris we haven't hard from him in over two years and neither have you though you're supposed to be friends, right!"

"Yes, if you must know the truth I'm petrified of you. Suddenly you've become a very powerful person overnight. A monster evolving before my very eyes. Don't laugh, it's not that funny. This can only lead to disaster and I'm utterly helpless before you. St. Austell clay in your malleable fingers. For the first time in my life you make me feel old and I'm shuddering inwardly. I don't just fuck people. What am I, a mechanical penis to be switched on and off at will! There is an emotional content to all sexual contact. That's what separates us from the beasts of the fields. Though looking about me today, I seriously begin to wonder. I believe in the psychic exchange of the sexual act. Don't smirk like that and stop showing off the shape of your body against the glass kitchen door. You're got my complete attention so let's try and act normal and talk this through. You're right. Without my realising it, you've become my best friend of late and I don't want to lose that. I never planned it that way it just happened. Yes, I know, I'm prevaricating and you just want to get on with it, but I'm scared! Once you believe something to be true, it happens. If I'm conscious of the psychic exchange during sexual intercourse then there's no going back. My emotions will open up and I will be helpless before you as a child. If Michelle ever finds out, she'll set the police onto me. And what about you? What's suddenly brought this on? Gerry and Michelle making love in the master bedroom in Sancreed has made you restless and just a tad envious? You're right. You could have any young buck you wanted. I'm sure the sparse male population of Sancreed is drooling over you. Farmers' sons fantasising about you every night as they reach orgasm with their complacent, put upon wives. Me. I take all this very seriously as you of all people should realise by now. I don't like the fact that my prick, Max, is getting hard as I'm talking to you. I know what is going to happen. My emotions will burst forth, my love life will get all made-up and I will be shattered, despairing and left for dead when it's over. I'm not into on-off or casual sexual liaisons, you know that. Before no time at all you'll want out and be embarrassed by what's happened and feel awful with yourself and you'll be right."

"Shush. Let's go up to your bedroom now. C'mon, I'm taking control. I don't care, I just want to fuck. I'm itching terribly between my legs, I've got love juice running down the inside of my thighs. Look, run your fingers over it and put them in your mouth. Good. I love that. Take your clothes off. You shouldn't be so awkward you've still got the body of a young man with all that yoga that you do. Do my bra and knickers turn you on?"

"What are they?"

"Silk bra and briefs in venetian red by Prada, very expensive. I ordered them from New York especially, just for this moment. I memorised the blurb to excite you. When the Belle Epoque meets the seventies, it's little girl looks with a decadent spin. You should see your face. Why are you drawing the curtains? There isn't a house for over two miles in that direction. Do you think the seagulls are going to spy on us and report you? Nobody is going to see us, don't be so afraid. What's that music you've put on, I like that. And that smell, what's that?"

"Billie Holiday and Spiritual Sky cedarwood incense sticks."

"See, if you were some randy farmhand you'd already be banging me senseless by now, but you're taking your time, I love that. Can we just lie naked next to one another and stroke each other's bodies. I want to stroke and gently squeeze your prick. God, look at it! It's jumping and juicing. Shall I lick it? Do you want me to suck it? I've done that before. Is that it? Are you coming?"

"No, Sweet Pea, that's my love juice."

"Please, you promised never to call me that again. Don't spoil it. I love the incense smell. it's so heavy and earthy. How shall we do it? Do you want me on my back or my front?"

"Just leave it to me. Yolande."

"Can I roll a spliff now? Are you finished?"

"I'm so sorry, Yo, I should never have gone at you like that. I told you it would be like a pent-up dam bursting. I just couldn't hold back nay longer. Please forgive me. I'm so sorry."

"But I loved it! It was great! Really wicked. I never imagined it would be as good as that! You mustn't feel so guilty. I wanted you to. You're worried and upset because you put your prick max into my arsehole. I loved it! At first, it all felt dark and strange then my arse took over and I couldn't stop. I was screaming with joy, not pain. What do you call it? Divine madness. I want to do it like that every day from now on. I thought it would hurt when you first put your prick in my vagina. Michelle sat me down a couple of years ago and said it would. But I didn't feel any pain. It was lovely. I just kept coming and coming, especially when you stuck your finger up my arsehole and started biting my nipples and ears. You were very kind and gentle with me, but I love it when you're animal. I'm in ecstasy. I want you to do it again and again. How much longer before Max is ready to go again? Can I help him along?"

"God, now I've started something and you're in control. There's no going back. Max has got a will of his own. This is crazy, I'm falling for you like a stupid kid and I can't help myself. I love the smell of you body. Your openness, freshness, simplicity. I know I shouldn't be behaving like this. It's madness. If anybody ever finds out, they'll lock me up and throw away the key. But I'm hooked, addicted to you after only ninety-odd minutes of fucking and lovemaking. You're so pliant and willing and that drives me crazy, spurs me on till I can't stop. Max is already raising his horny head again just looking at you. Suddenly every move you make is so sexual. At this rate I shall be a spent force in a couple of days. I love the way you put that lipstick on. What is it?"

"I'm doing it so I can put a red ring of lust around Max. Good, I got you to laugh. Loosen up, nobody's going to find us. Usually you're so relaxed. Here, listen to this one. 'Nothing says Vixen like a full red pout, the Bourjois effect in 3D in rouge volcanic.' See, it's working on Max already and I haven't even started licking and tonguing him yet. You know your problem, you're eaten up with guilt."
I used to watch Chris with Michelle. He was just the same. Who gives a fuck. Remember how open and free you felt as a child living under the Spirit of Georgy. How you once told me you never ever wanted to be thirteen because you somehow knew that would be the end. You loved being a child because you valued your innocence. You could see all the grown-up problems with money and sex. You were aware enough to enjoy your dreams, you were lucky you had the presence of the Dreamweaver. How you loved games, telling yourself stories, wandering off on your own, staying at your Gran's, going to senior school with no-one denying you freedom. Life has hurt and scarred you, living in the real world of grown-ups has taken its toll. Men aren't supposed to be emotional creatures, have feelings, be caring and kind, unless they're some bent priest. You've said so yourself. Male adulthood geared towards aggression and the ability to make money is the only accepted valid way to be. The drive towards power, self-control, with women secretly conducting the strings, egging men on. Well, I think that's all a crock of shit.

You're a living example of a man who's made money and developed as a human being without intentionally hurting anyone. That's why I really like you. I don't want to hear anymore about guilt or how I'm only an innocent girl. Fuck me and enjoy it for what it is. What's that word you use... ingenie?"

"Ingenue... thank you... the other way makes you sound like some temptress about to spring out of a magic bottle, a girl elixir of sexual fantasy."

"Listen, you tell Max to get ready before I lick and suck him to death. I'm going downstairs to make you a cup of your favourite Earl Grey tea and roll some more joints. Those posters in your front room. I know one's Marilyn Monroe, who's the other one?"

"Catherine Deneuvre."

"Right. Well, I've noticed you don't like skinny women so I'm going to eat the whole of that chocolate cake. I'm going to stuff myself all the time till you can't take your eyes and keep your hands off me! Neat, huh. See, Max likes the idea, look at him! I think I'll go blonde as well."

"No, no, don't do that, Yo. They are only poster pictures, pin-ups of actresses who turned me on in my youth."

"Fuck! You make it sound like you're ninety or something!"

"I like your hair the way it is. You don't often see genuine brown hair. God, this is getting ridiculous! Suddenly, I'm falling for your charms and contemplating a relationship with you. You've wormed your way inside of me without any effort. You shouldn't be here with a dirty old man like me. Go out into the world and explore. Go with boys of your own age or girls for that matter. Go and see bands, funfairs, festivals, protest demonstrations, street theatre. Stay up all night in smoky, drug-inspired clubs and dance yourself senseless . Experience everything..."

"You're annoying me. You haven't listened to anything I've said. If I didn't want to be here I wouldn't. Shit, you're stopping me making you a cup of tea and eating all that chocolate cake. People of my own age bore me. It would be different if I were living in London or Paris, then probably I'd meet a more interesting crowd. When I go and stay with my Gran in Nice I never spend time with anyone of my own age. Gran is always trying to get me off with a French man. Last summer it was a rich family friend. Alright, he's nowhere near as ancient as you, but he's got to be at least twenty-five. Gran seemed to think it was a good idea. She's always saying that English boys are very immature, how I should get myself a French man with prospects who will take care of me and teach me. You see, even my Gran believes I should go with someone a lot older."

"Well, she's definitely not going to like this!"

"Why? Are you going to tell her! She doesn't have to find out. Anyway, stuff her money, I'm not being blackmailed by her! You wouldn't mind if I told her to fuck her inheritance would you?"

"Well, being the Truth Dentist, I cannot lie to you, Yo. It's your mind and body I lust after, not your money."

"See, I know you're not a greedy son of a bastard. Anyway, you earn plenty of money. I can help you. You can teach me how to design film sites for the net, right?"

"It's not exactly rocket science, sweetheart. Sure, you can do it if you're prepared to put up with long hours of laborious tedium. The trial and error. The client will never be satisfied and will always propose changes. They will have their own ideas. It's funny about the net; everybody seems to think they're an expert. When you've spent weeks designing a magnificent site for some crummy two-man and a crippled lady outfit they'll want continual alterations and amendments because some casual acquaintance at a Hicksville party recommended they should. Then they'll try and beat you down over the agreed fee, drag their wanderlust heels over paying and you'll receive the grubby cheque three months later if you're lucky. Why isn't our site up and running? Because I haven't received your money yet, that's why! Oh, I'm sure we've paid you. In fact, I'm positive, I remember signing the cheque. Well, go tell my bank manager, I'm sure he will be very amused. It's rather akin to advertising, Yo, everybody thinks they're an expert though they've never spent two minutes working in the industry. Just because they've watched countless adverts on television and at the cinema, they believe that gives them the right to be considered a natural. Oh, I could do that. Here, what do you think of this idea. Good, huh. You advertising whiz kids should learn a lesson. What a doddle, earning all that money for a job you could handle in your sleep!"

"Fuck, you're getting really angry. Look at Max, he's shrivelled. I'm going to have to take good care of you. Smooth your furrowed brow and suck Max to death. Think up some neat ways of easing the pain. Now, at last, I'm going downstairs to make that cup of tea and stuff myself silly with all that chocolate cake. You roll some joints. You know what. We are going to make an unbeatable team. Nobody's going to stop us! Really wicked, huh..."

*

"What have you been up to? You look different. Leave that nut trifle alone. I've made that 'specially for Gerry. Don't pull a face like that. I'm not some old hag to be treated like a piece of shit! Don't flounce off like that! I'm pissed off with you, Little Madam, Miss High-and-Mighty attitude. Can't you try and make yourself agreeable for once, for me. Please, Yo, I'm trying hard and deserve better than this!"

"What's your problem?"

"We need to talk, Yo. I've made up my mind. Gerry's taken Luke into PZ to buy him a toy gun before the shops close. Have some of the trifle if you like. I've made two. Have you got worms or something? If you keep on eating like that you'll get fat and then none of the boys will look at you. Come upstairs to my bedroom, bring the trifle with you if you like, we need to have a serious chat before Gerry and Luke get back."

"I see you've taken to emptying half my wardrobe then!"

"Listen, honey, don't be mad, Gerry thinks that Louis Vuitton jacket is mine and the Bakelite bangles. What could I say? He likes them. They've become a part of my persona for him. In a funny sort of way it's a backhanded compliment to you, Yo. If I tell him now that they're not really mine he'll start becoming suspicious. You know what men are like! Well, maybe you don't, but you're sure as hell going to find out quickly in the next few years. You can never trust how they are going to react. Major things pass them by without a second thought, then some trivial, stupid event triggers them off and before you know where you are, they are interrogating you. Calling into questions all kind of crazy things like morals and ethics. Once you lose their trust you're on a slippery slope. Remember that, it may help you in your relationships. Don't yawn! I'm not that boring am I? I need your help, honey. I've made a decision. Gerry's asked me to marry him and I've accepted. Don't look so surprised. I know it's quick, but I feel like I've known him for years. He already loves Luke. They've taken to each other. It's different for you, Luke was only a baby when Chris left and has no memory of him. He desperately needs a father. His energy is too much for me now. I can't handle him. Look, I know you've been very good with him, Yo, but little boys need male company as well. All that yelling and screaming, the continual playing with guns is getting on my nerves. You were different. My life was different then. This is my chance and I've got to take it before life passes me by and I'm old like your Gran."

"I've slept with Paul. I've fallen in love with him and I think he feels the same."

"Great!"

"What. But I thought you..."

"This is perfect, honey, absolutely perfect. Heaven sent. Everything is working to a divine plan."

"You're not angry. What do you have planned?"

"You make me sound like a calculating bitch. I only want what's best for you, Yo. I hate it here in Sancreed. This house is starting to give me the spooks. Gerry coming along is a godsend. He owns a large house on the outskirts of Santa Fe. Luke will love it and by the time he's school age he will be fully acclimatised and integrated. What's been worrying me all day has been you. I don't want you to get the wrong idea, Yo, but you're no longer a young girl. I don't think it would be healthy if we all lived in the same house in Santa Fe.

I'm not saying that Gerry's funny in any way, but you have to be careful over these things. Human relationships are very delicate, you might say timely balanced. It doesn't take much to upset them."

"Fuck! I can't believe this! You're saying I'd be competition. I might query your pitch. You don't want me to go with you to Santa Fe in case I get in the way and Gerry takes a shine to me. He might try and get his nerdy American hands on my body...right!"

"Don't be ridiculous, Yo! I never even suggested that. Gerry has fallen in love with me and I'm more than enough woman for him. No, it's not that. But with just Luke we would be like a new family starting out. When I eventually meet his parents, all his relatives and friends, I'd be forever explaining who you are. I mean look at the size of you. You've really sprung up lately. You're taller than me now and it would look, well, rather strange. With just Luke there'd be nothing really to say. People would understand right off without the burning need to ask haunting questions..."

"How old have you told Gerry you are? C'mon, tell me."

"That's none of your bloody business, Yo. Alright, I told him I had you by mistake when I was seventeen. He felt sorry for me. Said it would never have happened in Santa Fe. Don't smirk like that miss. Always remember a girl's gotta do, what a girl's gotta do."

"Well, it's neat to learn I was just a mistake! Supposing he sees your passport or birth certificate? Numbers still read the same in French you know. What about at the marriage ceremony? I guess you're going to get hitched there as I suppose our Registry Offices won't be good enough for him! What then?"

"He won't find out, honey. If he does, we'll already be married. When I confirm my date of birth at the wedding ceremony it will be too late. I'll squeeze his hand hard and he won't even be thinking of it. Remember, it's easy to put men's' minds off things if you press your flesh against theirs. Men are always fantasising about sex. I read somewhere once that the average man thinks about sex over a hundred times every hour. Imagine that! There'd never be any time to think about anything else! Anyway, if Gerry does find out it will be too late by then. Look, don't set me off on to this. Don't spoil it! Ain't you happy for me, honey?"

"Sure, I'm ecstatic! Congratulations. And what the fuck about me! I don't count in all this, do I! What am I going to do?"

"That's easy, honey, you'll go and live with Paul. Perfect, see. You'll much prefer that. Paul's always had a thing about you, even when you were just a small girl. Do you remember when he used to live with us? You two were inseparable. Two peas in the same pod. Always sitting together. Always agreeing upon everything. When you were upset he was the only one who could do anything with you. Remember? Whatever Paul said was always right by you. It used to make Chris very angry. He's not her father. Why is she always cuddling up to him, hanging on his every word. Do you remember, Yo? When you were eight and nine, I used to say to Paul in front of you that he should marry you when you grew up. I've never seen a couple more ideally matched. Total harmony!"

"Oh, I see, just like that! Very convenient all round! If Gerry wasn't on the scene and I'd told you that Paul and I had fucked, you'd be up in arms calling him a perverted bastard. A dirty old man. You'd start threatening to get the police or have him shot by some mysterious French gangster friends of your's from Marseilles."

"That's not fair, Yo, and you know it! How did you know about Claude and his gang in Marseilles? Oh, never mind. I only want what's best for you. I care about you. You're very mature for your age, Yo, I know it must sound strange, everything happening so quickly and all, but I really believe that Paul will be good for you. I'm going to go visit him and sort out the best course of action. We will have to be extremely careful so as not to alert the authorities, you know how small-minded they are. Jesus, I hate it down here, the narrowness and gossip mongering of the Cornish really gets to me. We have to prepare the ground carefully, cover all eventualities, if that's what you want. Is it, honey? Tell me, don't look so off-hand and vacant like I'm a demoness or something."

"Yes, it's everything I want. Lucky you. Paul's a very neat person and loves me, I know. He's the only person who really cares about what happens to me. Shit! You've taken my silk chiffon dress, my Marni's cotton jacket. Fuck, you've even got my Girl Scout jacket, belt and tie by Angels of London. I was going to wear that especially for Paul. What are you planning? A little girl number for Gerry to remind him of the misspent schooldays in Santa Fe he never experienced. Is that it? Christ, you've even taken my cutworked leather gladiatorial boots! What are you up to! Dominatrix workouts! No wonder Gerry's asked you to marry him!"

"Think of it as a trade-off, honey. It's not a lot to ask, is it! You keep quiet and don't even breathe a word of any of this to Gerry. Luke will miss you and be upset for a while, but he'll soon stabilise with the excitement of the flight and new surroundings. I'm going to organise everything for you so don't go getting sullen or bitchy on me. Remember, you'll thank me in years to come. It's the best thing that could have happened for all of us."

*

"I've been banging on your front door and mashing your doorbell for over ten minutes! Have you gone completely deaf or something! I know, I know, you never receive unwelcome visitors anymore and I suppose you've given Yo a doorkey of her own. Well, don't just stand there gaping like a panic-stricken poodle, let me in!"

"I...eh...you'd better come in, Michelle. This is rather embarrassing."

"Oh, for godsakes, relax, I haven't come here to chop off your balls. Make me a cup of tea or, better still, give me a drink and we'll have a good talk."

"Chilled soave?"

"Well, at least you've remembered something. Don't be so nervous. You've got this house looking great. How long is it? It has to be at least four years since I've been here. Remember? Just after Beverley left, you invited us all over for dinner while I was carrying Luke."

"A little bird whispered in my ear that you've met a man. Do you ever hear from Chris now?"

"Oh, for godsakes, stop being so polite and making small talk! You already know all the answers so why ask the questions. You know, as I was driving over here I got to thinking that I've known you for over sixteen years and I still don't really understand you or know you at all. You remain a complete mystery to me. Don't look so hurt. You lived with us for over two years once and I was none the wiser when you left. You're typically English, all sang-froid and held in. That's why I feel Yo will be great for you, really loosen you up. Shake down that reserve, unsettle that cool exterior, get inside you and make you come alive again. Don't look so startled. You should see your face. Christ, honey, anyone would think I'd just crapped on your sofa. Yes, you heard right, I approve, but we have to sit here and work it all out, no loose ends. Nothing left to chance, otherwise the police will come down heavy on you and we don't want that, do we! Also, I could get into trouble, encouraging a minor, even if she is my daughter, into living and sleeping with an old freak like you. Your shoulders are all hunched up. Chill out. Roll us a joint. Don't worry, I'm not suddenly going to go all schizoid on you and produce a concealed hatchet to attack you with. Don't say anything, honey, don't speak, just listen, okay. I'm going to marry Gerry and move to Santa Fe. The three of us are flying out next Monday, somehow I've got to pack up the whole house in five days and arrange for flight and delivery. Everything's fallen divinely into place. John Robbins from Grumbla came over last night. I couldn't believe my luck. He wants to buy the house outright with cash, straightaway! Isn't that amazing! What do they call it? Serendipity. See how my English is perfect now. That's all those years of you and Chris taking the piss out of me. Always picking me up on my every word. Anyway, John wants the house as a wedding present for Amanda and Jed. Get them started. Do you remember them? Silly me. I forgot, you always remember everything, don't you, honey. I'm going to tell the school that Yo is leaving, coming with us to Santa Fe. I've already explained to Gerry that Yo can't come with us because of her school friends, plus it would disrupt her studying. He thinks you're married, an old family friend which, of course, you are except I've never felt we were friends somehow. We don't connect, I can never tell what you're thinking which puts me off. Every man I ever meet comes on to me. Tries to get inside my pants, but you never did. I found that strange. I know you're not into men, but I just couldn't believe that a friend of Chris's could be that loyal and never make at least one pass at me. Not one, in all the time I've known you, and here you are, fucking my daughter, I find that hard to take. All right so I'm vain, so what! The whole goddamn world is made up of vain people, ego trippers, it's just that most won't openly admit it. Anyway, Gerry believes me. The school's a cinch. I'll telephone my mother and explain the same. She hasn't recovered yet from finding out I'm marrying Gerry and moving to America next week. Blew her mind. She never picks up on what's happening to my friends, she gets very confused these days. She quite liked you and Beverley. She said you reminded her of a young English flyer she knew from the Second World War. She thinks you're cute. She probably thinks you're still living with Beverley so that shouldn't be a problem. Just remember to make sure that Yo telephones her every week as usual and goes for her monthly visit to Nice during the summer holidays and everything will be fine. Don't get so edgy, that's the easy part. Christ, I've never known you so quiet. You would usually have interrupted me at least ten times by now. That's a good sign. Yo must really have got to you. Now, small details...I'm getting Yo a year's supply of contraception pills, she can top up when she's in Nice, it's much easier for her over there. So that takes care of any pregnancy hassles. I'm not ready to be a grandmother yet! When she's sixteen I will give my written consent, then you can both get married. Now the house. I've always loved this house. It's so cut-off and quiet, secluded. Nobody would even know that you're here. So that's no problem. Nobody sees you come in or out, do they? You always use your car. It's okay you can nod if you like, I don't mind. Yo's made you tongue-tied, will miracles never cease. God, you seem in shock, pull yourself together you're gonna have to be smart if this is to work properly without any unwanted aggravations. Now, before you rediscover your voice and start shooting loads of questions at me, pour me another glass of that soave and roll another joint, will you."

"What about all of her school friends? The people around Sancreed? When they see her, they'll become suspicious. You know how it's almost impossible to do anything in a small community like this without anybody finding out. You know that old Cornish saying, Michelle. If you don't want anybody to bitch and gossip about you then make sure you're always the last person to leave any grouping."

"Jesus, this is a strong joint! Is this some of your home-grown gear Yo was telling me about? You should go into business. Don't get paranoid about Yo being spotted. Use your head. Be astute. Yo's not a fool. This is a big deal for her, I can't think why, but the silly little bitch is crazy about you. Firstly, you're a long way from Sancreed and the school in St. Just. Make sure you don't go over that way, easy, right! I noticed when you left me standing on your doorstep for ten minutes that you car's got those black tinted windows. So, honey, you can drive around with impunity. No-one's going to see Yo. You have to just remember to be careful and cautious that's all! It's only for the first eighteen months. I presume you are going to do the decent thing and marry her when she reaches sixteen, otherwise I will get angry and take a hand. You are? Do I hear a yes? Was that a definite nod?"

"What choice do I have in the matter. You and I both know what will happen. We'll get married. Everything will be fine until Yo hits around eighteen then she'll grow bored. Want to start going out to all-night raves and parties. Beach barbecues and hanging out with people of her own age. I will become an embarrassment. A yoke around her pretty neck. She'll try to pass me off as her uncle, shun me or ignore me in public altogether. But as you can see, I'm prepared for that. I know that disaster looms. I'm doomed, but, of course, I won't stand in her way when the time comes."

"That's what I've always liked about you. You're such a happy soul. So positive. Look on the bright side of things, honey, you could have five years of tranquil bliss. Who else is going to bring you any happiness. Who the fuck else would even bother to put up with you! I always used to say to Chris that you're a workaholic. I noticed that about you. You only ever seemed truly happy and content when you were writing or selling on the telephone. Then you started hiding away in your room playing on a computer. You have no sense of fun. No aptitude for the absurd. You've never learnt after all these years that life is a game, a slice of theatre. That's why Yo will be so great for you. I know you can relax completely with her. Enjoy it while it lasts. This of yourself as fortunate and you never know, you might get a pleasant surprise. Just think, I'm your future mother-in-law. Fuck! That strikes the fear of death into me. Still, Santa Fe is just about far enough away, isn't it, honey, and we won't have to go through this charade anymore, will we! Maybe I'll come over for the wedding, though with Gerry in mind, I'd better not."

"What if Chris should suddenly turn up out of the blue from Prague?"

"Honey, you can forget that one. I haven't even got a contact address for him anymore. He owes me over two year's maintenance money plus a host of other debts strewn all over West Penwith. I bet he still owes you money, right? I thought so. Put that one out of your mind. He won't show and he'll never have any money. I spent years with his grand ideas and slick schemes for getting rich quick. Look where it got us! He's useless with money, always will be! I'd still be living in abject poverty if my father hadn't died. That's when I made up my mind, Chris had to go. I can guess what you're thinking, but I can assure you the relationship was long dead before he took up with that cheap lying bitch Gloria! He never once asked me to get married in all our years together. Now is that all? I can't think of any other angle. Just remember, honey, to put your ego to one side and listen to Yo. She's very shrewd for her age and will organise the whole charade much better than you. I've always thought, believed, that too much thinking and calculating gets you into trouble. I was going to say it's none of my affair, but as I'm your future mother-in-law while you live in sin, it is, isn't it! Just think, honey, I'm aiding and abetting you to fuck my underage daughter. Don't look so worried I'm not going to pounce on you as a farewell, parting gift. You're already fucking one member in my family and that should be enough. As I said, at risk of repeating myself, leave all the details to Yo. Now, you gonna wish me luck or what!"

"Well, I hope it all works out for you in Santa Fe. That this Gerry is what he seems and not some fake or charlatan. If ever you're in trouble..."

"Well, thank you for that vote of confidence. I know it must have taken a huge effort on your part. Now, you look after my little girl, you hear, and don't corrupt her too much, honey!"

*

His presence is upon me, the kindly form without a face bearing down on me, drawing me onward. My whole body is lathered in sweat and I am afraid. The Dreamweaver touches my rattled brow with his magic essence, beckons me to follow him and I have no choice. Cannot resist this Dream reality where truths are exposed and demons met.

Walking at a hobble through the dust-strewn streets of an ancient city. Onlookers dressed in the shimmering colours of the spectrum of the rainbow have gathered in their doorways to jeer and mock me. Piles of dung and excrement are thrown at my twitching feet and splash over the broken, crooked nails of my mangled toes. Humility and shame are perched equally on my sagging shoulders. The claustrophobic air contains a stench and a whiff of alarm. The smell of a fetid calm before an earth-shattering storm, an earthquake that will render us all plastacine shaped subjects of a bygone age. Plunge us into the sea with our statues and treasures. We will lie submerged for thousands of years as we sink beneath the towering waves in a terrifying catastrophe. I sense this is coming, but the thought of it gives me no peace for now. I am disgraced completely. On I am lead by rough, callused bystanders. People push and prod at my tortured body. The light is so alive and clear. The colours of amber, dun and chocolate bounce off the clear blue brilliance of the Mediterranean sky. This dusty street is awash with noise and I am the joyfully acclaimed victim. I am the news dish of the day to be served up and spewed forth for the hunger lust of this citizenry. The all-consuming need to provide entertainment and sanction the moral codes of this ancient civilisation sanctified upon the massive hieroglyphic inscriptions adorning the temples. The Dreamweaver is there, though I cannot see him anymore, through the pressing, crushing crowd. I can no longer hear his commanding, penetrating voice through the hubbub and commotion. I know, without thinking it, that an amorous inclination has lead me to this. One stringently forbidden and taboo. One scorned and denied by these screaming, laughing, abusive people with their proud brown faces, their jerking, flailing arms of glinting golden amulets and jangling bracelets, dancing in the radiant sun glow, bouncing before my dazzled and confused eyes. I am looked down upon and chidden, my sacrifice eagerly anticipated. My crime, though of an inborn nature, was a sufficient cause. The streets widen and the crowds grow distant, held back by the disinterested brute strength of the armed soldiers. We are approaching the expansive opening of the gorging mouth of the main channel of the Nile delta. For all the magnificence and glory of this city, I am reminded, as I stumble and bumble blindly forward, gasping for air, as the dirt and odour of ass and camel dung march into my unprotected mouth, that this community is extremely puritan in nature. The colossal statue of Isis bears down on me from across the harbour wall, but brings no respite. I have been exposed by a communal process. Shunned and despised. Losing by slow degrees my money, which was never a lot. Then the dwindling of community position and, finally, all my reputation. Expansive houses and friends that once welcomed me in closed their doors. Old friends turned their faces away and muttered out of the sides of their mouths and drank freely from silver goblets etched with fold in finely traced lines of amun. The creator supports them and I am now an outcast. Unclean, nearing forty without having made one years' livelihood of work in the last three years. Scanning the backs of people I was once happy to call my friends. The rich clothes end. All finery in tatters, the people who so admired me have turned a cold shoulder towards me. Forced to scrounge and beg. Sometimes used and abused by the darker elements of the denizens of this glorious city. The gateway to the ancient wonders of the world. Thankful to earn expenses, to act as a go-between in the margins of unspeakable acts thought to be too shameful to even image in ones mind. I became such a sort, out of hunger and the slow remorseless unhinging of my brain. My breeding and former station despised. Loathed by the high-minded citizens. Fully and utterly comprised in my life. All this is a searing, burning part of me as I am lead forward to await my fate and judgement. The disconnected moralising of my peers. There is no escape, but these flickering scenes of impending doom, the glimpsed internal flashes of a volcanic eruption, blinding in their ferocity and speed, are leavening my load. These vengeful people protect their own shortcomings and murky secrets, but they too have only a short while to live. The pressing throng parts and the noise and tumult subsides as I am dragged, pushed and prodded across the statue-adorned square to receive the pronouncement of the counsel of elders. Long beaked, hooded priests who view me from a distance with disdain. And yet, even now, I cannot help, but think of her. It is only proper to be fair and just. To mention her absorbing nature and subtle beauty that betrayed my trust. There is a point of view, seen from which, she appears more attractively guised. Her angelic face is leavened from behind a fluffy cirrus cloud that flouts strangely out of place above the harbour wall, the tops of masts of ships clustered together, bobbing up and down. The cries of the different sea birds are piercingly clear, so savagely shrill and beautiful. Brought so sharply into focus by imminent death. She appears to me from behind this cirrus cloud. When I dwell on her as genuine, a sweet child of love, who began above her honour and delight to forge a ray of glittering light, to forbid reputation to put aside her fears and qualms. She did not hesitate to unleash her presence, the pure flesh that gives bewildering succulent wholeness, wicked and divine, fragrant and earthy movements that give pure pleasure to man, and I am undone. I do not hear their voices, the sneering comments or feel the stifling heat beneath the tortuous sun. Only I glance upwards and am surprised that the cirrus cloud has vanished from the Mediterranean sky. Evaporated and only remains in the memory of my mind's eye.

The Dreamweaver is leaving me. I am scared and forlorn, but only have my weak-willed self to be. The fanfare of trumpets and pronouncements follow, declarations and pagan edicts resounding in compromise and order. I forgave reputation for her, but the community, so very puritan, has all of its values wrong. The cirrus cloud has magically reappeared, but I am now trance-bound and it many only be in my imagination. What does it matter they are one and both the same. My sense of loss at the Dreamweaver is utter, total, inconsolable. From behind the fluffy white cirrus cloud her angelic face appears as if suspended above moonfields and is the face of Yolande. Shining and innocent. Severe and haunting, if you incline your head to a slight angle. I am being lead forward to great cheers, loud thrilling cheers that an outcast has been denounced and sentenced. My hobbled legs grow unsteady and start to wobble, my entire, spent body is encased and oozing reeking sweat. The air has grown stultifyingly close, hanging and heavy. The sea birds have gone, the blue of the sky has faded and the heavens have grown immensely dark. The women are wailing. The soldiers huddle together for comfort. The judges have fallen on their knees and are hiding under stone tables, offering up prayers and lamentations to Isis. The air is rent with the sickly sweet smell of death. Buildings totter and tumble. Masonry flies through the panic-stricken air in all directions. Great chasms appear and expose the shaking ground in a blink of an eye. The massive great monumental black basalt stone crashes across the sky. The harbour walls are breached and crumble and we are feeling the very ground beneath our feet giving way. Our senses cannot withstand the shockwaves and implosion. Flying stone slabs relieve some crying merchants of their heads. Children are thrown from the quaking earth and sob for the milk of their mothers. Scream for the life-giving strength and force of their fathers.

The Gods are angry and have decided to traumatise and terminate this glorious wonder of the ancient world. To cease our human bleating and end our existence. The foaming sea reaches out its' roaring bubbling arms to ensnare and embrace us and we are all swallowed whole to our deaths.

*

"Hi. I thought you would have a lot more gear than this."

"I have. Michelle thought it would be wise for me to pack all my belongings into large cardboard boxes and have them especially delivered by Red Rascal. In her words. So as not to arouse unnecessary suspicion. They're due to deliver tomorrow morning, if that's alright with you?"

"Sure, sure. You okay?"

"I'm so excited and happy. Everything's hunky dory. Heat beyond belief. Just imagine, no more school. No more homework. No more babysitting duties. Fuck, you look awful. You look all clammy and worried. Don't you want me to move in with you?"

"Of course I do, Yo. It's just...Well, I had a frightening dream last night, that's all. The sounds and image won't leave me alone. Ancient words and worlds keep spinning around my brain, making me feel dizzy."

"Was I in it? Was it about me? Did the Dreamweaver appear?"

"All of those things, yes. It's not often a dream really scares me, but it was so intense and vivid. The Dreamweaver deserted me. I was publicly disgraced and humiliated. Condemned to death and you were my downfall. Then everybody in the dream died. The city I was living in was hit by an earthquake and instantly crumbled, to be submerged under the sea."

"Don't let that worry you. If you have such a vivid dream life you can't expect it to be great all the time, can you. I'm sure the Dreamweaver will come back to you. It's just your fears. My moving here, the suddenness of it all. You're afraid we'll be found out and the police will come and get you, that's all. Listen, stop fretting, obey your Auntie Yo who knows best. Sit down and relax. Chill out. Do you like my Girl Scout jacket? I smuggled it away from Michelle especially for you. Thought it would turn you on. Roll a spliff, I'll make a pot of Earl Grey tea and we can talk. Smooth those crease lines away from 'round your eyes and ease your fears. It's only to be expected. God, listen to me. I sound so sane and in control. You know why? It's because I'm so wickedly happy and excited. Michelle's such a selfish shit dumping me like that in case I screwed things up for her with Gerry. But I'm really happy about it. I didn't want to go to Santa Fe with them anyway. I'd only have been in the way. Little Miss Awkward casting a shitty shadow over their blissful union. Their new life together. I'll miss Luke, but what the fuck, I've got you instead and that's much more fun. You know what? The best thing we can do is drink this tea, smoke these other spliffs and go to bed. That way you can stop fretting like an old dog and lose yourself in my body. We can fuck and fuck, stop for tea and spliffs, I can eat a whole chocolate gateau. Look, I'm putting on loads of weight already, I know that really turns you on. Wicked, huh! Then we can fuck and fuck again, make passionate love till we are really wasted. When you're completely exhausted and happy, you won't think about anything else. Don't look so worried, this is our own little island of paradise and no-one's going to get us or become suspicious and interfere if we're careful, right! Just leave everything to me, I'm gonna make sure that no harm ever comes to you. I love you so much I'm giddy with excitement. We'll have long days of endless pleasure. No more shitty Yo do this, Yo do that! Be here, go there, crap! What is it, Yo, honey, you look so downcast and sullen. Why are you so unhelpful to me, honey? God, this is heaven. We're really neat here, aren't we? Get yourself prepared, mister, cos I want to do it all the time so you're so shattered you just collapse into my arms and I can stroke you and cuddle you. Make everything all right again. Leave everything to me and we'll have a wicked time. Do you know what really surprises me?"

"No, what? Tell me..."

"That my arsehole doesn't get sore. I mean, that's some kind miracle, isn't it. I mean, I know you use that jelly stuff, but with the size of Max and us keep doing it, I thought it would... Hey, I just had a funny thought. Really neat. Max must be making my arsehole get bigger and bigger. At this rate, it'll get so massive I'll just be one huge walking arsehole, right."

"What's that music?"

"Well, I was getting fed up with us doing it all the time to Billie Holiday, Miles David and that Ro...What's his name again?"

"Roland Kirk."

"Yeah. Thought it was time you heard some music that's happening today. The first track was 'Want to tell me' by Spellbound. Did you like it? Don't look so enchanted! This is 'Blackout' by L'il Louis vs Hydrogen Rockers. You'll really like this one. Don't pull a face it's not that bad. I'm just fed up hearing all that old time jazz and acid rock music. What are you laughing at?"

"I don't know, Yo. I don't care. Play what music you like. You're right. I know what I like and it doesn't matter. Nothing matters. I don't know why I'm laughing. I suppose I've succumbed to your spell and don't care about anything anymore. Laughing gas invading my body. What the hell. An earthquake could hit Cornwall right now, straight off the Richter scale and I wouldn't worry. I'd quite happily die just like this."

"Is that good or bad? I don't want to die. At least not yet, while I'm having such a neat time. Tell me what you're thinking. What's going on in that brain of your's?"

"I was thinking about Peter Sellers."

"Who's he when he's at home?"

"An old English comic and actor. Great mimic. He died six or seven years before you were born."

"I think I know him. Isn't he the Pink Panther guy?"

"Yeah, that's the one. I was remembering when I was your age. A far less together or precocious lot than today, I think we were retarded by comparison. Anyway, in those days I used to go to the cinema at least twice a week. No television at home so the cinema, pictures, clicks, were a big deal, but I'd never seen an X rated film. I can't remember for sure, but I think it was sixteen in those days before you could get into an X on your own. I'm a bit hazy on that, it might have been seventeen, unaccompanied. They're always changing it which makes it hard to remember. Anyway, I'd arranged to go with a school friend, Rob Wainwright, known as the Prof."

"Why Prof?"

"Well, kids in those days with glasses were either Four-Eyes or Prof depending on their brain power. Prof and I arranged to rendezvous outside the Red Hall Cinema at Walham Green by Fulham Broadway and see if we could get in to see this X film. I touched myself up by using some of 'Liz's' mascara, not too much, to give a faint trace of a moustache and slightly blackened my eyebrows which must have looked very odd because I was very blonde then. I managed to borrow a pair of my father's black painted shoes without him knowing and wore a very tight dark-green Italian bum jacket."

"I can't imagine you like that. Though Max obviously can, he's woken up again."

"Well, the shoes were right and pinched horribly and it was pretty hot so I was sweating which made the mascara run. I had it all over my hands and handkerchief. The Prof and I met as pre-arranged, just around the corner form the Red Hall. Just in case, you understand. We puffed out our chests with bravado and walked tall. God, it sounds so stupid and pathetic now, but back then it was daring. We were the only ones at the ticket kiosk when we entered. Thinking back, the Red Hall was pretty run down by then and they were probably just pleased to receive any money. We weren't fooling anybody. Christ, the Prof and I barely looked fourteen. A real rush of adrenaline and we got in. Having to contain our excitement. Acting nonchalant. There couldn't have been more than twenty people in the audience. I really loved the Red Hall. It was a fleapit. A real old-fashioned cinema, seating about twelve hundred people with ageing plush red seats with discoloured studs running along the tops of the backs. I was fond of the place because I'd once performed there in a skiffle/rock band with some surrogate cousins when I was ten. A Saturday morning competition for a television show called 'Carroll Everett Discoveries' which we won. Sorry, I'm drifting. The Prof and I sat there, in those fading red seats, gazing at the lights dancing patterns on the red curtains covering the screen, praying for the lights to go down before the manager arrived and placed a large beefy arm on our shoulders and ejected us. I can remember the record that was playing over the P.A. system as clearly as I'm stroking your pink/brown nipples right now. It wasn't a song I particularly liked. But in that moment it somehow took on a greatness for me all of its own. Spanish Harlem by Jimmy Rodgers. A rose reared up in Spanish Harlem. It only comes out when the sun is on the run and all the stars are gleaming. We made it. No heavy hand on the shoulder and the lights went down. After all the Pearl and Dean ads, the Pathe News and the forthcoming trailed attractions our X rated film. Lolita by Stanley Kubrick."

"My teen fragrance."

"She's been many things. Parts of the film bored me stiff, but Peter Sellers was in it and he was riveting. He played this character called Clare Quilty, a playwright who secretly desires Lolita and follows her and the main protagonist, Humbert Humbert, around. Humbert doesn't know he's following them because he keeps disguising himself as different characters like a policeman and a psychiatrist. I could go on and on about the film, but somehow that performance by Peter Sellers is still one of the most dynamic I have ever seen by anyone. The fact that I was fourteen, the subject matter of the movie, that is/was Lolita, all jumped into my mind as I was feeling your body. It fitted. Lo-li-ta. The syllables that roll so sweetly off the tongue. So perfectly formed. The actress, Sue Lyon, was fourteen as well. Lolita is meant to be twelve, but heavy censorship in those days probably made it almost impossible for Stanley Kubrick to get the film made at all. Most of the movie is crap, but Sellers was amazing. What I'd like to do, if you could wave a magic want and stop wriggling your bottom like that which is driving me crazy, is get my hands on all of Kubrick's footage. Knowing him, I bet he shot at least twelve to fourteen hours of film. You could tell he was entranced by Peter Sellers' acting by all the time the camera lingers on him. I'd guess there's at least ten hours complete footage of Sellers stored in some family vault somewhere. All the other actors like James Mason and Shelley Winters seem uncomfortable, absolute crap compared to Peter Sellers. I'd like to take the modern version of Lolita by Adrian Lyne with Jeremy Irons, Melanie Griffiths and Dominique Swain as Lolita, and run them together. One of the problems with the original...stop doing that, you'll drive me crazy with lust...is that all the location shots were done separately. Stanley Kubrick had already reached the stage where he wouldn't film anywhere else, except England. In the story, Humbert Humbert and Lolita crisscross America by car, right. Well, I'd take the modern Lolita and put Sellers original Clare Quilty performance in it in place of Frank Langella. Take all that footage of Sellers by Stanley Kubrick and edit it down and cut it all into the modern Lyne version."

"Well, I can't wave a magic wand for that, but I can wave my nipples and shake my arse. Look, better still, why bother about two silly old movies when you've got me, your very own Lolita. I bet I'm a better fuck than she ever was and more fun!"

"She was only a fictional character."

"Oh yeah, it doesn't sound like it to me. That Kubrick guy and that Peter Sellers you keep going on about seem well into her. Who wrote it anyway?"

"Vladimir Nabokov."

"Right, well, how did he find her. She must have been a real person like me. Anyway, I'm fourteen, not a girl of twelve. Still, I liked you talking about it. Look how it turned you on. I tell you what we could do. We could buy both videos, watch the films together in bed and see if there is some way of cutting this Sellers guy into the other movie."

"You are truly wonderful. Do you know that? You truly are."

"I am now that I'm here with you. I feel released. Reborn. That's it! I've been reborn! And I'm going to take good care of you. Help you in your work and be your very own pleasure machine. That's what I want to be. A sex-driven pleasure machine. Wicked, huh! Doesn't that sound great! Look at you. Your face. You look like a cat who's grabbed all the cream. That's my purpose in life from now on. To make you happy. To make up for all the shit that's cascaded. Can I say that?"

"You can say and do whatever you like."

"Right, well, all the shit that has cascaded on you in your life. All those bitches I've seen you with over the years. None of them really cared for you. Even I could see that as a little girl. I never used to say anything because nobody would've paid any attention to me. That happens a lot when you're young. Grown-ups ignore you like a bad smell, just hoping you'll go away, disappear and they won't have to deal with you. But I could see it. Anyway, I bet I'm not the first fourteen year old you've ever slept with, am I? Tell me. Remember back and talk about them. Go on."

"I'd never really considered it till after Michelle's visit the other evening. God, she seemed so frantic and in control all at the same time. I've never seen her like that before. It struck me as an odd combination. Like she was on something, but I couldn't place it. Snorting sulphate perhaps? I got to thinking after she'd left and, you're right, I have slept with other fourteen-year-olds, but I'd never thought anything of it. There's more has over there in the bottom drawer cupboard...no, the bottom one...When I was fifteen, I went on a school cruise that took in West Germany, Denmark, Sweden, Russia and Finland. We cruised aboard an old troop ship called The Devonia. Three and a half weeks of heaven. Spending at least two days in five ports. We docked in Leningrad for five days. A brass band greeted us on the quayside as we were the first European school children to visit the Soviet Union on a cruise ship. I prefer the name St. Petersburg and I'm glad the city's reclaimed it, but in truth I went to Leningrad. You're getting better at rolling joints. They seem to smoke better when you roll them without any clothes on. About a third of us, say three hundred, had paid an extra eight pounds, sounds ridiculous now, doesn't it, and travelled overland by train to Moscow for three days and back. I don't know exactly what the split on the ship was, but it must have been something like five hundred girls and four hundred boys. I'd started this relationship when we were docked in Copenhagen with a girl named Janice Brook. She had what we used to call come-to-bed eyes. On the first day the Devonia docked in Leningrad harbour Janice Brook and I went down into the bowels of the ship to the drying rooms. Quietly picking our way through the lines and lines of damp smelling sheets and pillowcases. The uniform of the hour then was tie-dyed tee shirts, Lee jeans and sneakers. Janice Brooks was fourteen and we lay on the hard floor of the laundry room and fucked. In truth, I probably came before I'd fully penetrated her. Often happens to virgin boys, they get so excited and overly eager. She must have liked it well enough though because we repeated the act at least five more times before the cruise ship finally docked in Tilbury."

"Was her arse as pretty and as sexy as mine?"

"I don't know, I never really...never!!"

"Good! I'm pleased we got that straight. So you lost your virginity in the drying rooms of a ship docked in Leningrad harbour when you were fifteen, right!"

"I think that's about accurate. Yes, the fact that Janice Brook was only fourteen never even entered my head. When the cruise was over I pursued a younger friend of hers called Veronica Friday. She lived across the water from me in Plumstead. On my sixteenth birthday, I got a DKW 197cc motorbike with a left foot clutch and used to get a real kick out of riding through the Woolwich Tunnel on Mondays to see her. We used to both take the day off from school. She was fourteen and we used to make love in her front room on a settee with protruding springs. Her parents were both out at work all day so we had the place to ourselves. I suppose this went on for about twelve weeks till the DKW broke down and Veronica found someone else closer to home and more accommodating."

"Did you like her more than her friend, Janice?"

"Well, I used to speed through the Woolwich tunnel on that motorbike to see Veronica. Ride like the wind. Less traffic around in those days. If I'm honest, it was the thrill of that bike ride and the anticipation of Veronica rather than the act."

"See, that's what I was trying to explain to you the other week when you asked me about boys of my own age. They don't want to lay naked next to me and talk for hours. Stroke my body, get inside my head and find out all about me. Swap dreams and fantasies. Take their time and continually fuck me. Wham bam and it's all over. Off down the beach to surf. Then they ignore you in public till the next time they want a quick fuck. That's what I was saying, you see. You were just the same when you were their age. You said yourself the thrill and excitement of riding that bike meant more to you than the girl. They're just the same now about riding the surf at night off St. Ives. That's the real fuck, the danger."

"Staring at you right now, those boys must be mad. They don't know what a little gem they had right under their surfing noses. I went on other cruises after that one to Leningrad. When I was seventeen, we went on a three-week cruise that took in Vivo, Lisbon, Tangier and Madeira. Now, on the last day of a cruise, it's like the end of school. Everybody's elated. At long last, getting off the swaying, rolling ship, but sad at departing and saying goodbye to new-found friends. Everyone swaps addresses and promises to keep in touch. About a month after the cruise was over, I received a surprise visitor. I can't even remember exchanging addresses with her. She must have got mine from some other girls at her school. I can recall my father answering the front door and calling me with this big cheesy grin on his face. Sis came into the lounge a few minutes later, wrinkled her nose up and turned on her heels and left the room like she'd just encountered some evil pariah. Jules was extraordinary. She'd only just celebrated her fourteenth birthday and explained later that she'd waited because she thought she was too young for me on the cruise. If I'm truthful, Yo, I'd never even noticed her existence. Shows how one-eyed and blind we can all be. One of the reasons why my father had smiled was the way Jules was dressed. Way ahead of her time. She used to wear a black bowler hat tilted at a rakish angle. One long teardrop earring sparkling down. She was the first girl I ever encountered who wore black nail varnish. Waist hugging striped pantaloons with a gold belt with a large buckle and the head of an asp on the prong. High-heeled, fuck me black shoes and, under the pantaloons, a pair of black tights. She never wore a bra or knickers."

"Doesn't sound that wonderful to me. Must have made her look like a bit of a comedienne!"

"Miaow. She was unusual in her time that's all. Like you are now. Her father was a rich stockbroker which I suppose gave her the licence to experiment and do whatever she wanted. We used to spend our time in Hyde Park. At first, just petting, but caresses and kisses weren't what she'd come for. The jobsworth park-keepers were always hunting us down, but after a while we just accepted them and moved on every time they interrupted us. They always seemed to spring out from behind bushes brandishing a stick each time I was about to ejaculate. Jules was unbelievable for fourteen. She's stand there, half-naked in front of them and fuck and curse them. When the pinched-face park-keepers threatened to call the police she's tell them they were miserable job-serving peasants who'd forgotten what it was like to be young, have fun and make love in the open air. The park-keepers would usually grumble a bit at her and warn us, but she'd hit home and they knew it. Gradually, we discovered danker, more secluded, earthier places to do it, laid under the twilight sky, her writhing on top, fucking away. Christ, Yo, hang on that hurt!"

"I'm going to bite and suck Max dry while you talk. I'm not going to let that Jules have all the fun!"

"Look on the bright side, Yo. You've got thirty years on her now. She's probably been dead for ages. Met a horrible end. If not, her face will have shrivelled like a prune. Her father's long dead and she lost all her inherited wealth in the big bang bust of the early nineties. She's now an unhappy alcoholic and I wouldn't recognise her if you paraded her naked in front of me in this room right now."

"Fat chance of that. She's not coming anywhere near this room! You concentrate your eyes and hands on me, mister, and forget all about that little bitch!"

"The funny thing was I never ever thought about contraception. How come Janice Brook, Veronica Friday and Jules never got pregnant? I have no idea. Just luck or impotency I guess, but I know that wasn't so. I never considered I was going anything wrong or breaking the law. Why should I? That's the beauty about being amoral. All innocence and natural animal drive. Whatever you do is fine, okay, because you don't know any better."

"What have you been up to? Shit, I couldn't believe it! Are you totally out of your mind or what!"

"What are you so excited about, Yo?"

"Don't play that calm, serene game with me! You know fucking well. While I was waiting for the kettle to boil, I thought I'd play on your computer. And what a surprise I got! On your personal menu I found a heading under Truth Dentist. And what did I fucking well find! You're writing about us. Recording our relationship in graphic details and what's even worse you're posting it up on your website for people to read. I just can't believe that you could do this. That you could be so stupid. So unkind to me who loves you. You never mentioned it to me! You must have known I'd find out sooner or later. You should have spoken to me first. Don't I have a fucking right to know? Don't I have any say in this? Don't I deserve some fucking respect? Well!"

"I'm really sorry, Yo. Once I'd started I just couldn't stop. It's like I'm writing about a verboten subject. It just came pouring out of me in an avalanche and wouldn't cease. I didn't mean to offend you and you're right. It was shitty and disrespectful of me not to tell you, discuss it with you at least. But I suppose I was afraid you would object and say no. Also, it's like being permanently on camera. People never act the same way when they know they are being watched. Sure, they forget themselves sometimes and let their guard down, then they quickly remember the all-seeing camera eye and go back to acting what they think of as their superior personality. Showing off their best possible side for the world to view with admiration. I didn't want that to happen here because I'm recording us. I want us to be natural. I know it's no excuse, but all of this is making me twitchy, nervous. Michelle's attitude the other night stunned me. I was badly shaken that week when our relationship started and I suddenly realised that you are a stronger person than me. More in control. After all, I've known you all of your life, somehow you never expect that will happen. That a young friend will turn into a monster and control you. Take over."

"So now I'm a fucking monster as well! What is going down here!"

"Only in the best possible sense, Yo. I'm putty in your malleable hands. Unable to resist. Utterly in thrall to you. Lost in the aromatic orifices of your body. Enraptured by the fragrance of your sweat and the tang of your flowing juices. I like the smell and taste of your shitty arsehole. Your unique thought processes and sibilating voice bedevil my every waking hour, climb right into my dreams and penetrate deeply into the hidden depths of my subconscious. I am entranced by you and I love and hate it at the same time. I've utterly surrendered myself to you against my better judgement. I'm not complaining or moaning, that's just the way it is. My will power is fading and I don't care. I've become weak and don't any longer recognise myself and now I'm afraid. Writing it out as the Truth Dentist and putting it up on the net is my way of retaining some sense of equilibrium. Justifying what is happening to me."

"Are you going to put it in book form and publish it?"

"Yes."

"Then we will be discovered and you will end up going to prison. You know that, don't you!"

"Yes."

"Why, when everything is so perfect and we are so happy? Why jeopardise that! Now every second we are together will be like living on a knife-edge. The most innocent 'phone call or knock at the front door will send earth tremors throughout the house. I can't stand the thought of you being arrested. I won't let them touch you! I won't."

"If we are meant to be discovered, then so be it. The thought-police, sex-police, dream-police, are out there, multiplying, mushrooming by the hour with the improving technological advances. The chances are we will be detected long before you've reached sixteen. They, the paranoid system of modern living and increasing human numbers, will contact your grandmother in Nice and track down Chris in Prague or wherever he is now. Your grandmother will get to you. Her pretty little grandchild, being corrupted by a middle-aged English ogre. She will take you to France, blame Michelle and cut her out of her will, promising everything to you alone. Private tuition and psychotherapy sessions will follow. She will have got what she's always desired. You to herself alone. Her own attractive granddaughter, a boon companion. Her own special girl, full of life force and energy, youth to sustain her later years, a prize possession all in one. Michelle will be interrogated, blamed and cut out of her mother's life all together. Chris will prove of a nuisance value, then when it's all over your grandmother will pay him off with a small lump sum and drop him like a soggy French baguette. She will hire the best solicitor and barrister that money can buy and have them flown in from London or Paris. Briefed to their shark-suited teeth with the vagaries of British and European law regarding sexual offences and under age molestation. I will be denied bail and put on trail in Truro crown court. Your grandmother will have got to you by then and you will have been brainwashed. On the day of your appearance in court, they will have you decked out in an old-fashioned school uniform. You will have lost weight and appear skinny and fragile. In the witness box you will be fifteen going on twelve and I won't stand a chance. With your barrister drawing the jurors' attention to all the hash, grass and magic mushrooms the police found. A polite clearing of the throat and the final clincher with regards to the special stash of crack cocaine secreted away for celebration on a wet Cornish spring day. I'll be looking at five years minimum, if I'm lucky. Your stern-faced, appalled grandmother will be calling for the guillotine and resembling a caricature of Madame Defarge. All jabbing knitting needles clicking with the perverse, screwy intent of the demented."

"Then why do it? If you stop now, we'll probably escape discovery. You'll be saved!"

"I can't. I'm drawn like a carnal moth to the flame flitting over your electric body. Look on the bright side. When you perch your pretty arse on the toilet seat and shit, sucking my dripping prick, the thrill will be heightened. Every second spent with each other will become totally meaningful. No turning back. Our time here together will be the most precious we can ever experience."

"Really neat, Paul. I love you and am going to bring about your downfall because you insist on exposing us to the world. Driven to writing it all out. Go get that crack cocaine now. We might as well get wrecked and celebrate while we still have the chance. Let's fuck now, be as really wicked as we possibly can, in case it's the last opportunity we ever get!"

Lightning Source UK Ltd.
Milton Keynes UK
UKHW050946140422
401506UK00010B/316